CITY
OF
GOD

PREVIOUS LT. BILL DONOVAN MYSTERIES:

NIGHT RITUALS
DEATH GAMES

CITY
OF
GOD

MICHAEL JAHN

A·THOMAS·DUNNE
BOOK

ST. MARTIN'S PRESS   NEW YORK

CITY OF GOD.

Copyright © 1992 by Michael Jahn. All rights reserved. Printed in the United States of America. No part of this book may be used or reproduced in any manner whatsoever without written permission except in the case of brief quotations embodied in critical articles or reviews. For information, address St. Martin's Press, 175 Fifth Avenue, New York, N.Y. 10010.

DESIGN BY JUDITH A. STAGNITTO

Library of Congress
Cataloging-in-Publication Data

Jahn, Mike.
　　　City of God / Michael Jahn.
　　　　　　p.　cm.
　　　"A Thomas Dunne book."
　　　ISBN 0-312-06927-8
　　　I. Title.
　　PS3560.A35C5　1992
　　813'.54—dc20　　　　　　　　　　91-40963
　　　　　　　　　　　　　　　　　　　　CIP

First Edition: March 1992
10 9 8 7 6 5 4 3 2 1

For Ellen

AUTHOR'S NOTE

In 1980, as *Night Rituals* was being written, America was fighting Iran. In 1990, as *City of God* was being written, America was at war with Iraq. America has come a long way in ten years, nearly as far as Donovan and I.

Donovan survived the 1980s better than I did. He solved a number of high-profile crimes, for which he received great acclaim and small cost-of-living increases from a perennially broke City of New York. He was shot at several times without fatal effect, and survived as well two self-inflicted wounds to his heart and mind. Rosie Rodriguez, who came into Donovan's life a few years into the decade, as America invaded Grenada, left it before the last palm tree was liberated.

Donovan's second wound? Alcohol, his companion when he wasn't chasing bad guys, lost its luster and he stopped drinking. Thus his heart survived one episode; his liver, another. Neither milestone proved as catastrophic as he feared, and Donovan easily slid back into his West Side bachelor's life of work, talk, and pickup basketball games. Then Marcia Barnes reappeared and announced her permanence. Donovan rewarded her with a marriage proposal and a vow of sincerity, sobriety, and stability befitting a man of his accomplishments and years. That left him to ponder issues of God, loyalty, and responsibility, which he does in *City of God*. He also chases a killer. Marcie does much the same thing. Arguable successes are achieved by hero and heroine (although, more so than usual, morals and ethics take a beating).

I was never as lucky as Donovan. During the 1980s I lost some of the best people I knew: Margaret Mary Loughlin, my aunt, and Jimmy Coughlin, a cousin. Friends at Columbia University passed away and will be missed: Mary Ann Gillies, John Murray, Manny Warman, and Bill Kahn. Don Zahner, a Broadway bartender who, at the dawn of the decade, suggested I write stories about our imaginary friends, went down fighting. My biggest loss of all was my father, Joseph C. Jahn, newspaperman and pacifist, who died in 1984. He would have liked to watch the Berlin Wall come down. (At least he saw his grandson, Evan, grow to fine young manhood.) I wish my father could have met Ellen.

Ellen Lebetkin came into my life as the sun was rising on the 1990s, and right away made it a far better decade. *City of God* is dedicated to her. The third Donovan novel, it was written largely in the first year of our marriage (Ellen is far more understanding than this old, ink-stained wretch deserves). The writing was begun by the docks in Sheepshead Bay, N.Y., when America was at arms against Panama, and finished across the street from the Kuwaiti mission to the United Nations, as American tanks rolled into Iraq. As Donovan rambled and reflected in the Cathedral of St. John the Divine, Ellen and I sat up nights watching the war on CNN and listening to the chants of the antiwar demonstrators down the block. For a while it was like being back at Columbia in 1968 (certainly a vintage West Side place and time).

I love her madly. Without Ellen, my life would still be the familiar West Side yarn of words and pickup basketball games played in the company of Donovan, Jefferson, Barnes, and the usual suspects: the writers, lawyers, cops, bartenders, freelance anarchists, Falstaffian felons, and other misanthropes who live on the Upper West Side of New York.

—Michael Jahn
February 7, 1991

I.

CITY OF GOD

B efore going out to kill, Marcus ran his finger down the chapter summary and read it: *I classify the human race into two branches: two societies of human beings, one of which is predestined to reign with God from all eternity, the other doomed to undergo eternal punishment with the devil.* The thick old book smelled of leather and parchment and the page crinkled faintly.

Mortal men walked in two cities: one, City of God eternal; the other, City of Man corrupt. They worshipped in two houses: one, Cathedral of God majestic whose spires grazed heaven; the other, an asphalt and concrete amphitheater distinguished only by the volume of blood and anguish flowing on its streets.

It had always been so, Marcus knew. From the very beginning two kinds of men occupied two kinds of worlds, and there were judges to intervene when the debased intruded upon the temple. The Marcus who guarded the temple into the fifth century was a judge as well as a holy man and was beatified under the name Augustine. The Marcus who would guard the temple into the twenty-first century would prove himself as worthy. Perhaps he would be more so, for his temple was confronted with a variety of evil such as could never have been imagined. And those who did that evil were destined for extinction by the hand of a most dedicated servant of the Lord.

Marcus lifted his finger from the page and tilted his head in the direction of the heavy wooden door. Through the black iron straps that bound the three-inch-thick oak boards came a majestic sound impossible to ignore. The City of God shook as the mighty organ's bass pipes filled the 16 million cubic feet inside the world's largest Gothic cathedral with a furious sound designed to overwhelm the devout with the glory of the Lord and terrify the sinner with His might. From the opposite end of the nave—500 feet away—the sixty-one silver pipes of the State Trumpet mimicked the fiery tones of the Royal Trumpeters at St. Paul's.

Marcus stood, hefted the bludgeon, and walked to the door of his cell. He pressed his palms against the vibrating oak door and absorbed the power of the organ. The power came through the old wood and up his arms and through his body, bringing strength and conviction; he said, "Thy will be done."

He closed the book and moved it to one side so that he could open the brass-bound chest in which he kept his tools. Marcus lifted the mallet and dropped it into his old leather shoulder bag.

When he pulled open the door the music had changed. The power was gone, drained, stolen. In its place was the breezy, weightless music that was played to accompany silent movies. Marcus closed his eyes, breathed in a deep breath of great fury, then went into the narrow corridor and down the steps.

—

2.

MY LOVEBIRD IS CHIRPING

Donovan had never been quite so happy. In fact, for much of his adult life the word "happy" had served only the purposes of sarcasm. "Happy" was smiling faces on lapel buttons, and Disney movies with singing deer. It was feel-good television, Coca-Cola commercials, miniature golf, and the Ice Capades. Starting with the very first time that someone tried to shoot him, "happy" was the first refuge of those too uncritical to wake up and smell the dung.

All that had changed. Donovan was a new man. Suddenly proud of himself and every step on the path that got him there, he stopped claiming thirty-seven years and was owning up to each of his forty-seven. He even admired the wisps of grey in his sideburns, and stopped getting angry with Marcie when, to pass time at the supermarket checkout, she counted the grey hairs on his pate. Now he thought it was cute.

The transformation came like a syzygy, at the confluence of several celestial events—his forty-fifth birthday, twenty-fifth anniversary with the New York Police Department, receipt of the opinion by several esteemed physicians that he was drinking himself to death and, finally, Marcie's brush with pregnancy. The combined gravity of all those moments impelled the inevitable. He sobered up, straightened out, and in Jefferson's words, "hauled his honkie ass into the gym for real this time."

The pregnancy was unplanned, the supposed conception occurring as it did on a patch of soft grass in the woods of eastern Long Island, and turned out to be a false alarm. But coming on top of everything else, Donovan took it as a sign from God that it was time to get real. No matter that he was an atheist. Signals of such clarity could not be ignored.

That was a year-and-a-half to two years ago. Now they were cleaning out his apartment, preparing to move in and turn it from a large bachelor pad to a family residence, with enough bedrooms for, as he put it, "two-point-seven children and a dog."

The number of children was under discussion. Long a mixture of high-living single woman, undercover police person, and feminist, Marcie had her own harmonic convergence to coincide with Donovan's. She'd turned thirty-six a few months before and, a year-and-a-half after the false pregnancy, sat more and more tremulously upon her ticking biological clock. For her as much as him, glamour, independence, and tales of valor to tell the grandchildren weren't much good *without* grandchildren.

So on a fine November evening they embarked upon the adventure of love and wisdom and, typically for them, got as far as sorting out the old clothes in the master bedroom before succumbing to passion on the bare mattress. Lying glistening with sweat and watching a crescent moon hover over the Hudson, Donovan found himself purring with unashamed pleasure.

"My lovebird is chirping," she said, grinning, running a slender fingertip up and down his spine.

"What did you say?" Donovan laughed.

She didn't answer exactly, but blew a soft breath on his cheek along the line of his cheekbone, choosing precisely that feature he had been admiring of late. Along with the weight he lost went the puffiness of too many wasted nights. He had recently grown cheekbones, the result being that he looked a bit less Irish than before and somewhat younger. Always deceptively young-looking, now Donovan also appeared more angular.

"We match better now," she said, giving him a big smack on the cheekbone before rolling onto her back and sitting up.

Donovan joined her, peering with mock suspicion at her alpine features.

"Are you sure you're black?" he asked.

"That's the passionate half of me," she said, placing his hand on her breast to augment the point.

"Very nice, Barnes. Now, are we going to get serious about cleaning up this dump? I've got to get to the hardware store and buy a scrub brush and some brown soap. We've been at this four hours and all we did was throw out my old clothes." He removed his hand.

"The ones that don't fit you any more. Donovan, where did this domestic streak come from? I tried for years to get you to clean up this place, and no dice. Now you can't wait to set up housekeeping."

"I'm nesting."

"What?" she laughed.

"Typical male nest-building behavior, designed to attract a mate."

"It worked. I'm attracted."

He used a toe to pick up an ancient moccasin and flip it across the room in the direction of a plastic garbage bag that was already half full.

"How many L.L. Bean things can one man *have?*" Marcie asked.

"It's not the number. It's the durability. Two last like ten."

"And smell like twenty. I hope that the room Jennifer is going to sleep in doesn't need to be fumigated."

Marcie's childhood friend was coming in that weekend for the New York Marathon, something both women had been training for all year. No long-distance runner but one of the city's most decorated and best-known police detectives, Donovan wangled an invitation to ride motorcycle escort for the marathon, mainly as a way of staying close to his honey.

"She called this afternoon. She wants to sleep on the *West Wind.*"

"Jennifer wants to stay on the boat? Does she know how cold it gets?"

"I couldn't talk her out of it. Hey, it's romantic. How many people get to visit Manhattan and sleep on a yacht?"

"The *West Wind* is an old boat, not a yacht."

"In Manhattan she's a yacht."

Donovan got to his feet, stretched, and pulled Marcie up. He picked up his pants, shaking the leg to let a balled-up argyle sock tumble to the floor. That went to the garbage bag with the moccasin.

"We can take this stuff to the recycling center on our way to work tomorrow morning," she said.

3.
THE PHANTOM OF THE CATHEDRAL

On the last night of his life, Dale Charbaux was savoring the glory of a long-awaited moment. His dream, to produce a silent movie festival at the Cathedral of St. John the Divine using the great organ to provide the music, had come true. As the immense pipes blared accompaniment, *The Phantom of the Opera* flickered on the big screen hung halfway between the narthex and the crossing. The crowd was two hundred strong and bearing bottles of wine and plastic cups and the self-satisfied grins of the truly hip—those who appreciated the irony of hearing silent-film music played on a cathedral organ. So what if the festival was making money only for the cathedral's homeless program? The publicity it generated would launch Charbaux into the fast lane of Manhattan classic-movie presentation. He orchestrated the production as if it were on a Hollywood set. Like Charbaux, ushers were grey-robed monks, hooded in rough garments, their eyes downcast and voices low. Moviegoers were led across a cold stone floor above which dry ice fumes crept, released from black boxes to curl around ankles and up to thrill white knuckles.

The evening was a palpable triumph. As Lon Chaney crept across the screen, Charbaux wandered away from the projection stand and toward the northwest nave, looking for a corner in which to savor his victory with a smoke. There was no time to go outdoors, and too cold that night anyway. Even the harsh, wide-weave cotton robe wouldn't keep out that autumn chill. He stepped into the Arts Chapel, one of the fourteen chapels or memorials set in the nave walls that had been dedicated, over the course of the century, to one or another form of human endeavor: sports, arts, crusades, education, law, the ecclesiastical, the historical, the armed forces, monastic life, medicine, the press, labor, missionary, and all souls. Until recently, the Sports Chapel had an exhibit of photographs that showed athletes and their muscles in closeup. Now the Arts Chapel had in it a monstrous contemporary sculpture, brown canvas stretched over steel framework, giving the overall effect of a gigantic vulture.

Charbaux thought that the vulture, poised in the chapel as if to spring from a nest, was as marvelously sardonic within the context of St. John's as was Lon Chaney, the monk-ushers, and the Rue Morgue-like dry ice fumes. He snuck behind it and lit a cigarette, plucking a pack of Merit Ultra-Lights from within the hood of his robe. The smoke had barely singed his lungs when he realized that he was not alone.

Marcus stood in the darkness behind one of the vulture's wings, silhouetted by the glow of hundreds of lights on the great Christmas tree that just went up in the narthex, that western part of the cathedral traditionally reserved for women and penitents. The mallet was held suspended overhead. It came crashing down, ignoring Charbaux's gasp of terror and last desperate try at blocking it.

4.
"YOU'RE A MUSH BALL," MARCIE SAID

It was easy for Donovan to lapse into sentimentality. But only Marcie had been let in on the secret.

"You're a mush ball," Marcie told him with increasing frequency since he began promoting marriage and family. "The next step is for you to display emotion in public."

"I love you despite what you just said," he remarked.

With his New Age Man status came the fearlessness with which he opened up to reveal a soft and very sentimental interior that he had, for years, kept the best secret on the West Side. That secrecy had not been an expression of Irish-cop machismo. Being tough was a matter of survival, one that made it easier to deal with matters like the unavenged murder of his father.

It also made it simpler dealing with the slings and arrows of day-to-day life, an example being the boys at Riley's Saloon, who would turn Donovan's life into a living hell if they learned he turned to jelly when Marcie said she loved him. It was tough enough being a cop without being saddled with a reputation for softness. For his own sake and their future, it was best that Donovan go through life carrying on as if he really were an old fart. Fortunately, that also came easily to him.

It grew markedly colder after sundown, and by midnight Donovan felt an icy draft lick his cheek. He lay in bed in the bulky, autumn-brown sweater given him Christmas past by Marcie, who rested in half-sleep under his right arm. The *West Wind* was a fine old wooden boat, but she *was* made of wood, and the planks near the gunwale let in enough winter to make it clear that the season would be long. Even with sweaters and a thick comforter and the cabin's electric heater on full to warm him, an occasional draft touched his eyes, and he blinked and gave his lover a hug.

Unable to sleep and listening anyway to the sounds of wind and waves, he became aware of a shift in weight of the boat. Someone had stepped quietly onto the afterdeck and was walking toward the companionway, making a point of silence. A moonbeam lit up the old brass pitch meter, showing that the pendulum-like indicator had swung slightly aft.

Donovan reached into the bedside drawer for his Smith & Wesson and, holding the .44 magnum in his left hand so as not to disturb Marcie, aimed it at the door. From below the waves and through the hull came the low groaning of wharf timbers. Up on deck the footsteps halted, hesitated, and then came the sharp clink of an old brass key opening the companionway door.

"God must have a plan," Donovan grumbled, and put down the gun.

He slipped his arm out from beneath Marcie, and she moaned a complaint. "Where are you going?" she asked, just as came three knocks on the cabin door.

Jefferson said, "Bill . . . I got a weird one."

"So they say in the ladies' locker room," Marcie said, rolling onto her back and pulling the comforter up about her neck.

"Don't dis me, woman," Jefferson snapped, opening the door a crack and letting a bit of light into the cabin. Donovan rolled out of bed and pulled on his pants.

"What's up?"

"Some guy got his head bashed in at the cathedral. It was a real messy job. You gonna come alone or is Guinevere coming with you?"

Donovan asked Marcie by kissing her forehead. She smiled and said: "I'm going back to sleep. Have lots of fun bonding with your buddies." And she rolled over to face the wall.

Twenty minutes later and thoroughly briefed on the case by Jefferson, Donovan got out of the car and stood in the icy early-morning air looking up at the spotlit towers of the world's largest Gothic cathedral.

With an inside vista 600 feet long and twelve stories high, the cathedral towered over northern Manhattan from its site atop Morningside Heights. Its two spires, those of St. Peter and St. Paul, were still being built a century after the cornerstone was laid in 1892. When finished, the Indiana limestone would soar 323 feet above the altar. In the cavernous interior, the length of two football fields, seven private chapels were arrayed around the High Altar and Great Choir. The 248-foot nave held, in its north and south walls, the fourteen other chapels inside one of which rested the bones of Dale Charbaux. In all, the Cathedral of St. John the Divine was twice the size of Notre Dame and York Minster and only a bit smaller than St. Peter's in Rome.

Charbaux's body decorated the polished stone floor of the Arts Chapel, what remained of his head resting beneath the vulture's canvas talon. Far above it, the blindstory window showed St. Cecilia, the patron saint of music, a third-century celibate who was forced to marry a nobleman and with him suffered martyrdom, and St. Dunstan, the tenth-century Saxon who took monastic vows after being expelled from King Athelstan's court for practicing black arts.

Ubiquitous yellow crime-scene tape was strung from the nave wall to half a dozen rows of chairs and back again, helping to keep a small crowd of spectators from having their devotions spoiled. Buzzing around the scene were forensic technicians. Donovan wondered if cops and forensic guys weren't instinctively drawn to gore.

"It's primal, like winter and despair," he said.

"What?" Jefferson asked.

"Blood."

"There's been lotsa songs written about it. Anyway, the man's name is Dale Charbaux, spelled in the French manner. He runs a film festival that just started in the cathedral."

"I got the flyer in the mail," Donovan said.

"Yeah. Tonight they showed *The Phantom of the Opera,* the silent version. Early on in the show, Charbaux strolled over here, apparently to have a smoke. There are traces of cigarette filter stuck in his ear."

Donovan acknowledged the information as well as the way in which it was presented. As always in the body business, humor served to defuse tragedy. Not enough remained of Charbaux's head to account for more than a guffaw.

"What we got here is a fairly severe case of blunt instrument," Jefferson said. "The prelim puts it at four to six inches in diameter and delivered with sufficient force to scramble Charbaux's eggs. What's worse, he knew what hit him—his forearm was broken as he tried to ward off the blow."

Donovan asked, "Did you search the crowd for battering rams?"

"Not yet."

"So the killer is strong and also able to hide a hefty bludgeon in his clothes. What was the light like when it happened?"

Jefferson consulted the yellow legal pad that he carried everywhere, even to church. "I can duplicate it," he said.

"Chase the crowd first."

Fifteen minutes later the cathedral was dark except for a few small spotlights, the Christmas lights at one end of the vastness and the altar lights at the other, and floating in the middle the flickering image of Lon Chaney. With people gone and the organ silent, the ticking of the movie projector resounded like a slowing passing freight train.

Stepping carefully around the body, Donovan and Jefferson reenacted the crime, using all probable positions and approaches. They narrowed the probabilities down to one: The killer came from the narthex and caught Charbaux as he was having a smoke under the right wing of the vulture. One blow smashed the man's forearm and skull and left the corpse beneath the giant steel-and-canvas raptor.

"Lights," Donovan said, and the scene was illuminated once again. "The range of possibilities is limited. He came in the main door and walked the fifty feet to here, in which case he would have been seen on the street. The facade is floodlighted all night. Or he came from within the cathedral, more likely because he had to be able to see that Charbaux was here. This was no random killing."

Jefferson agreed. "You don't walk around with a battering ram looking for victims beneath modern art."

"Even if he hid the weapon in a bag or under clothes, it would be too heavy to take for a stroll," Donovan said. "No, Charbaux was killed very deliberately . . . but *why?*"

"There doesn't seem to be a reason in his background. From what I can tell this early in the game, he lived alone, had no obvious enemies, and the only thing he did that was odd was . . ."

"Dress up like a ghoul and run movie festivals in cathedrals.

Most folks come to pray. Still, that ain't much of a motive for murder. Let's go deeper into his background at the same time that Forensics goes deeper into his skull—maybe that weapon left a signature."

The morgue workers put Charbaux into a body bag and put the bag on a stretcher. That they carried out of the cathedral. In its place was a white outline, over which Donovan stood, holding his left fist aloft to simulate a lethal blow approaching his forehead.

He said, "Okay, *incoming!*" and hit himself on the forehead and did a good pantomime of collapsing in a dead heap, landing atop the outline but not exactly matching it.

Noting the difference between chalkline corpse and Donovan, Jefferson said, "You're taller than Charbaux," and touched pen to pad. "He's only five-ten. You got three inches on him. I make the killer to be six foot even."

"And right-handed and strong. Either a construction worker or a right-handed tennis player with one hell of a serve."

Jefferson said, "We'll get more background in the morning. See if he's rich or important or anything."

"They're aren't any stones missing from the wall, are there?" Donovan asked, hoisting himself back up and brushing some chalk dust from his pants. "It makes more sense if a solitary lunatic happened along, picked up a brick, and debrained the guy."

But there were no stones missing, and Donovan led Jefferson out of the cathedral into the morning, pausing only to give admittance to a television cameraman of his acquaintance. Donovan hadn't spent time in a house of worship since he was a kid, at least not quality time. There was always the odd funeral, of fallen colleagues and other loved ones. Churches made him nervous. Good people were forever being buried there, and one of the principles that guided Donovan's life was that good people should live forever. Spending more than cursory time in churches gave Donovan bad dreams of bleeding hearts of Jesus and the nuns' insistence that no one could reach heaven except Catholics from a white, Western European background, and then only if they led no kind of lives at all. Too bad none of the nuns of his childhood torments lived to meet Marcie.

Donovan opened the trunk of his car and pulled out three garbage bags stuffed with old clothes.

"What's this?" Jefferson asked. "Donating your garbage to the church?"

"And why not? They filled me up with theirs."

"A lot of you white guys really got a hardon against religion, don't you?"

"What do you know? The worst thing you had to deal with on Sundays was Mahalia Jackson. Help me get this to the Recycling Center in the rear basement, would you?"

"Old clothes?" Jefferson asked, feeling the bag Donovan thrust into his arms.

"I'm throwing out my old wardrobe."

"Bullshit! It died of natural causes."

They walked along the cobblestone path that paralleled the south wall of the cathedral until reaching St. John's Cathedral Recycling Center, open from 11 A.M. through midnight seven days a week. Conceived in 1974 as a reaction to urban pollution and expanded in 1988 when the Rain Forest Coalition moved into the office of the Cathedral Community Ministry, the Recycling Center took in refuse from all over the West Side and Harlem and sold it to recycling firms. The profit from this refuse-forwarding service went for conservation measures in the Amazon jungle.

After depositing the clothes in the huge deposit box, painted green with a splendid rainbow splashed across, Donovan and Jefferson drove to the funky all-night diner on West Street across from the Javits Convention Center, where they sat down to bacon and eggs and the morning joust with *The Times'* crossword puzzle, and Donovan quietly swore to let the matter of Dale Charbaux be resolved by someone in the West Side Major Crimes Unit other than himself. The Charbaux murder would be assigned to Moskowitz, who thought that the cathedral was amusing because the bishop seemed more interested in his social-activist, gay-rights, arts, and AIDS-awareness programs than he did in praising the Lord.

"Moskowitz will plotz when he gets this case," Donovan said.

"Amen, brother," Jefferson agreed.

"What's the name of the actress in *The House on 92nd Street?*"

"How many letters?"

Donovan counted ten.

"I don't know," Jefferson said. "Anywhere south of 110th has too many white guys. Ask me about uptown."

Donovan sighed and put down his pencil. "It think it's Simone Signoret but I'm short a letter. What's on for this morning?"

Jefferson peered at his pad, then said: "Tieman has a court appearance. Bonaci is at Midtown South checking background on his bunko case. Corrigan is staked out with TNT watching a crack house on 107th Street. That could be more than usually entertaining. TNT is going to bust it in half an hour."

"A Tactical Narcotics crack bust ain't my idea of a hot time," Donovan said. "The big excitement is betting on which West Indies island the perps come from. Where on 107th does this extravaganza occur?"

"The first floor at 507 West."

Donovan drained his coffee cup, then set it down. "I used to play stickball on that block. The building rings a bell."

5.

Off-the-wall, Basketball, Chinese Handball, and the Mill Luncheonette's Egg Creams

The 507 block of 107th Street lingered in Donovan's mind as the stickball equivalent of Tidewater in the Triple-A baseball league. All of the West Side's major league stickball stars played there at one time or another. Timmy Reilly hit homers there before going on to an illustrious career at Brooklyn South Detectives. Mel Lieber learned to put smoke on a Spaldeen that made it pop in Harry Rothstein's palm before they got together and opened the funeral home that would serve as a way-station to the afterlife for some of Timmy's clients. Donovan saw a past in stickball as a necessary credential for a Native New Yorker, like off-the-wall, basketball, Chinese handball, and the Mill Luncheonette's egg creams.

As always, the 507 block had no stores, apart from the Chinese laundry that alternated with the candy store on Amsterdam Avenue as the illegal numbers joint, and served up bets or starched collars depending on how diligent the street cops were at a given time. A block-improvement effort in the 1960s resulted in three scrawny maple trees, two of which had trash cans chained to them, and a color scheme for the wrought iron railing—red on the uptown side of the street and green on the downtown—nobody remembered why.

Apart from that, the block was poised between going to seed and being gentrified. Real estate developers had bought all the buildings that weren't already owned by the City of New York due to tax default, and were waiting for mortgage rates to go down while arguing lease-buyouts with grandmothers who had lived in rent-controlled apartments since the 1930s. The street was in stasis, and the only action came from the crack dealers who had opened shop in a large, rambling, ground-floor apartment in 507 W. 107th.

In the handful of years since it devolved from cocaine and turned into the drug of choice of the urban poor, crack had rewritten the street politics of New York. The epidemic turned teenagers into murderous drug dealers armed with automatic weapons and as likely to blow their way out of trouble as run from it. Ninth- and tenth-graders, relatively immune from prosecution even for murder, roamed the sidewalks, playgrounds, and public schools either selling crack or steering customers to houses where it could be bought.

Their bosses were only a few years older and replaceable. For every twenty-year-old drug czar put in jail, ten emerged. Command structures ebbed and flowed with the whim of the moment and the quality of the weapons. It wasn't like the old days of the Mafia, where you could put away a few bosses and shut down crime for a while. Organizations, like people, were replaceable. As the millennium approached there seemed no solution to the problem other than to throw money and cops' lives at it. The West Side Major Crimes Unit wasn't often involved, an individual crack deal being a tip-of-the-iceberg crime perpetrated by an amorphous body capable of slipping out of handcuffs. Special Tactical Narcotics Teams, called TNTs as if fancy acronyms could make the bad things go away, were assigned to go into neighborhoods and make a show of arresting replaceable bad guys. TNT sweeps were nonsense, everyone knew, but pleased the block associations, made good headlines, and had become political weapons. Donovan regarded them as sideshows whose only significance was in being more entertaining than daytime television.

"This bullshit changes nothing," was one of Donovan's sayings.

The sweep was directed at the Estrada brothers, Paco and Frank, who had been dealing crack out of a two-bedroom apartment since July, and might have stayed in business another four months had not a nine-year-old neighborhood girl been caught between two groups of high schoolers vying for control of drug traffic on two blocks of Central Park West and killed in the crossfire. Even as her blood dried on the pavement outside 507 West, TNT set up shop in a Consolidated Edison utility van across the street.

The setup was familiar: the van served as mobile HQ and electronic eavesdropping center, with videocameras taping both the street and the entrance to 507 West. Muted radio calls came in from undercover cops impersonating, variously, Con Ed workers, crack addicts, motorists double-parked or in some kind of distress, and traffic enforcement agents (who, being unarmed, were universally ignored). One Jefferson-trained electronics wiz was atop a cherry picker changing the light in a street lamp while providing an eye-in-the-sky for the team. It was his cussing (also learned from Jefferson) that helped convince the Estrada brothers that the loudmouth atop the telephone pole was indeed a city worker upholding the finest tradition of civil service.

Jefferson parked by a hydrant on Duke Ellington Boulevard—106th Street to cops and old-timers—and tuned his walkie-talkie to the TNT frequency. Mobile HQ had just announced a three-minute countdown to breaking in the door to the Estrada apartment, and the cop in the cherry picker had reported no indication of alarm on the part of the dealers. It was seven in the morning and the junior high and high school crowd was beginning to pour in for their morning fixes, to buy crack to smoke in the hallways of 507 West preparatory to terrorizing legitimate tenants and everyone else.

Donovan led the way down a flight of stone steps leading to the walkway beneath 510 West *106th* Street, just to the south of the crack house and built by the same turn-of-the-century developer. Like so many West Side blocks, 106th and 107th were developed after the subway was built up Broadway in 1904, connecting midtown with what then was the suburban Harlem Heights, now Morningside Heights, and Manhattanville, now West Harlem. Many of the original buildings were identical, with identical walkways beneath and between buildings, leading to internal courtyards and airshafts and other blocks. Originally service corridors, they had become convenient passages of transit for dope smoking, apartment robbery, and escape.

Donovan pulled his .44 magnum and poked the barrel in between two battered aluminum trash cans that reeked of salsa and rancid tomatoes on the curb across the street from the crack house. The pavement had fallen empty, as it sometimes did before busts, the ozone smelling as it did of anticipation. Donovan forever worried about civilians being caught in the line of fire. As if on cue, the pavement often dried up and the civilians blew away just before the bust. Donovan called it luck, Moskowitz a mitzvah; by whatever name, it worked. The parting of the innocents just before busts in which Donovan was involved was something he cited as evidence that God was on his side, at least during those moments that Donovan chose to believe in God.

The radio crackled. "We've been spotted," Jefferson said.

"By whom?"

"Ashley, the guy in the cherry picker."

"Make it official."

Jefferson spoke into the walkie-talkie: "Mobile HQ, this is Donovan and Jefferson of the West Side MCU, observing from across the street. You guys need help?"

"Negative, 'kay. We're going."

The radio acknowledgement " 'kay,' short for "okay," replaced the archaic "roger" in NYPD radio etiquette.

"I remember that building now," Donovan said. "There's a walkway like this one but it was bricked up thirty years ago. Runs between 507 and 509 and the parking garage down the block. It comes out in the elevator mechanical room in the garage."

Jefferson gave a concerned look down the block, then spoke into the radio: "Jefferson again, are you covering the walkway leading to the garage?"

"It's bricked up, 'kay," was the response.

"Brick walls break down," Donovan said. "Follow me."

He backed away from the trash cans that sheltered them from the street and led the way back to the building's airshaft. Donovan skirted the bottom of the six-story cavern meant to bring air to inner tenement apartments but carrying only soot, mildew, cooking smells, and babies' cries, and hurried down a narrow stone passage painted white and flecked with rust stains from steam lines. Two buildings' boilers were roaring and the pipes steaming and the temperature over 100.

Donovan said, "We used to hide out in here when we skipped school and the truant officer came around. The only one who could find us was my dad. He used to hide out here when he was a kid, too."

"You really think that the Estradas broke down that wall?" Jefferson asked.

"Their reputation is they're mendacious motherfuckers who don't like to be caught. This way."

Donovan turned two corners, crossed a second airshaft and a courtyard, and ran up the iron steps leading from the garbage room to the sidewalk at the corner building on 107th, safely down the street from 507 West. As they scurried across the street and into the basement of yet another building, bullhorns shrieked down the block and there were gunshots.

"Shots fired," Jefferson said.

"Gotcha. In here." Donovan kicked aside a stack of old plastic milk cartons that were being used to store spare parts from an elevator-repair job that had been going on for a least a month. He yanked open a dented metal door and the two of them were smacked in the face by a cold blast of outside air blowing down a disused shaft. Machine oil and pigeon droppings were on the floor along with soot-covered tools. On the West Side no job was ever finished; there was always more.

A decades-old elevator counterweight was propped against the far wall alongside a dark hole and a pile of broken bricks. There was no soot atop the bricks, as there was atop everything else.

"Bingo," Jefferson said.

Donovan motioned his partner to a crouch, then joined him. "Lights in the tunnel."

"Too late to call for help."

"No need. It's narrow. No escape," Donovan said, aiming his massive magnum down the tunnel through the spot where the Estradas had broken through.

Jefferson felt naked. They were exposed, with nothing to hide behind except firepower, and suddenly his standard .38 seemed like a popgun. It was too small for the New York City crack wars, whose major players were armed with automatic weapons like Uzis and Macs. Donovan's .44 magnum could stop a small car, if he aimed right. But it only had six shots, and you had to pull the trigger for each one. An Uzi could eviscerate a Volkswagen with the squeeze of a trigger.

There was a curse in Spanish and the flashlight scraped the wall. Donovan shouted "Police! Freeze" and sucked in his breath as the flashlight was thrown aside and replaced with the muzzle of a machine pistol.

Jefferson's .38 crackled and Donovan's magnum roared. Four rounds from an Uzi ripped up the old brick wall of the tunnel before the gun slipped from dead fingers and clattered to the floor.

A small, frightened voice cried out "No mas! No mas!"

Jefferson shook off the stunning effect of gunshots in a confined space and, shouting Spanish, ordered the surviving Estrada brother out into the elevator room and down on the floor. Donovan found the flashlight, inspected the riddled corpse of Paco Estrada, and returned rubbing his arm.

"I got to get this looked after," he said.

"What, the dead guy?" Jefferson asked.

"My elbow," Donovan said. "I'm getting too old for large-bore weapons."

6.

Turkish Coffee in a Finjon and Kashkaval Cheese

A t six A.M., a coastal oil tanker making its way up the Hudson to Albany from the Mobil terminal on Kill Van Kull with a boatful of number-two home heating oil left a wake that rolled the *West Wind* from side to side.

Marcie rolled with it and the blanket slipped off far enough to let in a cold draft. She grumbled and sat up, swinging her legs off the bed and sitting on the edge.

"Donovan!" she shouted, and got no reply. She mumbled, "Always getting up in the middle of the damn night and running off. This will change when we're married."

She pulled on her Reeboks but didn't tie them, then stood and straightened her sweat suit, pulling the pants up and the top down to cover the cold air that was tickling her midsection. Dawn light was flooding the main saloon through the open door to the cabin. She went to the galley, put sugar and two scoops of Turkish coffee in a *finjon* and poured in boiling water. Kashkaval cheese, melted over a bagel in the microwave, followed the coffee that she soon set on the table which, by then, had stopped rolling.

Marcie switched on "Good Morning America" and watched a pair of twin brother Kung Fu stars describe their new movie. A doctor, a social worker, and a blonde reporter who wore a $1,000 outfit comforted an AIDS victim. And, on the local news, Manhattan impresario Dale Charbaux was described as having been killed in the Cathedral of St. John the Divine, "apparently by a mugger."

Sipping coffee, she muttered, "So now we're getting out of bed to chase muggers."

7.
Still a Bad Case of Clint Eastwood Elbow

What I got is a bad case of Clint Eastwood Elbow," Donovan said. "It's worse in the morning."

"So stop firing that cannon and go back to your .38," Jefferson replied, having heard it all many times without ever being impressed.

Donovan laid the Smith & Wesson magnum on Riley's bar and stared at it dolefully. "The history of warfare has been an unrelenting struggle between the sword-makers and the shield-smiths," he said.

"Shield-smiths?"

"We've gotten to where tanks have ceramic armor and missiles are neutron particle beams," Donovan went on. He extended his hand to his buddy. "Your weapon, please."

Jefferson put the regulation .38 in Donovan's hand, where it was hefted lovingly. "A more elegant weapon from a more civilized age," he said, quoting Obi-wan Kenobi, a sage from an earlier age in the Donovan household.

"Don't tell me you're giving up the Clint Eastwood Special?"

Donovan returned the man's weapon and rubbed his elbow again.

"I'll have no part of the continuing escalation of firepower in the City of New York. My brain will be my weapon. At least until someone makes a snub-nosed neutron particle beam. Where did I leave my old .38?"

"In the shoe box where you keep your medals, where else?" Jefferson replied, glad that the cause of the pain in Donovan's elbow was removed, for along with it would go one more excuse to complain.

George the bartender came up, eyeballing the magnum as one might an irresistible new toy. Easily six-four, he sported a beer belly of superhuman proportions, and had a big wooly beard that gave him the look of a mountain man. He scowled at the lieutenant.

Bill Donovan and George Kohler had been friends for years, but only keen observers could tell. For all appearances they only talked because their establishments—the West Side Major Crimes Unit and Riley's Saloon—shared the same building, and would likely kill each other if left alone long enough.

Formed around the nucleus of Donovan's strong personality, which blended a certain nonchalance that disarmed critics with an impressive arrest record, the Unit (or House, as police outposts are called) served the burgeoning strip of Manhattan between Central Park and the Hudson River. Donovan's men roamed from Lincoln Center for the Performing Arts on the south to Columbia University and the Cathedral of St. John the Divine on the north, tackling major crimes in a crazy-quilt of ethnic neighborhoods and nouveau-riche condo farms.

Donovan was a second-generation police presence in the area. His father, a legendary cop-on-the-beat before him, willed to his son an enormous, rent-controlled Riverside Drive apartment which Donovan lived in before moving onto the *West Wind* with Marcie Barnes a few years back. With Marcie and Jefferson, Donovan's black chief aide and best friend, they were a family of sorts, but one composed of three black sheep. Their disputes were as famous as their arrest records, to the point where life on Broadway seemed vaguely empty if Donovan, Jefferson, and Marcie weren't squabbling over something.

Sometimes George got involved in it. Currently the dispute involved Donovan's magnum.

"You planning to get rid of that?" George asked.

"Yeah. Wanna buy it?"

"How many notches does it have?"

"Two. The 'Rican gang leader on 106th Street . . ."

". . . Duke Ellington Boulevard," Jefferson corrected.

"And Paco Estrada."

"What about the broad in Newport?" George asked.

"Marcie nailed her with a shotgun," Donovan said. "Sorry, only two notches in this model. You wanna make an offer for the .38?"

"I can't afford it. I'll give you twenty bucks for the magnum."

George reached for his wallet, but Donovan snatched the revolver. "What do you need a gun for?" he asked.

"Jake is supposed to get his money any day now. The vultures are gathering."

Jake was Jake Nakima, but only half of that was his real name. His first name proved to be unpronounceable and someone long ago hung the moniker Irving on him. He disliked that and began calling himself Jake, after "it's Jake with me," which perfectly fit his agreeable personality, and it stuck. The aging Japanese was known around Riley's for his preposterous claim to be the only Kamikaze pilot to have flown twenty-nine missions. That was not the cause of his current difficulty. He had spent several childhood years in a internment camp for Japanese-Americans built at the Santa Anita, California, race track, which gave him his lifelong addiction to gambling in general and horse racing in particular, and also entitled him to a $20,000 settlement from the United States Government. That was what caused the vultures at Riley's to flock.

Jake had talked about the $20,000 for all of the ten years the government had promised it to him. The Civil Liberties Act of 1988 brought the check a step closer, and Riley's regulars began assuming that Jake would spend the money on his rapidly growing roster of friends. The Justice Department sent Jake a promissory letter during the summer of 1991 and he made the mistake of showing it around the bar. Now he had more friends than ever, and George was thinking of buying a gun to hold the crowd at bay.

"Why don't you just advertise how much you're charging for Jack Daniels?" Donovan suggested, tucking the magnum safely away so George wouldn't shoot *him*. "You won't have problems with customers *then.*"

The bartender folded his tattooed arms and bristled. "You haven't bought a drink in a year-and-a-half and you haven't stopped busting my nuts. Either get over this health kick and start drinking like a man or pay for the club sodas and shut up."

"Police protection ain't cheap," Donovan said, taking the soda gun and refilling his glass.

Jefferson said: "Have Jake put a C-note on the bar and everyone can drink from that."

"Not good enough. Guys been losing money on the horses he picks for twenty years. He owes big to the community. I need a gun so I can limit the crowd to locals. The last I heard, guys were coming in from Brooklyn waiting for him to get the check."

Donovan said, "I sense that this yarn is going to drag on some. I may fall off the wagon before it's done."

The door swung open then and in came a puff of early autumn breeze. Along with it came Marcia Barnes and Jennifer Peel, her friend from Massachusetts who was in town for the marathon. There were six sets of eyes in the bar and all focused on the women.

Jennifer was taller than Marcie and a shade or two blacker, a former Ivy League volleyball champion who now coached the women's team at Amherst. Her hair was short and her face carried the unmistakable features of an Igneri Indian from Trinidad.

Donovan had never met Jennifer, only talked with her on the phone and been charmed by her slight island accent. But Jefferson, who professed to only like urbane black women from central Harlem, was in love.

Jennifer also was smitten. She spied Jefferson across the slightly crowded room and her expression said, "Welcome." She had frankly been rather suspicious of Marcie's falling in love with an Irish cop, especially a highly decorated one. In one moment, her opinion of Marcie's taste in friends went up a thousand percent.

"It took an hour-and-a-half to drive in from the airport," Marcie said.

"It was worth the wait," Jefferson said, assisting Jennifer onto a bar stool.

"You're not Donovan," Jennifer said, with a slight laugh.

"I'm Thomas Jefferson."

"I *like* the name."

"My daddy didn't name me after no ball player. This here white guy is Donovan. He was named after the spy who founded the CIA, and he's been stickin' his nose in other folks' business ever since."

"Hi," Jennifer said to Donovan, who shook her hand.

George the bartender said, "This is charming. Do any of these people drink?"

"Go away," Donovan snarled.

"I'm *so* glad you could come to New York," Jefferson said, using his best Billy Dee Williams savoir faire.

"He's gay," Marcie said.

"What a shame," Jennifer replied, looking genuinely sad.

"No I'm not! Just because I'm good-lookin' I have to put up with shit like that! Innkeeper, you ever see me with a guy?"

"Nope," George replied.

"Anybody here ever seen me with a guy?"

"A couple of dogs maybe," Donovan said. "Never a guy."

"What did I tell you? That gay stuff is a vicious rumor that Donovan started so he could keep all the women for himself."

Marcie said, "He's got the best now."

Jennifer laughed, "Thanks, guys. But I really came to town for the marathon."

"I am devastated," Jefferson said, slumping against the bar. "Innkeeper!"

"What?" George asked hungrily.

"A club soda, please."

"Someone is going to get hurt in here tonight," George grumbled.

"Let me make your day," Marcie said. "The *women* are running for their lives tomorrow and need to load up on carbohydrates. Two beers."

"What brand?"

"What's expensive?"

"Guinness."

"I'll drink to that. We'll have two."

She slapped a twenty on the bar, but George pushed it away.

"Donovan pays, for once," he said, with a vengeful grin.

Pondering his club soda, Donovan mused, "As we enter the stretch to the millennium, the men speak gently of soft drinks while the women slug down booze and run foot races."

8.

A Boys Choir of Death Masks

The nine-inch television screen flickered softly in the late night air aboard the *West Wind,* the death masks flipping past the eye like patterns on the backs of shuffling cards. As seen on "Nightline," the death toll mounted as the expressions of horror poured in. New York's new mayor warned that illegal social clubs with no fire exits or sprinklers were death traps, and threatened yet another crackdown, the first of the 1990s. The fire chief reminded the public of the many failed fire inspections and the need for an increased budget for inspectors. The chief of the Buildings Department preached on the topic of fire exits and also asked for more money for inspectors. The head of the Patrolmen's Benevolent Association warned against nascent plans to divert cops from their regular duties to the mayor's unlicensed social-club crackdown.

Two sociologists sought to understand, but also warned that the current estimate of 700 such death traps in the City of New York would swell to 2,800 by the turn of the millennium. And the Republican National Chairman, who also was a Pentecostal minister, noted that the arsonist who torched the club and instantly became America's newest mass murderer had come into the U.S. under the auspices of a Democratic administration.

By midnight, 147 had died in the Trinidad and Tobago Social Club fire in East Flatbush, Brooklyn. Donovan and Marcie and their guests watched in near-silence as the camera panned along the rows of victims. They were childlike in death, a boys choir of death masks. Suffocation came on within seconds, so fast that some still held drinks; couples' hands were entwined; and the club's disk jockey fell, still clutching a platter entitled "Young Lover," by reggae singer Coco Tea. Several young smiles had scarcely faded from teenage faces. Burns weren't shown on camera, having been judged horrible by network censors. Only the peaceful (or, at least, nongory) dead made muster.

"Why did we have to watch that?" Jefferson asked.

"Reality check," Donovan said. "We've eaten too well and had too much fun this evening. Time to recall we're still living in the City of New York."

"Those dead ones are my people, yet I feel almost nothing," Jennifer said. "There are too many of them, and they don't look dead."

"Man, who would go into a place like that?" Jefferson asked.

"Back home we never crowded by the hundreds into a shoe box," Jennifer agreed.

"What gets me is the motivation of the perp," Donovan said. "I can understand being pissed off at your girl. But then to torch her and 146 of her closest friends . . ."

"It must be easier to nuke a crowded room than to look one man in the eye and kill him," Marcie said.

Donovan switched off the television. "Have you girls drunk enough for one evening? If not, I can have Budweiser make an air drop."

Jennifer giggled, and Marcie said, "We're fine, Donovan. We'll run like the wind tomorrow."

"With a brewery and a pizzeria inside you?" Jefferson asked.

"It's called carbohydrate loading, Einstein," Marcie shot back.

"My momma called it gluttony." Jefferson got to his feet and stretched, pressing his palms against the roof of the yacht's cabin. "I put on ten pounds just watching you. Well, girls, it's been fun, but I'm outta here."

"We'll see you at eleven A.M. at the finish line," Donovan said.

"Nice meeting you, Thomas," Jennifer said, suppressing a ladylike burp.

Donovan went up onto the deck and escorted Jefferson to the dock. It was midnight and crisp, and several wisps of smoke emerged from the stoves of nearby boats at the 79th Street Boat Basin. Up above on the West Side Highway, a lonely siren from a solitary police car wailed its distant way toward midtown.

"So, what do you think of her?" Donovan asked.

"A nice girl. Tall and athletic, too. I like 'em that way. It's too bad she's a damn yuppie, like your wife."

"Marcie and I aren't getting married until Christmas. Don't rush things."

"I got to lower my standards to be best man at a damn yuppie wedding, and on Christmas Day. Next you'll be trying to marry me off to Jennifer the Yuppie Jock. She is cute, though. How long did you say she'll be in town?"

"Three or four days."

"And I'm in on the party tomorrow night?"

"Absolutely. As soon as the women get back from their foot race."

"I'll see if I can scare up some theater tickets," Jefferson said. "And there's a couple of restaurants and clubs I want to try out on her."

"Good deal," Donovan said, slapping his friend on the back.

Jefferson stepped onto the dock and said, "She's not really black enough for me, but she's an improvement over your wife. Have a nice night, Bill."

9.

THE EVIL THAT MEN DO

Jennifer Peel ran with the wind at her back, twenty-five thousand people to the left and the right, coming down the slope towards the Brooklyn side of the Verrazano-Narrows Bridge.

The running of the New York Marathon was why she was in the city: to fulfill a promise to herself and to see her old friend, Marcie, finish with a personal record of three hours. Jennifer had no thought of keeping up with Marcie, who would pull away soon after they reached the Brooklyn shore. It was enough to offer encouragement at the start. That and bathe in the rush off the Verrazano, the glorious moment when twenty-five thousand souls descended the slope of the world's longest bridge, accompanied by helicopters, blimps, television cameras, motorcycle escorts, and the cheers of a million spectators.

The women ran side-by-side down the off ramp, pushing the pace to stay ahead of the wave of humanity that looked, in television sets across the nation, like a sea of colored pebbles rolling off the sweeping steel sculpture of the bridge. They ran a 5:42 pace that, if she could keep it up, would bring Marcie to the finish line in Central Park in two hours and twenty-nine minutes. She would slow once securely ahead of the mob and, God willing, stay healthy for the next three hours. Jennifer would be happy simply to finish, then enjoy the post-race party on the *West Wind*.

They ran onto the Brooklyn shore and past Fort Hamilton, where Generals Grant, Jackson, and Lee were stationed before the Civil War, and up Fourth Avenue in Bay Ridge. Spectators were four-deep on the sidewalk in front of Kelly's Tavern, and a young boy stood atop an old car parked at the Amoco station.

"Wow," Jennifer said, the first thing said since the mayor fired the cannon to start the race, and Marcie responded with a quick smile. A burst of wind hit Jennifer in the face and ruffled her hair.

A shiny-new, blue-and-white police escort motorcycle pulled alongside, its red lights flashing. Most impressive in polished black boots, fully laden Sam Browne gun belt, and NYPD helmet, the driver looked at the two women and said, "You're on top of the world, girls."

"Hi!" Jennifer replied.

"Just clear a path, Donovan, we're coming through," Marcie shouted.

He waved a gloved hand and pulled to the side of the road, intent on staying with his lover for most of her grandest moment. Borrowing the motorcycle and uniform and talking his way into the role of escort was simple for the highest-profile cop in New York. Keeping track of Marcie for all twenty-six miles would be harder.

As seen in the rear-view mirror, they were quite a pair: Marcie's cocoa skin covered the body of a limber athlete; Jennifer's darker brown was stretched over a taller, more muscled body. The identical blue-and-white running outfits—obtained from the Patrolman's Benevolent Association's clothing cooperative—and the look of comradeship revealed them as friends.

Donovan adjusted the mirror so he could see them better, and pulled ahead into a gap between groups of runners and moved to the center of Fourth Avenue's southbound lane. As the runners moved out of Bay Ridge and into South Brooklyn, the mod shops, Irish bars, and Italian restaurants gave way to a succession of ethnic neighborhoods before reaching the towering chrome ego of Manhattan.

Twenty-five thousand affluent marathon runners from eighty nations ran through the Silk Stocking district on the East Side and Donovan stayed with them, riding the motorcycle as if it were Secretariat, gliding along with the ribbon of humanity and gunning the engine on the steady incline up First Avenue into Harlem. Jennifer had dropped back in Brooklyn, as planned.

Donovan rode with her as the pretty woman from Worcester, Massachusetts, who had known Marcie since both were little girls, negotiated the streets of New York City for the first time. When he roared ahead to find Marcie, he left Jennifer with a wave and the confidence that, surrounded by so many people on such a tightly controlled course, nothing bad could happen.

Donovan found Marcie an hour later as she coursed through the Bronx and back into Manhattan, with Central Park the destination. She was still on pace, running confidently and preparing for the loop around the park to the finish line. Donovan thought that she never looked better than she did that day, the day she had trained for the past five years. "You're beautiful," he shouted.

She accepted a cup of water from a marathon volunteer at 110th Street, drank half of it, and threw the other half at Donovan. With a laugh and a toss of the head, she disappeared into the park.

10.
HOT FOR A KILL

As the runners streamed into Central Park, a horde of a different order swept out of Harlem, hot for a kill.

They were out-of-work black and Hispanic teenagers who sold and used crack and otherwise prowled the subways, sidewalks, and parks of Manhattan to raise hell. Civilization as represented by 25,000 mostly white runners with expensive watches and sneakers ate at the kids. It was a red flag, an invitation for chaos.

On Marathon Day, the horde was drawn to the periphery of the marathon route, jostling one another and chanting a rap song. Then they moved along 110th, swelling in numbers and knives and becoming what police had come to call a wolf pack.

It was such a group that ran amok at a Diana Ross concert in the park in 1983, beating and robbing anyone who got in their way. Another wolf pack struck two years later, breaking up a March of Dimes Walkathon that ventured through the park too close to Harlem. In 1989 thirty or so teenagers again rampaged through the northern regions of the park, gang-raping and nearly beating to death a twenty-eight-year-old woman who had committed the crime of being female and vulnerable. A special task force clamped down for two years, and nothing much happened save for the clamor of social scientists writing about what they called wolf-pack behavior and the kids called wilding.

Scott Carter and Darryl Weems were looking for adventure outside the cuchifritos shop at the corner of Fifth Avenue and 117th Street and found it on the periphery of the wolf pack that had turned into the park looking for prey. There should be no trouble finding that, they thought, what with 25,000 marathon runners in the park and a few hundred thousand watching. With the police guarding the busier sections of the marathon route, Park Drive North near Harlem was relatively deserted.

As the crowd of teenagers jostled along, looking menacing with their adrenaline high, Carter took out a stiletto and hefted it. The hilt, black ivory decorated with a gold letter S and inscribed with his name, grated against the huge, S-shaped gold ring that was his proudest possession, something to make the other kids jealous as they stood on the corner of Jackson Avenue, his turf. The ring was new and a bit loose; Carter took it off and stuck it and the knife in the pocket of his eight-ball jacket, also new. Harlem kids who weren't properly armed were killed for their eight-ball jackets.

The fun began in a crunch of blood. A twenty-year-old man on a bike was run off the road and beaten with a pipe, then chased into the woods amidst great laughter while his bike was driven off by a ninth-grader. A middle-aged jogger was knocked down and kicked and had his watch stolen, and a taxi driver who went to his aid had his windshield smashed.

A siren blast from a passing patrol car sent the wolf pack

scurrying into the woods atop the granite escarpment that faced 110th Street. There it split into three factions, two heading across the flat ground to the southeast, and the third along the escarpment to above Harlem Meer, the lake on the northeast corner near where the marathon route entered Central Park.

Carter and Weems were eager to pick up a little extra money. Not that they didn't have enough, what with the street price of pharmaceuticals more than keeping pace with inflation. But crack meant easy money, chump change, and they wanted something they had to work for. Perhaps break a sweat. Separated from the rest of the pack, they walked quickly along the half-overgrown trails they knew so well from a lifetime on the prowl. That part of the park, from the reservoir to 110th Street, was to a large extent still wild, and only the adventurous or foolhardy went into it alone. For most of its travelers, it was mainly an escape route for muggers and apartment robbers who preyed on the wealthy neighborhoods of the Upper West Side.

They headed down a trail that led east to where the East Drive curved around Harlem Meer and joined with 110th Street. The newly installed bells of the Cathedral of St. John the Divine began to peal the noon hour as Carter and Weems rested atop a hill fifty feet from the roadway, to look for prey.

At that part of the marathon course, perhaps the most desolate, there were no race officials and few spectators, only runners following other runners. For a stretch of a few hundred yards where the race course rounded the lake, runners were alone with the woods and their hundred-dollar watches. Two of the groups that had split from the wolf pack re-formed a way down the road, where the curve ended and the drive began its headlong plunge south paralleling Fifth Avenue. As the bells tolled noon, the wolf pack struck at the New York City Marathon.

Twenty-four teenage boys burst from the woods and onto the route, scattering runners and ripping at the women's jerseys. One woman was thrown to the ground and had her watch torn off; another was surrounded by young hands thrusting at her breasts and thighs. A male runner was tripped up and went down with a pulled hamstring. Two other men ran straight into a half-dozen kids and elbowed four out of the way, then wrestled two to the pavement and held them.

It was over in half a minute, the wolf pack dispersing back into the woods south of Harlem as police cars and foot patrols arrived on the scene. Four teenagers were held by runners and cops, but the rest of the pack was lost in the still-wild northern sector of the park. Within ten minutes, runners passed by patrol cars and ambulances with little notice or concern. Once again, the sheer pace of life in New York City had rendered a crime commonplace.

Back up the road, Carter grinned at Weems. They were thrilled, though in running and tumbling through the woods Carter had fallen and Weems tripped over him, laughing.

"Let's go down there and see what we can find," Carter said, his stumbling over the W betraying a slight speech impediment. They eased their way along thirty more feet of trail until they reached a patch of grass that widened to join the west shoulder of the road.

They crouched behind a bush. The nearest runners were so close they could almost hear their hearts beat.

—

II.

RUNNING WITH PAIN

Jennifer Peel had only run one marathon, the Boston, and that in the unremarkable time of four hours. She was a weekend jogger, not committed to running the extraordinary distance of twenty-six miles like Marcie, who even as a girl living on her father's estate in Croton-on-Hudson, New York, took her body quite seriously. To take her mind off the increasingly nagging pain in her right thigh, Jennifer periodically checked her expensive and flashy running watch as she recalled the times they shared as teenagers. If she played tennis for fun, Marcie played to win, and won acceptance at the country club despite having a black father.

Jennifer enjoyed the thought of her lifelong friend's seriousness, and how it was often disguised by a flippant attitude. Donovan was the only man who both saw through that and fancied it. Maybe that was why they made such a delightful couple. Jennifer welcomed the thought of partying with them that night.

The growing pain in her thigh had stopped her twice—once going uptown on First Avenue, and again heading down Fifth Avenue in Harlem. That second time she took three blocks to walk off the cramp. That damned cramp. It first came to her in the heat of the 1976 Olympic trials, and ended her playing career in volleyball. The heat was starting to get to her, too. Sixty-five was a bit too warm for a marathon, especially in New York City, where the concrete held in the sun's rays and made midday last well into evening.

Jennifer drank a cup of water and dumped another on her head and wiped off her forehead with her wrist band. *I'm going to finish this,* she swore, and started running again.

Running with pain, but determined that Marcie wouldn't be the only winner that day, Jennifer ran with the crowd down Fifth Avenue and out of Harlem. She passed a solitary TV cameraman who focused on the contrast of glamorous, mostly white runners and rundown buildings. A few blocks past 110th Street, the course turned into the park in the start of a broad curve that would take the runners near Harlem Meer, tucked into the northeast corner of the park.

As she turned into the park and left behind the huge crowds lining Fifth Avenue, Jennifer's thigh began to cramp up again. Going into the curve she tried to run it out, but had to stumble to a halt, hot and frustrated. Around the course ahead of her and unseen, police and reporters had begun to gather at the scene of the wolf-pack attack. Noting that the sirens and commotion had slowed the pace a bit, she checked her watch, hobbled to the side of the road and stretched, touching the ground. That didn't help, and neither did slow walking. Jennifer had to push on something, a fence post or a tree, so she could stretch her hamstring. A maple grew ferociously just beyond the wood line at the edge of a small, wooded hill. She went to it, placed her hands against it, and started to stretch.

From nowhere, angry hands grasped her. One held her shoulder and spun her about. Another held a bright object, sharp and deadly. Jennifer gasped and tried to wrestle away. She stammered, "Get away from me," and tried to break free, but was immobilized in fear. Then the slender knife went up into her belly, over and over again.

As she slipped to the ground her ears roared with blood and fury. Then Jennifer felt her cheek smack the cold dirt beneath the maple and everything went quiet and black.

—

12.

Donovan Does His Famous Impression of Rommel

Marcie ran the final hundred yards in a fury, spurred on by the 100,000 spectators roaring on the sidelines and the grandstands as much as by the sight of the big overhead clock ticking perilously close to three hours. With a sprinter's kick she passed two other women and dashed across the finish line in two hours, fifty-seven minutes, seven seconds, then let out a big burst of air and nearly fell into the arms of Sgt. T.L. Jefferson. He wrapped her in a great sheet of light foil, designed to prevent sudden heat loss, that reflected a spectrum of color from the midday sun.

"I made it," she gasped, as he put an arm around her and walked her off into the rest area.

"With enough time left to take a vacation in," he said.

The rest area was strewn with recuperating runners and their solicitous friends. Jefferson walked her around, the foil wrapped around her, until she was okay to sit down. Once on the grass, he rubbed her leg muscles.

"How'd you find me?" she asked.

"I get paid to make sure you don't get in no trouble. Today is just an extension of what I do on the job."

She laughed, and said "I feel like a baked potato."

"You're corn, babe. Pure country corn. You want a towel?"

She said that she did, and one was produced. Marcie shrugged off the foil and towelled herself off. Then she jumped to her feet as a pair of black motorcycle boots came into view.

"Donovan!" she exclaimed, and wrapped her arms around him. "I did it!"

"You sure did."

"Take off your helmet and kiss me."

He did, and they kissed. Then he held her at arm's length, looked her over, and said "A little sweaty but otherwise intact."

Jefferson said, "Yeah. Let's take her home and toss her in the river."

Marcie said, "Wow. Where do I get my tee shirt?"

"Your what?"

"My souvenir tee shirt. Come on, Donovan, it's part of the prize. Anyway, *you're* all dressed up. You look like Rommel."

"Thanks," he said and slapped her on the bottom.

He checked his watch, and said, "The last time I saw Jennifer she was running a pace that should get her into the park in about twenty minutes. I'm going up to 110th to see if I can find her."

"Okay. We'll hang out here 'till you get back."

Donovan found his motorcycle, put his helmet back on, and headed away from the crowd and up the West Drive toward Harlem. As he approached Harlem, the radio burst to life with riot calls and warnings about a wolf pack having assaulted several runners and passersby near Harlem Meer. Donovan raced across the North Drive, which paralleled 110th Street, until he reached the point where the marathon came out of Fifth Avenue and into the park. Further south, police and ambulance radios crackled through the trees. A little way into the curve near the lake, a small crowd had gathered. A woman was crying and being consoled by an older man; another man waved at Donovan.

"What now?" he muttered, and gunned the motorcycle.

As he pulled to a halt and got off the cycle, the woman cried, "She's so young" and went back to sobbing.

Donovan brushed past the crowd and into the bushes to the foot of the maple. Jennifer Peel was laying on her back, blood staining her running shirt.

"No," Donovan said, and felt beneath her watchband for a pulse, but there was none. Fury rose within him, and when his clenching fingers began to close on her lifeless wrist he pulled them away. He stood, his breath coming in great gobs of anger for a minute, maybe longer, until he got himself under control.

The gold ring with the huge letter S caught his eye a few feet away. Donovan scooped it up and looked at it, then dropped it into a pocket when another officer came over and someone yelled "Up there!"

Scott Carter and Darryl Weems were atop the hill, staring at the scene below. For a few seconds that stretched like taffy, their eyes met Donovan's. He saw them as deer whose eyes had been frozen by a poacher's jacklight; they read his fury and were scared to death.

"Seal off the area," Donovan ordered, and got back onto his cycle. As Carter and Weems began running, Donovan raced along the edge of the road and turned into the woods as soon as he could, trying to turn a low-slung escort motorcycle into a dirt bike. The last he saw of the two young men, they were running along the crest of the hill toward thicker woods above Harlem Meer.

He gunned the cycle deep into the underbrush after them, and got halfway up the hill before hitting a log and flipping over, the engine stalling. Donovan scrambled up the hill but, when he got to the crest, he was alone.

He ripped off his helmet and smashed it to the ground.

13.
"THAT'S A HOME-BOY RING," HE SAID

The body was already zipped shut in the body bag when Jefferson and Marcie arrived in a squad car. She walked, then ran, toward the body, but Donovan caught and held her.

"Jennifer . . ."

"It was too late when I found her. I'm sorry."

"Let me see."

"No," Donovan said firmly, holding her until she stopped struggling.

Runners kept going by on a course that had been reduced by half by the addition of several police cars and a coroner's wagon.

"How did it happen?"

"A knife, I guess. I found this on the ground." He held up an evidence bag with the ring inside it. Marcie barely gazed at it, but Jefferson took a close look.

"That's a home-boy ring," he said. "Crack money."

"Yeah. Two black kids ran into the woods. I tried to catch them, but no dice."

"They *got away* from you?" Marcie asked, pulling away.

"Sorry," he said, with a sad shrug. "The bike wasn't designed to go up hills."

"I had better call her parents."

"I'll take care of that. They'll want to fly down from Worcester. Let's go home."

"I want to stay with her," Marcie insisted.

"Home," Donovan said, softly but firmly, and took her arm to lead her back to the car. She wrenched free.

"You go home," she snapped. "I'm staying here to find out who did this."

As she stepped back from Donovan, she bumped into a coroner's aide and would have stumbled if Jefferson hadn't been there. He took her by the shoulders and said, "You're going back to the boat. Bill will stay with Jennifer. You're in no condition to help."

Marcie tensed up even more, then her shoulders slumped as she accepted the inevitable. There would be plenty of time for vengeance after the crying was done. She walked slowly to the car.

"I'll catch them," Donovan said, but she didn't reply or even look back.

Donovan watched as Jefferson eased the car away from the crowd and headed off westward, taking her to the *West Wind* at its berth at the 79th Street Boat Basin. The morgue technicians carried the body to the wagon and put it in, then that too drove away.

The area was sealed off with yellow crime-scene tape and patrolled by two uniformed officers. Forensics experts were scouring the scene, coordinated by Howard Bonaci, one of Donovan's best men at the West Side Major Crimes Unit.

The melancholy that had descended upon the bright autumn day made Donovan feel suddenly foolish in the motorcycle-cop's uniform. The black boots that seemed so snazzy an hour before had become silly. He longed for his corduroy pants and penny loafers. He looked around uneasily, then decided that work was the best therapy and stepped over the tape into the crime scene.

Bonaci said, "Yo, Lieutenant," and used a stick to point to a massively scuffled area near the base of the maple.

"Footprints?"

"One partial and one clear. The girl must have planted one foot pretty good about five feet from the base of the tree and the other closer. We got a good print of the front of her left shoe."

"She was stretching," Donovan said. "Marcie does it all the time. She must have had to work out a cramp. This *would* be the spot where there's no fence alongside the road."

"You said she was from out of town?"

"Massachusetts."

"Then she didn't know not to go into parks, even a little bit into parks. It's not your fault, Lieutenant. Those guys nailed her less than thirty feet from the road. The sector cops chased a couple dozen kids through these woods at about the same time."

"There's another print?"

"Yeah, but not good. It could be one, it could be two or more. There's a partial of what looks like a cowboy boot."

He pointed at it with the stick, and Donovan crouched to get a look. The heel of a narrow, perhaps fancy boot was indeed pressed into the soil several feet behind the tree. Around it, leaves and soil were displaced by the signs of a fierce struggle that involved too many footprints to identify or even count. Most looked like sneaker smudges. Dirt and grass clumps were torn up and tossed around.

"You get photos of this?"

"Yeah, a whole bunch. It looks like the two guys grabbed her over here, one of them stabbed her, and she got tossed over there." Bonaci pointed at the spot where Jennifer's body was found.

"It looks a damn war was fought here, but I only saw two kids. Don't know how two kids could dig up so much dirt."

Donovan stood and looked around. Jennifer died at the base of one of a half-dozen maples that the city planted along that edge of the road a few years back, replacing a thicket of scrub oak. Apart from the striplings, only an older oak stood nearby.

Donovan looked up the hill to where he had seen the young black men standing. He wished he had gotten a clearer view of them. All he could say for sure was that one was taller than the other and both looked startled.

He began up the hill, following the same trail that Carter had followed, occasionally spotting the hint of a footprint. Once at the top, Donovan found the spot where Carter and Weems had been standing. The leaves were much-trampled there, but there were no clear prints. Five cigarette butts lay near the roots of an aging pitch pine into the trunk of which was carved a rough Maltese cross. The butts looked fresh, and he put them in an evidence bag. That was it, nothing more to look at other than a glint of light off Harlem Meer through the trees.

Donovan pushed his way through the underbrush to the spot where his bike flipped over, then descended the rest of the hill and walked back along the race course to the crime scene. He gave Bonaci the evidence bag, then leaned against a tree and watched runners go by until it was time to go home. He was afraid to face Marcie. Her friend, who had been staying with them, was dead. He should at least have the heads of the perps as trophies, to make her, and maybe him, feel better.

14.
UNTIL FORENSICS AND THE CORONER CHECK IN

The *West Wind* was a fine old wooden ketch, lovingly maintained on deck and below, with a mahogany wheel and wooden spars that swung appealingly in an early autumn evening breeze. Donovan thought her the finest boat in the marina, a splendid contrast to the many fiberglass houseboats, most of which hadn't left dock in years.

Still, as he walked down the dock to where she was berthed, he felt a growing anxiety. He was going home without having served vengeance on the killer of Jennifer Peel; it was just a matter of time before that failing came home to roost. Sure,

Marcie was an experienced, objective police detective as well as his fiancee, but Jennifer was special to her. The night before, when she slept in the aft cabin, Jennifer was overwhelmed with kindness: is the bed soft enough, are you warm enough, would you like a cup of cocoa? And now . . .

Donovan stepped onto the deck and down into the cockpit, averting his eyes from the several boxes of catered food sitting amidships waiting for a post-marathon party that would never occur. He was three steps down the companionway to the main saloon when Jefferson came up.

"Keep it down, man. I finally got her to sleep."

Donovan looked forward toward the closed door of the owner's cabin. "How bad is it?" he asked.

"I never seen her this whacked. She was telling me about what they did as kids and all. She's really upset, Bill."

Donovan nodded. "Thanks for looking after her."

"Did you find anything else at the site?"

"Just fragments—cigarette butts and footprints. Bonaci is in charge. And I just got a glimpse of those kids," Donovan said.

"There's nothing we can do until Forensics and the coroner check in," Jefferson said. "Why don't you rest up. I'm going home to change for the wake."

The word "wake" smacked Donovan's face. It wasn't right to ask Mr. and Mrs. Peel to mourn their daughter on a boat. It would have to be at his apartment, which he hadn't lived in since Marcie rented the boat. The apartment would have to be opened, aired out, cleaned and stocked with food and drink. The plans to create in it a family residence with enough bedrooms for two-point-seven children and a dog seemed inestimably further off.

He said goodbye to Jefferson, got himself a glass of water, and sat on the starboard lounge. The ship's chronometer sounded seven bells as he took off his Sam Browne and laid the heavy belt on the coffee table. Next to him was a small pile of cotton; Marcie's New York Marathon tee shirt, given to winners. He held it up and watched the light come through it. *Some winners,* he thought, and put it down.

Marcie came out of the cabin bundled in his old terrycloth robe. She draped herself over his lap and put her arms around him and held him very tight.

She avoided his eyes for a long time, and he avoided hers. But finally their eyes met and he saw that hers were red from the tears, and swollen.

Marcie said, softly, "You still can't cry. My friend is dead and you can't cry."

He replied, quieter than her, "I'm sorry."

"I love you anyway. I'm just trying to understand."

Donovan held her tighter still, and once again she lapsed into silence.

15.

TREMBLING CLOSE TO YOU

*That is what you did. You died. You did not
know what it was about. You never had time to learn.
They threw you in and told you the rules
and the first time they caught you off base they
killed you.* —Ernest Hemingway

I t smells like Paris on payday," Donovan said, looking with suspicion at the uncorked bottle of florid liqueur that George had proudly shown him.

George offered one of his scowls.

"You're like a squirrel, Donovan," he said. "You bust my nuts."

Donovan was not put off. "What did you buy this crap for?"

"I'm trying to improve the image of the place. Attract more people."

"Why don't you lower the prices? What's Jack Daniels go for these days?"

George whisked the bottle of liqueur off the bar and recorked it. "Don't start!" he growled. "You never drank Jack Daniels and you never will. You just bring it up to bust my nuts."

"How much?" Donovan asked.

"Three-fifty," George growled.

Donovan whipped out his calculator, tapped out some figures, and said, "Three dollars and fifty cents for seven-eighths of an ounce of Jack Daniels works out to $128 a quart, for which you should get the electric chair."

George tried to glare holes through Donovan's skull, and when that didn't work he opened a bottle of beer and sat down on his stool, giving a panic-stricken bar the impression that he had quit work for the day.

Donovan reached over the bar, took the soda gun and squirted himself some club soda, then sat down next to George.

"Did you get my volunteers?" he asked.

"I got four of 'em," George said. "Jake, Gus, D'Amato, and Waldo Pepper. They'll be at your place in an hour. Gimme the keys."

Donovan slid a spare set of keys across the bar, along with a piece of paper. George plucked a pair of reading glasses from behind the bar and balanced them on his nose.

"Dust. Vacuum. Open windows and doors to air out. Clean up beer bottles. Come on. You don't live in the place no more. How long have those bottles been there?"

"When was the last time you borrowed the place for a poker game?"

George harrumphed, and continued reading: "Pick up the food from the boat and lay out a buffet. Donovan . . ."

"Gus can do that. He has a talent."

George folded the paper and put it in his pocket along with the reading glasses.

Donovan said, "We're picking up Jennifer's parents at La Guardia at six. Try to have everything done by then." He handed George a fifty-dollar bill. "Buy the boys some beer, but make sure they clean up that mess, too."

"It's a shame about her," George said. "Are you gonna catch the guys who did it?"

"Don't I always?"

"No."

From down the bar, someone called for service by waggling his glass. It was Chico Brewer, a Brazilian ethnologist in town for post-doc work at Columbia but mainly known for sitting at the bar in Riley's, fingering a gold earring, and reciting the day's AIDS deaths from the obituary page of *The Times*. George glared holes in the man's skull, and shouted, "Go to the Puerto Rican joint if you don't like the service!"

Donovan checked his watch, then got off the stool. "You're a gentleman, Mr. Kohler."

"Take it easy, Bill."

Donovan left the bar and walked to his car, which was parked in the marked spot near the door that led, in turn, to Riley's, the Yangtze Pantry ("New Gourmetian Pleasures, like treasures found at the bottom of a lashing sea"), and, upstairs, the West Side Major Crimes Unit.

On that November Sunday, Donovan and Marcie drove to La Guardia Airport to pick up Jennifer Peel's parents while Jefferson went to his home in the Harlem Historical District to change for the wake. Donovan and Marcie were tense with each other through the ordeal that followed: two nights of tears and mourning in Donovan's apartment, the nightmare of arranging for the body to be transported to Worcester, and the awkward moment of Marcie's leaving to take the Peel family and their daughter home. By Tuesday evening Donovan was exhausted and alone on the *West Wind*, wrapped in a down coat and knit cap and sitting on the foredeck, listening to Tom Waits sing "Jersey Girl" and staring at the cold glistening wavetops.

The forensics reports had come in. The bootprint was as yet unidentified. It was definitely laid down since the last rain—twenty-four hours before the killing. The cigarettes were unfiltered Camels and both were smoked the day Jennifer died. There was a partial thumb print on the gold ring. As for the murder weapon, the tip was sharp and the blade narrow—a stiletto. The wounds contained shards of nylon fabric from Jennifer's jersey, and other junk—bits and pieces that tend to get into wounds when people are killed in the woods, such as detritus from a pitch pine, including sap. That was it. *Got to find two faceless teenage crack dealers,* Donovan thought. *Two kids who went on a rampage with a couple dozen other kids and, in the course of it, took a life. Nothing to it.*

There came a rustling on the dock, a bumping of suitcases. Jefferson helped Marcie over the stern rail and followed with her bags. Donovan's spine straightened but he didn't turn his gaze away from the wavetops. Jefferson looked forward at his boss and best friend, recognized the mood, and said "Try to get some sleep. Him too," and squeezed Marcie's arm.

"Thanks, Thomas."

Jefferson's footfalls receded in the direction of land.

Marcie dragged the suitcases into the cockpit, stared at them for a bit, then kicked both down the main companionway. She pondered the silhouette of her lover, caught some strains of the music—Tom Waits was singing "And I remember quiet evenings trembling close to you"—and walked slowly along the starboard rail to the bow.

When she stood behind him, he looked over his shoulder, smiled faintly, and laid his right hand, palm up, over his shoulder for her to touch. Marcie touched her fingertips to his, then ran her hand over his until they could grasp each other's wrists with their fingers.

Her silence and her touch told him that she was back; the funeral was over, the mourning set aside if not forgotten, and she was home. Any vengeance-taking for the murder of Jennifer Peel would come later, and they would have their vengeance together.

There was the lonesome murmur of a tugboat's fog horn.

Donovan's head tilted backwards and his lips parted. Marcie lowered her lips onto his, her long straight hair framing him, her pointed tongue touching his.

"Welcome home," he thought.

48

16.

FIREFLIES ACROSS THE GRAVEYARD

Just before the curtain rang down, Michael Avignon roamed the pallid moonscape of the Stone Yard, ever on the prowl for a good story.

Avignon was a freelance telejournalist, pushing fifty, who roamed the city in a 1957 Chevy hot rod that was his first car and which he had lovingly maintained for thirty-five years. He was unquestionably the best there was at finding news—be it a Hollywood superstar newly arrived for a weekend with her latest beefcake lover, a politician caught in a police sting operation, a plane crash, or some similar event of the sort that he called "photogenic catastrophes."

He made good money selling the footage to the wire services and local TV stations, and had become something of a legend in the news industry, admired by younger reporters but feared and ofttimes hated by his less-talented and energetic contemporaries. Avignon was a friend of cops who knew he would make them look good in the papers, and loved by bribable maitres d'hotel who he paid well for tips about when Cher was around with her latest lover. He went back a long way with Donovan, and on several occasions was the conduit for one of the lieutenant's legendary leaks to the press. It was Avignon whom Donovan admitted to the scene of the Charbaux killing on the first night that Marcus struck.

Like Donovan, Avignon was cursed by curiosity and introspection. He wondered why he was fascinated by the city's revolting madness and glitter, and why God made him so good at ferreting it out. He wondered what it would be like to be an old man in a young man's profession. He wondered why he couldn't fall as much in love with his lover as she was with him. His constant wondering about why things were so bad and why he couldn't resist chronicling civilization's downfall kept him up all night, listening to the police scanners for photogenic bad news and racing off in his boyhood hot rod to shoot it.

The murder of Dale Charbaux was tailor-made for Avignon. There was an unusually good mix of irony and gore. Given time, he thought, Donovan would even get a chuckle out of the denouement. For the time being, he was happy stalking a strange figure he had just seen mucking about the front door of the gigantic structure.

The Stone Yard was on the north side of the cathedral, occupying the field where kids formerly played soccer. Now it was a moonscape of building stone and the sheds in which the stones were cut.

Avignon was drawn to the cathedral because the Charbaux murder was *weird*. Once there, he was further drawn to the Stone Yard, where the eccentricity had crystallized in the bizarre notion of helping underprivileged black and Hispanic youths by teaching them to build cathedrals. "What a wonderful marketing concept," Avignon gushed when the bishop first sold the idea to his flock. "The bottom falls out of the co-op conversion market, there's no longer a building boom to use semiskilled labor, so let's teach the poor how to carve gargoyles."

Donovan, who counted Avignon as a friend, concurred in this judgment. But Donovan, as a general rule, hated religion too much to go to God's house unless someone was murdered there. He declined Avignon's telephone request to join in an exploration of the cathedral, preferring to spend the night in bed with Marcie. Once again, the buck was passed to Detective Moskowitz. He too thought Avignon's request amusing but frivolous, and left the curious photographer to prowl the cathedral grounds on his own.

At midnight, with a three-quarter moon glistening off the stacks of Indiana limestone, Avignon crept slowly, his jogging shoes crinkling softly in the thin layer of stone shavings. It was a

Wednesday evening, and nothing was doing inside the monumental structure. To the north and across 114th Street, the Emergency Room at St. Luke's was doing its normally brisk business, with a steady stream of ambulances, police cars, and private vehicles dropping off victims of the city for whatever patching up could be done. The flashing red lights swept over the heaps of moonlit stone without brightening a thing. They were fireflies across the graveyard.

Avignon went to the Stone Yard by instinct. He smelled blood. The scent of prey had always been strong with him, and he swore to an ability to detect stories by their pheromones. Avignon's senses tingled. Between the emergency room and the cathedral, amidst the piles of virgin stone waiting to be carved into gargoyles, he poked the lens of his Ikegami videocamera.

It was ghastly quiet. The ambulances and police cars were running with their sirens off and the red lights flashed by silently. There was no wind to rustle the leaves of the solitary maple tree. Avignon crept up to the corrugated steel carving shed that housed the gargoyle project, and found the door unlocked and ajar.

There was nothing inside to steal but stone slabs, grotesques, and gargoyles, and who needed them on 114th Street? Still, no one in New York City left the door open, even if there was nothing to steal. An open door invited squatters; a bunch held down the tenements across Amsterdam Avenue for nearly two decades.

"The sonofabitch must have gone in here," he thought.

Avignon pushed the door open and stepped inside, carrying the Ikegami as if it were a shield. That was an old habit, germinated in the days when he carried a four-by-five Speed Graphic and shot black-and-white stills for the tabloids. There was nothing like a sturdy, *big* camera to push crowds aside and ward off blows from outraged macho actors who had just been snapped in the company of women not their wives.

He heard nothing, but the sense of blood went from a rumor to a roar. A three-foot-high grotesque, shaped like a furious Pekinese with four sets of jowls and a maw that gaped wide enough to swallow an arm, looked down on him from atop a stone column. The air was alive with anger and death, and then there was movement. Out of the darkness behind a nine-foot stack of granite slabs came a blur of robes and a hand raised overhead, waving a cudgel.

The word *Jesus* got half the way out Avignon's mouth when something big and heavy crashed down on him, smashing the camera between it and the side of his head. He was thrown to the dirt, and the last thing he recalled was the powdery feel of limestone dust and blood against his cheek.

17.

420 HORSES, DUAL QUADS

Licking his lips, Donovan said, "She has a 396 cubic inch Corvette engine; high lift cams pushing 420 horsepower; Mallory ignition; dual quads; four-speed Corvette transmission; a Hurst speed shifter; and a four-eleven rear end."

"Don't call a car 'she,' " Marcie grumbled.

"What kind of mileage does she get?" Jefferson asked, looking with a mixture of fear and awe at the mint-condition 1957 Chevy, which was flame red with a black interior, sitting in a cathedral parking spot.

"Ten gallons per mile," Donovan replied, patting the left front fender, which bore a carefully executed painting of a busty woman holding a fat and phallic bomb, and the legend "Enola Gay." He dangled the keys enticingly. "Want to take a spin?"

"Donovan, your friend is in the hospital and all you can think of is stealing his car?" Marcie said.

"Who's stealing? He gave me the keys years ago. I'm the only other one he trusts to drive her."

"Bill sees it as his sacred duty to look after the Enola Gay while

Avignon is healing," Jefferson interpreted, earning himself a look of admiration from the boss.

"How is he?"

Jefferson replied, "A bad concussion so far as the doctors can tell. He has to have a CAT scan, but that will wait until he wakes up and recovers from the monster headache he's gonna have. X-rays show some fracturing in his skull bones. He's gonna be out of action for a while."

"How long?" Donovan asked.

"Long enough for you go get your driving rocks off. I assume you're gonna keep the car in the precinct garage, 'cause Avignon will be real pissed off it she's stolen."

"Trust me," Donovan said.

He got behind the wheel and turned over the engine, listening appreciatively to its roar. He revved it once, then shut it off.

"No way that muffler is legal," Jefferson said.

"The sound is subject to interpretation," Donovan replied, getting back out of the car.

It was half-past dawn, and the city was stirring. Though St. Luke's Emergency Room was quiet—stabbings and crack deaths traditionally abated with the approach of dawn—commuter traffic was brisk on Amsterdam Avenue. Cars, trucks, and buses poured downtown to the city's commercial center, and just to the north, early morning classes were getting under way at Columbia University.

Jefferson said, "The night watchman found him at 2 A.M. He managed to pick the lock on the gate and drive into the Stone Yard."

"Mike always was good with burglar tools," Donovan responded. "He let me into my apartment one time when I was locked out."

"Where was I when this happened?" Marcie asked.

"Getting your hair straightened," Jefferson spat gleefully.

"Avignon was found on the floor of the carving shed," Donovan went on. "What the hell did he see in there?"

"Nothing that didn't see him first. The prelim holds that he could have been hit with the same boulder that refried Charbaux's beans. We'll know better after the doctors pick the pieces of videocamera out of his head."

"I don't suppose he taped the assailant."

"Not that much of the camera survived. Maybe Avignon *saw* something, but we won't know until he wakes up. *If* he wakes up."

"Go find out when that will be," Donovan said.

When Jefferson was out of earshot, Marcie said, "Who is Charbaux?"

"The first victim. Some guy with an absolutely spotless background who got killed for no reason."

"The first victim of whom?"

"I don't know of whom. I know that there have been two murderous assaults at this place in a week, both using an extremely blunt instrument. The previous crime incident at the cathedral was a purse-snatching in 1987."

He led the way into the carving shed, where the crime-scene tape was coming down and the cathedral's black and Hispanic apprentice stonecutters were ready to resume work on ashlars, sills, cluster mullions, traceries, apexes, cornices, and capitals, as well as on grotesques and gargoyles.

Bonaci, an indefatigable crime-scene busybody, had dissected everything and was finishing his notes.

"Same as the first one, Lieutenant. The perp was tall and right-handed and hit the victim with significant force. He was wearing fancy boots with a star design on the sole. This limestone dust sticks to everything. You may recall . . ."

"The lab found traces of limestone dust on Charbaux's shoulder," Donovan said. "At the time there was no way of explaining it, there being no free limestone near where he got hit."

Marcie said, "Limestone dust? Is that why you're calling these crimes related? Is that what's keeping you here?"

"I'm here because my friend was almost killed," Donovan said, then regretted the words before they were out of his mouth.

"My friend *was* killed," Marcie snapped.

"Come outside," Donovan shot back, and dragged her outside into the daylight.

She said, "I'm serious, Donovan. Let's get to work finding Jennifer's killer. Leave this to Moskowitz."

"Don't ever contradict me in front of my men," he said tersely.

She glared at him for an instant, feeling the incredible, contradicted fury that wells up when a loved one is the adversary. Then she turned and stalked off, tossing a "See you in the office" over her shoulder.

Donovan returned to Bonaci, who said, "Sorry."

"That won't happen again," the lieutenant said, a bit sheepishly.

"I can't imagine what it would be like to work with my wife," Bonaci said.

"We ain't married yet," Donovan grumbled.

"Well, to continue. We got a pretty good idea what the perp's boots look like, but not enough to estimate the size. The hardwood floor holds the dust, but not enough dust to make a complete print in."

"And where he came from?"

"Yeah, we got that too. He walked in here through the same door Avignon did. A little before him, I guess. He went behind that stack of stones over there and waited for the victim."

"An ambush? Led him in and attacked him? Can you tell the perp's movements outside the shed?"

"Nope. The ground is too hard."

"Very strange," Donovan said. "I'm going to talk to Avignon."

"Tell him that I still think he's an asshole but hope he gets better soon," Bonaci said.

He barely spoke when Jefferson came in, spotted the grotesque atop the pillar, and said, "I know that guy from Riley's. He's one of the bums you used to drink with."

"What about Avignon?"

"He's not as bad as they thought, and should be able to talk in an hour."

Donovan said, "Moskowitz can take over here. Let's grab some breakfast and then talk to Avignon."

18.

SLAPSY MAXIE ROSENBLOOM

H e was one of my gods when I was a kid," Avignon said, closing his eyes as a wave of migraine pained him. "Slapsy Maxie Rosenbloom was battered and also bloodied but he never gave up and always came back for more, usually with a smile."

"He never was a contender," Donovan noted.

"That's the difference between us—I'm a contender. And I'll be proven the best when I get my Oscar."

"For what?" Jefferson sniffed.

"For the documentary I'm shooting on the dissolution of Western civilization as seen in New York City as the year 2000 approaches," the battered cameraman said proudly.

"I think your project needs a mite broader scope," Donovan contended.

"No, Donovan! I have it under control! I have the perfect focus—murders in the cathedral, and more! Murders of the defilers of the temple, *in* the temple."

"What *are* you talking about?"

"The cathedral is run like Timothy Leary is the padre. Nobody *prays* in there. They run film festivals and waste-recycling projects. They put up art for AIDS victims and give readings of gay and lesbian poetry. Their idea of helping the poor is teaching black kids to carve gargoyles. Get with it, Donovan. A religious zealot who thinks he's Saint Augustine is killing the perps for defiling the temple."

"Including Charbaux?" Donovan asked.

"Starting with him. Read this."

He handed over a sheet of heavy, rag-bond paper with handwriting on it.

"I found it nailed to the door of the cathedral at one in the morning. Just like Martin Luther nailed his ninety-five theses to the door of All Saints Church in Wittenberg. Donovan, I nearly got the guy on tape doing the nailing. I followed him, and that's why he ambushed me. I'm telling you, we're on to something here."

The parchment seared Donovan's fingertips. "Of course you smudged any prints," he said, then laid it out on the serving tray next to the bowl of ice chips and the half-pint of orange juice.

"Hey, the guy was nailing theses to the door. I wanted to see what they said."

"Which is?" Jefferson asked.

"Read it and weep. You got another nut job on your hands, Donovan."

"I've decided to specialize in them," Donovan said, proud at finally being able to admit what was common knowledge around One Police Plaza: that the cases involving sickies, weirdos, and exotic weapons didn't land on Donovan's desk entirely by accident.

He read slowly, shaking his head at the words, occasionally lifting an eyebrow:

" 'Live not in revelry and drunkenness, not in debauchery and licentiousness, not in quarreling and jealousy, but put on the Lord Jesus Christ and make no provision for the flesh to gratify its desires.' "

"So what?" Jefferson asked.

"Don't ask me, I'm no fan of God," Donovan said. "The last time we spoke He told me to take a hike."

Avignon sighed, "Those words are from the Bible. Romans

13, if I'm not mistaken. That was the passage that got Marcus Aurelius to take up Christianity."

"Marcus who?"

"St. Augustine's original moniker. Read on."

Donovan read: " 'The pleasure seekers of the City of Man will be punished for encroaching on the City of God. I am the protector of this temple, and I speak for Him.' Signed, Marcus Aurelius. Avignon, did you make this up?"

"I only tape peculiarity, Donovan. I don't create it. The guy thinks he's St. Augustine and is popping off defilers of the temple."

"All Charbaux did was run a film festival in there."

"That's enough. The place was built for worship, not watching movies. When there isn't a service going on, you're supposed to kneel and pray. Okay, they're protestants—*sit* and pray. Or meditate. But not watch fuckin' movies. Think about it. You did time in the system."

"Did what in the what?" Jefferson asked.

"Spent eight years in Catholic school," Donovan translated.

"Is that where you got this piousness that just drips off of you?"

"That's where I got it. Put this in an evidence bag and see if there are any prints left. Also check for limestone dust."

He gave the paper to Jefferson, who folded it carefully into a plastic bag.

To Avignon Donovan said, "Tell me about this Marcus."

"Well, I drove up from my studio to check out the scene where Charbaux got bashed. I picked the lock on the Stone Yard and drove inside. I can't just leave the Enola Gay out on the street, capiche? Where is she, by the way?"

"Safe," Donovan said, with a wicked smile.

"One dent and you're a dead man. But if you got to try her out, the Cross Island Parkway south of Howard Beach is a sensational drag strip. Anyway, I was circling toward the front of the cathedral when I see this guy come from across the street . . ."

"Where across the street?" Jefferson asked.

"Plaza Caribe. The six-story tenement the squatters took over twenty years ago."

"It's been gentrified now. Yuppies live there."

"Marcus has a point about defiling the temple. Things were bad enough when the neighbors were squatters. Now they're damn yups. So he comes from in front of the building, crosses Amsterdam, and walks up the steps to the main door. Not the door on the right they keep open for tourists—the center door that's only opened in November when they have the blessing of the animals and need to get the camels and elephants in and out. I tell you, I got primo pictures of *that* for my masterpiece. So he walks up to the door, takes his hammer in his hand, and nails the thesis to the door."

"Did you at least leave the nail so we can tell how tall he is?" Donovan asked.

"I left it. He goes six foot, easy. He didn't even have to stretch to do the nailing."

"Then what happened?"

"I must have made some noise and he sees me. He scoots around the south side of the cathedral past the scaffolding where they're finishing the South Tower, with me in hot pursuit. I lost him in the Biblical Garden. You know, where the rooster and peacock beg for bread crumbs during the day."

"But you figured he went around to the north side of the cathedral," Donovan said.

"Yeah. It was there or down the hill through Morningside Park into Harlem, and I didn't figure he was up to *that*. This guy was real white bread. Not even as dark as Marcie."

"Don't start trouble or I'll pull your life support," Donovan retorted. It was his fervent hope that the "degrees of blackness" arguments between Marcie and Jefferson were of the past.

Avignon continued: "I went around to the north side and through the Stone Yard. I saw the door to the carving shed was open, and I went inside. The guy must have been hiding behind a pile of stone. He bashed me. How's my camera look?"

"A mess. Were you taping when you went in? Maybe we can save the tape."

"No such luck. I may be the best cameraman in the world, but even I need light. I did tape the thesis hanging from the nail, if that will do us any good."

"Us?" Jefferson asked.

"Yeah, well I got a masterpiece to finish and you got a nut to catch. We *need* each other, Donovan."

"I haven't needed you since that time I got locked out of my apartment," Donovan sniffed.

"You want to keep the keys to the car?"

"Hey . . . don't threaten. I can impound her."

"Not without filling out a lot of forms. Let's keep this informal. You let me in on the case and I'll let you drive the car until I get out of here. The doctor tells me I can go home in twenty-four hours."

"Let me get this straight—I get to drive the Enola Gay for twenty-four hours in exchange for having you as a pain in my ass for the next couple of weeks?"

"We *need* each other," Avignon insisted, reaching out with a sun-gnarled hand and lightly touching Donovan's arm.

"Forget it," Jefferson cut in. "Donovan ain't handling this anyway. Moskowitz is."

"I haven't absolutely made up my mind on that," Donovan said, a bit uneasily.

Jefferson said, "If you work with this clown, what am I gonna do?"

"Help Marcie catch the creep who killed Jennifer," Donovan said.

"We got to talk," Jefferson replied, edging toward the door.

"Remember, the Cross Island Parkway at four in the morning," Avignon advised. "Don't get into a money race with the *cujine* in the maroon Iroc 4000, and don't get dents in the car," Avignon cautioned.

19.
BLACKS FOR THE SPICE AND JEWS FOR THE CONVERSATION

The dual quads sucked Atlantic Ocean sea breezes into the 420 horsepower Corvette engine as Donovan raced around the southeastern rim of New York City. Moving through the gears with the zeal of a car buff who had been starved too long by residency in Manhattan, Donovan took the Enola Gay eastbound along Beach Channel Drive from Breezy Point to Rockaway Beach. Then he turned north across Cross Bay Boulevard through the Jamaica Bay Wildlife Refuge and the tiny meadow's edge community of Broad Channel, and found that the road was, indeed, perfect for drag racing, even at midday.

Donovan did a zero-to-sixty without alerting the local uniformed constabulary, but forgot to time the run. Just as well, he reckoned. The car would never be as fast in practice as it was in his memory. His blood lust for fast cars temporarily sated, Donovan pulled the '57 Chevy up in front of the New Park Pizzeria in Howard Beach and went up with Jefferson for a couple of slices. The two friends made regular appearances there, usually on the anniversary of the killing of a black man by a white mob at the spot, to make a point and, perhaps, to dare the locals into making smart comments. That never happened.

"These guys know it's a setup," Jefferson said, staring balefully at a limp slice of lukewarm pizza. "Only a salt-and-pepper cop team would be crazy enough to show their faces in Howard Beach in a '57 Chevy, looking for trouble."

"Is that what we're looking for?" Donovan asked.

"It sure ain't a culinary experience. You know what's gonna drive us outta here? The lousy food."

"I haven't finished making my point. So, what's your problem with working with Marcie?"

"Other than having to hold the mirror while she fixes her hair? Nothing."

"Come on," Donovan prompted.

"I mean it, man. The Peel case is about teenage wolf packs, probably the same bunch that's been coming out of Brooklyn and busting up tourists in the Village. The D-train banditos. I can't go chasin' after them if I've got your yuppie fiancee slowing me down."

"She needs to work on the case personally. You're the only one who can help her."

"What's wrong with *you?*"

"I ain't black."

"You think of these things late in the game. The girl's been in your life for fifteen years, and now it occurs to you that this minor difference in your races could be a complication?"

"It doesn't get in the way of the relationship," Donovan said. "It does prevent me from going undercover in black neighborhoods. Come on, Thomas . . . yield to the logic of the situation."

"I don't wanna work with no yuppie," Jefferson insisted.

"And therein lies the real problem. Marcie just isn't black enough for you. She's not pure African and she's not street."

"We worked that out, her and me."

"Sure you did."

"Did you bring me to Howard Beach to discuss degrees of blackness?"

"No, but I might leave you here if you don't do what I ask," Donovan said.

"Oh, *man,*" Jefferson moaned. "There's no way out of this for me, is there?"

"Not really."

"It's not bad enough I got to chase teenage punks through Harlem, but I got to have the Afrap with me."

"The what?" Donovan asked.

"African-American Princess."

"Just don't get on her because her mother's white."

"I'll give you this: her mother's Jewish, which ain't as bad as bein' white-bread Christian."

"The best of both things I like," Donovan said happily. "Blacks for the spice and Jews for the conversation. I love New York."

"What are you gonna be doing? Hanging out at the cathedral with Avignon?"

"Maybe. This case is shaping up interestingly."

"You just be sure to separate Avignon's imagination from reality. He dreams a bit, and he's looking for hot items to edit into his video masterpiece. Remember that time you found him in Riverside Park at dawn trying to tape a voodoo ritual? The guy's a freak for weirdness. That's what you and him got in common."

"Everybody loves a good yarn," Donovan said, happy that Jefferson was going along with his plan. "Sometimes the bizarre ones are the best."

20.

Marcie Does Her Famous Impression of Greta Garbo

G et out of my life!" she snapped, spilling coffee as she walked across the main saloon of the *West Wind* to sit on the starboard lounge.

"Don't do this," Donovan pleaded.

"I want to be alone. Maybe just for a couple of nights, but go!"

"I *need* to work my way. I can't always explain myself. There are instincts I have to follow, and a very strong one is telling me that the answer lies in the cathedral."

"The answer to what?"

"To everything."

"My God, another mid-life crisis! How many of them must you have? I thought that those days were over when you stopped drinking."

"I see things more clearly now that I'm straight," Donovan argued.

"You are so full of shit that it's coming out of your ears. You just want to hang around the cathedral with Avignon because he's the only one more obsessed with strangeness than you."

"I'm chasing a murderer."

"So am I, and if I have to work with Jefferson instead of you, I won't live with you. Go sleep on a park bench."

Donovan said, "You'll be chasing teenage wolfpacks. Those kids I chased were Harlem boys. The investigation will have to be in Harlem, and that rules me out."

"You could *still help!*" she insisted, spilling so much coffee that she gave up trying to hold the cup.

"Sure . . . if I didn't have a murder in the cathedral."

"Dammit, William . . . I can't do this alone," she said, finally coming to the heart of what was bothering her.

"You can do anything," Donovan said, repeating the phrase she so often applied to herself in the days before becoming a bride and possibly a mother ruled her thoughts. To that she had no reply.

He picked up the L.L. Bean bag that Marcie had filled with his underwear and socks. "I'm going back to my apartment," he said. "Come and join me when you're ready."

"I know now why you like that place," she exclaimed. "It's empty, like your heart."

No smart retort occurred to Donovan, so he just left. Without a word of goodbye, he left the *West Wind* and trudged through Riverside Park to his building, at the corner of Riverside Drive and 89th Street across from the Soldiers and Sailors Monument.

The argument had raged for all the previous night and half the following day before being resolved by his removal from her presence. It was not the first time they had broken up. Twice before they parted, once for several years. But they always came back together, complete with pronouncements of great love and eternal faith. After a time, their friends sensed a rhythm to the whole thing; the relationship breathed like a wild animal, occasionally growling and baring teeth.

"One of these days it's going to be forever, one way or the other," Donovan muttered as he opened his mailbox and withdrew the phone bill, the gas bill, a card from an upholstery cleaning company, and a copy of *Aviation Week & Space Technology* magazine. When the Persian Gulf War gave way to the War Against the Central American Drug Barons, Donovan the information junkie had sworn to remedy his appalling lack of knowledge about modern warfare.

He rode the elevator alongside a school girl accompanying a golden retriever, then walked listlessly down the hall to his apartment. Then he stood by the door, rattling around in his pants pockets, and realized his latest mistake—the keys were still in the hands of the boys from Riley's who cleaned up the apartment for the wake.

He thought: *How could I be such a fuckup? Maybe I should get religion. Or at least learn to keep track of my house keys. Damn, I feel like having a drink.* That was the value of alcohol that no nondrinker could ever understand, he knew—it allowed him to shut down his overactive imagination for a couple of hours. For the duration of a few beers the weight of no tragedies lay on his shoulders; he would be just another guy watching a ball game in a bar.

Besides, that's where the keys are, he thought, and rode the elevator back down and walked up to Broadway and the bar.

George scrutinized him through eyes made squinty by too many unfiltered Camels, and sized up the situation: "A shooter and a beer will cure that," he said.

"Have I grown so obvious?" Donovan asked.

"What is it, the Commissioner? The press? The body in the cathedral? The body in the park?"

"Women," Donovan replied, and took his customary seat at the end of the bar by the window, where he could see the pedestrian traffic on Broadway.

"When you start drinking like a man I'll listen to your woman problems," George said, pouring a shot of Fleischmann's down his throat. "What'll it be?"

"Club soda."

"It can't be so bad, then."

"With a lime."

It was midnight in Riley's and the Knicks were losing to the New Jersey Nets in the final minutes of the last quarter. A pall had descended over the bar. In a neighborhood bar in New York City it was bad enough to watch the Knicks lose, but losing to a hapless team from the wrong side of the Hudson was a blow to the guts of all true New Yorkers. Three thirsty-looking men quietly fixed their attention on Jake Nakima, who took Donovan's appearance as the excuse to move to his end of the bar.

"The buzzards are circling," he told the lieutenant, casting an especially wary glance at Brewer, the obituary page-dweller who had just finished reporting on the passing of a San Francisco choreographer and a Chelsea art director.

"Is there any word on the check?" Donovan asked.

"Nada. But the rumors are flying faster than the buzzards. One guy came in from the Bronx claiming to be my cousin."

"Was he?"

"My cousin Moishe?" Nakima asked.

Donovan sipped his soda, and said, "When the check comes, you better take a couple hundred and throw a beer party for everyone. The way I see it you got two choices—a beer party in the park, or a bloodbath in the street."

"At which point it becomes your problem," Nakima said.

"Where are my keys?" Donovan asked, miffed that the subject had been changed back to him.

"What keys?" George asked, shifting his weight uncomfortably.

"My house keys."

"What do you need them for?"

"Do I sense a problem here? Now I got to give a reason for wanting my house keys back?"

"You live on a boat," George said.

"Not any more," Donovan admitted, glad that it was out in the open.

"Oh, *those* kind of woman problems! Why didn't you say so? A shooter and a beer will straighten you right out. The first is on the house."

"I am *not* falling off the wagon over this," Donovan vowed.

Jake clasped his arm comradely, and said, "Good for you. You been looking a lot better since you stopped drinking. As a matter of fact, I been thinking of giving it up, too."

"I'm not hearing this," George said, preparing for the worst by pouring himself another.

"I mean it. The way I figure, if everyone thinks I've gone straight maybe they'll stop trying to get a piece of my twenty-thousand dollars."

George growled, "Donovan, this is your fault. You've been encouraging them to get healthy. I got to pay seven-thousand dollars a month rent on this place and I can't go it catering to a bunch of seltzer-suckers."

"Sell Perrier," Donovan said. "And find my keys."

"I lost your fuckin' keys and am proud of it," George said, stalking off toward the ice machine.

21.

'Twas Like the Howling of Irish Wolves Against the Moon

D onovan's soul ached. In the pale glow of the front window's Budweiser sign, he felt alone and in a cruel universe. He had been tossed off his honey's yacht, and his friend had lost his house keys. Worse yet, booze and a nap in Riley's beer locker was no longer a viable option.

" 'Twas like the howling of Irish wolves against the moon," he mourned.

"What was?" Nakima asked.

"The torment in my soul."

"So what happened, Marcie toss you out?"

"Yeah. This is the third time. No . . . the last time, *I* threw *her* out. Or maybe not. I don't remember. I was drunk at the time."

"What did you do this time?"

"I sent her out to work in the fields. You know, gathering roots and tubers. But it's not like she's alone. I gave her Jefferson to help out. You see, I got a problem to work out that she can't be a part of. I have to do it alone. I'll tell you about it some day."

"Fair enough."

"So now I'm sleeping alone. *If* I can find a place to lay my head. *Innkeeper!*"

George replied from the end of the bar by elevating his middle finger, so Donovan reached over the bar for the soda gun and refilled his glass.

Nakima filched a new lime wedge, and Donovan was squeezing it into the glass when Avignon burst through the doors, looking like a war refugee with a dirty white bandage around his head.

"Which way to the front?" he asked.

"I thought you were dead," Donovan said.

"I only smell that way, my friend. I get a little woozy now and then, but don't worry about it. When do we start?"

"Right away. You can let me into my apartment."

"Not again!"

George hurried down the bar, sensing a new customer, then paled when he recognized the haggard-looking cameraman. "Another teetotaler," George snarled.

"Haven't had a drop in years," Avignon bragged.

"The man gets high on strangeness," Donovan said.

"It's a fuckin' epidemic," George replied.

22.

ARROW POISON AND PURPLE TREE FROGS

Avignon picked the lock on Donovan's apartment and, after wiping out the supply of Ritz Crackers and Velveeta Cheese, they slept in the splendid isolation of the three-bedroom, three-bath flat fifteen stories above Riverside Drive and the Hudson. Far below, the *West Wind* bobbed gently in the ebb tide.

Donovan awoke at six, as was his habit, put on his Columbia sweats, and went down into the park for his morning mile. At the end of it he swung by the boat basin and jogged out onto the dock, but Marcie was already gone. To work, he knew. He walked back to the apartment and got Avignon out of the sack by tossing a copy of the *Daily News* at him.

"Wake up, killer. They're gettin' away on us."

"Who's getting away?" the cameraman said, sliding out of bed.

"Rapists, murderers, dope dealers, and used-car salesmen. I'll make the coffee."

"No stimulants. And I only want to catch the killer in the cathedral."

"St. Augustine."

"Marcus Aurelius, he's calling himself, with appropriate modesty. The bastard is leaving the canonization to posterity. You got anything to eat in this palace?"

"It's the cook's day off. I'll buy you breakfast at Dunkin' Donuts," Donovan said, and went into the kitchen to make Sanka.

Five minutes later they drank decaf while riding the elevator down to the lobby. With Avignon around and Donovan temporarily single, life was in motion again: checking out of hospitals early and still bandaged; eating Ritz Crackers and bullshitting half the night like college roommates; and having coffee on the run to the scene of the crime. Appealing, Donovan thought; he had gotten too sedentary living with Marcie. And she had grown dependent and predictable. Well, a little predictable. Even a whirlwind gets familiar when you sleep with it. Donovan wondered if by pushing her off on her own for a while he was only fighting his own pushing-fifty tendency to slow down.

Avignon hadn't slowed a bit. He was still as hyper as ever, and after breakfast whisked Donovan down to SoHo to pick up a new camera. Then they drove to the Cathedral of St. John the Divine, where Avignon wanted to shoot some footage and Donovan wanted to take a quiet prowl around the nave.

Not much was happening. The tourists were being shown the site of the Charbaux killing as part of their hour-long jaunt around the edifice, the stone cutters were back at work making gargoyles, and the Crusaders Chapel had just been fitted with an exhibit about efforts to save the Amazon rain forest.

Donovan took in the exhibit and was moved, recalling all those old issues of *National Geographic* with stories about piranha and Stone-Age Indians, tree sloths and lemurs, arrow poison and purple tree frogs. Now the Brazilian cattle-herders were chain-sawing the rain forest to make grazing land. The Rain Forest Defense was holding a pop concert that night to raise money to preserve the Amazon for future generations of tree sloths and lemurs.

"Sounds like a good cause," he said to Avignon, who taped the exhibit as well as a stage that was being set up, near the choir, for the concert.

"Do you want to save the whales, too?" Avignon asked.

"Yeah. Why not? And the tree frogs. Piranha I got no use for, but that's just the bigot in me talking."

"I always had a peculiar admiration for piranha," Avignon admitted. "They strike me as very cosmopolitan fish: kill anony-mously and in packs."

"Very New York," Donovan agreed.

"I'm gonna try to get back here tonight to tape the concert. I tell you, Donovan, I love it every time they bring mammon in here to defile the temple. Christie Gaynor is Liza Minelli with a chest. I can't wait to shoot her wiggling in front of the altar."

"Who's Christie Gaynor?" Donovan asked.

"Only the hottest act in Great Britain and the continent. Don't you like music?"

"If she's anything like Thelonius Monk or Duke Ellington, I like her."

"Never mind. I'm gonna shoot her tonight."

"I wouldn't be surprised if *Marcus* didn't shoot her tonight. That would make sense—he killed Charbaux for running a film festival in this hallowed hall, and has got to be real pissed off at the prospect of a concert."

"You'd have to be crazy to pull off a murder with the cops watching and me taping it," Avignon said.

"Welcome to my world," Donovan replied. "Some of the most interesting people are crazy."

"We'll be waiting for this one. Me taping and you arresting. Donovan, we are gonna make some team."

23.

"One of His Servants," Donovan Said. "Not Him."

It's everywhere, Lieutenant," Bonaci said. "It's all over the paper."

"Limestone dust," Donovan noted.

"The same dust we found on Charbaux's shoulder is on the note that was nailed to the cathedral door. It was also on the shirt that Avignon here was wearing when he got hit. And on the camera he was carrying."

"What does this Marcus do, swim in it?" Donovan asked.

"There were no useful prints on the paper, though. Just some smudges. Marcus is lucky."

"He has God on his side," Donovan noted.

"Beg pardon?"

"This guy thinks he's God's hit man. My only question is, where around here is there a lot of limestone dust?"

"In the Stone Yard," Bonaci said.

"How many people work there?"

"Five or six, including the neighborhood kids who are being trained to carve gargoyles. But almost anyone could go in there and pick up dust on his shoes. Tourists walk through it every day—hundreds of 'em. I lined up their boss: Steven Langton, a Limey. He's the one who can tell you about the apprentice cutters."

"What about the murder weapon? After Charbaux we thought it was a battering ram."

"Whatever hit me was big," Avignon said.

"That's true, Lieutenant," Bonaci went on. "The lab says that the weapon that smashed Avignon's camera was at least six inches in diameter."

"Jesus Christ!" Avignon swore.

"One of His servants," Donovan corrected. "Not Him. Marcus could be a priest for all we know. Do Episcopalians have priests? I think so. One thing for sure is he's big. Six-one or two and able to wield a battering ram."

Bonaci said, "The lab says that a man would have to go six-two in his stocking feet to drive the nail into the cathedral door at the angle he did. Avignon didn't see him standing on no chair. Yeah, and there's limestone dust on the door too."

"We're gonna have to search the Stone Yard," Donovan said. "He has got to work there, or at least have frequent access."

Bonaci said, "More specifically, access within an hour or two of the Charbaux killing and the attack on Avignon. That's the only way he could keep enough limestone dust on his person to deposit at the scenes of the crimes."

Donovan said, "Let's see this Langton and get a list of all those working in the Stone Yard at those times. Let's ask *all* cathedral employees where they were."

"Including the bishop?"

"Especially him," Donovan said. "Apprentice cutters . . . I like the sound of that. You want to come with me?"

24.
GARGOYLE WITH LISTERINE

That's how long my family has served the Church of England, Lieutenant," the man said. He pronounced the title *lef*tenant in the British manner, which always gave Donovan a thrill.

"What happened seven hundred seventy-seven years ago?"

"The barons forced King John to sign the Magna Carta. My ancestor presided."

"Your ancestor was King John? What are you doing teaching New York neighborhood kids to carve gargoyles?"

"No, no. My ancestor and namesake was Stephen Langton, archbishop of Canterbury and the first man to witness the Magna Carta."

"Really? That's a coincidence. There's a piece of it here someplace."

"Yes, in the choir . . . part of the altar from the Abbey of Bury St. Edmunds. I spent many happy hours there as a lad, recounting family history. My ancestor was something of an enforcer, you know, devising church laws. Many of his laws are still in effect today, remarkable as that may sound."

"And you're carving gargoyles."

"Actually, my preference is for grotesques. Gargoyles are less open to interpretation. You must remember that they have to serve as drain spouts. The word derives from the Latin for throat."

"As in 'gargoyle with Listerine,' " Donovan said.

"Consequently, function overrides form. On the other hand, grotesques are mere decoration, fantastic creations that allow the artist much latitude. In the same cathedral you may have sinners into whose ear the Devil whispers evil, fools' heads with lalling tongues, wretches looking downcast, and dogs with human features. It's common to fashion them after co-workers or friends. The National Cathedral in Washington has carvings that depict golfers, hippies, and bureaucrats."

"I plan to commission the likeness of a certain innkeeper," Donovan said.

The contemporary Stephen Langton was a tall man, six-two at least, with grey-white hair surrounding a bald pate. His arms and shoulders were massive, as thick as his legs were strong; the legacy of a lifetime spent hauling and carving stone. Langton was burly, red-faced and, one would say, typically country English, save for a quirky preference for expensive cowboy boots. One of several master stone carvers imported from England to pass on their craft to a new generation, Langton presided over a large studio in the stone cutting shed in which four apprentices toiled over massive stone decorations.

"I'm proud of my lads," he told Donovan. "I've trained thirty-seven well enough for them to get high-paying jobs working stone for midtown office buildings."

"I didn't think there was that much call for the craft anymore," Donovan said.

"A mistake, that attitude. There's plenty of new construction . . . nothing beats a good stone building . . . and during hard times there's restoration work to be done. I have one boy working on the Chrysler Building reornamentation right now, and making a lot of money, too."

Donovan said that he was impressed.

"So you want to know if any of my lads are killers?"

"I just want to know where all of them were when the killings occurred. And where you were, too. Nothing personal."

"I understand," Langton said. "I gave your Sergeant Bonaci a list of the apprentices and their home addresses. Most of them live in the neighborhood; two are from East Harlem and a third is from the South Bronx."

"Where do you live?"

"I sublet a flat on 107th and Manhattan. The rent is cheap."

"But the neighborhood is bad. There are lots of drugs. A cop was killed there not too long ago."

Langton nodded. "It's bad on my block. There are crack deals all the time, and shooting at odd hours of the night. It's like your Wild West came back. What was the name of that frontier town that's become synonymous for shootings?"

"Dodge City," Donovan said. "Last summer the mayor of that town publicly debunked comparisons between the Big Apple and his town; said that even at its worst, things were much less violent there."

"I know how to handle myself," Langton said. "I'd like to

think I could make a difference. My family has always stood for law and order."

"Just keep teaching kids to carve gargoyles. And give us a statement telling where you were at certain key moments."

Langton tossed up his hands. "I didn't kill anyone, though I'll shed no tears for the film-festival man."

"Is that a confession?" Donovan asked.

"It's a confession that some men don't deserve to live, for they have no respect for the works of God or anyone else."

25.

A KILLER IN A STONE-GREY MAZE

The huge belly of the cathedral throbbed as the stacks of Marshall amplifiers filled it with bass sounds and guitar. The lights were down except for a few spots, and the tastefully illuminated altar that formed a backdrop for the concert. Wisps of dry-ice fumes rose from around the feet of the hyped-up Vegas nightclub singer Christie Gaynor, a pencil-thin, pasty-faced Briton clad in pastel velvet whose only principal asset was a reedlike voice that spiralled out from behind huge breasts that made her look like she was about to topple over. She sang beneath the high altar in front of a neon backdrop that showed a handful of lush trees and the initials RFD.

"What does RFD mean?" Donovan asked.

"Rain Forest Defense," said Gaynor's manager, an equally skinny Englishman who, over the course of the late 1980s and early 1990s, had earned a reputation for raising millions to save the Amazon forests. As earlier music promoters had built their reputations by crusading against world hunger and AIDS, Terry

Loomis recently made the cover of *Time, Newsweek,* and *Rolling Stone* by running "singathons" to save the rain forest.

The concert at the cathedral was a comparatively modest affair when compared with the fundraisers at Wembley Stadium and the Los Angeles Coliseum. But it was the only New York appearance, and had a closed audience.

It was being held in conjunction with the annual meeting of the American Medical Association, and was designed to win the audience of several thousand doctors over to the Rain Forest Defense point of view.

"The idea being that medical professionals, who have a huge trust factor with their patients, will best be able to convince others to contribute to us," Loomis explained.

"Surveys show that eighty-seven percent of doctors recommend the rain forest above ordinary forests," Avignon ad-libbed.

"Something like that."

The audience filled most of the nave; what few seats weren't taken up by conventioneering doctors and their wives were filled with media people. There were crews from all local TV stations and the networks, and a three-man crew from "Entertainment Tonight" prowled the center aisle focusing on celebrity onlookers. In the rush to tape a certified event, the Charbaux killing had been forgotten. By all but Donovan, who left Avignon and was prowling the perimeter, looking for the trouble that a sixth sense told him would surely come. He hunted alone, for the most part. For a time he was joined by Arturo Vega, one of the half-dozen Brazilians in the entourage, whom Donovan at first pegged as a Rain Forest activist but who turned out to be Terry Loomis's gregarious, expensively dressed security chief.

Donovan thought: How do you ferret out a killer in a stone-grey maze? The cathedral rushed overhead and dwarfed everything inside it. Its power was enormous and, compared with its scope, even the throbbing music seemed tiny and termitelike.

For an hour or more he walked the outskirts of the crowded concert, trying the cold walls with his fingertips, looking for the worm hole that he was convinced Marcus would come out of.

The killer was in there someplace, he knew. The walls of the edifice were as thick and impenetrable as the shell of Riverside Park and its interlaced tunnels beneath, where he had successfully fought a killer years before. But this was different. It was a house of God, whatever little that meant anymore, and the worm holes could not be seen.

As midnight beckoned, the music stopped. Loomis had scheduled a half-hour intermission to allow a new audience to file in for the second set. While feet shuffled in and out, Christie Gaynor had scheduled a break for a rest, a smoke or two, and a costume change. As was her habit, the break would be taken alone, in a dressing room that lay south of the choir. And as was *his* wont, driven by a long-time association with celebrities and knowledge of their often rampant desires, Avignon had schemed to deliver unto her the person of the lieutenant, figuring that his Celtic bluster would fit her notion of manliness. Besides, Donovan was temporarily single; of course, Avignon checked out this bit of manipulation with no one.

"Donovan will thank me in time," he chuckled as he closed the dressing room door, locking Gaynor inside, and went off in search of the lieutenant.

26.
CITY OF GOD (2)

The smell of leather and parchment oozed from the pages of the thick old book, thrilling Marcus, just as it did every time he opened it to read or write. He moved the quill from side to side and down, filling a new page with a droll scrawl and a quotation from Macaulay: *"Those trees in whose dim shadow/ the ghastly priest doth reign; the priest who slew the slayer/ and shall himself be slain."*

Marcus tilted his head in the direction of the heavy wooden door, through whose thick oak boards came a new abomination, another cacophony of mammon. The City of God shook anew with the roar of electronic music and the unruly clamor of the crowds shuffling in and out.

Marcus walked to the door and pressed his palms against oak and again the fury rose inside him and took form. He whispered, "Thy will be done." He opened the brass-bound chest in which he kept his tools. The mallet came up and out and again slipped into his shoulder bag.

He pulled open the door, his nostrils flaring in anger, then went into the narrow corridor and down the steps.

The crowd swelled to fill the cathedral. It was like a sleeping giant had taken a great breath, filling its lungs with musty air. In the corridor that connected the dressing room with the choir, a few show-biz business functionaries mingled with security men and the TV crew from "Entertainment Tonight."

Avignon lingered outside the dressing room, waiting for Donovan, with one hand on the knob. A few minutes into the intermission Donovan came down the corridor, checking to see if all was well. According to his earlier premonition, Marcus was a threat to Gaynor, who indeed was the soul of this newest desecration of God's house. The last thing he needed was a murder while he was guarding the victim. That could not happen, he thought, quickening his step. That was unthinkable.

"Who's in there with her?" he demanded to know.

"No one," Avignon said. "Liza Minelli and Barry Manilow tried to butt in but I had them thrown out."

"You left her alone? Where's Loomis?"

"Went out for a smoke. The bishop forbade smoking in the cathedral. Monkeys, lemurs, and Hollywood is okay, though. Fuckin' liberals."

"Open up and let me in," Donovan said, trying the door.

It was, indeed, locked.

He knocked on it. There was no response.

Donovan knocked again, this time using a clenched fist.

"Police Department, Miss Gaynor," he intoned.

The door faltered and swung open. A rush of marijuana smoke burst out into the corridor. Avignon smiled. "Just like the old days, William," he said.

"Gimme a fuckin' break," Donovan said, and stepped inside.

Christie Gaynor stood before him, wearing tight black spandex pants, a silver belt, and a halter top that was more like dental floss strung over her heaving globes.

"Who are you and what are you doing later?" she asked, in a slightly intoxicated London accent.

Smart remarks eluded him, as they had the last time he saw Marcie. And just as he was about to utter a pedestrian inquiry about Gaynor's health, a shriek came down the corridor from the outer shell of the cathedral.

"What's that?" Donovan asked, whipping his head around.

"It's Mister Loomis!" a voice cried.

"Stay with her!" Donovan yelled at a rent-a-cop before running down the hall with Avignon on his heels.

27.

THIS DOOR IS ALARMED

Loomis had been laid low with a massive blow from overhead and to his left. His frail body resembled a pale wax museum figure that was partly melted and splayed across the cathedral floor. His head was merely a suggestion, and his upper torso was soaked with blood. A river of blood flowed across the floor and down a slight incline and under a locked door that led to the outside; an emergency fire exit with a sign reading: "This door is alarmed."

"Me too," Donovan said as he pushed open the door, setting off the alarm.

Two security guards appeared, one from the area near the choir and the other from the staff parking lot, south of the cathedral. Donovan identified himself and said, "Keep everyone out of this area! You from the parking lot! You see anyone open this door?"

"Just you."

"Shut off the alarm and stand by. When the city cops come up, tell them that Lieutenant Donovan said rope off the crime scene."

"Will do, Lieutenant."

"Dammit! Where the hell did he go?" Donovan said, thinking that only Avignon was videotaping him. But it was also the crew from "Entertainment Tonight."

"Where did who go?" a blond, dolled-up reporter asked.

"Marcus," Donovan reported, before he realized he was talking not to an old friend but to the world.

Upon catching his mistake, he shooed them out of the area and used the indoor security guard to block the corridor.

Avignon said, "There's no way here except through the door or down he corridor."

Donovan looked down the corridor away from the choir; the only way that Marcus could have gotten there. It dead-ended in an ancient iron door that looked like it hadn't been opened in generations. Beside the door, a raggy old tapestry hung from brass fittings. A scene of deer grazing in a woodland dell was nearly obscured by decades of dust and city grime.

"Who screamed just before?" Donovan asked.

"Don't know. A woman ran past me and out into the crowd. Did Marcus get away through that door?"

Donovan tried it, but it wouldn't budge. He shrugged and said "Videotape everything. The walls. The floor. The body. Get me a copy of the tape."

"Done," Avignon said, and set about doing it.

The uniformed cops weren't far off and showed up within minutes, and Bonaci wasn't far behind. He had the scene roped off and the bystanders chased. Then he said to the lieutenant, "Boy, you sure don't waste time, do you?"

"When you have Jefferson's seniority you can be a wiseass," Donovan snarled.

"The TV guys want a statement from you. They want to know who Marcus is."

"I blurted out the name. Tell them it's the working name we have for the suspect. Then get them the hell away. Encourage them to interview Christie Gaynor about the death of her manager."

"It's kind of refreshing to have a show-biz guy who didn't OD," Avignon said.

Bonaci said, "They also want to know why Avignon can stay and they can't."

"Tell them I deputized the sonofabitch," Donovan said.

He stood aside while the forensics guys went over the scene with a fine-toothed comb, and blow-dried it as well. The concert had resumed, the demands of show biz (and the expense of satellite time) looming larger than grief. Gaynor got over her grief—that from the death, as well as from not having scored Donovan—and gave a whale of a performance in defense of the rain forest.

Donovan moved back into the scene and went over it with Bonaci while Avignon taped them. Loomis got his while smoking a cigarette near the fire exit. Marcus had gotten to him in any of three ways, all of them unlikely—from the crowd, in which case he would have been seen; through the fire door from the outside, but the parking lot security guard saw no one; or through the old iron door, which led into the bowels of the cathedral.

Donovan got some help in opening the door. No known key worked, but about 200 pounds of pressure applied to a pry bar pulled the door open into the corridor. Behind it was a dark and damp stairwell that ran down to the basement and another old, wedged-in door, and up to an open walkway that ran along the south wall at the blindstory level.

Donovan led the party up to that level and followed the

walkway west, walking beneath forty-four-foot high stained-glass panels on one side and the open nave with the rampaging concert on the other. It connected with four other stairwells, one at each end and two in the middle. All had doors that opened with the application of varying degrees of force.

"You can get anywhere in the cathedral from here," Donovan observed.

"Daedalus designed this place," Avignon concurred.

The thought was depressing. The world's largest Gothic cathedral had become the battlefield for a mad killer who had set out to avenge slights against the sanctity of the Lord's house. And he had done his newest murder when the place was full of TV cameras. Donovan even had *his own* TV cameraman at work. For a fleeting moment he longed for the comforting presence of Jefferson and Marcie, who by the force of their personalities tended to make catastrophe easier to live with.

"The press is gonna have a field day," he observed.

"No shit! I'm already getting five-figure offers for my tape," Avignon said.

"You wouldn't!" Donovan said, aghast at the thought that his friend would sell out on him.

"No promises if the bidding goes over twenty-five thousand dollars. That failing, I'll hang onto the footage until this is resolved."

Bonaci consulted with his forensics people and returned to his boss, who was looking forlornly down on the concert from his perch on the blindstory gallery. As dry-ice haze rose from beneath her feet and wrapped around her spandex-clad thighs, Christie Gaynor sang her version of "I'm in a New York State of Mind."

"We're ready to haul off the corpse, boss," Bonaci reported.

"Take him away. Just cover him up before you march him past the press."

"We're taking him out the fire exit to the parking lot."

Avignon said, "If you go down the stairs instead and through that basement room, you can come out through the Recycling Center. The press can't get to you there."

"How do you know that?" Donovan asked.

"I'm a professional. I know how to get out of buildings as well as into them. Besides, if the other TV crews can't get to the corpse it increases the value of my tape."

Donovan said, "You got to hang onto the footage until I say so."

"Very well," Avignon agreed.

Bonaci said, "Loomis was killed by the same blunt instrument that was used on Charbaux. Yeah, and there's limestone dust all over the place."

"All over where?"

"Loomis's head and shoulders. The wound. What's left of his head."

"The walls and floor?"

"Some on the floor in the vicinity of the door. None elsewhere."

"What door? The one to the outside?"

"Nope. The one leading up to the blindstory gallery. And there's a trace of it on the stairwell side of the door. It looks like Marcus left some dust on the floor while pushing open the door from the other side, and then dropped some more while waiting at the dark end of the corridor by the tapestry."

"Waiting for what? For Loomis to come out there?"

"There's no way Marcus could have picked his victim. Remember you thought that Gaynor might be a target."

"She was the logical target, assuming Marcus was pissed off by this concert. But she was harder to get to, although I will confess to a major case of butterflies when I heard she had been left alone in the dressing room."

"What were you afraid of?" Avignon asked. "Secret doors and passages?"

"That's exactly what I was afraid of."

"This is a Victorian cathedral, Donovan, not a medieval one."

"The Victorians didn't have secrecy and subterfuge? What

about Jack the Ripper? Nobody figured out how he came and went, either."

"Maybe this *is* Jack the Ripper," Avignon said.

"Nothing is impossible in my world," Donovan replied.

"Marcus could have known about Loomis. The sonofabitch *was* on the cover of *Time,* for God's sake."

"Maybe. But he couldn't have known that Loomis would walk away from the crowd for a smoke. Nor could Marcus have known that Charbaux would have walked away from his crowd for a smoke. One thing's for sure—smoking is hazardous to your health. No wonder the bishop outlawed it."

"I think that anyone at this concert would have served as a target," Avignon said.

"You got it," Donovan agreed.

Bonaci added, "Time of death was midnight or thereabouts. Considering that Loomis was only by himself for a few minutes— his cigarette was smoked halfway down—I would say that Marcus was laying in wait for *someone* associated with the concert and got the promoter."

28.
THE GARDEN SPOT OF THE UNIVERSE

As Marcie saw it, the Harlem doorway was huge, old, made of wood and broken glass over metal, and dark. It stood two stories high, like the gate to an armory, and still retained its architectural decoration—wavy strands of metal, iron that had been wrought in the form of undulating musical notations, flanking the doors. A fist had crashed in the glass over a cardboard sign reading "Keep out," and at eye level was a sticker, "Housing Now! National March October 7, 1992, U.S. Capitol."

Beneath the door the garbage and fast-food wrappers had been swept aside to make room for the nervously shuffling feet of the crack dealers. They had held that corner of Jackson Avenue and 117th Street for nearly six months, something of a record in the neighborhood. They took it from three older men, aged twenty and twenty-two, and defended their cache of smokeable cocaine against all usurpers, using 9mm pistols and an oft-threatened but never produced Uzi machine pistol. The police, in the form of the Tactical Narcotics Team, had made a sweep down a three-block stretch of Jackson only two months before, which meant only that the dealers had lain low for a few weeks. Soon they were back and as brazen as ever, shuffling their feet and sneering at the gaggle of teenage prostitutes who worked Jackson and 118th in order to raise money for crack.

Marcie watched them through sleepy eyes, occasionally sharing a pair of binoculars with Jefferson and their Uptown Narcotics colleague, Ed James. The trio was hunkered down in an old Mercury parked across the street and down the block a little in the direction of Central Park. Through the binoculars, and with a little help from the light of a nearby liquor store, they watched the parade of cars pull to the curb at the corner to make a buy.

"This is really the garden spot of the universe," she said, suppressing a yawn. "What time is it?"

"Quarter to three," James said. "And yeah, it gets better further uptown."

"Who are those guys?" Jefferson asked.

"The tall one's street name is Air Man. The short kid is Turk. We don't know the real names yet. Do these guys look like your Central Park perps?"

Marcie said, "All we know is that one is taller than the other and they're fast on their feet."

"Which doesn't necessarily make them crack dealers," James said. "The notion of street dealers as being athletic has gone out the window. They don't have to be fast anymore. They have lawyers to deal with the cops and enforcers to fight off the competition. Some of these kids are real fat cats, just sitting in their Jeeps with their women and their gold."

"What about the ring?"

"A gold ring with the initial S could mean that the perp's name is Sam. Or Snake. It doesn't mean a whole lot in the absence of other information. What did the lab give you on the ring?"

"It's coming in tomorrow," Jefferson said. "We're getting a rundown on the composition of the gold, manufacture of the ring, and local outlets."

"There are dozens of jewelry shops in Harlem that sell heavy gold. Dozens of shops and thousands of customers, most of them in their teens. You guys are in for a lot of work."

"What else have we got to do?" Marcie asked, emitting a yawn that she didn't even try to suppress.

"Donovan thinks that the Central Park perps are local Harlem boys," Jefferson said.

"How so?"

"Local knowledge. They knew the trails in the park pretty good."

"That sounds local to me," James said. "I played in those woods when I was a kid, and it's not something you pick up in an hour."

Marcie took the binoculars and trained them on the taller of the two drug dealers, the one called Air Man. The boy had left his post leaning against the old broken door and was walking to his car, a black Suzuki Samurai parked halfway down the block.

"The kid limps," she said.

"What?" Jefferson asked, and took the binoculars. "Dammit, he does."

"Air Man ain't runnin' through no woods," James said. "He picked up that limp a couple of months ago. Damned if I know how."

"These aren't the two guys we're looking for," Marcie said.

"You're never gonna find them this way," James said. "Going

street corner to street corner will get you nowhere. Trace the ring to a store and see if you can get a name out of the jeweler."

Marcie sighed and handed off the binoculars. "At least this is better than hanging out at the cathedral with Donovan."

"Yeah, I really miss bein' inside a nice warm building with food and comfort when we can spend another night watching Harlem crack dealers," Jefferson said.

"This isn't so bad," Marcie argued.

"For you, this is *new*. You never been in Harlem except maybe passin' through on the way to your dad's estate in Larchmont."

"It's in Croton-on-Hudson," she said.

"Same difference. Lotsa white bread and mayonnaise. Come on, babe, let me take you home."

"I'm enjoying this. Let's try another street corner."

"I'm taking you *home*. It's something I been gettin' good at lately. We'll go again tomorrow."

James said, "I'll drive you back to your car," and started the Mercury's engine. Soon they had turned around and were heading south, out of Harlem.

"There's something else wrong with the idea of your Central Park perps being crack dealers," James said. "The murder weapon was a knife."

Jefferson said, "Or a stiletto. That's what the autopsy said anyway."

"No self-respecting dealer would kill someone with a faggot stiletto. Ninety percent of 'em wouldn't use a knife. They have Uzis, for God's sake."

"The man has a point," Jefferson said.

"You have to be ready for the possibility that the perp bought his gold ring with money he earned by working at McDonald's. I wouldn't hold my breath on that, but it could be."

Once back in his own car, Jefferson started the engine and began driving with Marcie across 110th Street toward Broadway. The radio came on with a news flash: Rain Forest Defense promoter Terry Loomis had been brutally murdered at the Cathedral of St. John the Divine. A mad killer who went by the name of Marcus was blamed for it. A news conference would be held at the West Side Major Crimes Unit in the morning.

"Donovan," Marcie said quietly.

"See what we're missing?" Jefferson asked.

29.

"You Pissed on My Date and You're Sorry?!"

The story was one of Donovan's chestnuts, but it always got a laugh. Some held it up as the perfect New York City story, one that defined the indefinable humor of living there.

It was a true story, like all good ones, and came from his misspent youth. On one occasion he had to kill several hours in Times Square in August, and as was customary in those days (the late 1950s) he elected to spend them in air-conditioned luxury at the movies. In pre-porn Times Square, it was possible to see three Richard Widmark westerns for ninety-nine cents, and the credits had just finished rolling on the first one. The camera panned across the Great Prairie, and all was silence save for the whistling of a forlorn wind when an irate male voice cried, "You're sorry? You *pissed* on my date and you're *sorry?!*"

George said, "Hey Avignon, I didn't know you hung out in Times Square."

Donovan looked at himself in the backbar mirror, imagined for an instant that he was on horseback riding across the Great Prairie, and said, "I think I look like Richard Widmark, don't you?"

"Not again," Jake moaned. One of Donovan's foibles was imagining that he looked like celebrities. Usually it was Clint Eastwood, although Harrison Ford enjoyed a brief popularity.

Avignon shook his head. "You like to think of yourself as this big, tough, two-fisted hunk. That's the Irish in you, and maybe the cop."

"Nick Nolte and me," Donovan said, admiring his bicep.

"But you're really a William Hurt kind of guy."

"William *Holden,*" Donovan said, imagining himself instead standing knee deep in the River Kwai.

It was five in the morning, an hour past closing, and Riley's was locked and shuttered. Only "the cleaning crew," a euphemism for those of George's friends who were allowed to tarry past the legal closing hour, remained. Outside in the street three TV crews stood by, waiting for some word, official or otherwise, from the West Side Major Crimes Unit above.

Donovan was always popular with the press, good for an outrageous quote or two, and never more so than in the hours following the bloody demise of Terry Loomis. So after doing what he had to do at the Unit, he made an unheralded and secret approach to the bar using the fire escape in the alley. Avignon went with him and patched the video output of his camera into the bar's TV so they could watch the footage from the cathedral.

It went past their eyes like a firestorm of silent fury, and George and Jake were again reminded of the risky nature of their friend's business. It was their second introduction to the nitty-gritty of Donovan's career. Some time before, a local mobster was rubbed out while sitting on a Riley's barstool, but no video-cameras rolled to record that particular messiness.

Jake broke the silence, saying, "Gee, I wonder how they're gonna clean that up."

"The bishop is trucking in water from the rain forest," Donovan said.

George asked, "What did the Commissioner say to you?"

"Same thing he always says: 'Better you than me.' Of course, he still doesn't believe that I'm chasing a guy who thinks he's St. Augustine."

"It's so nice to have an understanding boss. When I think of the flak I had to take from Morty the time he found you sleeping in the beer locker."

"Another moment from my misspent youth," Donovan mused.

"It happened last year," George replied.

"Bullshit! It was at least two, maybe three years ago. And I was only taking a nap."

"With a quart of vodka in you."

"It was Scotch. And I regret none of it. Those were my halcyon days, filled with adventure, and I slept o' nights. When misfortune called I repaired to the beer locker and slept like a baby, and in the morning had only to confront the disapproving face of Morty the bar-owner. Now every call from the police commissioner or Eyewitness News is like a blast of caffeine. I shall sleep no more."

George regarded him suspiciously, then said, "It's too late for you. No amount of alcohol can bring you back to the real world. You'll be eating bean sprouts soon."

"He already does," Avignon said.

"Look at yourself," George went on. "A year-and-a-half ago you had three grey hairs. Now there are at least three thousand. The lines under your eyes look like meteor strikes. You've lost your famous ability to look thirty-seven."

"I never claimed a day under thirty-eight," Donovan replied.

"You're pushing fifty, slugger. Without the pickling agent in your veins you're falling apart."

"I know. I looked at the portrait in my attic and it's edging on a hundred and two. But I've decided to cast my lot with the sober."

George said, "I don't even care if you drink anymore. I can take the hit on my income. Just don't drag this bar down with you. Don't recruit any more of my patrons to sobriety. Jake here saw the light, fortunately, and fell off the wagon five minutes after you hoisted him onto it."

"I ain't no crusader," Donovan said.

"Terry Loomis was a crusader," Avignon said.

"God grant him peace," Donovan replied solemnly.

30.

ANOTHER SEASON OF TERROR AND MURDER ON THE UPPER WEST SIDE

A t a press conference filled with *sturm und drang,* the questions were typified by those of an Eyewitness News reporter: "Does this signal the start of another season of terror and murder on the Upper West Side?" Donovan didn't exactly respond to that one, but in the course of a prepared statement said, "As a God-fearing man, I understand the need to drive the money-changers from the temple. I shall myself make a scourge of small cords." He also said some other stuff, the expected pep-talk containing references to Churchill . . . everything short of praise for the RAF.

"You're a what-fearing man?" Jefferson asked later. He had been hovering on the sidelines, still hopeful of a reprieve.

"God-fearing, son," Donovan replied. "I have reestablished connections with Him."

"Have you really?"

"Absolutely. Did you catch my message?"

"I been missing your messages for years. Oh, you mean the line about the chords of fame or whatever."

"A scourge of cords," Donovan said. "I wanted Marcus to know that I have read the Bible."

"And you be into whips," Jefferson said, affecting a street accent. "No wonder your woman ran off to the ghetto with a brother."

Donovan hmmph'd. "How is she?"

"Dedicated, m'man. Wants to spend twenty-four hours a day chasin' the Central Park perps."

"I appreciate your help on this," Donovan said.

"Yeah, well, anytime you want me back . . ."

"I have to go to the cathedral," Donovan said, and went there.

With Avignon and his ubiquitous videocamera trailing along, Donovan kept an appointment with William Stewart, cathedral administrator.

"Cathedral administrator?" Donovan asked. "Isn't that a job for a deacon?"

"In the old days perhaps," Stewart said. "But running a modern cathedral is like running a business. It's not just a matter of services and prayer. It has to do with our mission in the community."

"I always thought that was to hold services and pray."

"You *are* old-fashioned. No institution functions without modern business techniques and public relations. Just last year I completed long and arduous negotiations that replaced the cathedral's old cross fitchee with a new Maltese cross built with the sweat and tears of death-row prisoners across the United States. Which brings me to my next point."

"You're a busy man. I should catch the killer and go away," Donovan said.

"Approximately. This Marcus, whoever he is, is a nightmare for us as well as for his victims. In a sense, we *are* his victims. If he isn't stopped, the work of God may grind to a halt. And the holy days are coming up."

"God forbid."

"Ironically, the tour buses are doing better than ever. Apparently, blood is a good draw."

"You should put up an exhibit based on it," Donovan replied. "I can give you lots of tips."

Stewart walked down the blindstory gallery, following the route that Donovan and Avignon took the night before while looking for Marcus. The area had been thoroughly swept by technicians, who found nothing more than Donovan had already seen. Even the conclusion that the killer had to be extra-strong in order to open the old doors evaporated; scuff marks from boot heels showed that he pushed against the bottom step of the stairs nearest the murder scene.

"So you think that Marcus came along this way?" Stewart said. "That tells you nothing; this passage connects with many others, and anyone with a basic familiarity with the cathedral can get inside. Besides, God's house is open to all, at least during business hours. We have many homeless programs that allow the humblest of God's children to come in from the outdoors."

"The guy could be living in here," Donovan said.

"Are you suggesting that we're harboring a maniac?"

"I'm suggesting that you have your own homicidal little Quasimodo running around popping off the parishioners. And I need free run of the joint if I'm to find him."

"My God, you can't fill up the cathedral with cops!" Stewart said, shocked. "The holy days are coming."

"I don't mean to load the cathedral with cops. Just me. And my cameraman here."

"Just you?"

"And Avignon. We'll try to be unobtrusive."

"And you can catch Marcus by yourself?"

"I've done this sort of thing before. Okay, the only comparable occasion was chasing a serial killer through the tunnels beneath Riverside Park. But there are parallels. He was a religious nut, too."

Stewart thought for a time, resting his frame beneath a monumental stained glass window from which sunlight poured through in all imaginable colors. That blindstory window, forty-four feet high like all those in the nave on the second level, rose above the Sports Chapel and showed St. Hubert, patron saint of hunters, the eighth-century bishop of Liege and Maestricht who was converted while hunting by the sight of a stag that bore a luminous cross on its head. Also pictured was Nimrod, son of Cush, of whom the Bible notes was the first on Earth to be a mighty man; he was "a mighty hunter before the Lord."

"Well very, Lieutenant. We'll cooperate. How may I help you?"

"I need the plans of the cathedral. Architect's drawings, blueprints of the new towers that are going up."

Stewart sighed. "There are many plans and no plans. The original drawings are over a century old, and even then were never complete. The best complete set I have is pre-war."

"Which war?" Donovan asked.

"World War II."

"I was afraid it was the Boer. Okay, that will do. And the new stuff."

"I'll get it for you right away. But remember that this is a monumental structure, and nobody knows where all the rooms are. Some were bricked over. Others were created anew. There are dozens, if not hundreds, of storerooms that nobody has entered in generations. The keys are long lost."

"I'll need as many master keys as you can lay your hands on," Donovan said.

"And I can get you into the rest," Avignon said.

"My colleague used to pick locks on motel rooms while holding a videocamera in his teeth. It was kind of a parlor trick," Donovan said.

"Very nice," Stewart said flatly. "Is there anything else that you need?"

"A room of my own. Somewhere central, where I can quickly get to other parts of the cathedral."

"No one place is terribly near any other."

"Take your best shot. But make it comfortable for two men, a camera, and a couple of guns."

"There won't be any shooting, will there?"

"Meaning I should restrict the carnage to that done with bludgeons?" Donovan said.

"The point is well taken, regrettably," Stewart admitted.

"I'll be discreet in the house of the Lord."

"I know that you will," Stewart said, stepping away from the stained-glass window and shaking the lieutenant's hand. "Your reputation is excellent. When this nightmare is over, I shall be forever in your debt."

"There is one favor, and I'd like it kept just between us."

Donovan had lowered his voice, and Avignon leaned forward to better hear the request.

"Consider it done."

"I want to be married here," Donovan said.

Avignon blanched, and said, "What?"

—

31.

"THIS ISN'T A CHURCH, THIS IS A RELIGIOUS THEME PARK."

I want to be married in style," Donovan said later on, when he and Avignon walked alone together down the main aisle in the center of the nave. Groups of tourists oohed and aahed and took pictures, and apprentice cutters came and went from the Stone Yard. The day after Loomis's murder, life was again normal.

"I know you're engaged, but I always sort of thought it was a bad joke. That, or something you'd get over. I mean, she did throw you out the other night."

"It's happened before. She'll get over it. Besides, it had to be done. Solving the cathedral murders requires patience and subtlety, something Marcie sorely lacks. Jefferson too. And I need them to do something for me in Harlem. In short, I can't work there and they can't work here. It's the race thing come back to haunt me. Jefferson was right. I didn't think it out fully when I fell in love with her."

"Would you have done anything different if you had thought it out?"

"Not a damn thing."

"Marry her then. But in the cathedral?"

"She likes ceremony. Me too."

Avignon said, "This is bizarre. She's a Jewish Baptist and you're an ex-Catholic atheist. So you have to get married at the Episcopal cathedral?"

"It's the best place in the world," Donovan said. "For me, religion is mainly a matter of music and architecture. Nobody does music and architecture better than Episcopalians."

"That makes as much sense as anything," Avignon said, tapping a fingertip on the pews as they walked up the main aisle. "So where are you going to do it—in the private chapel?"

"No way. I want the main altar. I don't expect to get it at eleven Sunday morning, but I want the big one. I see it this way: If I'm gonna walk down the aisle, I'm gonna walk down a fuckin' *aisle!* Got it?"

"Perfectly. Can I tape the ceremony for you?"

"I wouldn't have anyone else," Donovan said.

They reached the altar, and Donovan peered up in awe and admiration at the towering edifice that embraced him. "This isn't a church, this is a religious theme park. I love it!" he exclaimed.

32.

SOMETHING FOUND IN A BOX OF CRACKER JACK

Marcie and Jefferson found the Sixth Avenue Gold and Silver Exchange on the Avenue of the Americas, which is what used to be Sixth Avenue in the days before public relations struck the real-estate business in the city. Actually, it was off Sixth Avenue on 47th Street, which was the gold and jewelry center. As always in New York, retail and wholesale shops of a feather flocked together: electronics on Canal; linens and draperies on Grand; lighting fixtures on Bowery; flowers in the west 20s; garments in the west 30s; pornography in Times Square, and jewelry on 47th Street. No matter that ninety percent of the city's extravagant gold jewelry was sold in the black communities of Harlem, Brownsville, and Bedford-Stuyvesant, it was channeled through 47th, two blocks from Rockefeller Center.

Sol Wexler was a jeweler by trade and a detective by avocation. As some men raised bonsai trees or Siamese cats to keep their minds off business, Wexler was a police buff and whole-hearted contributor of gossip to visiting detectives. In his forty years on 47th Street, he had served as gold and silver consultant to police investigations into the Plaza and Drake hotel holdups; the Metropolitan Museum artifact theft; the Texas hording scheme to inflate the silver market; and scores of homicides involving robbery.

Jefferson loved the man. He was street-smart and cooperative, and Jefferson greeted him like a brother: "Yo, Sol . . . shalom!"

"Sergeant Jefferson and the lovely Marcie Barnes, to what do I owe this honor?"

"Gold, m'man, what else."

"What, for you? It's not your style. Maybe a nice diamond earring. That I can help you with."

"I don't want no earring. I want you to tell me where this came from."

He dumped Scott Carter's gold ring on the counter for Wexler's inspection. Seen in the cold florescent light of the exchange, it seemed even larger than before. The S-shaped face covered three fingers and could easily have served as a weapon, if the gold itself wasn't so soft. Wexler gave it a quick scan.

"Where did this come from? It came from the paucity of the modern American soul."

"Aside from there," Jefferson asked patiently. He had grown

accustomed to the fact that many of Donovan's friends talked exactly like him.

"Abel Casting in the Bronx does this sort of thing," Wexler said, giving the ring a closer look through an eye loop. "I knew Murray Abel when he did work you could be proud of, take home and show your grandchildren. Then he found a way to make money off the blood of children. That's what this is, you know. Selling vanity to children, who then steal or sell drugs to afford it."

"I seem to remember bein' real keen on this pair of Pro Keds," Jefferson said.

"Did you steal to get them?"

"Of course not. My daddy would have kicked the livin' shit out of me."

"Today's kids would shoot their own fathers with automatic weapons," Wexler said. "So, what happened to the owner of this ring? What did he do to bring you to my door?"

"We think he killed a woman in Central Park. Remember, during the Marathon?"

"That was vicious, that was. So, Murray Abel has *real* blood on his hands. You'll find him in the Bronx—across the bridge near Yankee Stadium. But this work, I can tell you, is *cheap*. Murray will tell you there's three ounces of gold in this ring, enough to make it cost over a thousand right there. But it's all fill and other crap. This ring is worth maybe two hundred and probably sold for five. The sucker who bought it should have killed Murray instead."

"These things are sold all over Harlem," Jefferson said. "It covers three fingers on your hand. You can't even unzip your fly with this thing on. I don't know why any self-respecting stud would want one."

"Self-respect is a rare commodity these days," Wexler said, returning the ring. "So, where's the boss? Where's Donovan?"

"Taking holy orders," Jefferson said. "He's working a church uptown."

"Donovan getting religion. Now *that* is news. What do you think, Sergeant Barnes?"

"I'm trying not to think about him," Marcie said.

Jefferson translated: "They announced their engagement recently, so the first thing they do is have a fight. She ran off to Harlem with me, and Donovan's in a church. Tell me why I'm the only one praying."

"Engaged? You're engaged?" Wexler twisted his *peyess* and gaped at her barren ring finger.

"It was never formally announced," she said.

"Of course it wasn't. You don't have a ring. Now *that* is something we can work on."

Jefferson said, hurriedly, "We got to be on our way to the Bronx."

"Hold on. This woman is engaged to one of New York's finest and doesn't have a ring? There is a great tragedy here. Sergeant Barnes, I can do a deal for you on a five-carat diamond that used to belong to Elizabeth Taylor."

"It's out of our price range."

"Our? What's this 'our?' Your husband-to-be has to pay."

"Donovan's been payin' ever since he met her," Jefferson said.

"Shut up, Thomas!" she warned.

"And now I'm payin'," he replied, undaunted.

"Donovan can't afford five carats," she said. "He was hoping to get something in a box of Cracker Jack."

Wexler said, "I have a two-carat diamond that shines so bright it would blind you on a sunny day. It comes with a bottle of number fifteen sunscreen."

Marcie said, "Thanks, Sol. I'll send Donovan around to talk to you—if I ever see him again."

Wexler said, "Don't tell Murray Abel that you're engaged. He'll try to sell you a ring that *should be* in a box of Cracker Jack."

33.
SOMEWHERE BETWEEN
THOMAS MOORE AND
PETER PAN

The room was a crypt, really, located just off the cathedral's actual crypt, but never, apparently, used as a burial spot for bishops. It was, most recently, a storeroom for the Cathedral Repertory Company. The small theater company, which put on plays in the old choir practice area near the crypt, kept props in the room. Some of them remained: a stylized wooden horse from *Equus,* a half-dead tree with two leaves from *Waiting for Godot,* and a plain pine coffin from *Dracula.*

There was also a wooden desk, one drawer of which held a collection of tax receipts from fiscal year 1957, a file cabinet, a manual typewriter that looked as if it had been scavenged from the city room of the old *New York Mirror,* assorted chairs, and two Army cots that Stewart had set up.

"I slept in worse," Avignon said, setting up a video playback deck and monitor atop the filing cabinet.

"This reminds me of my first apartment, the one I got for my twenty-first birthday," Donovan said. "It was 1964 and Vietnam was getting real hot. I decided that the war was not for me, a decision that caused my dad to toss me out of the Riverside Drive apartment. I got a one-bedroom on 113th Street, on the same block with the Columbia frat houses. For a solid year my life was beer parties and Thelonious Monk and living in this shitbox with a window that opened onto the air shaft. I owned a mattress and a record player and that was all that mattered to me. Other than being a cop, which also kept me out of Vietnam."

"What did you pay in rent?"

"One-seventeen a month. I thought it was outrageous."

"The same shitbox goes for a thousand now," Avignon said. "You know the duplex I built over my studio in SoHo? I recently got offered half a million for it."

"If you're so rich what are you doing this for?" Donovan asked.

"I'm a video genius, Donovan. I'm working on the primo project for the year 2000—a summing up of man's foibles as the millennium beckons—and Marcus is going to provide the key."

"Marcus is just another serial killer."

"Now you *know* that's not true. Marcus is a man consumed by the passion that's consumed the Western world for the past two-thousand years—Christianity. Marcus is Torquemada, the embodiment of the Spanish Inquisition, only time-warped to the brink of the twenty-first century and given a set of victims who are totally innocent of the crime they committed. At least during the Inquisition, the condemned had an idea what they did. There was a notion of guilt. Here, nothing. Run a Lon Chaney movie, put on a concert, and *whop!* Off with your head."

"The guy came after you, too," Donovan noted.

"Only because I followed him," Avignon said. "You don't think for a moment that he considers journalists worth killing, do you?"

"I've been tempted on occasion."

"That's different. But seriously, don't you see what a great cast I have here? Marcus is the avenging hand of God. The cathedral is the embodiment of religion as secular politics. The victims are do-gooders who mean well. And producing this play is God, if there is a God, probably having a good chuckle."

"Where do I figure in this cast? What part do I play?"

"I'm not sure, yet," Avignon said. "You're somewhere between Thomas More and Peter Pan. Stay tuned."

Donovan spread his Marcus file across the desk and stared at it while sipping a Diet Coke. There was a bizarre sense to it all, he knew, a pattern other than that of the bodies on the floor. Damned if he could tell what it was, though.

He scanned a batch of papers sent him by Stewart: schedules for the cathedral, which operated like a small city. There were lists of events, including the exhibitions that coincided with the deaths of Charbaux and Loomis. There was the building schedule for the towers, including the dates on which specific limestone blocks and carvings would be hoisted into place. Donovan learned that for $100 he could have his name carved into a limestone block, known as an ashlar, and hoisted far up one of the towers. For a few dollars more he could endow a gargoyle or grotesque. The notion appealed to him.

"I can take up a collection in Riley's and have a gargoyle named after George Kohler," he said.

"Make it a grotesque. A gargoyle is too good for the bastard."

Avignon flicked a switch and the monitor showed snow, then color bars, then some general footage of the cathedral. It was the tape he shot from the blindstory gallery. Donovan watched it again, and for the life of him saw no clue to where Marcus went.

"I know he's in here," Donovan said.

"Is he watching us?"

"Maybe not yet. But he'll find out we're here and look us up. I announced my presence well enough through Stewart as well as to the press."

"Do you think that Marcus *lives* in the cathedral?" Avignon asked.

"No one is supposed to live here. There are night watchmen, of course, to keep out the homeless. Curious that the bishop hasn't gotten around to letting them move in."

"Give him time. There's another Republican administration in Washington. There will be more homeless soon."

Donovan said, "No one is *believed* to live here, but the place is so damned big, how do you know? There are hundreds of rooms and thousands of nooks and crannies. Corridors up the kazoo. And that's just the places the architects bothered to jot down. Look at these blueprints . . ." He stretched one out across the desk and gesticulated at it. "On the tower of Saint Peter, due for completion in 1992, a complete schematic of the rooms and corridors. On the tower of Saint Paul, due for completion the same year, also complete plans. But in the adjoining structure, plans long forgotten and frequently elaborated upon.

"The design was changed a half-dozen times. The cathedral began life running north and south. Then it got changed to the traditional east-west orientation. The foundation goes down seventy-two feet into the bedrock. St. Luke's Hospital next door was built in toto while the hole for the cathedral was being dug. And, of course, the thing began as Romanesque and wound up Gothic, and they're just now finishing the towers designed in 1929."

"Still, in all, they're building it in one hundred years. Most European cathedrals took five hundred. Think of the politics involved in *that*."

"Think of the mortgage," Donovan replied, refolding the blueprint and leaning back, putting his feet up on the desk.

He checked his watch. "It's dinner time. You hungry?"

"Starved. How about the Hungarian joint down Amsterdam?"

"I have just moved into my new quarters, and am rather in the mood to order out."

"Send out for something? What do you want?"

"Pizza."

Avignon said, "We're living in the crypt of the cathedral, and you want to send out for pizza?"

"I want to let him know we've arrived," Donovan said.

——

34.
MURRAY PACKS A ROD

Murray Abel was a short, stocky man with a balding pate that was exaggerated by thinning black hair combed sideways in a desperate attempt to simulate growth. He swaggered a bit too much for a jewelry manufacturer from the Bronx, and wore a .32 in a belt holster.

"It's licensed, officer," he said defensively, whipping a laminated permit out of his shirt pocket and waving it in Marcie Barnes's face.

"So's the Bronx Sewage Treatment Plant, and it smells better than you," she replied, taking the permit and shoving it back in his pocket.

"What do you want from me?"

"The name of the store that sold this ring," Jefferson replied, showing Abel the thick, heavy ornament.

He looked the ring over several times, hefting it and scrutinizing it through several sizes of magnifier. He showed it to a man from the back shop, a heavy-set Puerto Rican with thick, dirty fingers, who was introduced as the chief designer.

"It's mine," Abel said at last, even looking a little proud.

"We *knew* that," Marcie replied.

"Not necessarily. There are two other places that make rings like this, but they all imitate me. We're class."

"Your address especially knocked me out," Marcie said.

"Don't knock the Bronx. It gave the world the Yankees."

"Okay," Marcie said. "What else? The Major Deegan Expressway and Fort Apache?"

Jefferson said, "The Bronx is so hot that Murray here has to pack a rod. You ever fire that thing, Murray?"

"Not in years, to tell the truth. But this is a rough neighborhood and I deal in gold."

"You mean there's enough gold in these rings to get a thief excited?" Marcie asked.

"They think there is," Abel shrugged. "This ring is from my design, all right. It's from my alphabet series, costs nine hundred ninety-nine dollars in most stores."

"What stores?" Jefferson asked.

"These," he said, producing a vinyl-bound distribution book. "I have fifty-three outlets in the City and can give you a computer printout of those that ordered an *S*-ring in the past year."

"Are there a lot?"

"*S* is a popular initial. Sid, Sol, Schlomo, Schmuel . . ."

"Schmuck," Marcie said.

"There's lots of names that begin with *S*. I'll get a printout for you."

Abel spoke to his secretary, and a minute later a printer spat out a list of stores. There were seven of them in Harlem. Each had sold at least one S-ring, and three had sold two or more. One, a large outlet on Lenox Avenue, had the record—seven.

"We'll be visiting these places tomorrow," Marcie said. "And I don't want to find out that you've been calling the stores and warning them."

"Would I do that?"

"If you do," Jefferson said, "We'll tell your customers how much their precious rings are really worth."

35.
AS QUIET AS A CHURCH MOUSE

At four on a weekday morning the Cathedral of St. John the Divine was as quiet as a church mouse.

The night watchmen were told to sit by their monitors and doors and do nothing else. Avignon was set up taping the nave and crossing from a vantage point far up the east front.

Donovan walked slowly up the main aisle, his footfalls echoing eerily off the cold stone walls. The nave—the long leg of the cross-shaped cathedral—was 124 feet from floor to ceiling, and even walking softly his steps sounded like cannon shots. The piers, alternately six and sixteen feet thick, rose 100 feet to the springing of the vaulted ceiling, which hung overhead like a dark, distant circus tent.

Between the piers were nestled the fourteen chapels, each with a twenty-five-foot-high stained glass window that was, at that hour, dark as ebony. To the exhibit in the Crusaders' Chapel had already been added a photograph of the late Terry Loomis, who died not far from it. In the nearby Ecclesiastical Chapel, a testimonial to the religious life was nearing completion. Further along the wall, in the Lawyers' Chapel, an exhibit was being erected in praise of lawyers.

Donovan wandered through the nave and crossing, where the short arms of the cross met, and into the choir. He revisited an old favorite, the Magna Carta Pedestal, beside which was carved: "The adjoining shaft was once a part of the high altar of the Abbey of Bury St. Edmunds upon which on November 20, 1214, the barons swore fealty to each other in wresting the great charter from King John. It is placed here as a symbol of the community of political tradition, laws, and liberties which is the inheritance of the English-speaking commonwealths throughout the world."

"Laws and liberties, huh," Donovan said, loudly enough to hear his words echo back to him from throughout the hollow belly of the cathedral.

He looked around him, and up and down the eight great columns surrounding the altar. Fifty-five feet high and weighing 130 tons each, they broke every manhole cover over which they passed when, in 1903, they were winched down Amsterdam Avenue from the 134th Street dock.

A chill like a Maine coastal fog settled over Donovan's shoulders and froze his spine. Every fiber of him said he was being watched by Marcus. Donovan turned up his collar and sat on the steps leading up the great altar. Facing east, he looked down the 600-foot length of the cathedral to the Rose Window, from which Avignon's spy camera was whirling.

"You're watching me, aren't you," he said loudly enough for Marcus to hear.

Then Donovan opened a small bag, and from it took his 4 A.M. snack. With the killer watching, Donovan opened a can of Coke and enjoyed it with a slice of cold pizza.

36.

DONOVAN ACHIEVES SELF-REALIZATION

My mother thought she was the most sensible person in the world," Donovan said. "My father thought he was the most moral and ethical person in the world. And I'm the only one in the world who believes that it's sensible to be moral and ethical."

"You're an only child, aren't you?" Avignon asked.

37.

TWO MEN SITTING ON THE STEPS TALKING ABOUT WOMEN

No one goes into police work to get rich," Donovan said.

"But few have stayed so aggressively poor as you," Avignon said. "The world throws money at me when I show it the footage of its own weirdness. But when you do the same thing, perhaps tossing in a jail sentence, all you get is accused of self-righteousness."

"Which is morals and ethics run amok," Donovan said. "Is that your point?"

"I'm saying that either you should go into show biz, so the

world will throw money at you too, or Marcie should put it in writing that she loves morals and ethics, and poverty, as much as you do. Which is what this conversation is really about, isn't it?"

Donovan sighed, and said, "Have I grown so shallow?" He folded his pizza crust into his jacket pocket and looked down the centerline of the nave to the Rose Window, which in the pre-dawn hours glowed with faint hope and optimism.

Avignon sat next to him on the steps to the altar. Their attempt to provoke Marcus had produced no obvious results. If the lunatic heard or saw Donovan's performance, no indication was given. Given that slight failing of the night's plans, it seemed reasonable to sit on the altar steps and talk about women.

"I see things about you that your friend, Jefferson, can't see or won't tell you about because you're also his boss, and which Marcie won't acknowledge. You *believe* in what you do, to the point of obsession. You really think that good people should live forever, and are willing to sacrifice everything to make the world that way. You're a crusader, Donovan, a true believer, one of the last. You should take Holy Orders while you're here in the cathedral."

"I don't believe in God and think even less of His hired help," Donovan snarled. "I'm only here for the music and architecture. Do you know how to play the organ? There's a pretty neat one over your right shoulder." He glanced up at some of the instrument's 8,000 pipes.

Avignon said, "You're afraid that Marcie doesn't share your dedication to the crusade. You think she's only in police business for the excitement, which is not at all the same as being in it for the morals and ethics. You think that she's interested in you because of the novelty of living with a white guy. You'd like to marry her and have kids but you're afraid that one day she'll find out that you love the crusade more than her, and will recall that making money wasn't such a sin after all, and that will be the end of it. You're terrified that she'll run off with some yuppie lawyer and leave you alone in that big apartment that you keep losing the keys to."

Donovan admitted, "She *is* better at the details than I am. I can trust her to see that the bills are paid and the dog is walked. She wants a dog, did I tell you? A golden retriever. A big dog and two kids."

Avignon said, "You were always more abstract and intuitive than her."

"She's also a better shot. Dammit, Mike, what girl in her right mind would marry an Irish cop? She was going to be a lawyer until she got sidetracked by me. It's only a matter of time before she realizes her mistake and splits."

"How long have you guys been together?"

"Off and on for twelve or thirteen years."

Avignon laughed, and said, "I kind of think that the novelty of falling for an Irish cop has worn off, as has the novelty of your falling for a black woman. In my opinion, if you're still with each other it was meant to be. Marry the girl and stop worrying about it."

Donovan frowned, and said, "Life seemed a lot simpler to figure out when I was drinking."

"Life *was* simpler. All you did was chase bad guys and drink."

"It seemed like quite enough at the time," Donovan shot back. "Occasionally it seemed like a full life."

"But no more."

Donovan shook his head. "I want more."

"What? A wife, I suppose?"

"Maybe."

"And after that, what? Peace of mind?"

"One thing at a time," Donovan said quickly.

38.
CITY OF GOD (3)

The limestone dust was everywhere, even on the gold leaf that bordered the pages of his book. When a new page was laid bare, the dust settled on the page in a fine mist, and was caught in the ink from the quill, faintly blurring the strokes.

Marcus set aside his quill and glared at the page, which now more than ever resembled a desert, barren of ideas, containing only dust. The agents of mammon had come into God's house to kill the ghostly priest, the ghastly priest. Marcus wasn't even sure which word applied anymore. His anger was too great. He couldn't write. He couldn't continue to carve. All he could do was trace a finger in the dust and burn with vile anger at the mocking intrusion.

He had expected that the City of Man would send agents, but that the power of God would turn them back at the gate. The only earthly power within the church would be that of Marcus himself and he would be safe there, unreachable. But this Donovan had gotten inside and was living there himself, with his friend, and was making a mockery of God, Marcus, and his work.

Worse yet, Marcus could no longer go out and walk freely in the cathedral, well after dark, when he was accustomed to having the house to himself. For three-score days, since the workmen had turned the cornice on the tower of St. Peter, Marcus was able to move freely from his cell, unseen. That was no longer possible. Donovan was there, in the crypt and elsewhere, making jokes and carrying on as if God's house were a picnic ground.

Marcus shut the book and watched as a puff of dust escaped the closing pages. Donovan or no, there was more work to be done. Abominations remained; God's house needed more cleaning.

The policeman would have to be avoided. That failing, he too would have to die.

Dawn came to the cathedral in a flutter not of songbirds but of flyers. Marcus laid atop his closed journal a handful of broadsides, schedules, and brochures, giving the details of the continuing violation of the temple. Despite two cleansings and the warning nailed to the door, the City of Man continued to intrude. Marcus shuffled through the papers, reading them with intense scrutiny; so many quarries, he thought, so little time.

39.
DEATH AS A 'JEOPARDY' QUESTION

W ho said 'let's kill all the lawyers?' " Brewer asked.
Jake answered, "Who was Shakespeare?"
"I *know* that. I mean, what play was it in?"
Jake quoted, " 'The first thing we do, let's kill all the lawyers.' *Henry VI, Part II.''*

Nakima was Riley's arbiter of barroom arguments because he was a voracious reader (albeit, mainly of the *Racing Form*) and because his regular seat was nearest to the drawer that held the essential saloon library: *The World Almanac, Webster's Biographical Dictionary, The Guinness Book of World Records,* and *Bartlett's Familiar Quotations.* But Nakima knew that particular Shakespeare quote well ahead of time; he looked it up as soon as he saw Herbert Spenser get out of a cab and go up the stairs to the West Side Major Crimes Unit.

Spenser was the attorney of record in many of New York City's most political cases, and could always be expected to defend cop killers, rapists (if the victim was rich), and muggers (on the principle that anyone with money in his pocket was a lapdog of the capitalist war-mongering conspiracy). Unlike Communism (he also defended the Castro government against its victims), Spenser never saw himself as being obsolete, and revelled in the revulsion that police held for him. His vigorous defense of an especially brutal cop killer from the Bronx earned him the eternal enmity of the police, but also assured him police protection. The Commissioner made it plain that should Spenser die anywhere but in his sleep, the nearest police officer was automatically suspect.

Shortly before he died, Spenser planned to go to the Cathedral of St. John the Divine to raise hell. To him, the mission was simple and direct. His client Terry Loomis had been killed—not by a raging lunatic who thought he was St. Augustine, but by an assassin dispatched by the fascist government of Brazil which, in league with the Central Intelligence Agency and the New York Police Department, wanted to eliminate the promoter who was responsible for disrupting the aforementioned fascist government's plans to turn the Amazon rain forest into pasture land for steer destined to become McDonald's hamburgers.

Spenser intended to make his point loudly and in front of the press, which he had summoned to a press conference on the front steps of the cathedral. The press conference was scheduled for 11 A.M., which would allow plenty of time to make the 5 P.M. newscasts. Before it, Spenser planned a provocateur's visit to the West Side Major Crimes Unit, nominally in the hopes that Donovan, an old adversary, would lose his temper and say something intemperate that would then be used to bolster the argument that the NYPD was in on the Loomis assassination conspiracy.

Donovan wasn't there, having moved into the cathedral the night before. Jefferson and Marcie were in Harlem, leaving Howard Bonaci the only one to comment. His comment was made in Italian and unprintable anyway, so Spenser headed uptown to the cathedral to keep his rendezvous with the press.

Disappointment covered him with irony. A Consolidated Edison generating plant on Randall's Island blew up, killing two workmen and injuring seven others and plunging sections of Harlem, the South Bronx, and Astoria into darkness. Every available TV crew was diverted to the scene of the catastrophe. The only reporter to show up for Spenser's press conference was a student from the Columbia Graduate School of Journalism who was working on a class project.

Said Donovan, "Fortune smiled on the misbegotten today," upon hearing that a disappointed lawyer was muttering loudly in the nave.

"I had the chance to run over that asshole once," Avignon remembered. "He was crossing Seventh Avenue en route to the Lion's Head with a woman who looked young enough to be his granddaughter. All I had to do was drop the Enola Gay down into second and floor it. But, you know . . ."

"A '57 Chevy in mint condition is a sacred object."

"What are you going to do about Spenser?"

"I guess I'll talk to him," Donovan said. "You want to come along?"

"No. He'll want me to tape him for the nightly news. I haven't stuck a camera in his face since he claimed that the teenage guys that raped the Central Park jogger were expressing justifiable outrage over their systematic degradation at the hands of society."

"I won't be gone long," Donovan said, and left his HQ in the crypt and went up to the nave.

Spenser was wearing a pea-green cloth coat, ragged at the collar, and adorned with a cashmere scarf and kidskin gloves. His wave of pure white hair was tussled by the November wind, and his cheeks were red from both cold and frustration.

Donovan avoided a handshake. "What do you want?" he asked.

"I would like an update on your investigation," Spenser said, his voice taking on a tone that assumed he wouldn't get anywhere.

"What's your connection with the case? I mean, other than being the guardian of truth and justice in the Third World."

"Terry Loomis was a client of mine. I understand you were present when he was killed."

"Actually, I was down the hall. I intend to catch his killer, Spenser. As the saying goes, I'm working on it."

"Uh huh," the lawyer said, nodding perfunctorily. Donovan sensed that he wanted to launch an accusation about NYPD involvement in a conspiracy, but was worried that the lieutenant might have an actual mean streak to go along with the rumored one.

"If you have any information, I'd like to hear it." Donovan knew that making such a request was risky, but it had to be done. God knows what Spenser would suggest as a lead; perhaps to track down the Brazilian Consul General and subject him to some patented NYPD abridgement of Fourth Amendment rights.

"There *is* something. Can we discuss it alone?"

Spenser looked around like a paranoid at a Republican Party convention. He flicked his hand inside his lapel, going for a bit of information or a gun. Donovan quick-decided that Spenser wasn't armed, and allowed himself to be intrigued. What did the man have in his pocket? He had never cooperated with the police before. As a general rule, cops got more cooperation out of the Mafia than they did from Spenser.

"We're alone," Donovan said, looking around at the basically empty nave. To be sure, a church group was taking the tour, but there were only twenty of them and they were halfway to the choir; about a football field away.

"Can we be more alone? Someone could be watching."

Donovan thought, *If I follow this guy into a dark corner and he drops dead of a heart attack, I'm going up the river for life.*

Nonetheless, he let Spenser lead him to St. Martin's Chapel, at the east end of the cathedral near the Biblical Garden. The chapel, the size of a normal church and its altar, was one of seven large chapels that surrounded the tip of the cathedral's cross. The

Chapel of St. Martin of Tours was named after the fourth-century Frenchman who, Donovan knew, was the patron saint of publicans and innkeepers. A statue of Joan of Arc graced one wall, and beneath it was displayed a stone taken from the very cell in Rouen from which she was led to the stake.

"There's no talking in here," Donovan said, respecting the sign on the door.

"This won't take long," Spenser said, finally producing something from inside his lapel—several snapshots of small crowds standing behind police lines. "Look at these. Look at the man in the blue jacket."

Donovan studied the prints and saw that one man was in all three photos. He was in his late twenties or early thirties, unshaven, with short brown hair and what looked like a small gold earring. Chico Brewer wore different pants in all three shots, but the same light blue team jacket.

"So what?" Donovan asked.

"This man has been following Loomis for two months—during the entire Rain Forest tour."

"He looks like a Columbia graduate student. That's Columbia blue."

"Columbia has many foreign students. I believe he's an agent of the Brazilian government sent to kill my client. Did you know that the university was endowed by money from the tea barons?"

Donovan frowned. Spenser saw the frown.

"I don't expect you to fully appreciate the sensitive nature of the Rain Forest crusade."

"Oh, I do. Tree frogs and piranha. I appreciate it better than you could possibly imagine. I never use plastic bags and I only buy recycled paper. So you think this guy killed Terry Loomis?"

"Why else would he have followed Loomis and the band?"

"Maybe he wants to get into Christie Gaynor's pants. That sounds more plausible."

"Sure. Go for the easy sexist explanation."

Donovan bristled. "My New-Age-Man credentials are impeccable, for a cop anyway. Do you have anything on this guy other than suspicions?"

"There were threats against my client. He could have made them."

"Any in writing? Any on tape?"

"No," the lawyer admitted.

"I'll see what I can do," Donovan said. "I suppose that now you're going to hold a press conference and announce that the New York Police Department has agreed to investigate your allegations of an assassination conspiracy."

"I sense your resistance to the idea."

"I've never been big on conspiracy theories. I read millions of words on the subject, and still think that Oswald shot JFK and Sirhan shot RFK. Granted there are evil men out there—fewer now that Communism has crashed and burned—but I don't think that this kid in the pictures got Loomis. A madman named Marcus got Loomis, and I mean to prove it."

"At least look into my theory," Spenser said.

"I'll look into it," Donovan agreed, leading the way out of the chapel, past a dark-robed man with silvery hair who looked askance at them for chatting in the officially silent St. Martin's Chapel. Donovan went back down to the crypt to make some calls. Spenser tarried in the cathedral for a few minutes, lighting a cigarette. Then when the curling smoke provoked angry stares from an elderly tourist, the lawyer pushed his way out the door alongside St. James's Chapel.

It was still cold in the early afternoon, with a northeast wind that blew up the hill from Harlem and chilled the bones of all those willing to linger outdoors. Spenser turned up the collar of his coat and sat on a simple stone bench in the Biblical Garden, a cathedral appendage in which volunteers tried to keep alive various forms of flora mentioned in the Bible. In the cold Northeast this was nearly impossible, and the most obvious example of Biblical shrubbery was an olive tree, newly planted that summer, already half-dead.

A goat shivered beneath it, nibbling on crusts of bread tossed out from the morning soup kitchen. Nearby, a largely royal-blue peacock sat atop a bright red pickup truck, making its decision to get in on the free feed. Spenser pulled his Russian wool cap down over his ears and watched as the bird fluttered down to the ground, then walked tentatively into the Garden to join the goat.

The peacock traversed scrubby gardens with brown and deadened tropical plants, each with a valiantly inscribed plastic tag identifying the species and its Biblical connection. As the goat munched happily, the bird walked down a crude stone border toward the olive grove in which sat the bench.

Past the fence and Morningside Drive and down the hill in Harlem, a lonesome police siren wailed. On Morningside, a traffic enforcement agent ticketed an Oldsmobile that was parked at a fire hydrant. A stiff November breeze rustled a browning olive branch alongside Spenser's head, masking the sound of a heavy wooden door opening behind the lawyer.

The goat stopped munching and looked up. The peacock froze in its tracks. And the huge wooden mallet crashed down on the lawyer's head from directly behind, driving the jawbone deep into his breast and snapping his neck.

The body slumped forward and did a semi-cartwheel in the dead leaves, blood dripping onto the ground where it was soaked up by the loaves of stale bread. Marcus stood tall and panting, his breath making great geysers of vapor in the chill air. Then, as silently as he came, he ducked back inside the skeleton of the cathedral.

40.
"I Think, He Talks, She Shoots."

I t ain't fair," Donovan moaned.

"Life itself ain't fair," said the Police Commissioner. He was trying to be helpful, in his way.

"To begin with, I have an alibi for the entire time. I was downstairs in the crypt talking on the phone with Bonaci when Spenser's number came up. Avignon will swear to the timing."

"Oh, *he's* reliable."

"Dammit, it was my dream for years to personally shoot Spenser, using my father's gun. If I killed the sonofabitch I would be bragging about it. I'm mainly embarrassed that it happened on my watch."

"That is a bit problematical. I mean, you were there to put a stop to the killings which, by the way, we all now admit were done by a madman who thinks he's St. Augustine."

"Thank you for that much," Donovan said.

"From now on you get as much help as you need. Men, resources, whatever. Do you want to shut down the cathedral and search it?"

"Yes, but the bishop won't allow it. The best I can get out of him is a watch put on the doors. I want comings and goings monitored, at least well-enough to pick up a tall and muscular lunatic carrying a battering ram."

"That seems sensible enough," the Commissioner agreed.

"And the joint closes down at ten every night. No more open-door policy twenty-four hours a day. That will give me all night to search the corridors."

"You really think he's living in there?"

"I know that he is. I plan to go door-to-door within those walls and ferret him out."

"I suggest putting men in every hallway. Outside every locked room until it's opened and searched."

Donovan shook his head. "That will only drive him somewhere else. There are lots of churches in this town, and at no time has he said he's devoted only to this one. How would you like it if he turned up in St. Patrick's?"

The Commissioner turned green. St. Patrick's was the Roman Catholic cathedral located in midtown, and its archbishop was politically connected as well as a connoisseur of public relations.

Donovan continued, "Let me have enough men to make a show of it. I'll station them in halls and walk them around the joint for a few days. That will hold down the body count long enough to let me conduct a search."

"Take whatever you need. Get them from division."

"I also need my team back. They're off in Harlem on the Marathon murder case."

"That would be Sergeant Jefferson, if memory serves."

"Yeah, and my sharpshooter."

"I didn't know he was that good a shot."

"He's not. I meant my fiancee, Marcia Barnes."

"The black girl you live with? So you're making it official?"

"I even picked out the altar," Donovan said proudly. "Of course, I have to make it safe for marriages first."

"You work better with your team," the Commissioner observed.

Donovan beamed. "We're good together. I think, he talks, she shoots."

"And what role does Avignon play?"

"Mike is my old friend and alter ego. He smells blood better than anyone I know."

"Don't get him killed."

"It will never happen. He's been trying to get himself killed for fifty years and it ain't happened yet."

41.
HOORAY FOR HOLLYWOOD

Academy Award!" Avignon exclaimed, focusing the Ikegami videocamera on the thick oak door that was set in the cathedral wall just behind the stone bench where Spenser met his maker.

Donovan requested an explanation.

"I got this worked out. I got *him* worked out. It's theater. It's Hollywood. Dammit, *it's show biz!* And you're getting into it just in time to save your career."

Donovan chased off the forensics technicians, who were done anyway, and Bonaci, who was looking at Avignon as one looks at a geek.

"I still don't understand," Donovan said.

"This tape I'm making is gonna win me an Oscar, the one I should have gotten years ago. Look at this door—straight out of Dracula's castle. Look at *everything* Marcus has done. He set himself up as the defender of the house of God against the works of man. He nailed a warning to the front door—straight out of Martin Luther and the whole fucking Protestant Reformation. He killed a promoter in the middle of *The Phantom of the Opera*. He killed a crusading environmentalist in the middle of a benefit concert beamed around the world via satellite. He tried to kill America's premier video genius while a couple of dozen gargoyles stood as silent witness. And most recently, he bashed in the brains of New York's most flamboyant radical lawyer while he was sitting under a garland of olive leaves. What theater! What *balls!*"

"On the other hand, maybe it *was* a conspiracy of the fascist Brazilian government and the CIA," Donovan said dryly.

"Too bad that Brewer has an alibi," Avignon said.

"Yeah, he was drinking with Jake, who is the most honest man I know. If I'm ever accused of murder, I want him as my alibi. Still, this is the first time somebody showed me a picture of a man he said was a killer and then got killed himself. The mere idea pisses me off."

"I'll shoot it as a TV movie," Avignon said.

"Odd, though, that an eminent ethnologist would spend time following Christie Gaynor around. Maybe he *did* want to get into her pants, like I told Spenser. Maybe I should have done the same."

"Too late now, so you might as well concentrate on Marcus. He may be crazy as a loon, but his finger is on the pulse of America. He understands the media. He wants his message broadcast. I think he let me live so I could go on taping his deeds. He's hiding within these walls knowing that you can't resist going in after him. He's researched you, Donovan. He knows that you'll bring the eyes of the world in with you."

"I brought *you.*"

"Exactly. Just as he knew you would. Anyone familiar with big-time crime on the West Side knows that if the murder is weird enough and/or done with some exotic weapon . . ."

"A battering ram qualifies."

". . . that Donovan will turn up, bringing along the usual headlines. Marcus has played you like a Stradivarius, my friend."

"And you too," Donovan said.

"It doesn't matter about me," Avignon said. "I'm in show biz, and the tape I'm making of this whole affair is gonna make me a million bucks. And you're getting better. That stunt with the pizza was pure street theater, the best kind."

Donovan sat on the stone bench, his feet resting on the chalk outline that marked where Spenser's body fell, and stared at the oak door. It was ten feet high and crisscrossed with black iron straps and rosettes. What Avignon said was right on the mark. Okay, maybe there was a slight exaggeration of the role of premeditation; maybe Marcus didn't consciously plan to lure Donovan in particular into it and to get so much attention, but that was the result. And one thing was undeniable—Donovan liked it; found it irresistible. He *would* go into the uncharted bowels of the cathedral after Marcus, tear it apart gargoyle by gargoyle, if need be.

"God help me, I love it so," he murmured, repeating a phrase attributed to Patton.

"The trail begins behind that door, Donovan," Avignon said, waggling the camera in its direction.

"I know that."

"It will get hot for you."

"It often does."

"After you," Avignon said, and the Ikegami started whirring as the lieutenant strode to the door and yanked it open.

The door swung up with surprising ease, and no squeaks, but it was dark inside. Donovan drew his .38 and poked it inside. He felt the hot breath of Avignon's lens on his shoulder, and stage-whispered, "Stay behind me."

Avignon said, "Remember, he's right-handed. The blow will come from your left."

As Donovan's eyes adjusted to the light, he saw a passage damp with mold and thick with history. Ten feet in there was another door, jammed shut and locked. A metal stairway ran up inside the walls, the faces of which were bare stone etched with algae and dirt.

Four flights up, daylight seeped through a rooftop vent. Donovan crept up the stairs, his weight bending the worn iron steps. The air was cold and damp, and he felt it crawl down his throat to his lungs with each breath. He paused on the second floor landing, which was no more than a square of metal webbing bolted to the stone walls. There was another door, this one slightly ajar, as if to invite him in.

"This is the place, this is the way he went," Donovan whispered, and then was shocked by how loud his voice was in the stone stairwell.

With the muzzle of the .38 in the lead, Donovan pulled open the door. It came open slowly and with deep grunts of old hinges, and there was another door, a wooden door, behind it. That door was locked. A brass lock cylinder had been poked at recently with a key. Tracks made by an unsteady hand fumbling in the dark could be seen in the film of dirt that covered the cylinder face.

"Somebody's been through here recently," Donovan said.

Avignon set down the camera and pulled his burglar's tools from a back pocket.

42.
"SMACK ADDICTS WERE MELLOW DUDES, IN RETROSPECT."

Marcie was in a Harlem still blackened out by the Con Ed explosion that diverted the local TV stations from covering Spenser's press conference. But the glow in the Lenox Avenue Gold Mine was awesome, especially considering that it came from half a dozen candles.

The candles were what Jefferson called "spook lights," thick, scented candles in glass sheaths sold in Caribbean bodegas as quasi-religious charms meant to ward off evil spells and house demons. Their scent filled the huge shop with perfume, and their light glittered off the dazzling array of gold body decorations.

Gold was everywhere, in display cases and on the walls, protected by a snarly pit bull and an Uzi. There were earrings the size of cantaloupes that, when applied, dragged the ear lobes down halfway to Florida. There were gold rope chains, plain and with pie-sized watches dangling. Gold breast-plates and cod-pieces adorned a mannequin. And an immense display case was chock-a-block with rings, the single-finger variety and those that were more like gold brass knuckles.

"Kind of makes you miss the good old days of heroin," Jefferson noted.

"Indeed it does," Marcie agreed.

"Smack addicts were mellow dudes, in retrospect," Jefferson said, "nodding quietly in alleys, not rampaging through crowds of civilized people stealing money to buy crack."

Sam the Gold Man pondered the S-shaped ring with faint recognition. "That's a home-boy ring all right," he said. "I sold seven like it in the past year."

"That's all?" Marcie asked.

"They go for a thousand a pop. Not everybody with the initial S and this kind of taste can afford that much."

"Crack money," Jefferson said.

"I don't ask them where they get it," Sam said quickly.

"You're the last store we've checked. The other ones didn't pan out. That means that our perp bought this ring here. Look at it harder and give me a name."

"They never have *names,*" Sam said, looking closer. After inspection, he said, "It's a size eleven. That's kind of big for a kid, and kids are the only customers for these rings. I know who bought it . . . but a *name?*"

"I'll take whatever you got," Marcie said.

"He's a local kid . . . Jackson Avenue. Calls himself RapStar. That's a joke."

Sam laughed.

Jefferson asked what was funny.

"The kid never talks. Gary Cooper had more to say than him. I can tell you this, though. He was real fond of jewelry. Had the S ring and this stiletto with a black handle that also had an S on it."

"Where's he hang out?" Marcie asked. "What's his turf?"

"That I don't know. I haven't seen him in a couple of weeks, although he said he'd be back for some chains. He was real proud of this ring. How'd he lose it?"

"It was left behind at a homicide," Jefferson said.

Sam gave the ring back, and for an instant the flash of gold in the store faded to black. He looked down, embarrassed.

"Heroin wasn't so bad after all," he acknowledged.

Jefferson's radio went off, and they went out in the street to take the call. It was Bonaci, relaying a message from Donovan.

"We have to call home," Jefferson said. "Donovan wants us at the cathedral."

"We've been summoned, have we?" Marcie snarled.

"He says he needs us. But we're just starting to catch up to Jennifer's killer."

"Donovan can wait."

"You want to be the one to tell him?"

"I would be delighted," Marcie said.

43.
DONOVAN'S EVIL TWIN, SKIPPY

Donovan told Jefferson and Marcie about Avignon: "He's my evil twin, Skippy. He *lives* the things that I can't even put into words. I approach evil like a parish priest, slapping the wrist—handy metaphor there—of the teenage boy for jerking off. But Avignon is the omniscient God, watching the evil that men do, getting it all down on tape but never soiling his own hands. He will see that they are punished, but later, at the millennium, when all sins come due for payment. Me, I could get killed off anytime and that would be the end of it. But Avignon is timeless, God as voyeur, the all-seeing, never-sleeping journalist."

"Newspaperman," Avignon interrupted. "*Journalists* are newspapermen who are out of work."

Donovan continued, "Avignon will outlive us all, watching the world and taking notes right up to the day the trumpet sounds."

"Which is about New Year's of the year 2000, by the latest reckoning," Avignon said.

"Are you *done* with that?" Jefferson asked, impatiently. Avignon was still working to unlock the old door when Jefferson and Marcie caught up with him and Donovan.

"Rome didn't come unhinged in a day. This lock is befouled with something."

"Limestone dust, perhaps," Donovan said.

"It's coming loose now . . . Got it!"

Avignon gloated as the latch clicked open, the sound rippling up and down the stone stairwell.

Donovan pushed the door open an inch, then recoiled slightly as a puff of stale air came out, smelling of damp stone and mold. Marcie sneezed, and that too echoed. He opened the door wide enough to step inside, then did so, the .38 again leading the way.

The hall was seventy-five feet long and empty, with doors slightly recessed every fifteen feet along the left wall. The right-hand wall was blank, bare stone, strangely clean as if it had been polished. The floor too was clean, swept, and the hall was lit by 40-watt bulbs placed every so often down the ceiling. There was no On and Off switch. The lights seemed to be on permanently. At the far end was another door, leading God-knows-where. While the others crept cautiously into the hallway, Donovan hurried down the corridor trying doors, including the last one. "All locked," he said. "This is not going to go quickly."

Jefferson said, "Bring in teams and open every door. Fumigate the place."

"No. It will only drive him out into the city, where he could go on killing forever."

Avignon focused his Ikegami on Donovan, who leaned against the far door while putting away his pistol. Then Avignon put down the camera and stepped to the first door, again brandishing his burglar's tools.

"We don't have time to hang out while you pick locks and

peep in doors," Marcie said, walking down the hall to her lover and standing close to him for the first time in a few days. She stood close enough to acknowledge the relationship but far enough away to give him pause as to its longevity.

"I need you now," Donovan said.

"Why now and not a week before? What's changed?"

"Marcus knows I'm after him. I went out in the open with it, waved a slice of pizza in his face."

Marcie offered a quizzical frown, then said, "Never mind. Don't explain. Just tell me why I couldn't be here when it was still a secret."

"You fit into an Episcopal cathedral as well as I fit into Harlem. Face it, there are some things we have to do alone."

"That's a crock of shit. You just want to creep around with your sick friend, lurking in shadows and imagining yourself in the cast of *The Third Man*."

"Is that what you think I do?"

"Most of the time you're a good investigator. But every so often you get a case that appeals to your sense of the dramatic and you go *crazy*. This Marcus has got you so turned around that you've lost perspective."

"I'm onto the guy," Donovan argued. "And I'll get him. But I need you here to take care of details, like always. This is a big place, bigger than I imagined, and I can't handle it alone."

She stepped back. "That's it, then? You're the star and I'm supporting cast? Is that the way it's always going to be? If so, I have to get back to Harlem."

He reached out to her, but she shrank from his touch. It was then that he saw the wall, both walls, the one that he had put up between them and the one that had always been there. She was black. He never quite got that before, as if the difference in their races was something cute to kid about, like her preference for gourmet food over his cheeseburgers and pizza.

When Jefferson, bored with watching Avignon pick a lock, joined them, Donovan felt another chill. For the first time ever, Jefferson and Marcie weren't squabbling. They were on a case together, and they were a team. They were black and working together and they didn't need him. It was so obvious, Donovan knew, and he should have thought of it before.

"I created this monster," he said, mostly to himself.

"Yes you did," she replied.

He shuffled his feet, like he had seen movie cowboys do, and offered, feebly, "Maybe when I wrap the Marcus murders I can help you with Peel."

"We've *got* a lead on the suspects," Marcie said, adding, with emphasis, *"In Harlem."*

"Bring them back alive," Donovan said. "There are questions I want to ask . . . problems with that case."

"We got to do this alone, Bill," Jefferson added, softly.

Donovan nodded, acquiescing, a bit sadly, and looked away from them and down at the floor. Marcie swung her eyes away as she turned and followed Jefferson down the hall toward the door.

The chill that had swept over him became glaciation. After all the years of living together and loving each other a wall had gone up. When Jennifer was killed, Marcie's sense of herself as a black woman had been violated, just as Jefferson's pride had been shaken. A bunch of black kids had come rampaging out of Harlem and maybe killed Jennifer Peel and now would be hunted down by their own race. Donovan was a white man, and although he was Marcie's lover, could have no part in the vengeance.

The chill got worse and he had to sit down on the cold, swept floor. He was no longer the sole guarantor of civilization on the West Side. And a wall had gone up.

Avignon called from down the hall. "I got the first one open. You know, I think I can make money breaking and entering. That is, if my TV career ever falls through."

"Break and enter into my broken heart," Donovan said, climbing wearily to his feet and trudging down the hall.

Avignon had the camera trained on the door as Donovan opened it. It swung open to shed light into a ten-by-ten storage room packed to the rafters with desks from a long-ago grade school. They were about the right size for ten-year-olds, and had sat unused and dusty for several decades. Whipping out a pocket flashlight, Donovan inspected closely. One kid had carved into his desktop, "Kilroy was here." Another favored "The Shadow Knows."

A fragment of newspaper wadded into an inkwell listed new apartments for rent on Columbus Avenue for $148.17 per month, two bedrooms, one-and-one-half baths.

An hour later they had searched the remainder of the cluster of rooms finding, in turn, storage rooms containing *The Book of Common Prayer;* 78-rpm recordings of psalms, Christmas carols, and renditions on the bagpipe of Irish melodies and "Amazing Grace"; bales of hay, tied with sisal cord; and children's shoes, various sizes and colors, with and without partners, dating from the 1940s.

"I don't think anyone has been in these rooms since the war," Avignon said.

"But Marcus has been down the hall. He even cleaned it. Swept it up. And someone left the lights burning," Donovan noted.

Avignon went to the door against which Donovan had leaned while speaking with Marcie, and picked that lock. Unlike the others, it popped right open.

Opening, it revealed another hallway, this one a bit longer and containing rooms on both sides. It too was clean and lit by low-wattage light bulbs.

"This strokes an ancient memory," Donovan said. "I was here before, a long time ago."

"On a case?"

"As a kid. The nuns used to bring us here every so often. I pretty much blocked all that. All I can say is there's no end to these hallways and storage rooms. A man could hide for years."

"Do you have anything better to do than watch while I pick locks?" Avignon asked.

Donovan tossed up his hands. "I thought I was getting married but I'm no longer certain," he said.

44.
THE RETURN OF
HALFTRACK

As day swept into evening, Donovan called it quits and emerged from the cathedral, pausing only to notify the plainclothesmen he had stationed around the perimeter to stay sharp. There were six of them in three cars strategically placed to allow screening of all those entering or leaving the edifice.

That pretty much fulfilled the barest requirement of Donovan's charge to protect the public safety. Anyone who looked vaguely like he could be Marcus—who was tall and strong enough to carry and wield a heavy blunt instrument—would be photographed and followed. But in Donovan's experience, traditional surveillance seldom replaced an observer in the know. That is, one capable of detecting the subtle rips in the fabric of life that occurred when evil was abroad. Donovan knew but one cop, himself, with that talent. Jefferson was a comer, but still too young and, anyway, occupied elsewhere. The six detectives assigned to watch the cathedral would have to do.

"As long as those boys can spot the more obvious suspects we'll be okay," Avignon said. "Besides, Marcus ain't goin' nowhere."

"Tomorrow we'll check out the Stone Yard and the guys who work there," Donovan said, after he procured a pastrami sandwich and led the way to Riley's.

It was seven o'clock of an average Thursday. This being the day before payday, most of the locals were broke and the bar only slightly tenanted. George sat with his feet up, leaning back against the cash register, his hands behind his head, watching a New York Rangers hockey pre-game show. At the bar were, working inward from the door, Jake Nakima, Chico Brewer, Little Harold the electrician, Wes Jackson the lawyer, and Gus Keane, who recently quit as night bartender to open a furniture-moving business using an old Ford van. In the back room a handful of Columbia students were wearing out the jukebox.

Donovan brightened upon seeing the peaceful scene. "A neighborhood tavern in the full bloom of autumn, complete with hockey game and rock and roll," he said, taking one of the two seats between Jake and Chico.

"Fuck you," George said, without taking his eyes off the screen.

"I will have a club soda with a wedge, and my friend will have a Coke. The old Coke, naturally, not the new Coke."

"Eat shit and die," was the reply.

"I could not exist without this camaraderie," Donovan noted, leaning over the bar and getting the drinks himself.

Jake waggled a glass of Seven-Up at the lieutenant, and said, "Evening, Bill."

Donovan returned the toast. "To your health."

Brewer peered around his copy of *The Times* and smiled a toothy Brazilian smile.

Jake said, "Do you feel lucky?"

"Is that a question or a straight line?"

"A question. We got a pool going."

Donovan pondered, failed to come up with an answer, and said, "On what? The only game on is hockey, and hockey games are too low-scoring to get up pools on them. What can you bet on? How many fights and the number of injured?"

"Deaths."

"Nobody's died on the Rangers since the last coach was fired. I don't get it."

"Not hockey deaths," Brewer said, his smile taking on a leering tone. "Deaths in *here*."

He tapped his finger on the obituary page, which he had marked with small crosses denoting the demise of persons he found more than usually interesting.

Avignon's face lit up, so much so that he immediately hefted his Ikegami and began shooting, but Donovan was horrified and said so. "I will not countenance wagering on AIDS deaths," he said.

Jake shrugged, and said, "Pick a number from one to ten. We're betting on tomorrow. Fridays are big days in the death game. A summing up of the week's totals."

Avignon said, "There's a history to this sort of betting. Several of the big London wagering houses had their origin in medieval barroom disputes over the number of daily deaths from bubonic plague."

"I'm sure that's not true. Besides, we're supposed to be more enlightened now."

"We're not, but we count a whole lot more accurately."

Donovan grimaced in the direction of the Brazilian ethnologist and asked, "What are you drinking? Blood?"

"Seven-Up," Brewer said. "Are you buying?"

George rolled his head in Donovan's direction, and said, "It's happened, Donovan. The day I warned you about has come. They're all on the wagon. The whole damned lot of them."

"Everyone?" Donovan asked, then scanned the bar to confirm the claim. All six patrons, who with the exception of Brewer were long-time customers, were enjoying soft drinks.

"I have taken in seven dollars in the past hour."

"What about the Columbia kids in the back room?"

"Two pitchers of Diet Pepsi. This bar is down the tubes and it's your fault. I hope you're proud of yourself."

"I am rather pleased, actually," Donovan replied. "We're all better off without alcohol in our systems. What's that in your glass, by the way?"

"Jack Daniels. I consider myself the last real man on the Upper West Side. I only got one question—do you plan to support me when I go broke?"

"I supported you for all the years I was drinking," Donovan shot back.

"I got to admit you have a point," George said. "I count the day that you went on the wagon as the beginning of the end for this bar."

"What can I tell you?"

"If it was just you it would be okay. Problem is, all the cops who look up to you went on the wagon too. Then the junk bond scandal wiped out Wall Street. All the yups who bought big on Columbus Avenue couldn't afford to drink."

"Then came the recession, the hit on interest rates, and the yups couldn't sell their co-ops. Pretty soon everybody was sitting on the curb drinking tap water out of dirty glasses. I don't know, George . . . it sounds to me like the good old days are back on the West Side."

"If only I can stay afloat."

"Sell Perrier," Donovan said.

"Who can afford it?"

"Jug-a-lugging Perrier is cheaper than having your liver redecorated."

Brewer brightened, flicked the lapel of his blue Columbia team jacket, and said, "Liver failure!"

"Beg pardon?" Donovan asked.

"A forty-three-year-old set designer from Boston just died of liver failure. AIDS-related, of course. Did you notice how the epidemic has changed obituary writing?"

No one had.

"It's given us a new class of survivor—companion. It sounds funny, in a way."

Donovan looked at Brewer with distaste, then said, "Buy this man a drink. A real one. The strongest you got."

"Don't you think alcohol is poison?" Jake asked.

Donovan grinned evilly.

"I'll have a Perrier," Brewer said.

"A shipment is coming in tomorrow," George promised.

Donovan wasn't done with Brewer, and said, "Give this man an unfiltered Camel as well."

George muttered, "I'll have to sell to winos. They're my only market now."

Donovan got an idea, and cheered up like a sparrow in the full bloom of spring.

"Halftrack," he said.

"There's the perfect example," George replied, also brightening.

Joe Halftrack was one of the truly maddening people in the world's most maddening city. Now pushing seventy and sporting a Santa-like white beard, the paraplegic was generally credited with having given physical handicaps a bad name.

"Everyone feels for a guy in a wheelchair," Donovan once noted. "With Halftrack they feel like tossing a hand grenade."

For twenty years he panhandled on Broadway and in its bars, at first in an orthopedic walker, lately in a wheelchair. His chair was decorated with a lifetime's knick-knacks, everything from pots, pans, and a beer mug that was a souvenir of the World Series Champion 1969 Mets, to half-rotten plantains filched from the Korean fruit stands. All that stuff rattled and shook as he rolled down Broadway, making his approach resemble a cross between an armored personnel carrier and an gypsy caravan.

Halftrack got into fights. Sometimes he set neighbor against neighbor, slipping into bars and stealing money and drinks and blaming someone else. Other times he just set the wheels on his chair, grabbed a hapless victim by the arm, and pulled him from his barstool, secure in the knowledge that no one would punch out a guy in a wheelchair.

That wasn't precisely true. The bartender of the Puerto Rican joint down the street from Riley's once socked him in the snoot, much to the approval of the community, but only fell into a deep funk after the story sparked the disapproval of those unfamiliar with Halftrack's despicable ways.

Most bartenders simply refused to let Halftrack in the door, which seldom worked (he blocked the entrance until he was given money or beer), and once inside harassed customers by requesting help emptying his urine bag. One bar even narrowed the width of its door so he couldn't get his chair inside, only to find itself at the losing end of a civil-rights lawsuit brought, of course, by the late Herbert Spenser.

Halftrack lost the use of his legs in the early 1960s, when he welshed on a debt to a Broadway loan shark who then took him to New Jersey, shot him, and drove a car over his back, all without succeeding in causing death. "Halftrack is like the decedent in *Murder on the Orient Express*," Donovan observed. "You'd need a computer to keep track of the suspects should he ever be found dead."

But Halftrack did drink, and prodigiously, and so was starting to look better in the eyes of George Kohler. Long-barred from Riley's, Halftrack had taken up position on a nearby corner, where there was a liquor store as well as plenty of passersby to harass. "If he pays for his drinks he can come in here again," George said. "Maybe he'll also drive the soft drinkers back to Columbus Avenue where they belong."

Donovan bought a bottle of beer—the first George had sold in two hours—and delivered it to Halftrack in a brown paper bag. The old man peered warily at it, then at Donovan, then at the front door of Riley's, where George Kohler stood with hairy arms folded across his chest.

"Did you get this from him?" Halftrack asked.

"What of it?"

"He peed in it, didn't he?"

"He mentioned something about strychnine. No pee that I know of."

Halftrack half smiled, and said, "Thanks, Lieutenant," and had a slug of beer.

"There's more where that came from."

"You *know* he won't let me in the bar. There was that one time five or ten years ago you bought me a drink, but not since."

"I can get you back inside. And subsidize your drinking for a week or so."

"No shit! Who do I have to kill?"

"Remember that job you did for me the last time? Looking for the Haitian?"

"Yeah. Did you lose him again?"

"He's dead. This time I'm looking for the guy who's killing

people at the Cathedral of St. John the Divine, including your counselor."

"My what?"

"Your lawyer, Herb Spenser."

"Is he dead? Damn, now I'm gonna have to rely on Legal Aid . . . guys just out of law school who are studying to pass the bar exam."

"If you would stop being a pain in the ass, you wouldn't need so many lawyers. So are you gonna help me?"

"Sure. What do I have to do?"

"Roll on over to Amsterdam Avenue and cruise the cathedral for a couple of days and nights. Check it out. I'm looking for a tall guy who may be wearing loose-fitting garments."

"He was a DOA two thousand years ago."

"Different guy. This one has muscles. He'll be going in and out of the cathedral at odd hours. Skulking around. I don't know . . . look for creeps. You know the type."

"Like him?" Halftrack said, gesturing in the direction of George Kohler.

"Yeah, only younger and holier. Christlike, but bearing a bludgeon instead of a cross. Drop a dime if you see him."

"Can you really get me back into Riley's?" Halftrack asked.

Donovan folded a $50 bill into the man's jacket pocket and gave his chair a shove toward the door.

Halftrack resisted. "Is the lighter fluid still there?" he asked.

"I'll see," Donovan said, and walked back into the bar. Halftrack rolled along behind, a cautious few yards back. As he passed the threshold and George's towering figure, he looked a mixture of frightened and garrulous. Redemption in the eyes of Riley's had been long-coming.

Donovan scooted around back of the bar and pulled open a drawer. From it he took a large, economy-size squirt can of Ronson lighter fluid. He gave the can to Halftrack, who sighed in relief.

For years, George had been threatening to douse Halftrack with lighter fluid and set him on fire. "The Westies may have not been able to kill the sonofabitch, but I can turn him into a torch," George said often, proudly comparing himself with the old West Side Irish gang that had a reputation for largely mindless slaughter, mostly in the 1950s and 1960s. It was they who tried to kill Halftrack in 1962 but only succeeded in starting his legend.

Donovan's father also had run-ins with the Westies, whom he considered to be the worst sort of shanty Irish ("skells," he called them). One theory on the death of the senior Donovan is that the Westies were involved. On the West Side, personal histories and local legends combined and grew together, sometimes inseparably. Donovan felt that his life and Halftrack's were intertwined in a small and peculiar way. It was nice that he could help the sick old man with the one vice that fate had allowed him to keep—drunkenness.

Halftrack slapped the $50 on the bar and said to George, "A shot and a beer, sir."

"Four Roses, right?" George said.

"See!" Halftrack beamed. "He hasn't served me in ten years and still remembers what I drink!"

George said, "I got this worked out, Donovan. I have a new theme for this place. One that will save it."

"You're going to sell Perrier?" Donovan asked.

"Nope. I'm gonna rename the joint Smoke 'N Drink and cater to all those in this city who still know how to live."

"I like the concept," Donovan said. "But you're not going far enough."

Avignon added, "Tack on a couple more banned substances just to make sure you're targeting your audience properly."

"Such as?"

"Smoke 'N Drink 'N Cholesterol. Serve booze and fatty food in a smoke-filled room."

"Sounds like the average Blarney Stone," Donovan said, referring to the popular New York chain of manque Irish pubs.

"Are you betting or not?" Brewer said, shaking the obituary page of *The Times* in Donovan's direction.

"Step into my office," Donovan said, grabbing the man by the collar and leading him into the men's room.

"Five to one Donovan busts him," Jake proclaimed, looking around for takers.

Donovan shoved the snapshot that Spenser had given him in Brewer's face. "This is you, ya fuck. What were you doing following Terry Loomis around?"

"What difference does it make? I didn't kill Spenser."

"I don't know that."

"I was drinking with Jake. He'll tell you. . . ."

"He already did, and I believed him. I just want to know how come Herbert Spenser ID'd you as a potential killer five minutes before he got killed."

"George saw me too."

"Why did Spenser have your picture?"

"It's none of your business," Brewer spat.

Donovan's own temper flared, and he said, "I'm not playing around."

"Sure you are. You have no other suspects, so you are harassing a foreigner. That is what American policemen do best. Can I go back to the bar?"

"Why were you photographed at Rain Forest concerts?"

"I grew up in the Amazon region before it became the popular thing to do. Its ecology is of interest to me. And that's all I'm telling you."

With that he pulled away from Donovan and left the men's room. He went back to the bar, but only long enough to pick up his change. Then he stalked out, leaving Donovan to stare at a devastated George.

"Now you drove *him* out," the bartender said.

45.

THE GEOPOLITICS OF
DRUGS AND WEAPONS

Jackson Avenue was an older commercial strip like many in New York City. Prior to the 1960s it was alive with small stores and fruit stands, but in the decades since had rotted like an old wino's teeth. Jackson burned in the political storms of the 1960s and never quite recovered. The old Jewish, Irish, and German shopkeepers moved out. Black neighborhood people were unable to get financing from the downtown banks to open shops of their own. And Koreans moved in, ignorant of local sensitivities but well-financed by their countrymen. Well-stocked and overpriced fruit stands and groceries were almost immediately the target of community boycotts, and on a given day chanting protesters marched outside Korean stores located in three contiguous blocks of Jackson Avenue. Two sweltering recycled-tire stores and a storefront livery service completed the paper-strewn strip of Jackson that Marcie and Jefferson finally targeted as the turf of the crack dealer known as RapStar, a.k.a. Scott Carter.

Sitting with Ed James, of Uptown Narcotics, in his old Mercury, they watched the facade of an abandoned four-story brick building that had been turned into a potent crack distribution center. From the outside, the building appeared little more than a battered shell. The windows were covered with sheet aluminum that, on the street floor, had been ripped out at the corners. The front door, also of aluminum but reinforced with two-by-fours, had an inch-square peephole cut in it through which a lookout's wary eye peered nervously. A wisp of pure white smoke curled out of a rooftop vent. The smoke froze in the crisp November air and curled straight up; Marcie and Jefferson looked through it to the Romanesque east facade of the Cathedral of St. John the Divine, which towered above it atop Morningside Heights.

"Looks like they're electing the damn Pope in there," Jefferson said, focusing his Nikon on the front door.

"People got to stay warm, even while doing drugs," James said.

Marcie said, "I don't get this. Here we have a four-story building that's been entirely taken over by drug dealers. Why can't we just go in there and arrest everyone?"

James said, "It's the geopolitics of drugs and weapons, Sergeant. We got .38s. They got Uzis and Macs and they ain't afraid to die."

"That's geopolitics?"

Jefferson said, "A house given over to drug use ain't so odd in Harlem. In a white neighborhood the pressure to get it out would be a whole lot stronger."

"Then there's nothing we can do?"

"A TNT bust will dislodge them. Those boys look pretty well dug in, though. We'd have to take them when they're vulnerable and with overwhelming force."

"They don't look too vulnerable," Jefferson said.

"I know a TNT guy who works it out with biorythms," James said. "He figures that the energy level of crack dealers is lowest at 5 A.M. . . ."

"Mine ain't too hot, either."

". . . And recommends busts at that hour. It's worked so far. If your perp is in that building, the only way to take him out is a TNT bust. And I don't know if I can arrange it."

"What do you mean, 'arrange?'" Marcie asked.

Jefferson replied, "He means he ain't got the juice. TNT busts are expensive and, therefore, political. Local politicians command them for their districts, usually when they're up for election."

"You got to be a big shot to get a TNT bust scheduled," James agreed. "Do you know any big shots?"

Jefferson gave Marcie a knowing look, which she took a few

seconds to decode, incorrectly as it turned out. "You can't mean . . . not my father."

"Who's your father?" James asked.

"D.A. during the Koch Administration," Jefferson said.

"Charles Barnes is your father?" James said, impressed.

"The old bro' who married kosher and produced my partner here," Jefferson said.

"If you come from *that* neighborhood, what the hell you doin' hangin' around with *this* nigger?" James asked, nodding at Jefferson.

"He's the best I could do on short notice. God, if my father heard you call him an *old bro'*. It's funny, actually. Anyway, there are drug dealers and murderers in that building. I can't believe that I have to go to my father upstate to get a TNT bust in Harlem."

"That's reality in the Big Apple," Jefferson said. "Your daddy may be black, but he has to call up the white folks to get anything done."

"Anything that costs money, anyway," James said. "I suppose we could steal a tank and blow the door down."

"There's another way," Jefferson said. "Someone else we can go to. The big shot I was referring to in the first place."

"Who?"

"Donovan. He can get it done quicker than anyone. He has the juice."

Marcie frowned, and said, "I don't like the way my options are working out."

"Like I said, welcome to reality."

"Donovan's no big shot."

James laughed, and Jefferson said, "Bull . . . *shit!*"

"Do you think that *just anyone* can get the Cathedral roped off for a few days so he can personally hunt down a lunatic?" James asked.

"I guess that is a little . . . extravagant," Marcie said, begrudgingly showing admiration.

"And have the commissioner drive all the way up there to

deliver the news personally. Donovan has the knack, babe . . . the juice. You'd do best to stop competing with him and lean back and enjoy it."

Her temper flared. "I'm not . . . oh, never mind."

"There's always the poor folks' way of doing things," James said.

"What's that?"

"On the street, baby. We watch and follow and take them on the sidewalk or in their vehicles. The guy you're looking for . . . RapStar . . . He's a new kid on the block. Went into business about six months ago as a steerer for this house. You know, steers customers inside. He hangs out with this other kid who's a lookout. This summer the both of them came into some money, and RapStar bought wheels. He's got a black Suzuki Samurai and I hear he's a big man with Pappy Bollis."

"Who's he?"

"A twenty-five-year-old, practically a senior citizen in this business. He runs this house and two others like it, all on Jackson. We'd love to nail him."

"Maybe it will happen," Marcie said.

"Anyway, I got the information on RapStar, as best we know. He's seventeen. Dropped out of high school at fifteen. Doesn't talk a lot. Somebody said he's got a bad stutter. I have no idea if that's true. He's been arrested plenty, but all his busts were as a juvenile. The kid's never been busted for a violent crime, although we've got about a dozen dead teenagers who bought their crack in that house, maybe even from RapStar and his buddy. Since you called me this morning I hung a name on the boy—Scott Carter."

"Scott?" Jefferson asked.

"Yeah, sounds like a damn golf pro, don't it? Tennis star or something."

"Like from Croton-on-Hudson," Jefferson said.

"I don't believe what folks name their kids these days. Scott. Todd. And the girls are all Tamara or Tamawa or Lashaka or some name that sounds like a brand of soy sauce."

"Where does Carter live?" Marcie asked.

"I got no idea. All I know is the name and a description of his wheels. Let's hang out here for a few days and see if he turns up."

"Few *days?*" Marcie exclaimed.

"This ain't AT&T," James explained. "Crack dealers don't punch time clocks."

Across the street and down a bit, life in and around the crack house went on. Two lookouts, neither of them Darryl Weems, watched passersby from in front of a tire shop and a vacant lot. A similarly anonymous steerer paced nervously in front of the building, occasionally greeting a car that pulled up and hustling one of its occupants inside. Directly across the street, one of the demonstrations outside a Korean fruit stand had turned noisy. Marcie craned her neck judiciously to note that an Eyewitness News van had pulled up, accelerating the protest.

The demonstrators, quiet all afternoon, began chanting "We will not be moved" with raised fists.

"I'm glad *something* newsworthy is happening on this block," she said.

"Yeah."

James asked, "What do you guys think of these protests?"

"I just wish people would get along," Marcie said.

"Yeah, well these Koreans come into a black neighborhood with all the money in the world. They don't hire no black folks to work in their stores. They don't smile or say hello to customers. And when a black man goes shopping, he gets followed around like he was a thief."

"The same thing happened in my neighborhood," Jefferson said. "I won't shop at the place."

"Where do you live?"

"Up in the Historic District off 155th."

"Nice area. But it's the same thing—the damn Koreans are taking over this city."

"*Foreigners* are taking over," Jefferson said. "The cab drivers are all from Saudi Arabia or someplace and don't talk no English. The fruit stands are owned by Koreans. Half the restaurants are

Japanese. All the news stands and gas stations are run by Indians. And the damn Hispanics have all the blue-collar jobs."

"You guys sound like Andrew Dice Clay. Or the old Irishmen in Riley's," Marcie said.

"What's Riley's?"

"A bar on Broadway that we hang out in," Jefferson explained.

"An Irish bar?"

"Owned by Jews," Jefferson said.

James said, "I'm going down the block to carry a protest sign for a while."

"Get me some juice," Marcie grumbled.

"Go home and get it yourself," Jefferson said.

46.
ART IS WHATEVER YOU CAN GET AWAY WITH

A seventh-century English Benedictine missionary from Devonshire, originally hung with the moniker Winfrid, made an early and particularly disastrous attempt to civilize Bavaria and other German locales (he was set upon by a mob and killed). As a reward, he was renamed Boniface and canonized and, early in the twentieth century, had a chapel dedicated to him at the Cathedral of St. John the Divine. By the late twentieth century, the chapel had become an occasional art gallery, featuring, when Donovan was there, the works of a modern sculptor and painter who used scrap metal and other found objects to make furniture and knick-knacks in the shape of cats and dogs.

As the evening wore closer to the cathedral's closing point, Donovan wandered into St. Boniface's Chapel and pondered a lifesized sculpture of a woman walking five lifesized dogs: a black Labrador, a setter, a Dalmatian, a dachshund, and a beagle.

"Next the dachshund will bite Boniface on the ass," Donovan muttered, walking around the chapel to look at shelf brackets in the form of dogs; a side table with four sitting-up-and-begging dachshunds supporting a glass tabletop on their heads; and a halfsized kitchen door complete with a cat bursting through a small, hinged door.

A guest book by the door invited comments. One visitor, from Yugoslavia, wrote, "Ingenious use of color and material." Other comments included, "captivating," "delightful," and "wonderfully creative and refreshing." Donovan whipped out a pen and added, "Art is whatever you can get away with," citing Andy Warhol.

Then he looked up to find a church employee watching him. The man was tall and thin but strong-looking, like a basketball player, with short, unevenly cropped brown hair, a black tee shirt that bore a line drawing of the finished cathedral, new jeans, and cowboy boots.

"What do you think of him?" the man said.

"Who?" Donovan asked, straightening up.

"The artist, of course."

"He's wonderfully creative and refreshing."

"I *know*. I'd love to own the woman walking dogs, but don't have the room in my apartment."

"Well, I have the room but probably can't afford it. How much is that thing?"

"Five thousand, I think."

"Definitely out of my league."

"The money is going to be a good cause."

"The Rain Forest?"

"Yes, insofar as the Rain Forest Project is part of the Gaia Concept."

"Unh huh," Donovan said, sensing that he had just stepped in something moist and unpleasant.

He knew that the Gaia Concept was the bishop's New Age Episcopalianism. He also knew that Gaia was the ancient Greek name for Mother Earth and had been appropriated in post-

Woodstock America to describe the notion that all things, living and nonliving, were interdependent and part of a unified, living, Earth. As described in cathedral literature, it was "the integration of human communities in the economy of nature and an understanding of the role of organisms in planetary processes."

"This happened right after people began referring to the Earth as 'the Planet,' " Donovan said once.

As redefined by the Bishop, the Gaia Concept equated an eager embrace of Mother Earth with spirituality. That was New Age Episcopalianism: music and architecture combined with Mother Earth and ecology. You didn't kneel and pray to God so much as kiss the bosom of Mother Earth and save the whales.

47.
"METAPHORS BE WITH YOU," DONOVAN SAID.

Regrettably, he said it out loud.

"Why, thank you," the man replied, sticking a clipboard full of papers under his arm and extending his hand to the lieutenant.

"I'm a cop," Donovan said, as a partial warning. His personal Miranda notification was a simple declaration of institutional affiliation.

"All are welcome here. I'm Jim Forrest. I do Prison Literacy."

"Beg pardon?"

"Follow me."

He led the way around the rosette of chapels that partially encircled the high altar, past St. James's Chapel, until reaching a wall alongside the door to the Biblical Garden. The wall was undecorated except for a three-part panel of black-painted cork-board to which were pinned several typewritten sheets.

"This is the Poetry Wall," Forrest said.

"Poetry wall?"

"The tradition started years ago. A few prisoners at Sing Sing wrote poems that were tacked up on the wall, partly to express themselves and partly as a way of getting pen pals. Now we have many prisoners who contribute to the wall. They put their names and addresses on their poems and anyone interested can jot them down and write back. This has been going on for ten years now. We get poems from all over the country, and I put them on the wall. People read them and take home the ones they want. . . ."

"Sort of a literary adoption agency," Donovan said.

"And write to the prisoners of their choice. So far nothing horrible has happened."

"No Hitchcock-style midnight visits by escaped pen pals?"

"Not one that I know of. And many of these men are on Death Row. Would you like to take one home?"

"No. I'm better known for putting them inside."

"Everything is in flux these days. You're Donovan, aren't you?"

He nodded.

"The man in charge of finding the killer. Does he really think he's the ghost of St. Augustine?"

"Apparently. What do you think?"

"Well, you could hide in here forever. Have you been up the spiral staircases?"

"Not yet. At least not all the way."

"They run from the crypt to the vault. Rumors are that some of the galleries are haunted. Last year, when workmen were testing the bells in the Tower of St. Peter, they heard strange howlings."

"I'll check it out. Maybe it's one or two of your literary jailbirds who've come home to roost."

Forrest looked sour, and hurt, and Donovan picked up on it.

"I offended," he said.

"I object to calling us 'jailbirds,' " Forrest said.

"Us?"

"It's no secret that I did time. The bishop knows."

"Where and for what?"

"Dannemora for armed robbery. I was very young, and no one was hurt. At least not physically."

"What did you steal?"

"I helped liberate a truckload of televisions from Kennedy Airport. It's not like it was never done. Anyway, I found Jesus while in prison and, when I got out, took a job that allowed me to work in His house."

"Did you expect to find Jesus in *here?*" Donovan asked. "I can understand finding the Anti-Fur Coalition."

"Helping the planet is the same thing as finding Jesus," Forrest said, a bit testily.

"I remain unconvinced."

"Would you like to read some poems?" Forrest asked, eager to change the subject.

"Why not?" Donovan read them as they were posted in a neat row, at eye level, across the black wall.

Of the thirteen that Forrest posted, eight were dreadful, four had promise, and one was a gem. Written by a Death-Row inmate from Florida about his childhood recollections of his mother, it had just the right combination of nostalgia and resentment, hope and anger, calm and fanaticism. It was signed Willie T. Jones, and had the man's prison ID number.

"Does anybody write to him?" Donovan asked.

"A few people. He's the best of our regular contributors. I hope they don't execute him."

"Who did *he* execute?"

"He killed his mother. I suppose you believe in capital punishment?"

"Only when I'm being shot at, which thankfully doesn't happen as often as it used to."

"I can't imagine what it's like to be shot at," Forrest said.

"There was no gunplay when you were busted?"

"I was caught by computer," Forrest said, and Donovan thought he was a little disappointed at the absence of glamour. "The warehouse we ripped off had a smart television system."

Avignon wandered up, shooting footage as he walked, and said, "Closed-circuit TV takes pictures every few seconds. The computer stores it in memory and compares the shots with ones it took a few minutes before. If the computer notices anything different, all hell breaks loose. Hello, Jim."

"How far did you get after all hell broke loose?" Donovan asked.

"Halfway down the block. Didn't even get the chance to use my gun."

"What were you carrying?"

"An Uzi that I bought from a kid in Hollis, Queens. The cops also tagged me for possession of an automatic weapon. It's tough to lay out the money for an Uzi and then never get to use it."

"Life's a bitch and then you die," Donovan said, a bit mindlessly. He had seen that slogan on a lapel button in Greenwich Village. He wondered if it were possible to get through life by speaking only slogans.

"Life isn't hard once you've found Him," Forrest said.

Avignon jiggled his burglar's tools and said, "Let's go open doors."

48.
A FLOCK OF TIN FLAMINGOS

The rooms beyond the doors were puzzling. Of the five in the newly explored corridor, two were filled with nothing of note: old clothes, donated years ago and forgotten, possibly including some of Donovan's, and music stands that stood, motionless yet awkward, like a flock of tin flamingos.

The three other rooms were oddly furnished, by mysterious design. One was entirely vacant save for a folding canasta table and a solitary, straight-backed chair. Those sat against a bare wall, and nothing else was in the room save a February, 1926, issue of *Collier's* tossed carelessly on an immaculately swept floor.

Another room was plain empty, but filthy. Walls and floor were covered with dust and the slightest, startlingly out-of-place odor of creosote.

The final room was filled, floor to ceiling, with cordwood. And the door was locked so securely that it took Avignon two hours to open it; extraordinary security for a roomful of old wood in an edifice lacking a wood-burning stove or fireplace. Whoever was in the room before Donovan had locked it very well, and to guard what? Old wood, one piece of which had a vague and unreadable handprint where a man's fist encircled it.

"Marcus?" Avignon asked, shooting a closeup of the print.

"It's recent, etched in the dust within the past week, I would say. Too bad we can't learn anything from it."

"We learned that Marcus was here. That he can get in and out of these rooms."

"I assume he's nearby, and can hear us at times. If I were him, I would keep track of me."

To keep him company while Avignon opened doors, Donovan brought his ghetto blaster, a twenty-pound monster of a radio that in warm weather accompanied pickup basketball games on the 106th Street courts. From it came chamber music and, at midnight, the switch to early morning programming, at first a phone-in discussion of personal bankruptcy.

"Time to party," Donovan said, hefting the radio.

"I've had it for tonight. I'm going down to the crypt and sleep for a few hours."

"Check my messages and see if anything is up. If not, I'll catch you in the morning."

"What are you going to do?"

"I'm gong looking for Jose."

"Who?"

"Somewhere in this building is a guy named Jose who knows every brick," Donovan said.

"A janitor? Do they have them in cathedrals?"

"Someone's got to snake the toilet and replace light bulbs."

"But the cathedral administrator said that no one knows all the ins and outs of this place," Avignon argued.

"The cathedral administrator means *no one he knows*. He doesn't function on the Jose level; knows only employees he can play tennis with. I'll find the man, probably at Riley's drinking with Halftrack."

Avignon said, "I'm not up to chasing janitors at midnight, but if I stumble over him in the crypt I'll give a shout. Good night."

"Watch the shadows on your way downstairs," Donovan warned.

When Avignon was gone, and his footfalls finally abated down the stairs leading to the crypt, Donovan sat on the floor leaning against the next door to be opened. Finding Jose, or whatever his name might be, was vintage Donovan—the knowledge that in any heirarchy there was someone, virtually unknown, who knew every brick—but it could wait until morning. For the moment Donovan wished to be alone, to lean his head against the door and absorb the smells and sounds.

The silence in the cathedral was awesome that night. When all the tourists were shooed out and the doors were locked and even the night watchmen were ordered out of the building—they were afraid to stay in it anyway—the silence crept up Donovan's backbone and into his soul. It made the slight chill in the air even colder, and exaggerated every ghostly wisp of convection current.

After a few serene moments, Donovan's ears adjusted. Like a blind man, he could hear sounds previously unsuspected. He was reminded of the time he spent in the tunnels beneath Riverside Park a few years back, while tracking the killer of young girls who used the tunnels for sanctuary and escape. There too the sounds were magnified and appeared to travel great distances, perhaps miles. Especially the low-frequency sounds. Donovan recalled hearing of a Columbia experiment where subsea sonic explosions off Australia or someplace were heard on the other side of the world. Just so, Donovan thought; like moans and desperation.

Then there came a soft hooting, and Donovan smiled at what he swore was a barn owl hooting from the belfry. But barn owls were certainly rare in New York City, and the cathedral didn't have a belfry as such. A few minutes later the sound went away, replaced by a rhythmic chirping.

More like a chipping, Donovan thought, the sound of metal on stone, a pinging, like you get from sonar or from tapping a ball peen hammer on the concrete wall of a house's basement. But it wasn't precisely rhythmic, and certainly involved neither a ball peen hammer nor concrete. It did seem to originate nearby, but came and went, depending on which ear Donovan cocked in its direction.

Got to get my hearing checked, he thought. At least the grey hairs on his head were attractive, giving him an air of gentility, and didn't interfere with earning a living. On occasion, when Marcie wasn't around, he allowed himself the luxury of lamenting the ravages of age.

The sound stopped for half a minute, then resumed, a bit more urgently than before. Donovan got to his knees and pressed his right ear against the door. Beyond it lay another stretch of corridor and, presumably, more rooms filled with odd bits of storage. But in one of them, something stirred; metal was working stone.

Donovan tried the door, though he knew it was hopeless. He got to his feet and put all his weight against the door, also to no avail.

From reading the charts of the cathedral, he knew that the corridor beyond that door ended in a spiral staircase that ran from the floor of the nave to the blindstory gallery almost directly above the Poetry Wall. A good guess would put another five rooms off that corridor. In one of them something like a ball peen hammer was working away.

Donovan turned and ran the other way, taking the open stairway down to the nave, then running across the cold, bare stone to the staircase. He yanked open the wrought-iron gate and went up the stairs, taking them two at a time. The door at the blindstory level was locked, which he expected. Donovan tore at the handle, then rammed his shoulder against the door. It didn't budge.

Frustrated, he pressed an ear to the door. Once again there was the sound, more slowly this time. Donovan strained to hear it over his own deep breathing. The chipping continued for a minute, then two minutes, then stopped. There was a scraping sound, something unknown.

Donovan banged his fist against the door, but it made only a dull thud against the heavy iron. Two times, then three he banged his fist, but the stranger within didn't hear. Then Donovan pulled out his gun and tried the butt. The steel of the Smith & Wesson hit the door with a satisfying click that went throughout the stairwell and out into the body of the cathedral, the sound coming back in several waves of echo. Three times Donovan banged the gun against the door before pausing to listen.

The scraping stopped. There was an odd muffled sound, then the ball peen hammer clattered to the floor. A momentary silence, then the soft shuffling of feet against stone, drawing nearer. "Marcus," Donovan whispered, switching the gun around in his hand so that the barrel was facing forward.

The footsteps drew up to the iron door, then stopped. Donovan held his breath, drawing back onto the landing, the gun clutched in both hands and aimed straight at the door. For half a minute, Donovan listened to absolute silence, and then to his own urgent breathing. The doorknob turned slightly.

The skin on Donovan's face tightened. Would the door spring wide open or only a little? Would Marcus come at him high, with a bludgeon, or low, with a gun? The knob twisted halfway, then stopped. More silence, then receding footfalls.

Donovan's face was streaked with fury. "Marcus!" he yelled, his voice booming in the damp stone stairwell.

The footsteps halted briefly, then resumed. Donovan went back to the door to listen. He heard some fumbling around, scraping and other motion, and then nothing.

49.
You Marry a Virgin Who Gets Knocked Up By a Ghost

And it came to pass that four thousand cops with picks and shovels descended upon the Cathedral of St. John the Divine, ripping out doors and scuffing up the marble with their hobnail boots," Avignon said, taping the event.

"I count ten cops and two crowbars," Donovan said.

"Numbers don't matter. *Drama* does."

Bonaci supervised as the work crew of detectives and technicians of Wrecking Crew One—as the Emergency Services unit that was frequently asked to take things apart was called—systematically busted open the newest section of corridor and the doors behind it.

Four of the doors held pretty much what Donovan expected: more wood, slats and boards that looked like they had been salvaged from an old barn; candles, various sizes, delivered in 1917, forgotten; and paintbrushes and paint, circa World War II.

"The stuff in these rooms makes no sense," said Avignon from behind his camera.

"Not so fast," Donovan said. "My memory is coming unblocked."

Bonaci nodded in assent to the Wrecking Crew men poised to rip open the door of the fifth and last room. As Avignon's camera rolled, the old iron door crashed out into the corridor, spewing puffs of dust.

"Hallelujah," Bonaci said.

A 300-watt work light burned in a newly cleaned ceiling fixture, illuminating an old but carefully restored woodworking shop. Benches lined the east and south walls. Drills, saws, augers, planes, and clamps hung neatly on wall-mounted racks. Old and massive vises clamped down on century-old air. In the center of the room a sculptor's bench, freshly and hastily abandoned, sat in the middle of a halo of limestone dust. That dust overlaid a frosting of sawdust. In the half-inch thickness of dust were footprints by the score, circling the sculptor's bench, coming and going from the now-demolished door and also making extraordinary progress straight up to an old and rickety wooden door, a utility door that lead somewhere, but where? According to the blueprints, there was nothing back there but stone.

Donovan was a kid in a candy shop. "Touch nothing!" he exclaimed, raising an index finger triumphantly into the air.

"It's a goddam carpenter's shop!" Avignon said.

"Hidden in a building dedicated to a goddam carpenter," Donovan said. "I *knew* that all this stuff makes sense."

"How so?"

"Every year the local school kids put on a Christmas pageant. I know 'cause I was in it for eight straight years. I never told this to anybody, and sort of forgot myself."

"You were an altar boy?" Avignon asked.

"Naw. I started out as a shepherd. That's the role you get by virtue of being in first grade in Catholic school hereabouts. In those days it was a big deal for the cathedral to let Catholics in. Now they have everything but Shiite Muslims, and for all I know that's on the bishop's agenda. Anyway, one time when I was about ten I snuck up the spiral staircase with Timmy Reilly to get away from the nuns and found this workshop."

"It was open? When was this?"

"About 1953, before this section was closed off. This old guy with no hair used the shop to build props for the Christmas pageants. That's what the stuff in the other rooms is for: logs and cut wood for the stable, hay for the animals, shoes for the kids to wear and candles for them to carry, and prayer books, of course. Funny, I remembered coming to the carpentry shop, but remembered it as being in the adjacent building. According to cathedral records, this corridor hasn't been used in thirty years, and the current carpentry shop *is* in another building."

Bonaci said, "Hey Lieutenant, in my Christmas pageant I got to play a Wise Man."

"Who'd you fuck to get *that* part?" Avignon asked.

"A shepherd was just my beginning," Donovan said. "By eighth grade I played Joseph, God's foster father."

"An admirable role," Avignon said.

"Yeah, it predicted what life was gonna be like for an Irish guy. You marry a virgin who gets knocked up by a ghost. You never lay a hand on her but wind up supporting the kid anyway. But hey, Timmy Reilly had it worse. There were no girls in our school, so he had to play Mary. It was the two of us up there that glorious Christmas of 1957, the last time I set foot in church. After Timmy and I endured years of cruel jokes, the only vengeance was to become cops with attitudes. I became a pillar of this here community, and Timmy went on to Brooklyn South

Detectives, where his first action was busting a priest for butt-fucking a Puerto Rican kid in the sanctuary. You wanna discuss religion with me, Bonaci?"

"No thanks, Lieutenant. The forensics guys are here to go over the workshop."

"Don't miss nothin'."

"It's infectious, isn't it?" Avignon said.

"What is?"

"Brooklyn. You mention Reilly's name and right away start talking like him."

"God forbid," Donovan said, and sat on his ghetto blaster to watch the forensics team at work.

At two in the morning, forensics and the Wrecking Crew went to lunch, leaving Donovan to prowl the workshop more or less alone. Bonaci was there with a summary of the findings, and Avignon's presence had become more or less inevitable.

"Let's hear it," Donovan said, taking his first tentative steps into the room since the 1950s and feeling the thrill of the hunt combined with intense deja vu.

"There are two layers of dust, with a recent deposition of limestone dust on top of old-fashioned sawdust." Bonaci read from copious notes written on a steno pad. "The sawdust is *years* old, and some of it might have been here since the cathedral was built. It's probably what you remember from when you were a kid."

"The carpenter's name was Jimmy, an old Irish guy. He used to do Irish shtick, you know. 'I see,' said the blind man, but he couldn't see at all. Sounds profound when you're ten years old. God, I spent a lifetime trying to forget this shit."

"Maybe you came back to remember."

"Nothing in my life is that planned."

Bonaci said, "There's limestone dust on the sculptor's bench, along with indications that Marcus was working something. You can see an oval area approximately five by seven inches where there's comparatively little dust."

"I wonder if he's any good," Avignon said.

"Great artists work in many media," Donovan replied. "Damn, I want everyone in the stone-cutting project interviewed. Get them out of bed and check alibis."

"Are you doing it yourself or you want a team on it?" Bonaci asked.

"I want a team. And find Jefferson and get him here. Enough already with the Harlem teenagers."

"Jefferson and Barnes say they're on the verge of picking up those perps," Bonaci said.

"Tell them to hurry it up. How long does it take to haul in two damn kids? And while you're on the phone, make sure that the cordon is tightened around this building. I don't want anybody out who's even *possibly* a suspect. Anybody who tries to leave the cathedral . . . unless he looks like Woody Allen, stop him."

"It may take a few hours to get enough men to make the cordon impenitrable."

"Start now. If this guy escaped through that old door . . ."

"Which leads into solid stone," Bonaci said, clearing his throat. "I never believed in secret passages, but we may have one."

"Don't I recall you as being one of the skeptics who thought there were no tunnels below Riverside Park?"

"Yeah, that was me. I got to admit it. It turned out there was not only the killer, but a whole army of homeless people. What about that door?"

He walked up to where the footsteps approached the old door.

"The blueprint says this shouldn't be here," Donovan said. "Behind it is supposed to be nothing but solid stone."

"Check it out," Avignon replied, imitating the patter of a Times Square street hawker.

The door was cedar and cut of boards that didn't quite fit. The face of it was clean, but dirt ground into the cracks looked to be many years old. Donovan took out his revolver and grasped the door handle.

The door groaned open into the workshop. Donovan poked

the muzzle of his Smith & Wesson into the darkness, which now was cut by room light.

Emerging in the darkness was another staircase, older and narrower than the ones that men in the 1990s knew about. It was a scant seven feet wide, and the steps were correspondingly steep and treacherous.

"This is an old work staircase. It must have been used by the original workmen a century ago."

"And forgotten in subsequent building," Avignon said. "Is anyone home?"

"Not that I can see. I'm going in. Bonaci?"

"Yo, boss," the sergeant replied, taking out his own weapon and pushing in front of Avignon.

The way down was dark and unlit. With a flashlight in one hand, Donovan stepped cautiously down the stairs, twisting his feet so they gripped the steep, narrow steps.

Unlike the other areas that Marcus frequented, these walls were filthy and the air stale. Nothing seemed to move therein, not the slightest wisp of convection current.

"This place is a tomb stood on edge," Donovan said.

A trickle of brown water rolled down the smooth, algae-covered stone. The stone was sweating condensation from where the hot air from the cathedral interior met the November chill. The stairwell plummeted down into the belly of the building, passing another cedar door, this one at the first level.

Donovan inspected it, shining the light around the rim of the door, paying careful attention to the hinges.

"This has been opened today," he said.

"Try it."

Donovan turned the handle and pushed, and met some resistance. The force holding the door in was mushy, a spring or something else soft. But beyond it Donovan sensed space and light. He put his shoulder to the door and shoved. There was a popping of cork as one of the black panels in the Poetry Wall swung open, leaving the lieutenant standing once again amidst the literary works of Death-Row inmates.

With the exception of Willie T. Jones's poem flapping in the rush of air from the cathedral into the stairwell, there was no sound or motion and no one was around.

" 'I see,' said the blind man, but he couldn't see at all," Donovan said, in a halfway authentic brogue.

"Yourself?" Avignon asked.

"I must be getting senile," Donovan said. "Bonaci, get on the horn and have Jim Forrest picked up. I told you about him. Prison Literacy me arse!"

"Do you think he's Marcus?" Bonaci asked.

"I don't know. He's big enough and he has a record. Right now I just want to nail him for taking my bad jokes too literally."

Bonaci said, "This panel is hinged and easy to use as a door. And you can't see that it's a door from the outside. Forrest has to know about this."

"He told me that some of the galleries are haunted. Maybe Forrest is hiding Willie T. Jones in here."

Bonaci asked who that was.

"A Florida con who fragged his mom," Donovan said.

While Avignon taped a closeup of the poem, Bonaci gave a series of orders over the radio. Then Donovan motioned the men back into the stairwell.

"He went further down," Avignon said. "I'm getting more of the sense of Marcus now. He's into basements and other dark places."

"And tiny rooms, no windows," Donovan agreed.

"But he needs access, or escape."

"Both. A way to come out and kill and a way back, to his sanctuary."

Bonaci tapped Donovan on the shoulder, then hooked a thumb in Avignon's direction. "This guy is just like you," he said. "I can't believe that God made two of you."

"Creepy, isn't it?" Donovan said.

"Marcus is down in the basement, Bill," Avignon said.

Donovan again moved down the stairs, taking them slowly, feeling the old wood bend and hearing it creak, the hand that felt its way down the wall slipping through the trickles of brown water.

The flashlight beam flashed around the stairwell, then reflected off a pool of brown water at the bottom.

"This hole has a bottom after all," Donovan said.

"There will be another door, coming out someplace unexpected. A con like Forrest would be comfortable with this setup."

The stairs ended in a concrete platform. Another cedar door showed evidence of having been recently opened.

"He's not gonna be there," Donovan said, trying the door knob.

"He came this way. I can feel it."

Donovan shoved on the door, which flew open amidst a clatter of aluminum cans.

"What the hell?" Donovan said, and stepped out into the Recycling Center. The door was hidden from plain view behind a seven-foot stack of plastic milk cartons filled brimming with cans donated for recycling. The stack went over when Donovan sprang the door, and cans were six inches thick on the floor in the narrow aisle between rows of stacks.

"This is the Recycling Center," Donovan exclaimed. "Marcie and I bring our old clothes here."

Bonaci said, "This is the room we used to get Loomis's body out of the cathedral. It was *his* idea." He indicated Avignon.

"Hey guys, I had no idea about this door. But I got to say I ain't surprised. The place is a labyrinth."

Donovan walked gingerly through the litter of soda cans until he reached the double steel doors that opened wide enough for a pickup truck to be loaded. Those doors opened readily out onto the ramp that led up to the courtyard and freight loading area between the cathedral and the complex of buildings that included the Cathedral School, Deanery, and Cathedral House. Donovan ran up into the night and looked around for cops, but there were none.

"Where are our guys?" he asked Bonaci.

"I told you it would take a few hours to get enough men to surround the place."

"Dammit. Isn't there anyone around?"

He ran from one end of the courtyard to another, finally finding a cathedral security guard asleep in a booth at the corner of the Sacristies near the south driveway. "Great," he said, walking away while Bonaci woke and berated the man.

Donovan hopped a hedge and walked across a small patch of lawn to sit on the base of "The Peace Fountain," a mammoth bronze celebrating the victory of good over evil. After taping the scene, Avignon put the camera on the ground and sat alongside his friend.

"Peace hasn't won yet," Donovan commented.

"No shit. You wanna fall off the wagon? I'll do it with you. I've had this really bitchin' headache ever since Marcus clobbered me."

"Nah. The memory of my soul aching is too strong. You know, Marcus had to have gotten out of the workshop by way of that stairs. If he exited the stairs through the first door, he's probably still in the cathedral. If he exited through the second door, he's on the loose in the city. I don't know which I fear more."

Avignon said, "I could have sworn he's living in the basement."

50.

"Kick the Shit out of 'Em and Cuff 'Em to the Radiator in My Office," Donovan Said.

A t four in the morning and a dozen blocks north of where Marcie, Jefferson, and James sat waiting, Scott Carter and Darryl Weems were voyeurs peering through the broken slats of a smashed louver door that did a poor job of separating a bordello room from the hall.

The brownstone on Adam Clayton Powell Jr. Boulevard had only been a bordello for a month and already it stunk of sweat, wine, and urine punctuated by the pungent smell of smoking cocaine. Rap music roared from loudspeakers inside the room, blending with similar music from other speakers in other rooms. A yellow light bulb hanging in a bare wire socket cast long shadows around the room, which held a stained mattress on a wire frame, a fiberboard folding table, and a chair; no more.

The room's paint peeled in long, forlorn, curling strips, partly obscuring black velvet paintings of Martin Luther King Jr. and Mother Hale. The mattress bent around the weight of two bodies; a lanky boy with spindly arms and droopy shoulders pumped frantically into a thirteen-year-old girl with sunken eyes and AIDS scars that flecked her skin. Her unfeeling body was shaped by his frenzy. It molded around him; she felt nothing but the euphoria of crack, which wiped out all else.

Five bucks a fuck to buy crack.

Carter and Weems watched until the john had spent himself and withdrew, then they stumbled across the room to the drugs on the table. They left in silence, pockets stuffed with money, and got into the Suzuki Samurai. The cold November wind cut inside the car's canvas top and under Weems's jacket, chilling his bones.

Carter drove south through streets largely devoid of human traffic. He made a right on 125th Street and for a few blocks cruised the afterhours street life on Harlem's main drag: at that hour, mainly homeless men and women, newspaper delivery trucks, and cops.

It was four-thirty when Carter drove down Jackson Avenue and pulled up in front of Pappy Bollis's headquarters, shutting off the ignition and, with Weems, exiting the car with a casual air that made Marcia Barnes jump so high she nearly went through the roof of the surveillance car.

"That's them!" she exclaimed in a loud whisper, grabbing her gun and the door knob.

"RapStar," James concurred.

Carter and Weems glanced briefly at the two pickets who remained on night watch in front of the Korean fruit stand, then ducked inside the house before Marcie could get out of the Mercury.

"Too late," James said.

She sat back down inside and jammed her gun angrily back into its holster.

"Lighten up, babe," Jefferson said, smiling at his Nikon. "I got good shots of 'em."

"What am I going to do with those?"

"Take 'em to Donovan and see if he can ID the punks," James said.

"This is going to take forever," Marcie lamented.

"We'll start right away," Jefferson said. "I'll call in a replacement surveillance team. You and me can run the film through the lab and have it to Donovan at the cathedral in two hours."

But it took five hours, including the hour that replacement surveillance took to arrive, two hours travel time (one spent in gridlock on Second Avenue near the United Nations; the Emir of Kuwait was in town with an entourage), an hour in the lab, and another hour tracking down Donovan. He had gone home to sleep, leaving the second that enough cops arrived to turn the casual ring that was set up around the cathedral into a formal cordon.

Marcie let herself into the Riverside Drive apartment and found him in the master bedroom. He had thrown off his clothes and fallen asleep diagonally across the bed, just like he did in the old days when he lived alone. *How quickly he slips back into that life,* she thought, a bit uneasily. *Next there will be beer cans lined up on the windowsill and the television will be tuned to Australian football or whatever else could be found on cable at that hour.*

Marcie peered out the window and saw the *West Wind* resting at her dock. Two years ago it seemed like such a romantic notion, living on a boat tied up at the 79th Street Boat Basin. Now the ketch mainly symbolized the distance between them. The boat had outlived her usefulness in Marcie's life, in exactly the same way that Riley's had outlived its usefulness in Donovan's. Both would have to go; the boat and the bar.

She took off her sneakers and climbed onto the bed, straddling him with her knees and massaging his shoulders until he awoke.

"Mmmf," he said, and rolled over to look up at her.

"No smart remarks?" she asked.

"I'm all out."

"That will be the day. You're just tired. Donovan, I found them."

"Carter and the other guy? Did you bring 'em in?"

"No. They went into a crack house on Jackson Avenue, and since then we've had a team following them to a market on 110th Street and then to the Schomberg Plaza Houses on Fifth Avenue. Are these the guys who killed Jennifer?"

She pulled a five-by-seven glossy from her bag and showed it to him.

He peered at it for a moment, then said, "Those are the kids I chased."

"Definitely?" she asked, her heart beating faster.

"Ten years ago and on level ground I would have had them. Bring 'em in."

"I'm going to do this personally."

"Good girl. Kick the shit out of 'em and cuff 'em to the radiator in my office."

She put away the photo and ran her fingers through his chest hair.

"If they go into that house, it may take a TNT bust to get them out."

"It can be arranged, but I'd rather not. Jefferson gave me the layout, and for one thing you have pickets across the street who might be caught in the crossfire. Take 'em on the street, but watch out for them. There's a lot of automatic weapons out there. In fact . . ."

He made the suggestion gently:

". . . Why not let James and Jefferson do it."

"I'm not capable?"

"Sure. But you're not street, and you never went up against crazies with Uzis."

"I can do it," she said. "I can drop them."

"No guns if possible. If you can't avoid a shootout, go for leg shots. In any event, be careful." He took both her hands.

"I will."

She leaned over and gave him a kiss; not a great passionate one, but closer to it than he had seen in days. "I better go."

"Stay with me and get a few hours sleep. You look like you need it."

"I can't relax now. I'm too close. Why aren't you at the cathedral?"

"Nothing important is going on. I ran Marcus back into his hole—wherever that is—last night, and now Bonaci and his team are going over the site. I want to shut my eyes for a couple hours. Take off your clothes and let's cuddle."

"No. I know what you're up to."

"Not that. I'm really too tired. Nothing personal."

"I mean, you're trying to get me to fall asleep so you can

phone Jefferson and tell him to take Carter and Weems. I appreciate that you're trying to protect me, and I love you. But this is something I have to do myself."

"The female ego speaks," he grumbled.

She got off the bed, took the comforter and pulled it up to his waist. Then she kissed him on the cheek.

"I love tucking you in bed and going out to work," she said.

"Sexist."

"You bet," Marcie said, and left.

51.
CITY OF GOD (4)

The limestone dust was mostly gone, evident only in the cracks between pages and along the filigreed spine of the book. Gone too was the sculptor's bench and carpenter's tools, abandoned along with the spacious workshop that had had the advantage of being centrally located as well as hidden.

Now the servant of God was back in his cell, tiny and dark but securely concealed within the old walls of the City of God. To find him, Donovan would need more than intuition and blind luck. But in order to continue his work, Marcus would have to travel further and risk more. No matter. It had to be done.

Marcus shuffled through the flyers he collected the previous morning in the nave. So much was wrong. So much to be punished. But there had to be a simpler way, a means of striking at the evil core of the problem. Behind all the desecrations was one force, a man who had sworn to keep God's house in order and who instead had let the City of Man intrude.

Marcus lifted his half-finished sculpture off the brass-bound chest in which his stone-working tools remained safe. The workshop was lost and he was back in his cell, where there was little room to carve. He opened the chest's lid and took out the mallet, which then slipped easily into his old leather shoulder bag. He reclosed the chest and put the bust back atop it, then went to the door and pulled it open.

The corridor outside was dark and narrow, but clean and, so far, still a secret. And like the other chambers within the stone walls, it conducted sound like an ear funnel. Two other corridors away, thick within the west facade, above and behind the horns of the State Trumpet, a servant of mammon worked alone.

With his final breaths William Stewart, cathedral administrator, supervised the erection of a display honoring the clergy. Put up in the Ecclesiastical Chapel on the north side of the nave next to the Lawyers' Chapel, the display celebrated the lives of radical clergymen and women who were persecuted for their social advocacy in Central and South America.

Stewart wasn't quite sure why he bothered. The cordon of cops that went up around the cathedral in the early morning hours had discouraged all the tour bus operators from bringing people inside. Tourism was down; donations and sales in the gift shops were almost nonexistent. No one had taken the tour of the Stone Cutting Yard in several days. The few tourists and pilgrims who dared step inside the walls kept to the wide-open central aisle and moved in small groups, rather like tiny schools of fish navigating shark-filled waters.

Three men had been brutally murdered and another savagely attacked. A threat had been nailed to the door. The cathedral had gone from being a center of social conscience and spiritual activism to being a bad joke featured nightly on the TV news. And most recently, a horde of cops in hobnail boots had trampled through God's vineyard, breaking down doors. Now Donovan and his men were out in the stone cutting yard, terrorizing the master craftsmen and their apprentices.

And coming up was the ultimate tragedy. Stewart had been summoned to an emergency meeting of the cathedral trustees, at which time he doubtless would be called upon to explain what the hell was going on in the house of the Lord.

Stewart needed badly to get away from it all. He had to do something with his hands, anything that would clear his head. And so he decided to do the final work on the Ecclesiastical Exhibit himself. To that end he climbed to the blindstory gallery beneath the Rose Window, above and behind the horns of the State Trumpet, there to hang a handmade patchwork banner glorifying religious social activism. The banner was a present from the Sisters of Cidade de Deux in Rio de Janeiro in gratitude for the cathedral's fundraising on behalf of Brazilian slum children. It was to be suspended below the Rose Window and State Trumpet, hanging down into the narthex in time for the upcoming Conference of the InterAmerican Social Accountability Program, a link between North and South American inner-city social workers.

"Not that anyone will show up after everything that's happened," Stewart said.

The banner was thirty feet long and made from rags salvaged from the clothes of 450 children and adolescents who were murdered in the Brazilian slum during the previous year. It had two twisted sisal ties that Stewart fastened to support struts behind the balustrade. For close to an hour, Steward loosened and tightened ties to make the furled banner perfectly even, stretched beneath the inner pipes of the State Trumpet.

He leaned over the balustrade and looked down to make sure that no one was below to be startled by the suddenly unfurling banner. Somewhat to his chagrin, Stewart saw that he was virtually alone. The cathedral was essentially empty, unheard of for a Friday. The only ones in sight were eight German tourists who were snapping photographs of the Ecclesiastical Exhibit, quite a distance to the northeast. Detective Sergeant Brian Moskowitz stood by the information booth, off to the north, going over the visitor sign-in book.

Three cords, also made of sisal, kept the banner rolled tight. Using a small pocket knife, he cut the end cords, then took another quick look down to the floor of the narthex. Stewart cut the final cord, and the banner rippled quickly downward, making an oddly high-pitched sound that echoed in the otherwise silent cathedral.

The lower end of the banner was of yellow fringe surrounding the message *pacem in terris*. It flapped happily, and made Stewart smile. It also made Detective Sergeant Moskowitz look up and smile, at least for an instant.

Moskowitz's smile froze, then turned strict and hard as his lips tightened. At the same time, Stewart became aware of a force behind him on the blindstory gallery.

Moskowitz dropped the book and produced his service revolver. "Get down!" he yelled, but it was too late.

The bludgeon came crashing down on Stewart's head, caving in his skull and breaking his spine in three places. The body, dead before it started to fall, pitched over the balustrade and rolled down the face of the still-swinging banner, landing on the narthex floor with a low thud.

Two shots roared from Moskowitz's revolver, but hit only air before impacting the west front of the cathedral. The figure on the balcony was gone.

52.
THE RESOLUTION OF THE JENNIFER PEEL MURDER CASE

History would record that the basic mistake came when Jefferson gave Marcie the keys to his car.

At first it seemed simple enough. He had to go back to the stakeout, and she had to show the photograph of Carter and Weems to Donovan. So he gave her the keys and she dropped him off before driving to Donovan's apartment building. All well and good so far. The problem came when she was driving back to the stakeout.

At quarter to noon on an average Friday halfway through November, Sam the Gold Man called Jefferson's extension at the West Side Major Crimes Unit to report that Scott Carter was due in his store at noon to pick up some gold rope chains he had ordered. The decorations were, said the jeweler, "enough to make the punk look like Mr. T." Since the call was urgent and Jefferson was on stakeout, the call was transferred to his car. Marcie got it just as she was driving up Broadway toward 125th Street.

At the same time, Carter and Weems exited the Schomberg Plaza Housing Project on Fifth Avenue in Harlem, got into the Suzuki Samurai, and headed north toward 125th Street with Jefferson and James following at a discreet distance.

Driving ever faster, Marcie cruised by the gates of Columbia University and descended the hill from Morningside Heights into Harlem, then hung a right on 125th. The Lenox Avenue Gold Mine wasn't far from 125th, and she wanted to be there well before Carter and Weems arrived. Taking them as they entered the store would be perfect.

But 125th Street *was* Harlem's main shopping drag, with car owners double-parking to run into shops or patronize street vendors. A crosstown bus was broken down at the corner of Seventh Avenue, and a rap video filming in front of the Apollo Theater had crowds of onlookers spilling out into the traffic lanes. Finally, lunchtime crowds from the New York State Office Building were slowing down traffic coming from Fifth Avenue. Jefferson and James fell a full avenue block behind the Suzuki, which Carter drove down the center line and through a red light.

Sitting at another red light at the corner of Amsterdam Avenue, Marcie unholstered her gun and laid it on on the seat beside her. Taking advantage of a break in the traffic on her side of town, Marcie pressed hard on the pedal of the Plymouth and raced across 125th. After negotiating the crowd in front of the

Apollo, she made the turn onto Lenox Avenue and drove the several blocks to the store.

There were no parking spots, of course. She made a U-turn and double parked across the street from the shop. She checked to make sure that the safety was off on her gun, then opened the door and slid out. The Suzuki was nowhere to be seen, though traffic was moving slowly in both directions. A white street-sweeping truck lumbered noisily uptown, backing up traffic behind it. Marcie started across the street, her gun partly concealed inside her jacket.

The street sweeper pulled abruptly into the oncoming lane to get around the Plymouth, and Marcie scurried out of its way. Then there was the blare of a horn and the black Suzuki came out of traffic, into the oncoming lane, and pulled up in front of the Lenox Avenue Gold Mine. Marcie spun towards it, standing ten feet in front of the bumper, and stared hard into the eyes of Scott Carter.

No one knows if he recognized her or was only looking at a beautiful woman, but he smiled and started to get out of the jeep, Weems behind him. Marcie was furious. She saw him smiling as he ambushed her friend, smiling as he drove the knife into Jennifer's heart. Down the block, Jefferson and James tore up Lenox Avenue, trying desperately to catch up. Too late.

Carter took a step toward Marcie then stopped in his tracks as she aimed her gun at his stomach. "Police! You're under arrest!" she shouted.

Weems looked at her, then behind at the commotion Jefferson and James were making.

"Cops!" he stammered.

Carter's smile disappeared. He froze, then suddenly rammed his hands downward, toward his waistband. No one ever knew what he was trying to reach.

Marcie squeezed the trigger twice. Her first shot hit Carter in the center of his chest, shoving him straight backwards into Carter. The second bullet hit Carter's shoulder as he fell, twisting him to one side.

Weems jerked toward the car, seeking God-knows-what. Marcie's third and fourth shots hit him in the chest and abdomen, slamming him into the hood of the Suzuki. He slid down the metal to the gutter.

She moved slowly towards them, her gun held in both hands in front of her. Jefferson ran up then, followed by James. "I got them," she said.

"You sure did," Jefferson replied, bending over the bodies.

"Carter went for his gun."

"We're on top of it," James said, joining Jefferson in a huddle over the bodies.

On both sides of the street, people never entirely jaded by the sound of gunfire were edging cautiously closer. Marcie saw them coming peripherally as she stared with increasing horror at the scene before her. Carter and Weems were down; dead probably. She had shot them and no gun had dropped. After warnings about crack dealers with automatic weapons, she stood over two unarmed bodies.

She slipped her own gun back into its holster and joined her partners. James was going through Carter's pockets. "It was in his waistband," she said. "I saw him go for it."

Jefferson and James looked up at her, and then at one another. Speaking too quietly for her to hear, James growled, "Get her outta here," and then Jefferson had her on her feet, walking back to his car.

"Come on, babe, let the man work. Sit in the car and call this in. Get us some backup and a morgue wagon."

"Unh, yeah," she said. "The gun . . ."

"We'll find it," Jefferson said, and went back to the bodies.

James was opening the trunk of his car and pulling out an old blanket. He carried it to the scene and draped it over the bodies, masking them as well as the sound of a metallic object falling from his fingers. Then he bent over Carter, tucking the blanket under the body, and then stood with a gun in his hand and a smile on his face.

"Got it!" he called to Marcie.

"Thank God," she whispered.

"It's a 9 millimeter semi," Jefferson yelled.

She leaned back in the driver's seat of the Plymouth and closed her eyes, too stunned to make the radio call. After a moment, Jefferson came over and did it. Soon the street in front of the Lenox Avenue Gold Mine was packed with official vehicles and, shortly thereafter, newspapermen and women come to witness the resolution of the Jennifer Peel murder case.

53.
"I Hope You Shot Better Than That in Israel," Donovan Said.

Moskowitz replied, "In Israel we used Uzis. Hitting the target wasn't the problem. Scraping up the remains afterwards was."

"Jesus, I close my eyes for a little while and all hell breaks loose on my beat."

"That'll teach you to lay down on the job," Bonaci said.

Donovan pulled on his clothes. It was two in afternoon, and his nap had come at the expense of three bodies. The Upper West Side and Harlem crawled with police brass and reporters, the front facade of the Cathedral of St. John the Divine resembled a television studio, and Jefferson looked like he had just crawled down forty miles of bad road.

And when Marcie came in the apartment door, the towering emotion building up inside her collapsed and she fell, sobbing, into Donovan's arms. Jefferson, Moskowitz, and Bonaci closed the bedroom door and repaired to the kitchen to exchange war stories.

"Are you all right?" Donovan asked, leading her back to the bed where she had left him to go to work just a few hours earlier.

"I'm . . . fine . . . I guess. Oh, I'm sorry. I'm embarrassed. I shouldn't be crying."

He brushed some tears from her cheek. "It's okay for women to cry. Really."

"I don't know why. I didn't feel this way the other time I shot someone."

"This one was personal. Believe me, I understand."

He sat her down on the bed and draped an arm around her shoulders. "Tell me what happened," he said.

"I left here and was driving uptown when I got the call that Carter and Weems were heading for Lenox Avenue. I went straight there, knowing that Jefferson and James would be following the perps. I guess I got there ahead of everyone. And Carter . . . the tall one . . . came at me from his jeep and he was smiling and, I don't know. I pulled my weapon and identified myself and he still went for a gun."

"You know that the kids in the crack trade have nothing to lose. Didn't I say that?"

"At least a million times," she nodded, drying her eyes with paper towels. "He had a 9 millimeter. God, I shot them both. All I could think of was Jennifer."

"She's avenged now."

"So why do I feel so *bad?*"

"You feel bad because you over-intellectualize everything, the same as we all do. We're civilized and educated and it shocks us to discover that brute force and revenge can be fun."

"It didn't upset me to kill Andrea Jones," she said, referring to a suspect she eviscerated with a shotgun.

"Jones was trying to kill me at the time. You were protecting your future husband."

"I didn't think of you that way then. Does this mean we're still getting married?"

"Yeah. I made some of the arrangements already. So look, Carter and Weems were certified bad guys. Ed James found eight thousand dollars' worth of crack in their vehicle. The thumb print on the gold ring matches Carter's left thumb. And he tried to shoot you. Stop worrying about it."

"You're right, of course."

"I'll remind you of those words after we're married."

She smiled faintly, then more broadly, and kissed him. "You're unique in the police department, Donovan," she said, hugging him.

"I'm unique, *period*. You too."

"No I'm not. I'm just a woman."

"Who can do anything."

"The last time I said that, I was a child. I don't believe it anymore. I'm not even sure how much I like the line of work I'm in. A couple of hours ago you were trying to get me to fall asleep so you could have Jefferson and James take the risk for me. That's what you were doing, wasn't it?"

"Maybe," he said.

"I should have laid down on this bed and fallen asleep."

"Lay down on it now. You haven't slept in two days."

"I could use a rest," she admitted.

"It's still warm," Donovan said, getting up and hoisting her feet onto the mattress. "And it's my turn to go to work."

"I wish you could stay."

"Sorry. I'll get back as quickly as I can, maybe even for dinner. If you feel like ordering out, I could go for Chinese. On the other hand, you might haul your ass into the kitchen and practice cooking. You know what the man said."

"What did the man say?"

Donovan imitated a rap song: " 'Get your biscuits in the oven. Get your buns in the bed. This women's liberation has gone to your head.' "

She said, "You're a swine. If I weren't so tired I'd kick your ass. Go away and let me sleep."

Donovan switched off the light and closed the door on her. He tucked his shirt into his pants as he walked down the hall and noticed that once again his apartment had become a command center. It happened occasionally, normally for a surveillance of Riverside Park below, sometimes to allow Unit detectives to work without TV cameras outside their windows. Donovan assumed that was the case this time, for an ungodly number of cops—including a few he didn't know—were manning cellular phones and walkie-talkies and comparing notes in his home. Their clearly happy patter hushed as he walked through the dining room.

"What am I, the Pope? It's okay to talk," he said.

"You're all right, Lieutenant," someone said, with a little laugh.

Jefferson, Moskowitz, and Bonaci were sitting at the kitchen table, taking hits from a bottle of Stolichnaya.

Donovan said, "I know why those guys out there are happy. Marcus is no longer a figment of Avignon's and my imagination. Dead Eye Moskowitz here pegged a couple of shots at him."

"We gotta lose these .38s," Moskowitz said.

"Where *is* Avignon, anyway?"

"Nobody's seen him, Lieutenant," Bonaci said. "He pulled a disappearing act shortly before Stewart was killed."

"Curious," Donovan said.

"Yeah, ain't it," Jefferson said, glaring angrily into his glass.

"What's your problem?"

"I ain't got no problem."

"I've never seen you drink. Not ever in the ten years we've worked together. Then Marcie plugs two crack dealers and all of a sudden you've got your snoot in my symbolic Stoli."

"I'll buy you another bottle."

"Is this bottle sacred?" Moskowitz asked. It was the first time he was invited to the Donovan household and already he worried about imposing.

"It was Marcie's. For some reason, single Jewish women living in Manhattan inevitably keep a bottle of Stoli in the freezer. Marcie's only half Jewish, so there's only half a bottle. I hung onto it to prove that I don't need booze any more. Drink it. *L'chaim!*"

He got himself a Diet Coke.

"So tell me, why is the Commissioner calling me again, and so soon? To tell me that Moskowitz is a lousy shot or Marcie is a good one?"

"Possibly both," Moskowitz said.

Jefferson shrugged and kept on drinking, but Bonaci offered an explanation. "Ah, you know how it is. Two black teenagers get shot in Harlem."

"They were armed drug dealers who pulled a gun on a cop. And a black cop at that. Well, arguably black."

"She's black," Jefferson said, pushing away from the table and standing to look out the window at the Hudson. "She proved herself. She's okay."

"She's a mensch," Moskowitz said.

"So why are you drinking?"

Jefferson shrugged his shoulders without turning around. Donovan sensed that he was avoiding eye contact.

Bonaci said, "Carter's parents have surfaced and are claiming that the gun was a plant. The Reverend Fred Handon is in on it."

"Just what I need," Donovan said.

A local Baptist minister and political ally of the late Herbert Spenser, Handon was famous for racing to the defense of black teenagers accused of heinous crimes. Spenser represented him as well as Halftrack and Terry Loomis.

"Was the gun a plant?" Donovan asked.

"No," Jefferson said, downing the last of his vodka.

"I gather you don't want to have a long conversation about this."

Jefferson turned around and slammed his glass down on the table. "I'm tired, Bill. I haven't slept in days. Do you mind if I use the guest room?"

"Of course not. You can look after Marcie while I'm out."

"I looked after her before and blew it," Jefferson said.

"Are you blaming yourself for what happened?"

"I shouldn't have lent her my car. I should have been on site ahead of her. I'm going to sleep."

He pushed past Donovan and disappeared down the hall in the direction of the bedrooms.

"Do you guys know more than I do?" Donovan asked, and was rewarded with shakes of the head.

"Where is Ed James?"

"With the Investigations Unit, the last I heard," Bonaci said.

"Keep me informed, willya? Now, Brian Moskowitz, tell me on the life of your dear Irish mother, how come you missed the sonofabitch?"

"Hey Lieutenant, you wanna check out the angle I was shooting at?"

"Take me to it," Donovan replied.

54.
MOSKOWITZ MAKES A STATEMENT

Donovan stood amidst the chalk outline that showed where Stewart stood at the moment of his death and gawked at the damage done to the Rose Window. The immense stained-glass jewel in the west front of the cathedral had holes shot in one of its more splendid frames. One slug tore up a Byzantine cross; another punctured the robe covering the torso of you-know-who.

"You did that on purpose," Donovan said. "You were making a statement."

"I swear on my mother's Irish eyes," Moskowitz said.

"Once was not enough, right?"

"Hey, you're not gonna pin that one on my people! It was Roman soldiers and you know it. I'll take the rap for missing Marcus, but no more!"

"Forget about it," Donovan said, punching the kid on the arm. "Like you said, the angle sucks."

He looked down over the State Trumpet to the spot from which Moskowitz fired his two shots, and could see that a hit would have been the wildest stroke of luck. So would have been a ground intercept. After firing, Moskowitz tore across the narthex and tried to get to the stairs that led up into the Tower of St. Paul, but the gate was locked.

Donovan led Bonaci and Moskowitz in an equally fruitless search for Marcus's escape route. The gallery on which he attacked Stewart connected with stairwells on both north and south sides of the nave as well as stairs running up and down both towers. At the juncture of the south face and the Tower of St. Paul, construction obstructed a passage that appeared to run off toward a linkage with the far-off corridor in which Donovan discovered the wood shop.

As the sun dropped below the apartment buildings across the street, Donovan looked down from the gallery upon the several hundred uniformed policemen and detectives who had filtered in. They milled about the nave, peering curiously at the monumental structure where few of them had ever set foot. Some of them were the men promised Donovan earlier that Friday. Others came in the afternoon, summoned at the behest of the Police Commissioner.

"The commissioner called to remind me about Sunday," Donovan explained to Bonaci and Moskowitz, who joined him in gazing down on the assembled task force.

"What's Sunday?" Moskowitz asked.

"The Feast of St. Francis. It's the day that the Cathedral stages the blessing of the animals."

"I don't want to miss that," Moskowitz said. "Five thousand people carrying their cats and dogs and canaries, come to church to be blessed by the bishop."

"And elephants and goats and camels outside," Donovan went on. "The whole thing presented in the context of a day-long celebration of the planet."

"I was here last year," Bonaci said. "The place smelled like a kennel."

"The jazz mass they play is pretty neat, though," Donovan said.

"So why does the Commissioner give a shit?" Moskowitz asked.

"Because the celebration is *still on!* Despite four murders and one assault, the Episcopal Church won't cancel its annual Earth Day. I have been instructed to abandon my personal quest for Marcus and call in a horde of cops in hobnail boots, who will take the place apart stone by stone. I still think this will drive Marcus out into the city, where there's no end to the harm he can do, but what do I know?"

"I got reinforcements here as fast as I could," Bonaci said proudly.

"Good man. In a way, I'm glad for the help. I have decided to attend the Blessing of Animals as a private citizen with his fiancee. They're running a puppy adoption service this Sunday. I plan to have two-point-seven children and a dog, and Sunday seems like a good time to start my collection."

"You're going to mass on Sunday?" Moskowitz asked, astonished.

"Only to catch the Winter Consort—that's the jazz group that plays the mass—and adopt a dog. Don't worry about me. I remain an atheist, but one with a weakness for music, architecture, and dogs, and they will have all three on Sunday." He raised his hand above the crowd and said, "Bless you, my children."

Bonaci brought his walkie-talkie to his lips. He asked, "Now, Lieutenant?"

"You may proceed."

"Begin your search patterns," Bonaci ordered. After subsequent orders by detectives below, the blue posse fanned out through the cathedral, carrying shotguns, flashlights, and video cameras.

"Which reminds me," Donovan said. "Where the fuck is Avignon?"

"He's now been missing more than five hours."

"I can't believe he's not taping this. It's like the miracle scene in *La Dolce Vita*. Avignon has got to be sick or dead."

"You want me to send some guys out looking for him?"

"Yeah, actually, I do. And while you're at it, find Jim Forrest."

"He's still missing too—lammed out of his apartment in a big hurry. We're checking buses, trains, and airports."

"Him I don't like. Cuff him to the radiator in my office. Space is available there now."

Bonaci said, "I'm gonna hang out here for a while, then go home to sleep. It's been a long couple of days."

His name came over the radio, but the sound was lost in the general clamor and Bonaci walked off by himself to hear the message.

Donovan said, "Moskowitz? What's on your schedule?"

"Home. It's *shabbos* in an hour."

"Oh, like *you're* gonna run back to Eastern Parkway and pray."

"Lieutenant, I'm a holy man. And I live in Canarsie."

Moskowitz was interrupted by the return of Bonaci, whose eyes were alive with breaking news. "It's Avignon," he said.

"Where?"

"We found him in his car. It's parked in the bishop's spot."

"Dead or alive?"

"Alive, but just barely. The sonofabitch had a worse concussion than he let on."

55.

SOME GUYS WILL DO ANYTHING FOR A PARKING SPOT

That's what Donovan told the incapacitated cameraman, to little avail. He replied: "Come on, Donovan, I can afford a parking garage. It's just that the bishop's spot is more convenient. What's he need a car for anyway? Can't he walk on water?"

"His boss does that. So tell me, how long have you been here?"

Avignon tried to sit up, but the Emergency Medical Services technician who was administering to him pushed him back down. His shirt was off, the better to attach EKG electrodes, and he lay across the front seat of the Enola Gay, the shadow of fuzzy dice in the moonlight quavering across his stomach. A fresh bandage was on his head and Donovan saw blood on the old one. Avignon had carefully hidden the severity of his concussion.

"The last thing I remember, we chased Marcus down into the Recycling Center. I remember a lot of tin cans. Then we all went outdoors and you ran off. I got weak, I remember, and my head hurt. I just made it to the car. How long have I been out?"

"Eight or nine hours, give or take a few."

"Eight *hours!* Did I miss anything?"

"Everything. Marcus squashed Stewart, the cathedral administrator, and Cecil B. deMille produced a police drama. Sorry, Mike . . . you missed the footage of the century."

"Oh, *man,*" he moaned, clenching his eyes shut.

The Emergency Services guy said, "We got to take him to St.

Luke's. His doctor has been looking for him ever since he injured himself."

"I didn't *injure myself,"* Avignon said testily. "I was attacked by a madman. Donovan, I'm sorry, but you're gonna have to finish this case yourself."

"What?" The lieutenant was more than a little astonished. Avignon had never willingly given up before. When he'd checked himself out of St. Luke's hours after getting his skull half caved in, Donovan assumed that Avignon was going as strong as ever.

"I don't seem to have it anymore," Avignon said.

Never one given to schmaltzy platitudes, Donovan found himself saying, "Come on, buddy, you're as young as you feel. You can do it."

Avignon shook his head. "I'm fifty and feel ninety. My head is shaking and my knees are weak. Despite my best attempts to the contrary, I have grown old."

"But what about your masterpiece? The tape you're finishing?"

"It's too much for me. Besides, you said that I missed the main event—the Cecil B. deMille production in the nave."

Donovan stepped back and watched as Avignon was carried from his car to the back of a city ambulance, the second time that had happened recently. As he was loaded into the back he called out, "Look after my car for me."

"You got it," Donovan replied as a set of keys came flying out of the ambulance and skittered across the asphalt.

As the ambulance drove off, Donovan returned to the Enola Gay. In the back seat was the Ikegami camera. The $50,000 machine was only one of four that Avignon owned. Donovan picked it up and took a tentative look through the viewfinder, then realized he didn't have the slightest idea how to operate the thing.

Langton walked up, attracted by the commotion. Donovan tried in vain to focus the camera on him, then put it down in embarrassment. Jefferson was the technology maven. "Tell me about stone cutting," Donovan said. "Is there a lot of limestone dust involved?"

"Surely you're joking," Langton laughed.

"Not quite."

"There's limestone dust all over the bloody place. It gets in your hair and you carry it home, where it gets in the cat food. The only way to rid yourself of it all is to take several showers. Is it important?"

"Maybe. I just noticed a sprinkling of it in Avignon's car."

"Well, if the man was in the Stone Yard, he got it in his knickers. I shouldn't be too hard on him for that."

"I was also wondering how he managed to sleep in the front seat of his car for nine hours in the bishop's parking spot without someone noticing," Donovan said.

"That's an easy one. The bishop *loves* his parking spot, and it's woe to him that takes it. In fact, the subject of parking is so sensitive that no one who works here will walk near a car that's parked in the spot. Do you see what I mean?"

Donovan scowled. "Where's the bishop today?"

"In Washington lobbying for the arts budget."

"A fifty-seven Chevy in mint condition with a fifty-thou-sand-dollar camera in the back seat sits unmolested for nine hours in the City of New York? Do you believe in Santa Claus as well?"

"I believe in the Lord, and this is His house," Langton said, apparently seriously, and Donovan changed the subject.

56.

A STRICTLY
DO-IT-YOURSELF
APOCALYPSE

Donovan cleaned his stuff out of the room near the crypt and packed it into the trunk of the Enola Gay. He put a police guard on *that*, not at all convinced that the bishop's parking spot was theft-proof.

Donovan visited Avignon in the hospital, but the man was asleep, sedated. Donovan went home to check on Marcie, only to find her dead to the world. He covered her with a down comforter, then tiptoed into the guest room, looking for Jefferson. *He* had gone home, and a phone call revealed only an answering machine. Once again, his long-time partner and best friend didn't want to talk.

On the return trip to the cathedral, Donovan picked up some noodles at the Yangtze Pantry and brought it into Riley's. It was eleven o'clock on Friday evening, and the place was deader than a Victorian door nail. Apart from a handful of kids playing the juke box in the back room, the only life came from the TV. The local news was recounting the latest scandal—according to projections, more than 2,500 New Yorkers would be murdered by the end of the year, making the Empire City more dangerous than Beirut.

Donovan sat at the front of the bar and leafed through the handful of flyers that people left in Riley's impromptu news-distribution system (a cardboard box next to the peppermint schnapps). Atop the pile was a broadside from Doom, the Society for Secular Armageddonism. It read, in part: "We believe the apocalypse is at hand, and the reasons for that belief are overwhelming: chemical and biological weapons, nuclear proliferation, deforestation, the greenhouse effect, ozone depletion, acid rain, the poisoning of our air and water, rising racism, massive species loss, toxic waste, the AIDS pandemic, the continuing population explosion, encroaching Big Brotherism, and at least a thousand points of blight. These aren't just conversation topics for yuppie cocktail parties; they're grade A, unadulterated harbingers of destruction, 100 percent bona fide specters of doom, and they're all proof that we don't need God to end it for us. The coming end will be a strictly do-it-yourself apocalypse."

"No wonder Marcus wants to kill everyone," Donovan muttered to Jake who, having tumbled from the wagon, nodded over a bottle of Schmidt's beer. "We *have* screwed up the world."

"Speak for yourself," he grumbled. "I was in the concentration camp in California when your people dropped the bomb."

"I understand Marcus better than ever. He's the conscience of the cathedral."

"Now you sound like Chico. I liked you better when you didn't believe in anything."

"What about Chico?"

"The day Spenser was killed he was carrying on about duty and responsibility and dead children. He sounded drunk."

"Dead children?" Donovan asked.

"Yeah, back home in Brazil. What do I know? The guy bet on AIDS deaths in the paper. He had a sick sense of humor. He was creepy. I'm glad he's gone, if you want to know the truth. Chico was a little scary. Remember Big Harold, who never talked?"

"How could I forget? He racked up a tidy little body count before we stopped him."

"You stopped him. Plugged him in a tunnel below the park. Anyway, Chico reminds me of him, only Chico talks more. Scary."

"Was he really with you the whole time that Spenser was killed?"

"As far as I know. Of course, I did go to the numbers joint a few times."

"I know. You told Bonaci."

"Yeah, I got interested in playing the Queens number, and . . ."

Donovan lay down his noodles and looked Jake squarely in the eye. "What number?"

"Queens. It's a new thing for me."

"The numbers joint doesn't handle the Queens number," Donovan said.

"Not *this* joint down the block. The one on 126th, up by the live poultry market."

Donovan squeezed his eyes shut, held them that way for a long time, then opened them to stare disappointedly at his old friend and former drinking buddy. "How did you get to and from 126th?"

"On the bus. Oh . . . I guess you mean I must have been gone for a while."

"How long?"

"I don't know. An hour, maybe."

Donovan sighed, and muttered, looking away at his image in the backbar mirror, "I hate drunks. I no longer find them interesting or amusing. I don't know how I wasted so many years of my life."

"What?" Jake asked, not quite hearing.

"Never mind. So, you really didn't see Chico the whole time. He had an hour to get to the cathedral, kill Spenser, and return."

"Could he have done that?"

"It's a lot closer, and he can afford a cab."

At the mention of money, and with the promise of changing the subject, Jake perked up. "Hey . . . it came!"

"What came?"

"My check! My twenty grand!"

"No shit!" Donovan exclaimed. "You got it with you?"

"No way. There's too much crime in this city. I don't know if you noticed that. It's in the bank, where it should be. Twenty thousand dollars in payment for the abuse I took at the hands of Uncle Sam."

"Look at it this way—you'd never have seen a penny if you'd flown a thirtieth mission as a kamikaze."

"That is true," Jake agreed. "And in celebration, I have decided to throw a beer party for the community. Well, for the regulars of this bar."

"The five or six of us left," Donovan said.

"And you're invited. Marcie, too. Hell, bring everyone. I plan to put $500 on the bar and let everyone drink from that. I'll make sure George gets a case of Coke for you."

"Forget it. I can't take the caffeine anymore, either. I'll have water. When is the party?"

"Tomorrow night. I'll let you know."

"What are your plans for the rest of the money?"

"I want to do something useful with it—maybe buy a liquor store."

"Twenty grand isn't enough, not even for a down payment. You'd better invest a tad down-market."

"What do you think?"

"I don't know," Donovan said, getting up and packing his Chinese food to take with him. "I'll ask around—see if anyone is looking for investors."

Back at the cathedral by midnight, Donovan found the task force winding up its extraordinary, stone-by-stone search. It had begun at the clerestory level and worked its way down to the crypt, inspecting everything.

The men looked behind every painting and tapestry; opened every door; went up and down every stairwell; and poked every crack that looked wide enough for a bug to crawl through. One team of cops even looked under the choir, pulpit, and altar, finding mainly dust. A pair of geologists from Columbia down the block used a portable rock sounder to thump the stone walls, looking for hollow sounds indicating hidden passages. They found nothing, and hunkered down in a pew near the AIDS Chapel, tired and disappointed.

It was in the stairwell leading down to the base of the Tower of St. Paul that the breakthrough came. It was relayed to Donovan just as he stood looking up at the high altar, mentally trying it out for a wedding. Bonaci was exhausted, but still his voice shook with excitement. "We got it, Lieutenant," he said.

Donovan turned and began to walk toward the Tower of St. Paul, languidly at first, sensing disappointment. It was too easy for it to end this way, in the predictable conclusion of an exhaustive search. You box a man in a confined space—no matter how big—and systematically hunt him down. What sport in that? Moreover, of the rest of the original hunting party, only Donovan remained. Avignon was back in the hospital, Marcie dozing, Jefferson asleep and incommunicado. Bonaci was the closest thing Donovan had to a fellow traveller in the Court of the Lion and the Lizard, and he wasn't really a buddy. Still, when he called again and there was greater urgency in his voice, Donovan caught some of the old fire and began to run, finally taking the stairs down to the crypt level in groups of three.

A narrow door was pressed into a stone wall moistened with darkness and lichens. The cast iron of its face covered thick oak timbers. Doubly heavy iron straps sprouted form the jamb and branched into rosettes.

Breathing heavily, his breath condensing in the frigid air, Bonaci presided over a three-man crew that held pry bars and shotguns. The sergeant's fingers were white clutching a spanking-new 9mm Penzler automatic.

"We just found it, Lieutenant. In the last place we looked. It's an old door, but it's been opened regularly. Check the hinges and leading edge."

He used the slender beam of a pencil light to illustrate.

Donovan drew his Smith & Wesson, then looked at it balefully and put it back. There were two shotguns and an automatic already in play; how many times did the man need to be shot before he died?

A cop pulled on the black iron ring that served as a handle. The door swung open and light from another bare forty-watt bulb split the darkness.

Gun barrels poked into the room, finding no targets. There was a mattress on a simple wooden frame, the whole deal draped in white. A square oak dining table, four square, was set with service for one, old but good sterling. A candle had burned down to nothing, but the smell of the wax lingered. Draped over a chair was a loose sackcloth robe, big enough to hide a bludgeon in.

Donovan stepped into the room and looked around. A wooden cupboard held canned goods, mostly fruits and vegetables and dried beef. A brass-bound wooden chest sat by the bed, a thick leather-bound book atop it. On a small, one-burner electric cookstove sat an unfinished bust. Donovan peered at the sloppy-jowled primordial human head the amateurish carving of which had left a layer of limestone dust here, there, and everywhere. Above the dining table was a figure of Christ. Donovan recognized the work; it was on sale every day at the Tip Top Bargains store on Broadway; $9.95, ink on black velvet.

"Here's the man who started all the trouble," Donovan said. "Two thousand years of intolerance and murder by the followers of this guy. Maybe Marcus is the first celebrant of the coming anniversary."

"What's in the book and the box?" Bonaci asked.

An hour later, after the room was dusted for fingerprints, they found out. The book was a mishmash of fragments from the Old and New Testaments, mixed in with incoherent rambling about duty and death. Bits from St. Augustine's *Confessions* and *City of God* lay alongside newspaper items chronicling recent inhumanities. There were child murders and tales of AIDS deaths; axe killings and abortions; political assassinations and prison tortures. As Donovan turned the pages, the handwritten fragments gave way to more and more newspaper clippings. At its end the book was merely a scrapbook of tabloid scare stories, the last being a tale of incest and matricide.

The chest opened with a faint squeak. Inside the limestone-dusty interior was a variety of tools. Donovan plucked them out one at a time. It was, he thought, like shopping at Sears. Marcus had assembled a hodgepodge of wood- and metal-working tools, nearly all of recent vintage, none with rust or other corrosion. A ball peen hammer still bore the price sticker of Columbia Hardware on Broadway and 113th.

Gingerly, Donovan hefted the exception: a stone-working mallet with a thin wooden handle barely supporting a massive, millstone-like head that was partly eaten away by years of pounding on steel chisels. The handle was worn smooth by men's sweaty hands, and the craters and cracks of the head were caked with blood. Donovan stared at it, awed and sickened. Embedded in there with the blood were traces of skull bone and brain, he was sure. That of Dale Charbaux, Terry Loomis, Herbert Spenser, and William Stewart.

Donovan held it aloft. "The murder weapon," he said.

"Where the hell is Marcus?" a cop with a shotgun asked.

Donovan looked around, shrugged. "Gone. Escaped. Flown the coop," he said. "On the loose in the city, just like I was afraid would happen."

57.
MY LOVEBIRD IS WARBLING

There are men who refuse to leave New York City because it's the home of Wall Street or the Theater District, the fashion industry or publishing, or because it has the best soul food or bagels. Donovan knew that he could never leave New York because he could get a good shower nowhere else.

Donovan's building was a PWE—pre-war elevator, huge and

fireproof and with a boiler large enough to propel the Battleship Iowa around the world twice. That was because it was an old luxury building, the pride of New York's Riviera, and also because it grew very cold alongside the Hudson in winter. A stiff breeze blew salty air against the windows of the highest buildings, corroding window seals and necessitating a massive boiler to heat apartments and water.

The water was crystal clear and roared out of the tap at high pressure, straight from the Croton Reservoir in the mountains upstate. It blasted the limestone dust and other of the day's accumulation off him, thrilled him to his toes and moved him to song. On that night the selection was "Try a Little Tenderness," and Donovan sang it to himself and the ceiling, the soap dripping off him as the words echoed off the walls.

The door opened, admitting a freshening blast of cooler air from the master bedroom. He saw Marcie's nude body stretching in the doorway.

"Hi, Honey," he called happily.

"My lovebird is warbling," she said.

"Absolutely."

"Otis Redding is singing in my shower. I waited a lifetime for this."

"Awright!"

"I have to pee," she said, then sat while he rinsed the shampoo out of his hair and shut off the shower. He stepped out to the sound of the toilet flushing, and she met him with a towel to dry off his chest.

"What time is it?" she asked, alternately dabbing his chest and kissing it.

"Early. Who cares?"

"You're in a good mood. Did you catch Marcus?"

"No."

"What happened?"

"He got away."

"Oh, I'm sorry. My honey had a bad day."

"No worse than yours. But I *am* in a good mood."

"Of course you are. You're home with me. Welcome home."

He smiled and hugged her. They both were home after a brief absence from one another. Her great quest was finished, and while the status of his was undetermined, they were reunited as man and woman.

"This feels great," he said, slipping her under his arm and leading her out into the bedroom.

She had lit candles. They gleamed from mirrory stainless holders mounted on the wall over the bed. The bedside radio, a replica of a 1932 GE cathedral radio, played softly tuned to WBGO, the jazz station across the river in Newark. A hand flicked out, and the electric lights went off.

"Do you want to talk about Marcus?" she asked.

"That's the last thing I want to talk about. Today I left my work at the office, where I will pick it up in . . ." He looked at his bare and still dripping wrist.

"Where's my watch? I could have sworn I had on my watch."

"You were in the shower," she said, smiling.

He shrugged. "I'll pick up the Marcus case when I get back to the office, whenever that may be. Right now, I'm home with my woman."

Marcie took the towel and balled it up and tossed it through the open door into the bathroom. Then she curled a hand around his neck and pulled his mouth down to hers. Their tongues met and slid along one another, reaching to the base while hot breath sucked in and out one another's throats.

His hands coursed over her skin, barely touching, gentle pressure all over from her shoulders to the base of her spine. His fingers slid down the crack of her behind, then traced up across her belly and cupped her breasts. She arched her back to press against his hands, breathing hard, her nostrils flaring, nipples hard against his palms.

Donovan had gone hard as a rock, and she held him in both hands, feeling his pulse throb. Then she dropped to her knees before him and sucked him into her mouth, and he moaned gently while running his fingers through her wild black cloud of hair.

He reached down to lift her, but she resisted. "I want to be inside you," he said hoarsely, the words barely escaping his mouth.

"I don't have my diaphragm in."

"I don't care."

Donovan hefted her, his strength nearly superhuman at that moment, and carried her to the bed, where the cover had already been thrown off. He lowered her onto the same bare mattress on which they made wild love before the whole horrible mess of the past few weeks happened.

She stretched out, as lithe as a cat, and purred gently while he ran his hands over her for a long time, stroking her and flattering her until the wetness dripped from her onto the mattress.

Marcie swivelled to face him, her legs open and welcoming. He knelt between her thighs and she reached to guide him in, her eyes wide as a doe's.

"Welcome home, honey," she gasped.

"I love you."

She whispered, pulling him in and drawing his head down alongside hers.

"Make me a baby," she said.

"Yes," he whispered back, and she began to come the moment he was inside her, and she kept coming, arching her back and crying out and scratching, while he moved strongly inside her, growing larger yet, then coiling his body and filling her with spreading fire.

58.
A BIG WOOFILY ONE

At three in the morning a cold front came through. They watched from the bed as the line of snow clouds came out of the American Heartland and over the Hudson, darkening the skies briefly before unleashing a cascade of brightening snow. Abruptly the land and night turned white, and snowflakes swirled against the window panes as the steam radiators hissed.

"I can't remember the last time it snowed this early in the season," Marcie said, entwining her fingers with his.

"God is urging change upon the land," Donovan said, only half-mockingly.

"I'm freezing."

He pulled the comforter up over her, and she snuggled around in it.

"It's only your mind."

"I want to stay in bed for a week. All weekend, anyway."

"Let's settle for all day Saturday," Donovan said. "Sunday is special."

"Why?"

"It's the Blessing of the Animals. I want to adopt a dog."

"Really? Can we really have a dog? I want a big woofily one, a St. Bernard or Newfoundland."

"English Sheepdog," Donovan countered.

"Irish Wolfhound."

"English setter. Let's see what they have."

"We can walk him together in the park. God, William, this is exciting. I wonder if I'm pregnant. What do you think?"

He ducked under the comforter and pressed his ear against her belly.

"I'm not sure. It's a possibility."

"I *could* be pregnant. I'm ovulating."

"You've been keeping track?" he asked.

"Yeah, well, sort of," she said, sheepishly.

"I'm crazy about you. If it's true, you can get maternity leave."

She rolled over to face him. "I've been thinking about that. And . . . honey . . . I'm not sure that I want to come back."

"What?" he asked, astonished, rolling toward *her*.

"I enjoyed being a cop when I was working Midtown South, and I did it for ten years. Then we got together for good and for the two years we've been working together I've been worried sick that it would end."

"What would end? Us?"

"That something would happen to you—or me. And if it did we'd leave no children. I'm not so afraid of dying as I am of dying without having had a child."

"Nobody's *dying,*" Donovan said.

"I'm thirty-six years old. I hope I'm pregnant."

"Me too."

"And if I am I'll have the baby and then see about going back to work. We can afford to live on your income."

"You'll get paid maternity leave."

"And they'll expect me to come back when the baby is six months old. Honey, I want to breast feed . . . I want to spend the first few years, at least, raising our child."

"Okay," he said, and kissed her.

"I want to get married and be a full-time mommy. I know that's not how you saw me."

"Oh, I always knew it was a possibility. But I'm afraid you'll get bored. Housewife ain't exactly your style."

"I don't mean to be a *housewife,* William. I'll find some way of keeping amused. I've been thinking of going back to law school."

"Yeah, I can see that. I could use free legal advice."

"Then you approve?" she asked excitedly.

"Yes," he laughed. "I *approve.*"

"Oh God I love you," she said, hugging him and covering his face with kisses.

"You're something else."

"Then it's settled. I'm going on maternity leave and . . ."

"Hey, wait a second. You have to get pregnant first."

She ignored that technicality. "I'm not going back on the street. I'm relieved of active duty anyway." It was customary to put officers on desk work following shootings, to allow Internal Affairs investigators time to assure the brass that all was up-and-up. "I simply won't go back. Thank God I don't have to get shot at anymore. To tell the truth, my life froze solid before my eyes when Carter and Weems got out of that jeep. I was terrified, and I never want to feel that way again. Or shoot anybody. And another thing: I want you taking it easy."

"I'm healthy as a bull," he protested.

"And nearly as intelligent. I mean, I don't want you getting into firefights."

"It ain't always my decision."

"Sure it is. You went out of your way to get shot at by the Estrada brothers. That's ending . . . *Daddy*. I want you to spend more time behind the desk."

Donovan harrumphed.

"No arguments! Maybe you can take the captain's exam. Work in a big office downtown."

"I'll never leave the streets. I'll never leave the West Side."

"We'll see about that."

A fierce wind came up and rattled the windows of the bedroom. Donovan got out of bed and fixed it, sticking a matchbook in the crack to create silence. The snow was falling harder, and he couldn't see the Jersey side of the river. Far below, the *West Wind* already had a white dusting of snow.

"We can move our stuff up from the boat this afternoon," he said.

"I am *not* getting out of bed."

"Okay . . . I'll carry it up."

"That's good. You're practicing being husbandly."

He slipped back under the comforter, beside her. She looped a leg over his.

"Do you think I'll have any problem with the Reverend Fred?"

"That idiot? He'll yell and scream but it will blow over. Let me handle it."

"Internal Affairs is supposed to report on Monday," she said.

"What can they complain about? Carter pulled a gun on you. You defended yourself. We have the gun. End of story. Let the Reverend Fred holler. He has to play to his constituency. Thank God that Spenser is dead."

"I was thinking of getting into social advocacy law," Marcie said.

" 'The saints preserve us, said Mrs. Jervis,' " Donovan said in a fake brogue. "How did you know about Fred Handon?"

"Jefferson called to apologize for drinking the Stoli. What was that all about?"

"He took a couple of hits from our bottle. He was in some mood."

"Nobody slept for days."

"Yeah," Donovan said. "That's what the problem was. Did he say anything else?"

"Only that he's ready to work with you on the Marcus case."

"Well, good. Things are returning to normal. Do you want a piece of Marcus, too? It can be your last, greatest moment."

She thought for a moment while toying with his chest hair.

"Is there anything to eat? I'm starved."

"I brought Chinese home with me. We can heat it up. Do you want to help me with Marcus or no?"

"I'll tell you," she said. "After I've eaten."

59.
"It Looked a Bit Like Lee Marvin to Me," Donovan Said.

Spending the first snow day of winter in bed was too good an idea to last. As had happened so often in the past, the arrival of Jefferson signalled the end of the good intentions.

He showed up at eleven, and rang the bell for a change. Donovan slipped the lock and his old friend walked in and into the kitchen, bearing bagels, which were fresh, and the morning papers.

He also had a liter of Stoli, which went in the freezer next to the remains of the old bottle. "Sorry about yesterday," he said to Donovan, who wore a terrycloth robe and made coffee.

"Forget it. Someone had to break the spell by drinking from that bottle. Best it was you."

"I meant sorry for the attitude. I was *tired,* y'dig?"

"I dig. Are you ready to talk about the shooting in Harlem?"

"Nothing to talk about. Carter pulled a gun on her and she plugged him. The other one, too. End of story. You want a bagel?"

"Yeah, toasted, with Swiss cheese."

"Me too," Marcie said, walking in wearing Donovan's white Oxford shirt and nothing else.

Jefferson smiled and said, "Hey, babe . . . *what it is!*"

"Whatever. What time is it?"

"Eleven."

"I'll have coffee too, decaf. I may go back to sleep."

"I'm making decaf," Donovan said, pressing the button on the coffee maker.

"You folks sure are living clean these days," Jefferson said.

"We're coming up hard on the year 2000. I want to greet the new millennium with a clear head."

"Clear this up first," Jefferson said, unfolding a copy of *The New York Times* and pointing to it. *"The Times,* which ain't exactly your sensational tabloid newspaper, has Page One'd the Marcus story. And of course the tabs are on it. Dig the *Post* headline—'MADMAN LOOSE IN CITY.' "

"Maybe let's all go back to bed," Donovan said.

"Can't do it. The Commissioner is on your case again—the brass and all the brasslets right down to the deputy-inspector level."

Donovan groaned. "What do they want me to do?"

"You got a one P.M. meeting at One Police Plaza, followed by a press conference."

"For once in my life, I don't have anything to say," Donovan said, pouring coffee.

"I guess they want you to explain."

"Explain what? That I warned them about driving Marcus out of the cathedral and into the city, but they did it anyway? The press will have a field day."

"What *is* a field day?" Marcie asked.

No one knew.

Jefferson said, "I suppose they want you to assure the thousands of people expected to show up for the Blessing of the Animals tomorrow that they have nothing to worry about."

"They don't. Marcus is currently haunting St. Pat's, in my opinion. Maybe he'll kill the cardinal and shift the focus of the investigation to midtown."

Marcie said, "Oh, that will reassure them. It will make midtown a desert island, and right in the middle of the Christmas shopping season."

"I am *not* in the business of guarding the Chamber of Commerce," Donovan said haughtily. He took a bite of bagel and Swiss cheese.

"Be that as it may, you better get ready for the Commissioner.

Since Bonaci went home and crashed, I picked up his files and spent a couple hours going over them."

He opened his briefcase and took out a thick folder. "I think I'm up to speed. Are you ready for a briefing?"

Donovan saw his quiet day in bed dissolving before his eyes. He turned to Marcie and tossed up his hands. "What can I do?" he asked.

"You have to work, I know how the game is played. Look, if you're going downtown I'm going to see my parents. Is that okay?"

"Sure. Of course. Take the Enola Gay if you like. She's in the garage."

"No, *thank you*. I'll use the Buick. Well, Thomas, you finally caught me in the act of going upstate to visit my terribly upscale parents. Any smart remarks? You want me to bring you a croquet ball or anything?"

"Not a word, babe. You're okay with me."

"Get on with the briefing," Donovan said.

Jefferson commandeered a roll of masking tape and stuck crime-scene pictures from all the murders up on the kitchen wall. The corpse photos were typically dispassionate, as if made using mannequins that had been decorated with phony blood. But the map of the cathedral and its grounds was alive with promise.

"The red crosses mark where the bodies were found," Jefferson said, taping the map to the wall. "Dale Charbaux got it in the Arts Chapel in the western end of the nave. Michael Avignon got it in the stone cutting shed north of the West Front and survived. Terry Loomis was murdered in a fire door off the choir. Herbert Spenser was killed in the Biblical Garden, which is south of the extreme eastern end of the building. And William Stewart got his halfway up the central portal of the west front. See any connections?"

Donovan said, "All but Avignon were killed within a few steps of the walls, which are ten or twenty feet thick and rife with old corridors, some of them forgotten. Marcus could have moved easily from his lair to all points where victims were found, with one exception."

"Avignon," Jefferson said.

"Yeah, I hate to say it, but I can't imagine where Marcus was going that night that Avignon followed him. There's something wrong with that whole yarn."

Jefferson said, "According to the report, Avignon followed Marcus all the way around the outside of the cathedral, from the front door to the Stone Cutting Yard."

"Practically a circumnavigation," Donovan said. "And entirely out of Marcus's pattern, which is to remain within the building and unseen. He ducked out of a stairwell to kill Spenser, but ducked right back in. What the hell was he doing prowling the perimeter the night that Avignon spotted him?"

"Nailing his theses to the wall," Jefferson said.

"Were that the case, he could have gone out the door, nailed up the paper, and gone right back inside. Poking around outside ain't his style."

"He turned on Avignon in the shed."

"And what was he doing *there?* Marcus, that is?" Donovan asked.

"Stealing limestone to sculpt on," Jefferson said. "I saw the photo of that bust he was working on. What the hell was it?"

"It looked like a bit like Lee Marvin to me," Donovan said. "Avignon must have spooked him by the door, which caused him to bolt south and east around the cathedral. Then, thinking he lost Avignon, he went on to the Stone Yard to steal material. After Avignon surprised him, Marcus ducked inside the nearest door, which is to the east, towards the gift shop."

Jefferson looked a bit soggy, disappointed, and admitted it. "I thought I had Avignon on that one," he said.

"I know you don't like him."

"The man is a psycho."

"Agreed, but he's a talented one. And his instincts are still among the best, nearly as good as mine. Did the lab come back with an analysis of the murder weapon?"

"Yes!" Jefferson said, "And that's the other thing." He shoved a piece of paper in Donovan's direction. "That mallet belonged to Langton, the master carver. It was one of his old ones, that he used in England. He claims he didn't know it was stolen until we asked about it."

"How many does he have?"

"Half a dozen. This one was last seen tucked under some old crap in the stone cutting shed, before Marcus got it."

"What did the lab say?"

"The head of that mallet looks like the Grand Canyon a hundred times over. There's all sorts of pits and scarrings. You couldn't wash the blood out of it if you used Drano. The lab identified four different blood groups in there, corresponding to the genotypes of Charbaux, Loomis, Spenser, and Williams."

"But not Avignon."

"Nope. And he lost some blood and scalp when he got hit."

"But not that much."

"Traces should be there. The lab was using high-end chromatography in the analysis and matching samples with preserved DNA from the victims."

"So what do you think? He hit himself on the head and made up the rest of the story?"

"I think that's possible," Jefferson said.

"Do you think that Avignon is Marcus?" Donovan asked. "All we really know about the man is that he's white. In the words of Brian Moskowitz, he's whiter than Dan Quayle."

"No one's that white. Avignon is a suspect. I know you don't want to hear that."

"On the contrary. I've wondered about him all along."

"What?" Jefferson asked.

"No one else has been able to get close to Marcus. Avignon practically fell over him. And, frankly, Avignon *is* a bit strange, even for my taste. I always figured he was merely suicidal, but when a morbid fascination with Armageddon keeps cropping up you have to wonder."

"You hung around with him," Marcie cut in. "You practically invited him to move in."

Donovan shrugged. "I was nice to the guy hoping to get him to talk. Look at it this way: Hitler loved dogs; while in his company it was a good idea to wag your tail. I did a passable imitation of an Alsatian. Which, by the way, I do *not* want. It's unbearable to think of two police persons owning a police dog."

"Are you guys going to the Blessing of the Animals?" Jefferson asked.

"Absolutely. Want to come?"

"Maybe. Who else do you have down as suspects?"

"Langton, of course. He hated Spenser and has no alibi, at least not for Spenser or Charbaux. He *was* accounted for during the other murders. Of course, we know now that Langton was the owner of the murder weapon."

"Motive?"

"Since when does a psychopath need a motive? The other suspects are Forrest, the prison poetry guy, and Brewer, the Brazilian ethnologist or whatever the fuck he is."

"Forrest is still missing," Jefferson said.

"Check on that. Try to find Brewer, too. The little prick has a lot of explaining to do. I discovered last night that he really doesn't have an alibi for the Spenser murder, and Brewer hit me with a real attitude the other day. I want to know why he was following Terry Loomis around."

"Will do."

"Brewer could be Marcus, even though he's not really big enough. Forensics's resident expert in Newtonian physics estimated from the angle of the blows and the height of the nail in the cathedral door that Marcus would run six-one or two and have a helluva right arm. Of all the suspects, only Langton fits that bill. Maybe Forrest; he's tall and lanky, and could work up a lot of angular momentum."

"If you say so."

"Avignon is a shrimp, only five-nine. Brewer ain't much

bigger. But I suppose you could leap in the air and . . . never mind, forget I said that."

"Already forgotten," Jefferson said.

"Did Bonaci ever get around to checking alibis on Langton's apprentices?" Donovan asked.

"Yeah, and all of 'em have alibis for at least two of the murders."

Half an hour and countless speculations later, Donovan and Jefferson finished breakfast and Marcie cleaned up the dishes. Jefferson took down the photos and packed up his files. "I'll get right on finding Forrest and Brewer."

"That's the first step," Donovan said. "And after we get back from downtown we'll go to St. Luke's and check on Avignon. I have a couple of questions for him."

"There *is* something you should know about the press conference," Jefferson said, in the queasy manner of someone avoiding the topic. "The Reverend Fred Handon."

Donovan groaned. "He's *not* going to be there."

"Rumor has it that he will."

"What's this about Handon?" Marcie asked, shutting off the hot water.

"You know how I feel about him, but there ain't nothing I can do about it. He's demanding a grand jury investigation of your shootings."

"So what? It's automatic when a suspect dies."

"It makes bigger headlines when he demands it," Donovan said.

"I'm not afraid to talk to a grand jury. It was a clean shoot."

"Of course it was," Jefferson said. "I'm just saying that Handon is making a stink. He may be at the press conference. He may drag a hundred of his paid supporters down to the Unit to picket us. Just so you know."

Marcie shook her head. "I don't have the patience for this nonsense. I really don't. I'm on desk duty anyway, and my commanding officer . . ."

"I like the sound of that," Donovan cut in. "Her *commanding officer.*"

"Just assigned me to drive upstate to visit my father. Didn't you, honey?"

"Absolutely."

"And that's where I'm going. I'll be there or in bed resting. Call me when the grand jury meets." She left the kitchen, heading for the bedroom to dress.

"Gutsy woman," Jefferson said.

"She's always been that way," Donovan said admiringly.

"Nice legs, too."

"Watch your mouth." He handed Jefferson a phone. "Make calls about Forrest and Brewer. I'll be ready in a few minutes."

60.

DONOVAN GETS PISSED

M aybe your stock would go up with the Commissioner if you didn't insist on riding to headquarters in a fifty-seven Chevy named after the plane that dropped the atomic bomb," Jefferson said, casting a wary eye on the gawking crowd of Christmas shoppers on Amsterdam Avenue to make sure he wasn't recognized.

"This is a *great* car," Donovan said, gunning the engine at a red light to make the point.

Amsterdam was filled with consumers despite the fact that the 1990s recession was in its second year. Couples with and without children lugged packages on both sides of the avenue and across the crosswalks. The small bodegas spilled lottery ticket buyers out onto the pavement, where they mixed with Saturday grocery shoppers and dog walkers and joggers trotting along to the sound of personal radios.

Donovan switched on the dashboard radio which, like every-thing else, was original equipment. "Please God, let me hear the voice of Murray the K," he said.

"You don't believe in God."

"But I do in Murray the K." Instead of an old DJ, the radio emitted a Vivaldi concerto. "I'll take it," Donovan said. "What did you think of the press conference?"

"I think you're lucky that Handon didn't show up."

"He'll be along. He always is. You know, I don't begrudge the black community a spokesman. Everyone needs an advocate who backs you totally. But I get a mite defensive when he goes after my woman."

"Handon ain't speakin' for me, Jack. Let's get that straight."

"I thought he was tied up with that protest in Jersey City. Let's not think about him. The Commissioner was pretty supportive."

Jefferson lowered his voice a register and mimicked a politi-cian: " 'The deranged individual who committed the horrible murders in the Cathedral of St. John the Divine is on the run and no longer a threat to the good people of this city. I have the utmost confidence in my men . . .' "

"The West Side Major Crimes Unit."

" '. . . to hunt down and bring to justice the worst serial killer in New York City since Son of Sam.' "

"You're very good," Donovan said, catching the green light and roaring on uptown, headed for St. Luke's Hospital.

"I only hope we catch the sonofabitch," Jefferson said.

"It'll be easier with you involved. Welcome back."

"Thank you, boss. Now, while you were gettin' your picture took I picked up some news on Forrest. His parole officer said he missed his weekly check-in and there was no answer at his apart-ment."

"Where's he live?"

"Four fifty-one Riverside. That's . . ."

"In the long block between 116th and 119th," Donovan said. "Nice block . . . one of the great ones on Riverside. How does an ex-con who pins poetry to a church wall afford that?"

"A good question. According to the cathedral, Forrest hasn't shown up for work since you found that hidden stairwell that pokes through the Poetry Wall. According to the parole officer, Forrest makes twenty thousand a year as a church aide."

"No way you can afford that address on that income. Forrest has got to be dirty. Do we still have an alarm out on him?"

"We sure do."

"Get us into his apartment. I want to check it out."

"I can have the key in an hour."

"Good. Now, what about Brewer?"

Peeking at papers on his clipboard, Jefferson said, "He's among the missing too. Hasn't been seen at the bar. Isn't at his apartment."

"Where's *he* live?"

"Broadway and 108th."

"Which corner?"

"Southwest."

"Above the Ideal?" he asked, mentioning a local Cuban restaurant.

"I think so."

"That building is more affordable, as much as any Manhattan building is affordable anymore. Did I mention that my landlord offered to slip me twenty-five thousand dollars if I give up the lease?"

"I hope you told him where to stick it."

"I do that every day of my life," Donovan said.

"Brewer has no visible means of support, so I don't know how he pays the rent."

"What do you mean? He's an ethnologist."

"What the hell's that?"

"Cross-cultural studies."

"Oh, that sounds like a booming field. I assume he teaches."

"He said he's at Columbia. Of course, what does that mean, *at* Columbia? Teaching, studying, or hanging out at the coffee shop?"

"Like I said, the man had no visible means of support."

"He could have been on a grant. Can you get me into his place, too?"

"Naturally."

"We'll go there after Forrest's place."

"What's next?"

"Avignon," Donovan said. "I want to see how his head is today."

Jefferson reconsulted his clipboard and came up with another fact. "His doctor's name is Baum, and he's at the hospital now."

Donovan ran an amber light, then crossed 110th Street and zoomed by the cathedral on his way to St. Luke's Hospital next door.

"Stewart's body ain't stopped bouncin' yet and already the cathedral is back in business."

Donovan asked what he meant, and got a flyer thrust into the air.

"How many trees do they cut down to print all these flyers?" Jefferson asked. "Now they're running an exhibit honoring American soldiers in South America. Did you know that the cathedral has an Armed Forces Chapel?"

"It must have slipped my mind," Donovan said, and pulled into a parking space reserved for official vehicles near the ambulance entrance.

Julian Baum, M.D., was an internist and neurologist who still made the time to drop in on the emergency room during peak hours which, on the Upper West Side, were late Friday and Saturday nights and on Welfare Check Day. A tall man with curly black hair and a cigar-thick mustache that he tinkered with while thinking, Baum had presided over several lifetimes worth of criminal head wounds.

Donovan and Jefferson found him in the doctor's lounge, drinking a Diet Coke and reading a *Medical Economics* article on investments. "I need your help," he told Donovan. "I need you to help me decide between a BMW and a Mercedes."

"I have never been able to understand why Jews buy German

cars," Donovan said. "One day they're going to drive you all back to Germany. Marcie's mother has one. It's insane."

"What do you drive?"

Jefferson said, "Lately, a bomb named after a bomb."

"A '57 Chevy that may be on the market if your patient upstairs dies," Donovan said.

"That would be Avignon. He told me about that car. He says it's worth a hundred thousand dollars. Is that true?"

"She's priceless, but not for sale. If Avignon kicks the bucket I plan to hold onto her. How *is* he doing?"

"Not bad. He'd be doing better if he listened to his friendly neighborhood neurologist, but does he?"

Donovan shook his head.

"Avignon has a fractured skull, a *bad* one. He lost quite a bit of blood before he was brought in, and if I can get him to hold still long enough I'll run a CAT scan."

"He says he blacked out the night before last—lost eight or nine hours and doesn't remember a thing."

"Entirely possible," Baum said. "I wouldn't be surprised by symptoms of brain damage, hopefully transient."

"Like?"

"Spatial disorientation. Crude visual hallucinations. Disorders of articulation. He took quite a blow to the left side of his brain."

"That's the logical side," Jefferson said. "He didn't use it much."

"Mainly I'm shocked that he walked out of here a few hours after his accident."

"After he was attacked."

"Right, attacked. So, Lieutenant, can you help me talk him into staying still for a CAT scan?"

"Sure. I'll threaten to drive his car off a pier if he doesn't cooperate."

"Let's go up and see the patient."

They followed Baum down the hall and rode an elevator to the fifth floor. Avignon's room was in the old wing on 113th street, off Morningside Drive. From all the windows on that side one could look almost directly down into the Stone Yard. In and around the cathedral, preparations were being made for the Blessing of the Animals. Workmen were erecting a wooden scaffold on the front steps from which the bishop would bless the elephant, camel, and other large beasts.

Avignon's door was ajar but the television blared with the old adventure show "Knight Rider," which featured a computerized car that talked.

Donovan smiled. "Here's what you should buy, Julie—a talking Trans Am."

"Just what I need."

Jefferson said, "I would like a talking car, but can you imagine trying to get laid in it? Having the damn car comment about your technique."

Baum swept open the door. "Visitors, Mr. Avignon," he announced, and then walked inside to find the room empty. "He's gone!" Baum exclaimed, then scurried to look in the bathroom. "He's run off again!"

Donovan looked out the window at the cathedral. "Now I'm really pissed," he said.

61.
WHEN THE GOING GETS WEIRD . . .

Four fifty-one Riverside was a seventy-year-old *I*-shaped building, painted white, with eight stories but a narrow frontage on one of New York's loveliest blocks. An awning covered the walk up to an entrance set between two arms of the *I*. Forrest's apartment was on the ground level, with unguarded thermal windows that opened just four feet above the pavement.

"Only a con would live in this place," Donovan said.

"A con or an eight-hundred-pound gorilla," Jefferson agreed.

"It's a snatch to lift this window and creep in to ransack the joint. Forrest must have bought another Uzi to keep under his pillow while he slept."

"It's easy to get out, though, for fast exits."

The janitor let them into a long studio, recently refurnished. It was basically one long room that had been divided by a new wall and a flimsy, hollow wooden door. A kitchenette was hidden behind louver doors, and a tiny bathroom occupied the space near the entrance.

The apartment was sparsely furnished but unexpectedly neat. Most of the furnishings were white and assembled from kits bought at Ikea, a Swedish furniture store in Elizabeth, New Jersey, across the river. "Check to see if Forrest has a car," Donovan said. "You can't get all this stuff from Jersey in cabs."

"I got no reference to a car, but I'll check."

There was a small square table set with a single place setting, a white candle in a white holder, and a pair of white salt and pepper shakers. A small computer desk, also white, held a Toshiba laptop computer and files for floppy disks. Donovan thumbed through them and found an annotated Bible as well as a chess program and one called "Tank Battle." There was also SmartCom, communications software that allowed Forrest to communicate with other computer users. Jefferson cranked it up and found within SmartCom's dialing memory the 800 number of a computer bulletin board in Austin, Texas, and another in Albany, New York.

"Computers are gonna revolutionize detective work," Jefferson said.

"They were supposed to do it ten years ago."

Prints carefully framed and hung depicted St. Bonaventure of Albano, author of *The Journey of the Soul to God,* Domenico Veneziano's "Saint Lucy Madonna," and da Vinci's "Virgin and Child with St. Anne." The closet was half full with clothes, mostly casual, but including one well-worn suit. The kitchen was well-stocked with healthful food and a few decorations. A color-ful poster revealed heart-healthy foods. A doodler had carved a Maltese cross in the wood frame of the spice rack.

A Rolodex gave Jefferson a list of contacts, including several in Bay Ridge, Brooklyn, where Forrest grew up.

"Have Moskowitz check out the addresses in Bay Ridge," Donovan said. "If I never go back to Brooklyn it will be too soon."

An hour spent perusing the apartment revealed nothing of certain importance, though Donovan thought that the computer bulletin board was promising. Computers are one thing cons can learn in prison, adding to what they already know about crime.

"No bus tickets, plane tickets, or hastily scribbled messages about midnight rides to Mexico," Jefferson noted.

"Check out the number in Austin," Donovan said.

Unlike Forrest's slice of prime real estate, Brewer lived in a classic West Side dive—a fifth floor walkup taken on short-term sublet from a Legal Aid lawyer who had decided to winter in Florida with his parents.

The tiny bedroom had a platform bed set smack in the middle of it, and two walls were lined with bookshelves. The lawyer's books were a mishmosh of legal tomes and leftist political trivia, and the only works that hinted at the owner's personality were half a dozen on growing up Jewish and a few more than that on surviving a divorce.

The living room was also tiny, with a nonworking fireplace that held the stereo and TV, and a red brick wall bearing a print of Max Beckmann's violent painting "The Night," as well as several cheaply framed photographs of Broadway crowd scenes. In the tiny kitchen, cockroaches ran dizzily around a cat dish.

"Where's the cat?" Jefferson asked.

"Try the bedroom closet. They always hide in there."

That's where they found the animal, a black-and-orange alley cat with a malformed left ear. Although professing a longstanding hatred of cats, Donovan opened a can of food for the beast.

Brewer's presence was sparsely indicated, mainly in the dining alcove. A corkboard by the seats-two dining table held phone messages, maps, and scribbled notes. There were lots of newspaper clippings about the Rain Forest Defense in general and Loomis and Spenser in particular. Donovan saw the clips and said, "So much for his wanting to get into Christie Gaynor's pants."

"Brewer is Marcus," Jefferson said.

"Either that or he had the hots for Terry Loomis, and nothing is out of the question these days."

"Why the clips about Spenser?"

Donovan tossed up his hands. "Don't know."

"What else is there around here?" Jefferson asked, and went on to uncover little. Brewer had packed his bags and split, leaving only a Sprint bill showing $405 in unpaid bills for telephone calls to Rio de Janeiro.

The calls were all to one number. "Trace them," Donovan said.

"Gotcha. But this guy is Marcus, no doubt about it. He doesn't care that we know. He left the clippings on the wall."

"I don't detect limestone dust around here, though," Donovan said.

"Maybe he showered before going home."

"An entertaining notion. I'll let you know what I think of it the next time I feel the call of nature. In the meantime, upgrade the alert on Brewer. I want him picked up for questioning in the murder of Herbert Spenser."

"Awright!" Jefferson exclaimed, sensing motion in the investigation and making the observation that it closely followed his arrival on the case.

"I wonder who the cat belongs to," Donovan said.

"Is it important?"

"No. It's just odd to sublet your cat along with your apartment."

"Maybe Brewer took her in. She looks like a stray."

"Odd sort of thing for a mass murderer to do," Donovan said.

"Maybe Brewer likes cats better than people. That would fit the psychological profile the department worked up."

"Humbug," said Donovan, who had less use for psychological profiles than he did for either computers or cats.

In their final burst of work for the day, Donovan and Jefferson let themselves into Avignon's studio in SoHo. The key ring that turned on the Enola Gay also opened the door to the studio, which was in a four-story converted loft building on Broome Street near the entrance to the Holland Tunnel. No one was home, at least not in the extravagantly expensive editing suite. The same could be said for the duplex apartment above. The door was locked with a code dialer and no one answered repeated rings. Nor was there excuse for a forced entry.

Clues to Avignon's whereabouts were nonexistent. He simply disappeared, leaving unattended a classic car and a multi-million-dollar television studio. He had been there, though, and shortly after clearing out of the crypt room he shared briefly with Donovan. Two tapes that had been shot in the Ikegami camera lay atop an editing machine, which Jefferson managed to get working.

They watched Avignon's tapes, more to fill Jefferson in on the sights and sounds of the first phase of the investigation than in hope of finding a clue to Avignon's whereabouts. The audio was erratic, film *noir*-ish, with voices coming and going in the general clamor. But the video was terrific, a real winner. "Two thumbs up," Donovan said enthusiastically, and Jefferson concurred.

"The man has talent, I admit. So maybe it helps to be a nut."

"Where the hell *is* he?" Donovan wondered, as he watched some of the last footage—that shot in and around the stairwell that led past the Poetry Wall to the crypt. In the dim light, Donovan saw reflections off the pool of water that stood, apparently forever, in the base of the stairwell. Then there was the Recycling Center, cans all over the floor, and a run across the side lot to the Peace Fountain. There, a disconsolate Donovan sat with head in hands.

"The Thinker," Jefferson said.

"I think I'm gonna have my portrait done in that position."

The tape went to black, and Jefferson shut it off. "When did he have time to run the tapes down here?" Jefferson asked.

"An excellent point. He said he passed out right after I saw him at the Peace Fountain."

"Are you sure you were with him during all of those murders?"

"Frankly, no. I have to think this over. Are you in the mood for an old-fashioned beer party? I mean, now that you drink."

"Unh . . . at Riley's? Jake's party?"

"Yeah. Let's meet Marcie there. She'll be on her way home from upstate by now. I've done some of my best thinking in Riley's."

"I remember one night you thought your liver was falling out," Jefferson said.

"You have that to look forward to if you keep drinking vodka straight," Donovan replied.

"Let's get back to Avignon—where was he when Charbaux was killed?"

"I never asked him. All I know is that he was one of the reporters who showed up to cover it. Remember, you and I let him into the cathedral. Then Avignon himself became the second victim, remember?"

"I dig. But there was no Avignon blood on the murder weapon, and if you ask me he could have faked it. Where was he during Loomis?"

"Well, he tried to get *me* into Christie Gaynor's pants . . ."

"Shit. Pasty-skinned Englishwomen are way too fey for you, bro. What then?"

"And then he split. Wait a second, I asked where Loomis was and I remember Avignon telling me that he went out for a smoke.' "

"How'd he know that Loomis was smoking unless he told him or spotted the motherfucker?"

"A good point," Donovan said. "There was a five minute period where Avignon could have been alone with Loomis."

"What about Spenser?"

"Let me think. No! He wasn't with me! I asked him if he wanted to go meet Spenser and he turned me down. I left

Avignon in the crypt and went up and talked with Spenser in St. Martin's Chapel, which is right by the Biblical Garden, where the body was found."

"That was when Spenser showed you the snapshots of Brewer," Jefferson said.

"Right. Spenser believed that Brewer was an agent of the Brazilian government sent to kill Loomis."

"Maybe he got his orders in the course of four hundred and five dollars' worth of phone calls to Rio," Jefferson said.

"Maybe."

"Brewer is Marcus and Avignon is in it with him. They faked the attack on Avignon to throw us off."

"Far from out of the question. Anyway, after talking with Spenser I went back down to the crypt to make some calls. Avignon wasn't there."

"And Spenser went out in the Biblical Garden to have a smoke. Hey—Charbaux, Loomis, and Spenser were all smokers. Maybe Marcus is being subsidized by the American Cancer Society."

"Stewart was the one who banned smoking in the cathedral," Donovan said. "Nice try, though."

"After Spenser's body was found, Avignon didn't turn up for two hours. Damn."

"He's in on it. I'm telling you. Him and Brewer. What happened at the Stewart murder?"

"That went down while Avignon was supposedly passed out in his car," Donovan said.

"During which time he was alive enough to get his tapes down to SoHo," Jefferson said, slapping a hand on the console. "The prosecution rests."

Donovan stood and stretched. "After Spenser's body was found and the Commissioner and I had our talk in the garden, Avignon talked me into plunging into the belly of the cathedral to track Marcus down. He said, 'He's hiding within these walls knowing that you can't resist going in after him.' And Avignon was right. In I went."

"With a killer two steps behind you, taping everything. Him and Brewer, I'm telling you. I can't say *why*, but that's how it happened."

"God, I hate television so," Donovan mused, glaring at the library of videotapes in a large display case that also held three Ikegami cameras. "Give me a snowy night, good food, pleasant company, and the Sunday *Times*."

"Amen. You wanna torch those tapes?"

"Nah. That's *Crystal Black*."

"Who?"

"Avignon's masterpiece, the compilation of depravity and gloom in New York City that he's been working on since Son of Sam. I've seen a bit of it; not bad. Maybe he *will* win the Academy Award."

"Can you accept the award from jail?"

Donovan ran his finger along the rows of tapes: "He's got every sickening moment this city has witnessed in the closing moments of the twentieth century. Including . . ."

Donovan went white and his finger froze on a black 3/4″ tape cartridge labelled, simply, "New York Marathon."

"What's that?" Jefferson asked, noticing the icicles forming on his boss's brow.

"Avignon never told me he shot the marathon," Donovan said.

"Give it here," Jefferson said, and soon plugged the tape into the machine.

"This is very strange," Donovan said, sitting down and gripping the edge of the console.

"What was that quote from that writer you like? Hunter Thompson?"

" 'When the going gets weird, the weird turn pro,' " Donovan said.

"Cueing the tape," Jefferson said, and the monitor again came to life.

They watched in muted horror as marathon runners coursed through Harlem and into north Central Park. That was what

Avignon wanted, of course, the contrast. White on black. Rich and poor. Well-heeled runners emerging from the dark gloom of Harlem into the white, upper-middle-class landscape of Central Park. Toward the end of the tape, there came a rumbling and a commotion. The camera shook as Avignon ran. Things blurred, and colors sped by. Then the shaking stopped and the focus settled down and Donovan saw himself, in the motorcycle cop's uniform, standing over the body of Jennifer Peel.

"Jennifer," Jefferson said.

"Yeah."

"That's you in your Rommel suit."

"Yeah."

On screen, Donovan looked up the hill and saw the two black teenagers frozen in time, staring down at him as they did in real life.

"That's them," Donovan said.

"Carter and Weems! That must have been shot right after they killed Jennifer!"

"That's what I thought, standing there."

"They were bad guys—killed Jennifer and sold death to teenagers. No tears for Carter and Weems. But what about Avignon?"

Donovan said, bitterly, "He shot the footage right after Jennifer died. Then he walked away and never mentioned it."

The tape went on a bit, but the camera wasn't being aimed anywhere in particular. It got mainly feet; runners and their shoes, Avignon's trademark sneakers, and a glimpse of cowboy boot before the tape ran out and that was that. No record of where Avignon went after shooting that footage. The next tape told the story of Marcus, beginning with coverage of the death of Dale Charbaux. Avignon was one of the horde of TV reporters who covered the story more or less anonymously. Donovan vaguely recalled letting him pass police lines that day.

"I am going to Jake's beer party," Donovan said. "And I am having a drink."

"I'm with you, Bill."

"We'll take these tapes with us."

62.

THE THIRTIETH MISSION

Riley's was done up like New Year's Eve and Independence Day combined, with red, white, and blue crepe streamers and multicolored metallic balloons festooned to the backbar mirror and the fake gaslights that pierced the old copper walls. The plantation of cacti in the front window was freshly scrubbed and watered, and even the old neon Budweiser sign in the window had been gone over with Lysol.

The juke box was outfitted with records that actually were recorded during the previous decade. The ice machine popped like a popcorn popper, churning out cubes for a crew of regulars half of whom had gone healthy and would use the ice for soda or sparkling water. No matter; the door had a sign reading "Closed for Private Party" and George Kohler stood by, admitting only those who had earned membership in the club by wrecking their livers and elevating their blood pressures.

The five or six who Donovan thought remained regulars had swollen to nearly a hundred, and Jake's contribution increased to $1000 to pay for it all. He dressed for the occasion in a rented tuxedo with a grand red cummerbund, and stood by the door next to George, the two of them forming a receiving line straight out of vaudeville, considering George's towering height, ponderous girth, and Paul Bunyan demeanor.

Donovan had gone home to meet Marcie. The two of them returned dressed somewhat more appropriately; he in his Harris tweed sports jacket with corduroy slacks, and she in a very short black wool sheath (Jefferson's compliment to her legs was duly reported, and she decided to show off), with three strands of pearls. Her normally straight hair was done in a pile of black curls, and she vowed to keep it that way.

Jefferson had gone to the Unit and then home to change and was expected within the hour. Everyone else was there. Gus Keane, the former bartender, showed up in his railroad engineer's cap, recalling the time he installed his childhood Lionel trains in the gutter along the bar and served customers by remote control. Another old bartender, Pat Fallon, a sports trivia expert and one-time "Jeopardy" finalist, was already winning bets based on 1956 Brooklyn Dodgers lore. Rounding out the roster of Riley's bartending alumni was Rosie Rodriguez, who during an earlier, less complicated age, was Donovan's beloved. Now married and gloriously pregnant, she wished Donovan and Marcie well and appeared to mean it.

Jack D'Amato was there with his new wife, who was Jewish, and before the night was done would engage Donovan in a long, nearly Talmudic discussion of why Upper West Siders seemed incapable of marrying their own kind. Little Harold the electrician still worked at the Museum of Natural History. He drank beer with Littler Harold the midget actor, whose main claim to fame (other than having once socked George in the knee) was having played an Ewok in *Return of the Jedi*. Waldo Pepper did something involving carpentry, though no one was really sure just what. Wes Jackson, the black lawyer, looked prosperous that year, as did Kevin Morgan, who claimed to be a Wall Street arbitrager. The few Riley's customers who knew what that meant had cast many wagers during the 1980s on when he would be indicted, but he never was.

"This was like the time I went to my high school reunion," Donovan said, seating Marcie in his favorite spot near the front window. "The ones who hadn't become priests were convicted felons."

"These are good people," she said, sweeping an arm around the crowd. "A little strange, but as we know you like that."

"I like *you*."

"That's all? Like?"

"I love you," he said, and kissed her.

"My parents send their love. We're expected for the holiday."

"Which one, Christmas or Hanukkah?"

"Hanukkah. *We're* making Christmas this year."

"Are we indeed? In my apartment?"

"Our apartment."

"We've got some heavy fixing up to do. Remind me to buy a scrub brush and brown soap so I can do the floors. And your stuff still has to be brought up from the *West Wind.*"

"As soon as we're finished with Marcus."

"We. Does that mean you're helping me?"

"From now on we do everything together," she said.

"And if you quit the police department and go back to law school?"

"I'll still help you on cases. I'll be a freelance detective. But I haven't made up my mind what to do. I spoke with my father about it and he'll support whatever decision I make."

"Meaning?"

"Meaning that you won't have to come up with tuition for Columbia Law, for one thing."

'Thank God," Donovan said. "Innkeeper!"

George came over, arms already folded in disapproval. "What are we having tonight, a Shirley Temple?"

"Gimme a Bud and shut the fuck up," Donovan said.

"What's the occasion?"

Donovan shrugged. "The country is deep in recession. There's a war brewing in South America. The banks are foreclosing on the co-ops. But I just saved ten or twenty grand a year and Jake just *made* twenty grand. The common people of the Upper West Side are in the chips again."

"And Avignon is out of our lives," Marcie said.

"So a madman is on the loose in New York City. What else is new?"

"Make that one Bud and one Guinness," Marcie said. "One of us has to have class."

"Coming up," George said, and shortly presented two bottles.

Donovan eyeballed his for a long moment, thinking of how bottles sustained him during the long years that followed the murder of his father, and then thinking of how badly his liver hurt and his soul ached as a result of it. He brought the bottle halfway to his lips, then said, "Nah," and put it back down.

"I'll have a club soda after all," he said.

"I'm very proud of you," Marcie said. "Now make it a seltzer. Club soda has too much sodium."

"Times have *really* changed," George said, and produced a seltzer.

Donovan sipped his seltzer and Marcie her stout. "Thanks for letting me make the decision not to drink that Bud," he said.

"I knew you didn't want to mutate back into a winged creature of the night."

"I was never that bad."

"No, but you were closing in on it."

George said, "I'm glad I'm making money tonight, 'cause this is it for this bar. A month more and we're bankrupt. Morty is putting the joint up for sale."

"What's he asking?" Donovan said idly.

"Four hundred grand. Normally a bar in this location would go for six hundred grand, but the market really sucks these days."

"A bit out of my range, even at four hundred," Donovan said, then got an idea and waved Jake over. "I got an investment for you."

"What?"

"Buy Riley's. Morty wants four hundred thousand and I think you can get financing with ten percent down."

"That's forty thousand down. I got twenty. Well, nineteen after tonight. And what good would this place be anyway? Nobody drinks anymore. The only places making money are those that sell food."

"Turn it into a restaurant," Donovan said.

"Can't be done," George said.

"Yes it can," Marcie said, her eyes blazing. "There's no decent restaurant for five blocks in either direction, so there's a need. And four hundred thousand *is* a steal. All we have to do is move the bar to the back and put tables in the front. Then we open up the facade and install a sidewalk cafe. It's perfect."

"We?" Donovan asked.

"Jake and me. I can get the rest of the down payment from my father for Christmas."

"Or Hanukkah," Donovan said.

"Better as a wedding present."

"You're serious about this, aren't you?"

"Of course I am. It's a way for us to be together. You work upstairs in the Unit and I work down here. That way I can keep an eye on you—make sure you're acting husbandly and not getting shot at all the time."

"Acting husbandly?"

"Responsibly. Remember, you could be a father in nine months."

"Are you guys having a blessed event?" Jake asked.

"We had a forgetful evening," Donovan explained. "Marcie forgot her diaphragm. Hell, we're getting married anyway." Suddenly excited, he said, "You can bring the baby to work in the restaurant with you. I can see him all the time."

"You can see *her* all the time. And I like the idea of you hanging around a classy restaurant better than a bar."

"What about law school?"

"It can wait. Donovan, I'm excited."

"Me too."

She wrapped her arms around him and gave him a gigantic hug, followed by a wraparound kiss that quickly grew so steamy that the revelers in the front end of the bar offered a round of applause.

When they broke apart, she said, "Where's Morty?"

"In the back taking inventory," George said.

"I'm going to make him an offer he can't refuse," Marcie said, and headed in that direction, the crowd parting to let her by.

"What have you gotten me into?" Jake asked, highly intrigued if a mite frightened.

Donovan put an arm around the shoulders of his old friend. "Warm up the sake, son," he said. "You are about to take off on your thirtieth mission."

63.
THAT UZI HE BOUGHT FROM AN URBAN ARMORER

At half past midnight Jefferson blew in, full of piss and vinegar. After clearing the receiving line and turning down a vodka in favor of a mineral water, he collared Donovan over by the peanut machine.

"What news?" Donovan asked.

"All three of 'em—Avignon, Brewer, and Forrest—are still missing, but I just checked the sensors and there indeed is activity."

"Let's hear it."

"Brewer has no known connection with Columbia. I got the faculty secretary out of bed and she never heard of him."

"I had a feeling that was a line. You like a guy and give him the benefit of the doubt. In this neighborhood, people *do* things like study cross-cultural differences. It was a wholly plausible yarn. Damn shame he made it up."

"Moreover, a call to the International Association of Ethnologists turned up zippo, too."

"Any hint what he really does? I mean, other than lie and maybe murder people?"

"He came into the country on a visitor's visa in September. Since you let your subscription to *People* lapse, you probably don't realize that was the same month that the Rain Forest Tour hit the northeast as part of its national circuit."

"I would never have made that connection. Thank you."

"The outfit played Boston, Hartford, Albany, Syracuse, Philly, and the Meadowlands before coming to New York. The snapshots that Spenser showed you with Brewer in them were taken in Boston, Hartford, and the Meadowlands. Apparently, Brewer followed Loomis and company on several occasions."

"I don't get it," Donovan said. "All that trouble just to get the occasion to ambush Loomis and Spenser . . . was Spenser on the tour?"

"No, just at the cathedral."

"Just to ambush Loomis with a stone-working mallet? Why didn't he just shoot the sonofabitch?"

"That's what I would have done."

"And why kill him anyway? Is there any connection between them?"

"Not that I can find," Jefferson said.

"What about the phone calls to Brazil?" Donovan asked.

"All went to a private residence in Rio. I'm trying to find out who lives there."

"What about Forrest?"

Jefferson checked his clipboard. "Moskowitz made a pass by his parents' house, which is on Fourth Avenue and 99th Street. You know that area?"

"I rode down it on a motorcycle recently, that's all. I'm not a Dodgers fan, Thomas, and have no fascination with Brooklyn lore. All the good people who grew up there left. Mel Brooks. Barbra Streisand. Woody Allen. I'm a third-generation Yankees fan, which is as much of a cross as I care to bear these days."

"Be that as it may, Forrest has not been seen. At least that's what his folks say. The last time he visited them was in October. They saw him once at the cathedral and once at his apartment, which they're subsidizing, by the way, but not in the past two weeks. He called home three days ago. That was the last contact."

"So they say," Donovan noted.

"Moskowitz also checked with the local cops and bartenders and other dignitaries. No mention of Forrest, other than his 1983 bust for armed robbery. The arresting officers considered him something of an amateur; they doubt he could shoot that Uzi he bought from an urban armorer."

"From a what?"

"As for the computer bulletin board in Austin, Texas, I rang it up myself from the Unit. Would you believe it belongs to the Prison Bible Study Society? They have this deal where you can download Bible study shit. You wanna know where Jesus and the Apostles hung out at a given time?"

"I'm going to church in the morning," Donovan said. "I'll ask around."

"No one at the Blessing of the Animals will know. Better ask about fleas. As for the Albany bulletin board, it's some social work kinda deal. Anyway, Forrest had a lot of correspondence with Prison Literacy. You said he hung up prisoners' poems."

"What about Avignon?"

"Yeah, well I had our experts go over his videotape and blow up the frames of Carter and Weems. That's them, all right. Practically caught in the act. That will make it easier for Marcie when dealing with Reverend Fred. In case you hadn't heard, he's announced a demonstration for Monday outside the grand jury room."

"That's wonderful," Donovan said.

"Where is the little lady?"

"Out back, negotiating to buy this bar so she can turn it into a restaurant."

"Say what?"

"A flight of fancy that will be forgotten by morning. You will join us tomorrow, won't you? I'm bringing home a big, woofily dog and will need your help getting him into the car."

"Okay. Did you pick a breed yet?"

"I'm homing in on an English setter."

"Sounds good. I . . ."

Jefferson was interrupted when Marcie came flying out of the back room, waving a napkin on which figures had been jotted. "Hi, Thomas," she said, and to Donovan, "Honey, I worked out a deal. Morty will take three hundred fifty thousand dollars if we get financing by the end of the year. I called my father, who will put up the rest of the money for the down payment. We'll get a loan for the renovations. This is a wonderful wedding present, honey. I love you."

"I thought you said she'd forget by morning," Jefferson said.

"Forget what?" Marcie asked.

"That you promised me an English setter," Donovan said hastily.

64.
"I Love the Smell of Wet Spaniels," Marcie Said.

D onovan was shocked to find that he liked it; more than that, he found that the Blessing of the Animals answered the question he had come to ask, however unwittingly: Why?

"Why did they put me through all that *crap?*" he asked, rhetorically.

Recognizing the symptoms of a monologue, Marcie simply held tight his arm and walked with him up the expanse of stone steps, the two of them tiny figures in a press of men, women, children, and animals.

"They said they loved me, then imprisoned me for eight years in a place where women were evil figures with white knuckles looming over you with a variety of punishments. For whispering, a whack on the back of the hands with a ruler. For talking, a shot across the back with a yardstick. For *talking back,* Timmy Reilly had his tiny head rammed into the blackboard. The nun put one hand on the back of his belt and the other on the back of his neck and ran him across the room and into the blackboard. That was in the 1950s. Nowadays if a nun did that she'd be on 'America's Most Wanted.' "

"No wonder Timmy went into homicide."

"And, once in the homicide field, it was only a stroke of luck that put him on the side of the good guys," Donovan said. "Enough of my classmates joined the battle on the side of the enemy. So I ask: Why?"

"Why what, exactly?"

"Why have the organized followers of a basically good man, maybe even a prophet, devised such a variety of evils? For two thousand years the church has done little more than create oppression, mainly against nonbelievers but also against women and children. I have hated organized religion since the day they put me in Catholic school. Yet today I find myself strangely drawn to this ceremony."

"That's because it's not a Catholic church."

"That's one plus."

"And there's music and architecture and animals."

"That's another. Where the hell is Jefferson?"

"He said he'll be an hour late but will find us. Get us two programs, would you?"

Donovan slipped a kid five bucks and got two guides to the eighth annual Feast of St. Francis. "Did I tell you that Francis is my confirmation name?"

He hadn't.

"Confirmation is kind of a Christian bar mitzvah, but you don't get presents. You do get to give yourself an optional fourth name if you can find a saint who grabs you. I took Francis after St. Francis of Assisi, who was into animals, or so the story goes. His actual feast day is October fourth, but they celebrate the Blessing of the Animals in November when it's colder so the smell isn't overwhelming."

They stepped inside the nave, and Marcie took a whiff and said, "Oh, *nice*. I love the smell of wet spaniels."

"I want an English setter," Donovan said.

The cathedral was packed, the most crowded that Donovan had ever seen it. The nave was an undulating carpet of men and women and pets, mainly dogs and cats but including caged birds and other small pets as well as snakes, monkeys, and ferrets. A camel, an elephant, and a yak were expected, but only outdoors. A platform had been erected on which the bishop would stand while blessing them. School children carried rabbits and hamsters, turtles and frogs. A couple carried brown and white gerbils.

The Paul Winter Consort played *Missa Gaia,* the earth mass, and celebrants held up programs to sing the praise of all living things. The music was fine and the singing spirited. Donovan recalled his jazz-club days, hitting every joint from Canal Street up to 155th. Standing tall amid the crowd was a robed black man with green-orange hair, swaying rhythmically, blissfully. Donovan thought of Sun Ra, whose jazz "solar arkestra" he used to hear at Slug's in the East Village in the mid-1960s.

They made their way to the front of the nave along the right side, far enough into the cathedral to note that while the barricades had come down from around the door in the Poetry Wall, the door itself stood slightly ajar, protected only by some yellow crime scene tape. That slight hint of police presence (undercover cops were everywhere, some with dogs) bothered no one. The celebrants carried on as if nothing had ever gone wrong in the cathedral, and soon Donovan forgot about business and enjoyed being swept up in the moment.

As had happened so often lately, a gentle breeze of happiness came over him. The Blessing of the Animals was neither smiling faces on lapel buttons nor singing deer in Disney movies. It wasn't feel-good television, Coca-Cola commercials with a heavenly choir atop a grassy knoll, and certainly not the Ice Capades. It was thousands of living things, men and women and children and animals, in a gigantic kennel that throbbed with music and barks and fleas. There was something bitingly real about the experience, and joyous. Donovan found himself swaying to the music, that and making eye contact with a sassy blue-and-yellow macaw that perched on the shoulder in front of him.

"Nice, isn't it, Lieutenant," a Portuguese-accented voice said.

Donovan and Marcie had been joined by Arturo Vega, security chief to the late Terry Loomis. A tall, swarthy man wearing a Burberry, he carried a brown, blue, and silver ball of fur that he identified as a four-month-old Yorkshire terrier puppy.

"He's beautiful," said Marcie, who stroked the animal atop its tiny head, between two gigantic ears.

"*You* are beautiful. The lieutenant did not tell me he had such a woman."

"I'm no secret. You must be new in town."

Donovan introduced them, then said, "What are you doing here, Vega? The Rain Forest Tour is off in Ohio someplace, isn't it?"

"Cleveland, yes. I was sacked."

He said it with a shrug, so having been fired didn't seem to have bothered him much. Vega had an incorrigibly cheery personality, leading others to believe that he should have been in politics or public relations.

The mass reached that portion known as the offertory, which in this case was trumpeted by elephant recordings and the Forces of Nature Dance. Between the jungle sounds and the barking and an occasional squawk from the macaw, conversation was conducted discreetly, but without interfering.

Donovan said, "I guess it's hard to hold onto a security job once your boss has been killed. Sorry."

"Actually, I was hired to protect Miss Gaynor, so to that extent I did my job. I would never have let *her* wander out for a cigarette. I was taking a chance in letting you in alone with her."

"Let's not make too much of that," Donovan said, *sotto voce*.

"I understand perfectly."

"What are you doing now?"

"Me? Oh, I think I will settle in New York. Already I have

family here. You have met Teddy. The two of us are looking for an apartment."

Donovan said, "The Yorkie is cute. I'm in the market for a setter myself."

"They are good dogs, too. I am telling you, Lieutenant, I like this celebration of animals. I come from a country with many wonderful species. I enjoyed being with the rain forest people, I really did. Don't care much for their music, though."

"We agree on both counts."

"In fact, because of my love for animals I intend to take communion today. Will you join me?"

"God forbid. I don't do religion. I only came here to buy a dog."

"Really, Lieutenant, it is a very special occasion. What harm would it do you to say a prayer for the animals? You must learn to loosen up. If you had a bad experience with religion—most Irishmen did—then do not pray for God or any of his minions, in whom I do not much believe myself. But pray for the animals. Pray for the earth."

"He's right, darling," Marcie said. "It won't kill you."

"The last time I prayed was in 1962 and I'm still ashamed of that."

She said, *"I* am going to, and you can join me."

"You're half Jewish," he said.

"Jews pray too."

"They don't *pray* to God. They *negotiate* with him. What am I getting myself into?"

"Stop arguing with your future wife. Arturo, may I hold the puppy for a moment?"

"Certainly," Vega said, gently laying the puppy in her cupped hands.

Marcie slipped to her knees just as began the *Sanctus and Benedictus qui venit*. Smiling, Vega squeezed Donovan's shoulder, urging him down to join her.

"In my country we have a strong feeling for inevitability," he said. "The woman loves you and you obviously love her. If not for the puppy, pray for her. Say a little prayer. What harm will it do? There may be a God and he may be listening."

"I'm going to regret this," Donovan said, but when he got to his knees beside his beloved and looked down at the helpless ball of fur in her hands, he saw something akin to holiness.

Vega was right. There was something wonderful about this *Missa Gaia,* the earth mass. Feeling good about it was wholly unexpected. Once again, his old hardbitten cynicism was fading before the new feelings coursing through his body. Together and healthy and in love, he *was* open enough to say a harmless prayer, if only to show Marcie that he would try anything for her.

Now if he could just remember the words to the Lord's Prayer.

No matter. Words are transient. He pressed his hands together and closed his eyes and thought of Marcie and how wonderful it was to be alive, straight, and in love.

Then out of the music and the murmurs and the animal sounds came the unmistakable click of an automatic pistol being cocked. Donovan heard a guttural rasp cry "murderer" followed by the roar of a 9mm. His muscles jerked tight and he grabbed his chest, a notion of death flicking across his eyes, and then he realized that it wasn't he who had been hit.

Arturo Vega jerked and tumbled to the floor, blood soaking his Burberry from a softball-size exit wound in his chest. Shot in the back, he sprawled next to Donovan and Marcie, who covered up the orphaned dog as one might a baby. "I don't have my gun!" she gasped, terrified to her soul.

Donovan drew his weapon as he rose, eyes ablaze with fury. Men and women screamed and a row of folding chairs went over as the assassin made a wild attempt at escape.

The crowd parted in panic and dogs barked frantically in fear. The assassin half stumbled, half ran, toward the door that was left ajar in the middle of the Poetry Wall. Donovan moved after him, not running so much as walking swiftly and deliberately and lining up a clear shot.

The man wore blue but had black hair. He grasped the door in his right hand and yanked it open, shredding the yellow crime scene tape that popped audibly amidst the organ music and the barking. He looked into the dark stairwell and then back at his pursuer, and in that instant their eyes met.

"Brewer," Donovan said, and raised his Smith & Wesson.

They were only ten feet apart.

"Donovan. I'm sorry."

And he jerked the gun upwards and fired a round toward the upper reaches of the cathedral. Donovan pulled the trigger three times and Brewer's body was hurled backwards through the Poetry Wall and slammed against the stone in the stairwell. The gun clattered downstairs followed by the body, which rolled and tumbled down a circular flight, coming to rest atop a square design etched into the dry bed of the stairwell.

65.

TOP COP KILLS KOOK; DETAILS P. 3

That was how the *Post* played the story, reflecting better than ever the tabloid headline-writer's nightmare— finding a monosyllabic alternative to the word "murderer." With more space as well as additional perspective, *The Times* ran its story far back in the Metro section, near the AIDS deaths, and even allowed the possibility that Chico Brewer was *not* the madman known as Marcus.

That was not a possibility that Donovan alluded to in public. He had long known that the tabloid press and television news, while pains in the ass always, were his friends. They were simple, predictable, and easy to manipulate, and loved his pithy statements. "I was into sound bites before Reagan ever heard of them," Donovan bragged on occasion. So when the first reporters showed up to cover the short life and sudden death of Chico Brewer, Donovan said, "Well, boys, I got him," and walked away with his bride-to-be and the Yorkshire terrier puppy she had inherited in a rather spectacular manner.

"Got who?" Jefferson asked upon finding Donovan and Marcie perched on the steps behind the Poetry Wall, looking down at the technicians who were scouring Brewer's remains.

"Brewer," Donovan said.

"Good work, boss! I *told* you he was Marcus."

"He ain't nobody," Donovan scoffed. "Just another poor dope grabbing a little revenge."

"He tried to kill you," Marcie stammered.

"And should have. I'll be damned if I'll ever get on my knees again except maybe to fix the kitchen sink."

"What's that furry thing in your lap?" Jefferson asked her.

"A puppy."

"Times sure do change. That's awful small for an English setter."

Donovan tossed up his hands. "The roll of the dice. The next dog will be a little bigger. But Brewer didn't try to kill me. His target was Vega."

"Who is he?" Jefferson asked.

"Terry Loomis's ex-security chief, a former Rio cop. Let's find out a little more about him. Here are his papers."

Donovan handed over a passport and other documents taken from Vega's pocket.

"Brewer took a shot at you before you shot him," Jefferson said.

"No he didn't. He said, 'Donovan, I'm sorry,' and fired at the ceiling. Is that what they call that thing way the hell up there? A ceiling?"

"Beats me."

"My gut reaction is that Brewer was following Vega, not Loomis and certainly not Spenser, and that's why his picture was taken in all those places. Brewer killed Vega after calling him a murderer, and then provoked me into killing *him*. Got it?"

"Not entirely."

"Brazil is a Catholic country. Catholics kill each other, not themselves."

"Then Brewer isn't Marcus?" Jefferson asked.

"He's still too short. No, he's not Marcus. I'm not absolutely sure, though. Check Vega's background and that phone number Brewer called in Rio."

"I did. The number was Brewer's house. No record of who he talked to."

"I don't mind letting everyone think that he's Marcus, in the hopes it may flush out the real item, which from where I sit on the steps of this delightful mausoleum is either Forrest or Langton."

"Or Avignon."

"He's also too short. Nonetheless, I would like to get my hands on the sonofabitch. He's guilty of *something,* and I plan to nail him for it."

A technician climbed the stairs and thrust a see-through document bag into Donovan's hands. "It's from him," the man said, indicating the body. "And it's addressed to you."

"Curiouser and curiouser," Donovan said, and read the handwritten note. It said: "Dear Lieutenant. I am truly sorry for causing you trouble, but you must know that I am no madman. Arturo Vega is responsible for the death of my son, Carman, who as a 14-year-old ran away from the home of his mother (my estranged wife) and joined a gang in the slum area of Rio de Janeiro known as City of God. Vega was the police sergeant who led the death squad that killed more than 300 children, including my only son, in City of God during the summers of 1988 and 1989. He escaped Brazilian justice but he shall not escape mine. This note is for you in the event of my death. Pray for me. Signed, Antonio (Chico) Brewer."

Jefferson whistled between his teeth. "Do you believe that?"

"Check Vega's background."

"And what was that phrase he used? City of God?"

"Three small words. The title of a book by St. Augustine. And

238

a phrase used by Marcus in the note he nailed to the door. The cathedral is the 'City of God' and he's its protector."

"Brewer using the same phrase is some coincidence," Jefferson said.

"As a symbol it works equally well with foolish hope and hopeless tyranny," Donovan replied.

"The press chooses to believe that Marcus is dead."

"And who am I to disappoint my friends in the press?" He got up and led the party out through the Poetry Wall and back into the nave, where he was gratified to see that the Blessing of the Animals was back in full swing. Music played, dogs barked, cats meowed, gerbils cowered terrified in cages, and the blue-and-yellow macaw was having a lively squawk with a yellow-casqued hornbill sitting a few shoulders away.

"The ability of New Yorkers to ignore tragedy is frightening," Donovan said.

"It's one thing that keeps us in business," Jefferson agreed.

"Tonight I prayed for the second time in thirty years, and the guy who talked me into doing it got blown away. I thought my number was up, Thomas. My first reaction was to protect my woman . . . sorry, honey, for that little burst of sexism . . ."

She nodded mutely, and he sensed the silent lump in her throat.

"My second reaction was that it teaches me right for putting faith in God. Now when I look at these people, all peaceful and in apparent bliss, praying with their dogs and cats and raising money to save the whales and the rain forest, I have to think. Organized religion has caused nothing but trouble, including a lot of personal grief in my life. Now, in the closing moments of the twentieth century some people have gathered together in the world's largest Gothic cathedral to save trees and whales. Upon reflection, I approve."

"You do?" Jefferson said, but only a little surprised.

"If religion must be organized, let it be organized to do something useful."

"It do beat all hell out of the Spanish Inquisition," Jefferson said.

"Not to mention burning abortion clinics."

He looked to Marcie for the approval he had come to expect whenever he stepped back from his policeman's role to voice a progressive opinion. But instead he saw her tight-lipped and shivering, not in cold but in fear, clutching the tiny dog to her bosom as if it were her own baby. Jefferson saw it, too, and glancing in Donovan's eyes exchanged the sort of compassion that men and women in uniform everywhere get when one of their own is shellshocked.

"This is like in wartime," Jefferson said, quietly so only Donovan could hear.

"I'm taking her home. I'll call you at the Unit in an hour or two."

66.
AN ONOMATOLOGIST'S NIGHTMARE

She sat on the couch by a window overlooking the Hudson, with a comforter wrapped around her like a baby's blanket and the puppy in her arms licking her face. Donovan sat on the arm of the couch playing with her hair.

The late afternoon sun was bright and flooded the room with healing brightness.

"I adore you," Donovan said. "I worship the ground you walk on. Let me take care of you forever."

"You're not disappointed in me?"

"Never."

"I don't know what happened."

"You're shellshocked. Too much has happened. You need time off. Maybe you *should* quit the force and buy Riley's."

"I intend to. I can't take it anymore. You're used to this life. Shooting people and getting shot at is something you take for granted."

"It was a lot easier when I could drink away the memory of it. And when I had no particular reason to live, other than to shoot and get shot at another day. Now I have more. I have you. I have it all."

"And that's something I never want to lose," she said. "To tell the truth, I never was much of a street cop. Sure, my marksmanship scores were great—on the firing range. But for the most part, I did undercover work in white-collar crime. Or played a hooker to trap johns. Remember those days?"

"Yeah. I dug the fishnet stockings with the garters."

"And the only time I was in a firefight before this week I had a shotgun and the perp carried an old six-shooter. Hardly fair, when you think about it. When I looked at Carter and Weems all I could feel was this incredible rage and I wanted to kill them. Not just to kill them, but to grind their ashes into the dust. Does that sound horrible?"

Donovan shook his head.

"And today at the cathedral, when that gun went off I had this image of you lying there dead, shot by Marcus or Frank Estrada or any of the dozens of guys who would love to kill you. Honey, I couldn't live if I lost you."

"I'd be lost without you, too."

"I'm finished being a cop. I'm opening a restaurant on Broadway. I hope you're not disappointed."

"Hell, I'll be your biggest customer. It will be kind of nice to have a place to hang out where I don't have to get into a big argument over booze."

She held up the puppy, which licked Donovan's nose. She laughed. "You have a very kissable nose."

"I do?"

"Very. Teddy—let's keep the name, he does look like a Teddy bear—is our first baby. We'll get you a setter next payday."

"Let's wait. I'm back on sheepdogs at the moment."

"Okay. But I want a baby, a regular baby, and I want it soon. I'm 36 years old. Like they said in *The Big Chill,* here I sit on my ticking biological clock. I want *two* babies . . ."

"And a big woofily dog."

"And I want to start now. If I'm not pregnant I want to be in a month. We'll take my severance pay and buy nursery furniture. No, that's bad luck."

"That's superstition."

"We'll deal with it when the rabbit dies. Isn't is possible to get pregnant without killing rabbits?"

"I'll ask Jefferson to look into it."

"He's been very good to us both lately."

"He always was."

"I don't blame him for getting on my case all those years. It *is* unusual to have a black father and a white mother."

"Not in New York it isn't. And our children will cover the gene pool of three continents, between the Irish, Black, and Jewish grandparents."

She smiled and rested her head against his chest. "It sounds nice the way you say it. Hey . . ."

"What?" he asked, when she twisted her head around to smile brightly up into his eyes.

"Let's pick baby names."

"Now you're *really* getting ahead of yourself."

"No, I'm not. I want appropriate names, covering everyone's ancestry."

"An onomatologist's nightmare," Donovan said.

"I want to sit up all night and think of names. If you go out, will you pick up a baby-name book on the way home?"

"Absolutely."

"Are you going out?"

"For a little while, and just to wrap up this case. And when that's done, I promise to stay with you for a very long time."

"If you're not back in two hours I'm coming after you."

67.

IF THE CHURCH ELDERS DIDN'T WANT IT FUNKY THEY SHOULD HAVE BUILT THE DAMN THING IN JERSEY

I found him!" Jefferson exulted, pointing proudly at the small and gnarly looking man who gave a fair impression of having been cuffed to the radiator in Donovan's office.

"Who *is* that?" Donovan asked, walking through the second-floor office of the West Side Major Crimes Unit carrying an armful of baby-name books.

"Jose, the janitor at the Cathedral."

"They really have a janitor?"

"Yeah, and that's actually his title, not Maintenance Engineer or some such newspeak."

"Does he know about Marcus?"

"Nada," Jefferson said. "He's not happy at being here at all. I got him out of an all-day domino game on Manhattan Avenue."

"Hang onto these," Donovan said, handing over the books.

"Yo, bro! The rabbit died?"

"Not yet, and I got to ask you about that. Let's talk to Jose."

Donovan introduced himself to the man, who was indeed irked at being hauled in by the cops. Janitors are so often the ones that cops turn to to get into apartments, go through garbage, or pick up loose gossip.

"I can't help you, Lieutenant," Jose said quickly.

"Just tell me one thing. You saw the cops go through the cathedral, didn't you?"

"I saw them."

"Was there any place they missed?"

"Yes. The bishop's bedroom."

"Other than that? Anything like a bomb shelter or potato cellar that only you know about?"

"Not that wasn't searched."

"A storm drain big enough to crawl into."

"No."

"Ten years ago I found a series of tunnels under Riverside Park that no one knew about but the killer hiding in them. You can't tell me that a structure the size of the cathedral was built without a few ratholes in the basement."

Jose shrugged.

Donovan said, "Is there a language problem here? Do you want money or anything?"

"Hey, officer. I got no problem with money or the cops. I just don't know anyplace like you're talking about. I practically live in the crypt area, and the cops took that apart and found nothing."

"The cops looked everywhere?"

"Yeah, and found zilch. You spent time there . . . I saw you around . . . with the photographer, and found nothing. So what do you want from me? Hey! There's someone you can talk to . . ."

"The photographer? Have you seen him lately?"

"No, and I don't mean him. I mean the drunk in the wheelchair who's been watching the cathedral all hours of the day and night."

"Halftrack!" Donovan exclaimed. "I forgot about him."

"I often wish you would," Jefferson said.

"He's in front of the cathedral right now, harassing tourists. They finally start coming back and right away some bum in a wheelchair that looks like a junk shop is harassing them."

"This is New York," Donovan said. "If the church elders

didn't want it funky they should have built the damn thing in Jersey."

Donovan and Jefferson found their man smack in front of the main entrance to the cathedral, rattling the pots and pans that dangled from his chair to attract panhandling victims. "You owe me fifty bucks," he said as Donovan hove into view.

The lieutenant waved a flash of green and asked, "How goes the fabric of life on this fine Sunday evening?"

"Say what?"

"Is evil on the loose?"

"Unh, yeah, always. Gimme the bread."

Donovan gave him the bread.

"Sorry I forgot you, but I've had problems of my own."

"I know. Every so often they haul a body out of there and remind me that you've got problems."

"What am I buying for my fifty bucks?" Donovan snarled.

"That crazy photographer who was taking pictures in Riley's? The friend of yours? He's not dead."

"Who says that he was?"

"He gave a pretty good impression of it the other day. It was real early in the morning and I saw you and him by the Peace Fountain. You were runnin' around before that, and then a whole army of cops came in and surrounded the place."

"I remember the day. What about Avignon?"

"He wandered around looking sick, you know, holding his head. Then he went to his car that was parked over in the bishop's spot and lay down. He looked like a goner, a stroke victim or something. *I* was hit by a stroke, you know. That's how I got to be in this chair."

"No you weren't. You were hit by the car that the shylock ran over your back. Tell me more."

"I was gonna go over and see if I could help him. He *is* a friend of yours. But then he got up and left."

"After how long?"

"Ten . . . fifteen minutes."

"Oh yeah," Jefferson said. "I *told* you he wasn't asleep for no nine hours."

"When did he come back?"

"I didn't see him for two or three hours, and then he wandered around some taking pictures in and out of the cathedral. About five hours after he first passed out in the car he passed out there again. After that you found him."

"The sonofabitch lied to me," Donovan said.

"You trust people who don't deserve it," Jefferson said. "Then you're shocked when you get screwed. This is a pattern with you. You never listen to me. I've been warning you about Avignon since this whole thing began."

"Let's go back to SoHo."

Avignon's studio was empty as before, but Donovan's newly angry eyes caught differences. The tape player had been left on, along with one of the monitors. Donovan knew that it was common to leave high-end electronics switched on. "The time these machines fail is the first time you plug them in and turn them on," Avignon told him over pizza in the crypt. "They like to run, like race horses."

"He's been here," Jefferson said.

"Someone has. And to the best of my knowledge, Avignon and I are the only ones with keys. But there's more. Do you see it?"

Jefferson scanned the room, then said "One of those fancy cameras is gone. When we were here before there were three in that case. Now there are two."

"I impounded the one left in the Enola Gay," Donovan said.

"So he came and got another."

"Which means there was something else for him to shoot—Marcus."

"The bastard has found him," Jefferson said.

"I know how it happened now," Donovan said. "Avignon saw Marcus outside the cathedral nailing stuff to the door. He followed him and got knocked down. Why Marcus didn't kill him is beyond me."

"Maybe he thought he did. It was dark in the stone cutting shed."

"So after we took him to the hospital the second time, Avignon is in a room that overlooks the cathedral. He's looking out the window one night and sees Marcus again, and takes off to find him."

"Why wouldn't Avignon just call us?"

"He wants Marcus all for himself."

"To do what? Give Marcus a second chance to bash his brains in?"

"Maybe not," Donovan said, turning to give closer inspection to the tape cabinet.

"What do you see?"

"There are two tapes missing. Two blank tapes from the top shelf."

"All those tapes labelled 'crystal black.' The name of his masterpiece."

"Yeah, except these are lower-case *c* and *b*. Fresh tape, never used before, processed in such a way to give it crystal black quality. Avignon told me he only uses this kind for *Crystal Black*."

"So the two missing tapes were . . ."

"Taken for use in taping something terribly important," Donovan said.

"And a camera was taken, which means . . ."

"Avignon was taping Marcus."

"Where?" Jefferson asked.

"Not at the cathedral. There were too many cops around and no place to hide. I mean, there *could be* . . . probably . . . a rathole or two to hide in, but nothing you could get into with another guy, a fifty thousand dollar videocamera, and lights."

"Where then?"

Donovan elevated his eyes to the ceiling, and then pointed at it. "Up there, in Avignon's apartment. Behind the expensive security system."

"It's a little far-fetched to think that Avignon, having nearly been killed by Marcus, would take him in and hide him. Not to mention talk him into doing an interview."

"Is it? Avignon always knew too much. He led me around, saying things like 'He's right down here . . . I can sense it.' Besides, the two of them in collusion makes an odd sort of sense. Avignon offers Marcus two things he doesn't have—forgiveness for having tried to kill him, and a place to hide. In return, Marcus gets to tell his story on tape—sell his goods."

Jefferson said, "I told you they were in it together and you dissed me."

"I apologize for the disrespect," Donovan said. "Get a court order to open the door to Avignon's apartment. He is now officially a suspect."

"Accessory to murder?"

"At the very least," Donovan snarled. "And post a guard—post ten guards—over every door and window of this place. I don't want *cockroaches* going in or out of there until I say so."

68.
BILL DONOVAN FROM MIAMI

Donovan paraphrased the paperback: "William is Old German, meaning 'resolute protector.' "

"Very appropriate," Marcie said, having a forkful of egg foo young.

"Famous Williams include William the Conqueror . . ."

"Not too shabby."

"William Randolph Hearst."

"As shabby as you get."

"William Shakespeare."

"Had a way with words, like you."

"Will Rogers."

"A sense of humor."

"And Willie Mays," Donovan said.

"Well awright!" Jefferson said, eating an egg roll while watching the technicians who were using an acetylene torch on the door leading to Avignon's living quarters. Stuffed with noodles, the Yorkshire terrier puppy slept on Donovan's lap.

"What about Michael?" Marcie asked.

Donovan looked up the name, then said, "Hebrew. I didn't know that."

"Okay," Marcie exclaimed.

"Pass the moo goo gai pan. The name derives from Mikhael, 'one who is like God.'"

"You do have an aura about you."

"Famous Michaels include the Archangel Michael."

"The right hand of God," Marcie said.

"Yeah, but it's his left hand he uses most often," Jefferson said, making a masturbatory gesture in the air.

"Those days are over," Marcie said. "Anyone else?"

"Mickey Mantle. Another baseball great."

"Like I always told you, I was named after presidents and you were named after ball players," Jefferson said.

"Mickey Rooney. No resemblance there. I can't dance."

"He can't?" Jefferson asked Marcie.

"You should see him out on the floor," she replied.

"Baby, I *have* seen him out on the floor."

"And Michael Avignon, producer, director, and cameraman. Leading exponent of video *noir*. How close are we coming to getting that door open?"

"A few more minutes," Jefferson said. "You think Marcus is up there?"

"Doubt it. But something is. Maybe the answer to what Avignon has been up to."

"It's settled then," Marcie said. "I want to name our first boy William Michael Donovan, Jr."

"No way. I can't saddle a poor kid with being called Junior. Besides, my name is too common. If I had it to do over, I'd name myself Izzy Schwartz."

"That's not very Irish."

"To tell the truth, I've never been much of an Irishman. Like to talk about it, mainly. Did I ever tell you about Bill Donovan from Miami?"

No one recalled if he had.

"Ten or fifteen years ago the phone company screwed up and listed my phone number in the book. You know that cops can't have listed phone numbers. Before I could change it back, I began getting calls from young women."

"The luck of the nominally Irish," Jefferson said.

"They came about eleven at night and always from a girl who sounded nineteen years old:

" 'Bill?'

" 'Yes.'

" 'Bill Donovan?'

" 'Yes.'

" 'Bill Donovan from Miami?'

" 'No. Sorry.'

"And after a disappointed pause, she would say 'He told me he was moving to New York.' "

"Who were these women?" Marcie asked, with a bit of wifely suspicion in her voice.

"Rejected suitors. Girls he loved and left. The calls came at least once a week, sometimes twice a week, and always from a different girl. And listen to this: usually from a different city."

Jefferson asked, "A travelling salesman?"

"A few of them found it hard to believe I wasn't him, disguising my voice. Then I got a call from a woman who sounded older, maybe in her thirties. By that time the conversation was going like this:

" 'Bill?'

" 'Yes?'

" 'Bill Donovan?'

" 'Do you want the one from Miami or the one from New York?' That only gave them the impression that I knew where my doppelganger was. A few accused me of harboring him. When *is* that door gonna be open?"

"Finish the story," Jefferson said.

"This older woman laughed and said, 'Let me guess. He's been screwing them and telling them he's moving to New York. You got caught in the middle because you have the same name, right?' "

"I said, 'who *is* this guy?' Turns out he's a distributor for a liquor company and travels the country making sales. He was also making out like a bandit. According to this woman, who went to college with him, Bill Donovan from Miami is one hell of a good-looking guy. I checked him out and basically confirmed the story. He lives in Miami, where he—wisely—has an unlisted phone number."

"You should find it out, call, and get his secret," Jefferson said.

"Too late for that now," Marcie said.

"So I changed my number and the calls stopped. Then one day at the Unit I had to call the Justice Department in Washington and the secretary who answered asked for my name. I said 'Bill Donovan.' "

"She said: 'from Miami?' "

"I said, 'No, dammit! I'm the one from New York!' "

"She said, 'That's too bad—he's really cute!' "

"You're cute," Marcie said.

"Is this what I have to look forward to from you guys?" Jefferson asked.

"I suppose," Donovan said. "But the point to the story is that I want my son named something else."

Jefferson got a signal from the technicians and said, "Work on baby names later, boss. We got the door open."

Donovan got up and took out his gun. "You coming?" he asked Marcie.

"No mas," she said, with a wave of the hand.

69.

THE RESOLUTION OF THE CATHEDRAL MURDERS

The door opened inward, and out came the scent of chili and beans and sour mash malt whiskey. Avignon didn't drink; hadn't in years. Donovan crept inside, leading with his Smith & Wesson.

The ground floor of Avignon's apartment held the living room, kitchen, dining room, and a den with a giant-screen TV as well as a wall full of audio and video equipment. All the lights were on, every single one.

While Jefferson crept through the dining room into the kitchen, Donovan went through the living room and into the den. The TV screen, which was four feet across if it was an inch, was turned to CNN and flickered with the silent images of American troops in Colombia.

The room was set up like a studio. The second Ikegami sat atop a tripod, aimed at the black leather couch that faced the huge monitor. Two tapes marked "crystal black" sat atop a playback machine.

One was unused. The other was half out of its cartridge, having been hastily reinserted. The coffee table held the remains of a bottle of Wild Turkey, a glass, and an ice bucket now holding only a residue of room-temperature water. There was also a half-empty bottle of Diet Coke, as well as a plastic mug that bore the logo of the Director's Guild of America. Two plates had been used to serve chili and beans.

"There's nobody on the first floor," Jefferson said in a loud stage whisper, standing in the door of the den and pointing his gun at the ceiling. "Jesus, this is some little recording studio Avignon set up here."

"Yeah. I can't wait to have a screening. Let's go upstairs."

Jefferson led the way this time, edging up the marble staircase. In contrast with the first floor, all the lights were off upstairs. They checked the bathrooms and two guest bedrooms before moving silently and with great caution into the master bedroom.

The only light came from another TV, a smaller one that stood on a platform at the end of the bed. Avignon lay spreadeagled on his back, unconscious head on a pillow, hand still gripping a remote.

"Is he dead?" Jefferson asked.

Donovan checked the pulse, and found a good one. "No. He's blacked out again. This time he's not faking it."

The door opened downstairs, and when it did Marcie's voice cried out for Donovan.

"Up here," he shouted back.

When the door opened a blast of cold air came in from a fire-escape window that had been left up. The security gates had also been pushed aside and the curtains flapped until she closed the downstairs door once again.

"Marcus was here," Donovan said. "He must have gone out the window, maybe when we arrived and began banging on the door. He's on the loose again."

"If Marcus ain't Avignon he must be Langton or Forrest," Jefferson said.

"He's Forrest. Look at this."

He pointed at the TV, which Jefferson came around to the head of the bed to see. It was freeze-framed on a close shot of the Prison Literacy volunteer as he sat on the black couch downstairs, drinking bourbon.

The man's face looked calm, almost peaceful. He had about him the look of one fresh from confession. Donovan recognized the bliss. It said, *I have sinned and been forgiven. I have gotten away with it.*

"This *will* win Avignon an Oscar," Jefferson said, shaking his head.

"Not if nobody sees it. Nobody but the jury, that is."

"What do you mean?"

"It's the law in New York State—you can't benefit from the commission of a crime."

"Avignon will never see a penny from this."

"He's not in it for the money. I wish it were that simple. You call an ambulance. I'll see if I can wake the bastard up."

Marcie came in, carrying Teddy. She looked at the unconscious photographer, and grimaced. "He's not quite dead," Jefferson said, dialing the phone.

"He's getting better," Donovan added, patting the man on the cheek until he stirred.

It took a minute, but Avignon murmured and opened his eyes. "Donovan," he groaned.

"I'm putting you away, you fuck," Donovan said.

"I was talking to him . . . getting him to confess. It's all on tape."

He handed over the remote.

"You knew it was Forrest all along, didn't you?"

Avignon nodded. "Met him at Dannemora, when I was shooting a project for Prison Literacy. He's one-of-a-kind, a true multiple personality. On one hand a likeable, not-particularly-smart boy from Brooklyn; on the other he's Marcus Aurelius, protector of the City of God. Jesus, my head hurts."

"The ambulance is coming."

"My legs feel like rubber; don't think I can move them. Play the tape. It has everything."

"I will."

"This will come as no surprise to you, but like most psychos he hasn't done much homework past the violent part. He doesn't know shit about St. Augustine and has got the theology screwed up. All he knows is that he burns with a rage against the twentieth century. The cathedral took him in and sponsored him while he was on parole, so he appointed himself its protector. He decided to defend it against everything he thinks is profane."

"Which includes most of what goes on there. Were you in on it from the beginning?"

"Oh no, no. I didn't get into it until after Charbaux. Forrest contacted me once he got out of the joint and told me he was working at the cathedral. I didn't think shit about that until Charbaux died and right away I thought—Forrest! So I prowled around and found him that night, just the way I said I did."

"And he really did hit you?"

"Yeah, with a damn brick! He only carried the mallet or the knife when he was stalking someone. He recognized me after he hit me, and called an ambulance before splitting."

"And you paid him back by hiding him from the law," Donovan said.

"He had nowhere to go after you surrounded the cathedral with cops and started searching every stone. At least that's what he said. I think there's still somewhere he hides out in, but that's just a feeling. Anyway, I have him on tape. It's a confession, Donovan. I did your job for you."

"You couldn't just tell me about him."

"Sorry, but this is show biz and I have rights under the First Amendment."

Donovan bristled, and said, "Forrest killed *three other guys*—Loomis, Spenser, and Stewart—while you were covering for him. That day I met him you came up and called him by his first name. You were the one who tipped him off as to where we were looking, and maybe you tried to steer me away from his lair. I found his workshop on my own, if you recall. So don't tell me about the First Amendment. You're a blight on the world, Avignon, a vulture. I always had this bad feeling about television journalists and you're the proof. And don't start rubbing your head and telling me how much you suffered. You faked a lot of that, too."

Through the window that opened on the alley they could hear the approaching sirens.

"Take good care of that tape, Donovan," Avignon said. "It's my property. My lawyer will be at your office in the morning to pick it up. I got a substantial offer from Geraldo Rivera's production company."

"So much for video art," Donovan said. "Your lawyer can find you at the prison ward at Bellevue. You're under arrest— accessory to murder, harboring a fugitive, and conspiracy. And that's all I can think of at the moment."

"It's just business, show business. You're never gonna understand that, are you?"

"Never."

"You're a lonely and bitter man, Bill Donovan," Avignon said, and closed his eyes.

"Once upon a time I was," Donovan said, looking up at his woman.

——

70.
DONOVAN LIVES LIFE TO THE FUCKIN' HILT

So that's all he knows," Donovan said, clicking off the videotape in disgust. This was much later, when Avignon had been hauled off. "St. Augustine was the bishop of Hippo during the fourth century. For all Forrest has to say, St. Augustine might have been the *zookeeper* of Hippo."

"Where's Hippo?" Jefferson asked.

"Somewhere in North Africa, I think. Forrest knows he was a bishop and that he wrote books including *City of God*. And that his original name was Marcus. Jesus, you would think that mad killers would do their homework better. I mean, if you're gonna *obsess* on someone . . ."

"You might be expected to familiarize yourself with his bio. I hear ya."

"Forrest tripped over his name in the prison library, learned that he defended the church, and made up the rest of it. When is this city gonna get a better class of criminals?"

"You don't know so much about religion," Jefferson said.

Donovan shrugged. "Forrest has good taste in boots, though," Donovan noted, nodding at the frozen screen. On it, Forrest sat with one leg perched atop the other and both on the coffee table. On the soles of his custom-made cowboy boots were round-tipped Texas stars, like you used to find on Wild West marshall's badges.

"That's the same star forensics found in the bootprints taken at the Charbaux killing and Avignon assault."

"I didn't know Forrest smoked," Donovan said, poking idly through the pile of unfiltered Camels found in a tea cup on the coffee table. Avignon had no ash trays.

Donovan removed the tape from the machine and gave it to Bonaci with the other tape. Bonaci was rested up and back in service as the consummate crime-scene busybody, directing the legion of technicians poring over Avignon's studio and apartment. Dawn was breaking over the City of New York. Once again, Donovan and Jefferson had been up all night.

Donovan woke Marcie, who had sacked out with the puppy in a spare bedroom for several hours. "Time to go to court," he said. "How do you feel?"

"I'm young and in love and getting married and having children and opening a restaurant on Broadway," she replied. "I feel great."

"Are you worried about the grand jury?"

"No. Carter and Weems were bad guys and I shot them fair and square. My conscience is clear. How do *you* feel?"

"One of my oldest friends betrayed me and I have yet to earn my pay this week. I was up all night staring at a giant-screen TV such as dreams are made of, and didn't see one minute of football. I don't smoke, eat anything that tastes like food, or drink anything stronger than seltzer. I'm hungry and pushing fifty and now must go downtown to get screamed at by the Reverend Fred and his jolly band of anarchists. How do I feel? I feel like I'm living life to the fuckin' hilt, like any native New Yorker would."

"I adore you," she said, scrambling eagerly to her feet. "Let's go see the grand jury."

71.
"No Justice! No Peace!"

Donovan paced the hall outside the grand jury room, carrying the Yorkie as if it were his own child. Suddenly aloof, Jefferson sat on a plain wooden bench reading the Monday sports pages, occasionally uttering an oath regarding the performance of the Knicks.

There had been a rip in the fabric of life (that was how Donovan put it during his drinking days, and he had never found a better cliché). He couldn't identify it or what was causing it, but something had grabbed the atmosphere by its margins and was stretching it until it tore.

It was true that Jefferson and he were both tired and hungry, and certainly some of the strain was caused by Marcus still being on the loose. It hardly mattered that they knew that Forrest was Marcus. He was out there hiding, probably at the cathedral, and Donovan didn't want to go back *there* again. His recent associations with the place included failure and assassination.

But the tear came from more than exhaustion, hunger, and Marcus. When Ed James showed up, Jefferson and he barely spoke, just exchanged grunts and a silent handclasp as James marched into the jury room. Now Jefferson, who normally couldn't resist commenting on everything, quietly read the paper while Marcie testified.

Even through the closed hallway window and the hissing radiators, Donovan could hear the amplified chants of the demonstrators outside. An electronic megaphone blared the Reverend Fred's high-pitched voice and the crowd's rhythmic response:

"No justice! No peace!
"No justice! No peace!"

And:

"What do we want?

"Justice!

"When do we want it?

"Now!"

Occasional sirens went by. Down the hall outside another jury room, a young black mother, her frame gaunt and wretched from AIDS or something nearly as bad, sobbed over a snapshot of a dead baby.

Donovan nodded down the hall at her and said, "The doctors at Bellevue used to call it 'the withers.' "

"What?" Jefferson asked, looking up, disconnectedly.

"The emergency room doctors at Bellevue who used to look at the heroin addicts who were dying of *something,* they didn't know what, used to call it 'the withers' and write it off as an unexplained consequence of heroin addiction. Bad nutrition or something."

"I didn't know that," he replied, and went back to the paper.

The grand jury room door opened. James came out, followed closely by Marcie. She smiled when she saw Donovan, did a little comic curtsy that she used to do when they first courted, and went into his arms. "Nothing to it," she said.

"That's good."

"Let's go eat," she said. "I'm starved."

"Bonaci has bagels in the car."

James slid by Donovan and past Jefferson, who sat with his fingers digging holes in his copy of *The Times*. "The Knicks are gonna pull this one out," James said.

"Yeah."

Jefferson flipped out his palm and James's fingers brushed over it. "Later," James said.

"Later."

Then he walked down the hall, his pace picking up as he went, and started whistling as he disappeared down the broad stairs to the street level.

"Let's *eat,"* Marcie said, and led the way down the hall.

Jefferson let out a sigh, then tried to fold the paper but botched the job and wound up abandoning it on the bench. For an instant, Donovan's eyes met his and Jefferson flicked them away in embarrassment before taking a few quick steps to catch up with Marcie.

Donovan shot a glance at the door to the grand jury room and then followed.

The roar of the demonstrators picked up when Marcie stepped out the door. There was something about her that infuriated them. Her beauty, neither black nor white, was something in-between and lofty. Her attitude and demeanor were confident and breezily unaware of life's little street problems. It was that attitude that first attracted Donovan, just as it irritated Jefferson for so many years until she grew on him, too.

As she went down the broad expanse of steps, Jefferson was alongside her. Carrying the puppy, Donovan was a few steps behind and catching up, a half-dozen uniformed cops forming a flying wedge to get them through the screaming crowd, when the Reverend Fred barged up. He waved a fist fat with gold rings.

The wedge of cops began to collapse. Donovan pushed forward. The Reverend Fred reached and pointed at Marcie, chanting, *"We want you! We want you!"*

Jefferson was caught in between as the man's arm brushed the side of his face.

"Get outta my face!" Jefferson yelled.

"You killed those boys! There never was no gun!"

Jefferson said, louder this time: "I said, get outta my face!"

Donovan surged forward, but a cop was wedged between him and Marcie. The roar of the crowd was maddening. Down the steps, Bonaci held the car door open.

The Reverend Fred grabbed for Marcie again, and she saw him this time and lurched away. "Murderer!" he yelled.

The crowd chanted, *"Justice now! Justice now!"*

Jefferson shouted, "Get your fuckin' hand off my partner!"

Donovan tried to shove the uniformed cop out of his way, but was too late. The Reverend was still reaching for Marcie when

Donovan saw Jefferson's fist cock back over his right shoulder and then go crashing into the fat man's chin. When recounting it later, Donovan would swear that he heard the rush of air over Jefferson's powerful right jab.

The Reverend's head snapped back and he tumbled backwards, toppling onto his ample bottom along with a brace of supporters. The crowd broke momentarily, long enough for Donovan to usher Jefferson and Marcie into the car and away.

"Nothing to it," she said.

They ate bagels and drank decaf while Bonaci drove uptown. Soon they were back at Donovan's apartment and, still tired from the night before, Marcie went into the bedroom with the puppy to sleep while Donovan and Jefferson sat in the living room trying to think of something to say.

When he was certain that she was out of earshot, Donovan forced Jefferson to look him in the eye and said: "There was no gun, was there?"

The sigh that Jefferson let out was a huge rush of air that puffed his cheeks. "You had to ask, didn't you? You just couldn't let the damn thing die."

"That was one hell of a right hand you threw at the Rev, with a lot of anger in it. Nobody told me there was no gun. Nobody had to."

Jefferson looked down at the carpet, then shook his head sadly from side to side. His head hung low, like a sidelined player on the Knicks' bench when they were down ten points late in the fourth quarter.

"What do you want me to say, Bill? She's my partner. She's your woman. Did you think we'd let her go to jail?"

"Does she know?"

"She has *no idea!* And if you're smart it will stay that way."

"Who planted the nine millimeter? You?"

"Ed. What difference does it make?"

"None. I was just curious."

Donovan thought for a long moment, then said "Well," not knowing what he meant by it other than as some sort of punctuation. And he, too, looked at the carpet for a while, until Jefferson said, "It looks like we got by the grand jury."

"Yeah," Donovan said, bobbing his head.

"You and me got to live with it. I'm not worried about Ed James. He's been out on the streets a long time."

"We'll manage, I suppose. We always do."

"You *do* know that Carter and Weems were certified bad guys. Crack dealers. Killers, and they killed Jennifer."

"The process of rationalization begins," Donovan said, with a crooked smile. "So it's all for the best that Marcie is quitting the force. She wants to run a restaurant. And there's some idea about freelancing as a private investigator, but I'm hoping she'll forget it."

"Me too."

Donovan snapped sharply to his feet and went to the VCR, atop which he had parked some of Avignon's tapes and one NYPD video. "There's something I remembered while we were driving uptown. Look at these and tell me what's wrong with the pictures."

Donovan played parts of two tapes, those showing the stairwell near the Poetry Wall. In the first tape, Donovan stood in a pool of water as he tried to open the door into the Recycling Center. In the second tape, the body of Chico Brewer lay bleeding atop a dry floor.

"The water's gone," Jefferson said. "Where did it go?"

Donovan shrugged. "And where did Brewer's blood go? He lost ten pints, and the cleanup squad scraped up two pints at most."

"Through the floor?"

"There's an outline there that I thought was a design. I've been thinking designs lately, like pitch pine on knife blades and how much a Maltese cross resembles an X with fishtails."

"What?" Jefferson asked, puzzled.

"I think that *this* design is a trap door."

Donovan handed Jefferson a sheaf of flyers. "Now look at these. I've made quite a collection."

Jefferson flipped through and quickly scanned advertisements for exhibits of photos, art, and sculpture, each set up in one of the fourteen chapels that lined the north and south walls of the nave.

"So what? What's the point?"

"The point is the pattern."

"A pattern to what? The killings? There was one?"

Donovan took back the flyers, reshuffled them, then handed them back one by one. "An exhibit of modern sculpture in the Arts Chapel is followed by the murder of Dale Charbaux. A photo exhibit about the crusade to save the rain forest, held in the Crusaders Chapel, is accompanied by the murder of Terry Loomis."

His eyes wide, Jefferson said, "A show in the Ecclesiastical Chapel opened just before Stewart, the Cathedral administrator, was killed."

"And a little homage to lawyers, held in the Lawyers' Chapel, was accompanied by the demise of Herbert Spenser. Marcus was making a point about the cathedral's ultimate insult to his beloved City of God—using it to celebrate man's earthly works and pleasures. Imagine a church having a chapel for lawyers, for God's sake."

"Damn," Jefferson said. "What's this last one about?"

He handed Donovan a flyer announcing a showing of photos by Mexican amateur photographers. The shots were made during the Pan American Games in Mexico City.

Jefferson read it and said, "So what?"

Donovan put it with the others. "I hope I'm wrong."

Jefferson got to his feet and, involuntarily, his hand touched his revolver. "Let's go finish this," he said.

72

CITY OF GOD (5)

T he cathedral at noon on the last Monday of November was empty save for the men cleaning up after the Blessing of the Animals. The faint smell of dogs was quickly swept away, replaced by the usual aura of still air and vastness.

Donovan and Jefferson walked swiftly up the right aisle, flanked by a few Emergency Services cops with pry bars, flashlights, and shotguns. Few of the cathedral workers bothered even to look in their direction; the blasé attitude common in the streets had come indoors, and no amount of bloodshed could shake it.

Donovan went down the stairs first, carrying a flashlight. The door to the Recycling Center was open slightly, and through it he could see the armed men he'd posted there. Donovan got down on his knees and inspected the outline of a square. He remembered thinking it was a concrete worker's line, like those cut in sidewalks to allow thermal expansion. But down on his knees and looking up close, he found himself poking at the outline of a liftaway door or hatch, metal that had been painted grey to match the concrete around it.

"This is where the water went," Donovan said. "This is where Marcus went. I remember Avignon saying he sensed that Marcus was down in this general area."

"Do you have any idea what's down there?" Jefferson asked, joining him.

"No. But this foundation was cut seventy feet into the bedrock. There could be lots of things." Donovan got to his feet and stood back to wave in two Emergency Services men, who brought down pry bars and heavy-duty flashlights.

"I'm going down after him," Donovan said as the trap door

was pried open. There was a slight hiss of damper, slightly compressed air from below.

"Not without your flak jacket you're not," Jefferson said.

"Marcus doesn't use a gun. It's not his style."

"No arguments! You're gonna be marrying my partner soon, and I got to make sure you stay healthy."

"I'm not at all sure I like the way things are turning out," Donovan lamented.

"She'd want me to mother you."

"You a mother all right," Donovan said, slipping on a Kevlar bulletproof vest handed down the stairs.

As the lid came up and was lifted and set standing against the wall, Donovan looked down a flashlight beam and saw a brick-lined compartment about nine feet square and six feet high. There was another smell, candle wax; twelve votive candles burned on an orange crate that had been turned on its side and made into a simple altar.

"Twelve for the twelve apostles, I guess," Jefferson said.

"Who the fuck cares? The guy is a nut. Help me get down there."

He let Jefferson and another cop lower him straight down until his feet touched the cold stone floor. Donovan had a heavy-duty light handed to him, and looked around.

The room was perfectly square and a mite claustrophobic, with a low ceiling that he had to duck under and nothing to sit on. The orange-crate altar was the only furniture in the place. All Donovan could say about it was that the short, fat candles had been lit no more than an hour before.

One wall ended short of another, the difference being a two-foot wide passage that appeared to head off to the east. The air that built up a slight pressure in the chamber came from there, and the flow was through the passage and up into the cathedral.

"Whatcha got, Bill?" Jefferson asked, sticking his head down.

"I know what this is—a catch basin and drainage passage built with the original structure to carry runoff water away from the foundation."

He shined the flashlight down it, then held up a candle and blew it out to watch the air flow.

"This is exactly what I thought Jose would know about, but he didn't."

"Where does it go?"

"Probably to the property line—did you ever check out the brick wall set in the earth just east of St. Savior's Chapel?"

"Must have escaped my attention."

"Well, go do it. See if there's a drainage gate."

"I'm sending somebody to check on the damn gate. I'm coming down with you."

"Don't forget your flak jacket," Donovan said.

A few minutes later and Jefferson too had swung down into the pit. With two flashlights, the details were clearer. Chico Brewer's dried blood speckled the brick floor as in a huge pointillist painting.

Apart from the altar, the place was newly occupied. "This is an emergency shelter," Donovan said. "Meant for escape or a last stand."

"A last stand. There's no other way out, in my opinion."

That opinion was confirmed a few minutes later, when cops covering the probable eastward route of the passage found no outlet big enough for a man to get through.

"There *is* a gate, like you said."

"I thought so. When I was a little nipper I lost a stickball down there. It's just inside the east fence and five to ten feet from the wall of St. Savior's."

"You got it."

"Maybe I can get my damn ball back," Donovan said. "Let's go."

"The gate is covered over with ivy that hasn't been tampered with. The place was kept for a last stand, no doubt."

"An Alamo."

"I hope it ain't as well-defended."

Donovan had to turn sideways a bit to fit into the passageway, which also was made of brick but only five feet high. He crouched low to fit in it, and crept along, trying to keep protected that part of his side not covered by Kevlar.

"How long is this passage, do you think?" Jefferson asked.

"Fifty feet. A hundred."

"You don't know better than that?"

"Hey . . . I'm making this up as I go along. Keep your powder dry and make notes. If we get Marcus you can take credit. It'll save your ass with the Commissioner, who has got to be a little pissed about your punching out the Rev."

"Bullshit! I'm the most popular man in New York right now. You know the joke: If you was in a closed room with Quaddafi, Saddam Hussein, and the Reverend Fred Handon, and only had two bullets in your gun, who would you shoot first?"

"Handon twice—to make sure he's dead," Donovan said.

"Man, I just get crazy when black guys get outta line, be they crooks or politicians or whatever. There must be something wrong with me."

"You're a conservative, Thomas. The only black cop in the world who wears Brooks Brothers suits. The only cop of any color I know whose living room looks like Bill Cosby's."

"Which reminds me, the city is paying the cleaning bill for today."

The passage was built on a slight decline so water flowed readily. Blue-green algae grew on the walls, and as they neared the halfway point spider webs connected walls and ceilings. The webs broke over Donovan's forehead as he inched along.

There was no sound but their own breathing. Unlike most other places in Manhattan that were near subway lines or major roads, the east end of the cathedral sat atop the highest point in the city, and was near only two-lane Morningside Drive, which few cars used.

Anywhere else, no matter how far you went underground, the city made noise, a heartbeat or pulse or a low moaning hum that city dwellers knew was a vital sign. There were subways or commuter rails or Con Edison steam tunnels or the creaking of roadbeds from the weight of heavy trucks. Add to that traffic

267

noise, sirens, and heavy-construction hammering and the city made its consumptive rasp everywhere you went.

Except here, where breathing and the scraping of feet were the only sounds.

"You got to get ready for some news," Donovan said, his voice dropping to the register that, when he used it, silenced people.

Jefferson made no reply.

"Remember that footage Avignon shot of the marathon?"

"Yeah," Jefferson replied cautiously.

"I was in it, looking down at Jennifer's body, then up at Carter and Weems atop the hill."

"I remember."

"Avignon shot it and never saw fit to tell me. Well, there was something else. You're not gonna like it, and Marcie can never . . ."

At that moment a bit of light came at them from ahead and they flicked off their flashlights. The light was simple and quavering; more candles, the flames teased by a slight draft that came in from the hard wintry ground-ivy that covered the gate.

Donovan sensed another presence, and moved slowly forward to greet it. As he did, he slipped his Smith & Wesson out of its holster and held it in front of him. The candle light grew with the smell of smoke and burning wax and Donovan moved silently until he could see.

There was another catch basin, but smaller than the first. It was only five feet high and round and had a brick ceiling, in the center of which was set a grate scarcely fourteen inches square.

Beside it was another orange-crate altar that held another twelve candles, along with a tin cup filled halfway with cigarette butts. The crate, stolen from the garbage outside a Broadway fruit stand, had come a long way from a Florida grove. In it Marcus had idly carved another Maltese cross. But the man himself was not there.

"He's slipped away again," Jefferson said.

From the ceiling grate came a small amount of daylight, and then an officer's voice. "Hey Lieutenant, you okay?" it asked.

"Just great," Donovan called back.

"The guy is like a ghost."

Donovan groaned. That ghost was haunting his imagination. "How long ago would you say these candles were lit?" Donovan asked.

Jefferson bent to peer at them. "Votive candles ain't my specialty, but I would say twenty minutes to half an hour. So he can't have gone far."

Donovan nodded. "Marcus is nearby. He lit those candles and left, meaning to come back. We showed up and spooked him. So he's in the cathedral someplace, watching and waiting."

"For what?"

"For me," Donovan said. "Avignon said that Marcus was focusing on me, and he was right. Clear out this cathedral one last time. I want to be alone with the sonofabitch."

73.
AN X WITH FISHTAILS

The afternoon sun came in low through the Rose Window, making a splash of colors along the north side of the nave. Straight lines of light pierced through the still inner atmosphere like swords, cutting parallel stripes in air that was thick with incense and cleaning fluid.

Alone again in the cathedral, Donovan found himself groping for appropriateness. He wanted badly to do the right thing, but it escaped him. The only other time he had the place essentially to himself, it was early morning with nothing but black night coming from the stained-glass windows that served as the most visible connection with the outside world. In the middle of the night, he hadn't had a crowd waiting outside the barred doors to hear the results of the contest. It was easy then to munch cold pizza sitting on the altar steps; knowing, waiting, for the insult to be acknowledged by the madman.

But this time, with the whole world waiting, Donovan found himself walking up the main aisle a bit awkwardly, hands in pockets, trying to think what to do. The burst of anger that impelled him to empty the cathedral was gone. Donovan thought: *I hope he's unarmed and stupid; I hope I don't blow it.*

Donovan reached the steps, fumbling for words. Then looking up piously at the high altar, declaimed, "Dear Lord, don't let me fuck up."

Not getting an answer, he turned and sat on the steps, same place as the last time. The cathedral was silent as a grave at midnight. None of the city could be heard. High above him, a large grey moth fluttered aimlessly, borne on a thermal that rose, unseen, to the dome. For a moment, he swore he could hear its heartbeat.

Then, above and to the left, a door opened. The hinges, old and sparingly used, creaked rustily, making a squeal that became a screech as it echoed throughout the cavernous cathedral. Of all the doors that Donovan opened during the previous few weeks, none made a sound half so horrid.

Donovan leaped to his feet, pistol in hand, the small hairs standing frozen on the back of his neck. He whipped his head around, looking up to the various balconies. There seemed to be dozens of places from which a man could look down: from behind the mammoth organ, with its forest of pipes; from above the south ambulatory and the Chapel of St. James; from above the Poetry Wall and its recently uncovered hidden passage; and from the clerestory-level balconies above the fourteen secular chapels that lined the nave.

The door slammed shut. The crash of metal reverberated around the cathedral, startling Donovan into the realization of his mistake: He faced a madman who was most famous for using a mallet, but who had expressed sorrow in never getting the chance to use an Uzi. Donovan glanced up at the personification of God and said, "I fucked up, didn't I?"

The answer came quickly, though not from God. The click of the weapon being armed was as clear as sin. Donovan wheeled toward that part of the balcony above the Poetry Wall and glimpsed Forrest—Marcus—grinning broadly and hefting the boxy machine pistol.

The madman laughed a mocking, triumphal laugh, a celebration of fatal victory. For a second his eyes met Donovan's, long enough for the lieutenant to read his fury and throw himself to one side just as a line of bullets ripped up the stone floor beneath him.

Donovan scrambled to his feet and half ran, half dived behind the pulpit. The huge chunk of Tennessee marble, taller than a man, was like a miniature of the cathedral facade, with ornate carvings of Jesus and the Apostles.

The gunshots echoed around the cathedral, seemingly for several minutes. Then Donovan's radio crackled to life and he fished it from his pocket.

"You okay?" Jefferson asked.

"I'm pinned down behind the pulpit."

"Still want me out of this?"

"No. Marcus is atop the Poetry Wall. Work your way through the narthex and up the tower staircase. Block that exit and wait till you hear from me."

"Where you going?"

"Where do you think?"

Donovan poked his head out from one side of the pulpit long enough to see that Marcus was still there, the Uzi still aimed in his general direction. Another burst of fire rang out as another several rounds sprayed the cathedral floor and the base of the massive stone column behind the pulpit.

Donovan raced to the other side of the pulpit and jumped out long enough to fire two shots at the lunatic. The Smith & Wesson sounded puny next to the Uzi, but its slugs had their effect. Marcus had only been shot at once before, and remained a novice. He ducked jerkily to one side, clambering back from the rail.

In that instant Donovan sprinted across the crossing, head down and feet flying. Marcus recovered and fired another several rounds, wilder this time. They splintered a row of wooden chairs in front of the choir screen, but Donovan was safe in the south ambulatory. Way down to the east, one of the main doors opened wide enough to admit Jefferson, who quickly moved into position.

The door in the Poetry Wall was open a crack, just as he'd left it half an hour earlier. Donovan hunkered down low and pushed it open with the barrel of his gun. The air inside was stale and smelled like fungus, same as before. Down on the lower level, the trap door was resealed, just as his men had left it. That much was unchanged.

The door leading to the balcony at the clerestory level was ajar, and a point source of light came from the very top of the old staircase. Built inside one of the main pillars of the cathedral, the staircase led from bedrock to roof, with a small square port yielding access to the roof of the nave.

Donovan sucked in his breath and stepped into the stairwell, the Smith & Wesson a tiny shield in front of him. He moved slowly upwards, acutely aware that his footfalls, however soft, resounded as loud as cannonshots. The door to the clerestory level remained open, and light from the cathedral flooded the dank stairwell.

Where was Marcus, on the balcony or gone up to the roof? A short burst from the Uzi would be the end of everything, if fired down the stairs. Marcus was a bad shot, but who needed to aim in those close quarters? Donovan thought these things as he crept up the steps, pausing outside the gallery door to think.

From the door he saw colors from a thousand stained-glass panels. And from the wall of the balcony outside there came a soft scraping, such as is made by a man's jacket brushing against a tapestry-covered wall as its owner crept along.

Marcus, Donovan thought, bursting into the open with his

finger straining against the tension of the trigger spring. He saw a gun, then, an automatic, but the fingers holding it were black.

"Jesus!" he exclaimed.

"He ain't here," Jefferson said, relaxing his own guard. The two men lowered the guns they had aimed at each other.

"Marcus is on the roof. There's no escape from there. I'm going after him."

"I'm with you," Jefferson said, waving his boss to go up the stairs and get on with it.

"I thought I told you to wait down there," Donovan said, indicating the narthex.

"I decided you weren't leaving me out of it again."

Donovan grumbled, "It's getting harder and harder to control you black guys."

"Wait till you're married to one of us," Jefferson said.

Donovan seldom fought the inevitable. He shrugged, and said, "Put men around the ways down from the roof and get the construction workers off the towers." Then he resumed his climb up the stairs, with Jefferson, having relayed the order over the radio, right on his heels.

The access port to the roof grew larger, the light from it brighter. A bitter November wind teased inside the portal, licking Donovan's face as he reached the top and peered outside.

The roof of the nave was a plain, pitched one. Shallow gutters with railings ran along the sides of it, from east to west.

"You take the north, I'll take the south," Donovan said.

"Be careful," Jefferson said, clambering up and over the peak of the roof and disappearing from sight.

Donovan walked slowly the length of the roof, working his way from pillar to pillar, pausing at the tops of each to look behind their ornate spires. It was late afternoon by then, the sun was lowering in the sky, and traffic helicopters followed the ribbon of cars making their way home along the West Side Highway. Two ambulances were racing toward St. Luke's Hospital, while across the grey rooftops of Harlem Donovan could see black, billowing smoke from an apartment fire. Ten stories below a crowd was forming, milling about like ants.

The construction workers had been evacuated from the still-unfinished towers and all ways down were blocked, as Donovan ordered. At last there was an uncomplicated and nearly empty playing field—the gargantuan roof.

The west front rose above the plain roof like the false facade of a western movie set. Highly ornamented in the medieval French manner, it was topped by a huge Maltese cross that had been installed the year before to replace the old cross fitchee that stood atop the cathedral for generations. *So that's the dingus Stewart bragged about,* Donovan thought, an *X* with fishtails; hard to notice from the road.

The rigging for the tower construction spilled over onto the roof and adjoined smaller scaffolding still in place from the erection of the Maltese cross. Bits of tarpaper and torn rags of fiberglass packing littered the roof alongside two-by-fours and buckets of roofing adhesive. Newly cut limestone blocks were stacked in several piles every score yards along the south gutter. They were waiting their place atop the tower of St. Paul, which rose above the roof and was still growing toward the sky. Here and there were smaller piles of grotesques and other ornamentation; three gargoyles were lined up on the peak of the roof, staring like pigeons at the twin towers of the World Trade Center far south across the Manhattan skyline.

The sun cast long shadows. The one from the gigantic cross was played across the copper roof sheeting, exaggerating an already exaggerated form. Donovan walked into it and the sun set abruptly behind this emblem of the medieval Knights of Malta. *I'm getting tired of seeing this thing around,* Donovan thought.

Suddenly there was a shriek of battle joined. Marcus burst out from behind a pile of limestone building blocks, silhouetted by the setting sun, a tall and angular fury holding an automatic weapon. His finger clutched at the trigger and a row of bullet holes ripped the copper sheeting atop the roof of the cathedral.

Donovan jerked away from the torrent of lead and, falling to his right, fired into the silhouette.

There was a gush of blood and a cry of pain and the madman staggered, the Uzi now held tenuously at the end of an arm that hung twitchingly from tendons shredded at the shoulder. His trigger finger contracted again, perhaps involuntarily this time, and another burst of slugs went wild.

Donovan fired again, hitting Marcus squarely in the middle. The Uzi slipped from his fingers and clattered to the roof, landing next to a pug-faced grotesque with huge, pie-shaped ears. He fell to his knees and looked down at the wave of blood spreading across the drawing of the Cathedral of St. John the Divine on his tee shirt.

Then he looked up at Donovan and, fleetingly, their eyes met. "I killed five demons," he gasped as he fell onto his side on the roof, his eyes open and staring up at the Lord.

Donovan walked up cautiously, taking his time, being careful. Being husbandly. Marcie was right—enough with madmen trying to kill him.

It was then that Marcus rose and swivelled his body, and from his belt came the black ivory-hilt stiletto that Scott Carter had lost in the woods alongside the marathon route. Its gold letter S twinkled in the half-light as Marcus drove it toward Donovan's gut. Two bodies with one knife; a black runner and her host in New York.

Another shot roared. It hit Forrest in the temple and killed him instantly. The body collapsed forward, straight down onto the copper roofing, and lay still without even the shudder of death.

Forrest's chest heaved a few times and then stopped. His blood poured out of him, across the roof, and through a grate below which was 270 feet of vertical shaft and then groundwater in the bedrock far below the cathedral. The blood was lost in the rocks deep below Manhattan, along with water that had been draining off the old stones of the cathedral for a century.

Donovan picked up the knife, peering at the gold S and the inscription, which clearly read "Scott Carter." Jefferson burst over the peak of the roof and down Donovan's side, checking the body before joining the lieutenant, who sat beside a gargoyle that reminded him of Casey Stengel.

"That knife," Jefferson said, the realization breaking over him, "I think . . ."

"This knife?" Donovan asked and, fumbling with it, dropped it through the grate. It tumbled in the air, falling for a good ten seconds before splashing, perhaps irretrievably, into the blood and water far below.

Donovan and Jefferson sat and stared at each other for a few long moments before Jefferson got his thoughts together.

"Forrest got that knife away from Carter somehow and used it to stab Jennifer," Jefferson said.

"What knife?" Donovan replied tiredly.

"The exhibit in the Sports Chapel was the thing that set Forrest off to kill an athlete—Jennifer. Avignon spotted him there. When the tape ran out is when Avignon started running after the sonofabitch. How did you know?"

"The pattern was an exhibit in a chapel followed by a murder. Jennifer was the only athlete killed in New York City in November. There were unfiltered Camels, which Forrest smoked, alongside a pitch pine atop the hill. Avignon mentioned that Marcus also carried a knife. Someone carved a Maltese cross . . ."

"An X with fishtails."

". . . into a pitch pine growing there. Forrest liked Maltese crosses—carved one in the spice rack in his apartment. You're sitting in the shadow of a particularly big one built by prisoners."

Jefferson looked up at the cross, which now cast its shadow halfway down the length of the roof.

"The sap of a pitch pine sticks to things like knife blades," Donovan said.

"There were traces of it in Jennifer's wound," Jefferson recalled.

"Here's how I think it happened: Carter lost his knife, probably in that crowd of kids that came out of Harlem before the murder. Forrest found it and used it to carve the cross before using it to kill Jennifer. He also left bootprints on the ground, and I saw his boots on Avignon's tape. And just before he died, Forrest bragged of killing five demons—Charbaux, Loomis, Spenser, Stewart . . . and Jennifer."

"Then Carter and Weems killed nobody except through selling crack. But *Avignon* is an accomplice."

"Which we'll never prove. He got away with it. I've always been amazed by what TV reporters get away with, but this beats all. I mean, we'll prosecute him but never convict. He'll get off on the First Amendment, which protects sleazeballs as well as honest men. He may even make it to Hollywood. So what *do* we do?"

"Jesus . . . I don't know."

"We do nothing. We bury Forrest for the murders of four men. We pat Marcie on the back for having avenged the death of Jennifer Peel. And we tell no one the truth, which we live with the rest of our lives."

74.
A Scrub Brush and Brown Soap

Somewhat later, Donovan and Jefferson walked down 110th Street, also known as Cathedral Parkway, toward Broadway. A wind had come up from off the Hudson, as it did late every winter afternoon, and was frosting the faces of New Yorkers. A brown-uniformed traffic enforcement agent ticketed double-parked cars on the north side of the street, while a white street-sweeping truck swept noisily along on the south side.

A passel of homeless men and women hunched over warm Con Edison manhole covers set in the outer edge of the sidewalk, their tattered blankets draped over them like pup tents. A Hispanic janitor argued loudly with a tenant, something about what night was the correct one to throw out a broken black-and-white television set.

Sweeping east across 110th was a blue-and-white police cruiser equipped with a loudspeaker. As it started down the hill to Harlem a taped voice blared, in English and then Spanish: "Attention! Toxic heroin was sold yesterday in New York City. Use of this heroin has resulted in overdoses and death. If you have used this toxic heroin, known by the street name Millennium, you are urged to seek medical attention immediately."

When the car was down in the ghetto and out of polite earshot, Donovan and Jefferson noticed that coursing up and down Broadway were Columbia students, all white and blond and corn-fed and looking very much like they just stepped off the bus from Des Moines.

"Have you ever seen so many white people in your life?" Donovan asked. "I don't mean just the skin. I mean, their *souls* are white!"

"Yeah, this city is goin' to hell fast. These touristas hit town and support things like Broadway shows with cats on roller skates and stuff."

"I remember when Broadway shows were real New York stories with blacks, Jews, and Irish in them," Donovan said.

"And I thought things would change when we got a black mayor. There's this little bar on the corner. I'll buy you a Coke."

Donovan shook his head. "Let's walk down to Riley's. I want to see how George is taking the news about who his new boss will be."

"Jake and Marcie opening a restaurant," Jefferson said, shaking his head. "The kamikaze pilot and the JAFRAP."

Donovan gave his friend a wary look. "I'm afraid to ask what that means."

"Jewish African-American Princess," Jefferson said gleefully.

Donovan waxed philosophical. "As the sun sets below the slum buildings on Broadway, life returns to normal on the Upper West Side. They're dyin' of crack and toxic heroin in the ghetto . . ." (He pronounced it *get*-tow, as Jefferson did when in a jaunty mood.) ". . . and gettin' MBAs and partnership offers up on Broadway."

Jefferson thought for a moment, then said, "You can't get married in the cathedral. That place ain't about you. Her either. And certainly not me. I grew up down the hill in Harlem and used to look up at that thing, and it sat there like a medieval castle and I never once felt it had anything to do with my life."

"You may be right," Donovan allowed.

He paused for a second to examine a window display of housewares.

"I got to get back to nesting," he went on.

"Say what?"

"Nest-building behavior designed to attract a mate. Don't you read *Scientific American?*"

"Not lately, boss. I got enough trouble keepin' track of my partner—make that *ex*-partner—and toxic heroin."

"If you did read *Scientific American,* you would know that Millenium is regular smack cut with fentanyl citrate, making it thirty times as powerful."

"Whatever. Welcome to the twenty-first century. Marcus knew what it was gonna be like."

Donovan shrugged, said, "I need some cleanin' equipment. My apartment ain't fit to conduct a marriage in."

"Maybe I'll help you clean it up. But hear me now—get married in my church in Harlem."

"Maybe," Donovan said, intrigued by the idea. "Yeah . . . why not? If Marcie agrees."

"You're more black than white now, and from what I hear of your performance in showers you don't sing so bad either. I'll talk to my preacher and see what I can do. I ain't gonna be best man in no cathedral."

Jefferson slipped an arm around Donovan's shoulders. This was his three-card-monte stance, the con-man pose he used while pulling a scam. "There's one more thing," he said.

"There always is," Donovan replied, failing to hide a smile.

"This restaurant your woman is opening—have you thought about what kind of cuisine you're gonna serve?"

"It's not my restaurant. Talk to the boss the next time you see her."

"I have not had good Southern cookin' in a long time, a very long time, and . . ."

"Talk to the boss," Donovan said, more emphatically this time.

"Listen to you. 'Talk to the boss.' You gonna be a *great* husband. You got the right attitude already. As I was saying, I used to go to this joint on 147th that had Southern cookin'— good Carolina cookin'—that you could die from, and . . ."

Shaking his head and smiling, Donovan steered Jefferson into the hardware store. "I got to buy a scrub brush and brown soap," he explained, and pushed open the door.